A
DANGEROUS
MOURNING

Also by Anne Perry
Published by Fawcett Books

Bluegate Fields

Callander Square

Cardington Crescent

The Cater Street Hangman

Death in the Devil's Acre

Paragon Walk

Resurrection Row

Rutland Place

Silence in Hanover Close

The Face of a Stranger

Highgate Rise

A
DANGEROUS
MOURNING

Anne Perry

Fawcett Columbine
New York

A Fawcett Columbine Book
Published by Ballantine Books
Copyright © 1991 by Anne Perry

All rights reserved under International and Pan-American Copyright
Conventions. Published in the United States by Ballantine Books, a division of
Random House, Inc., New York, and simultaneously in Canada by Random
House of Canada Limited, Toronto.

Library of Congress Cataloging-in-Publication Data
Perry, Anne.
    A dangerous mourning / Anne Perry. — 1st ed.
      p.   cm.
    ISBN 0-449-90554-3
    I. Title.
PR6066.E693D36   1991
823'.914—dc20   91-70655
                                        CIP

Design by Holly Johnson

Manufactured in the United States of America

First Edition: September 1991

10 9 8 7 6 5 4 3 2 1

To John and Mary MacKenzie,
and my friends in Alness,
for making me welcome.

A
DANGEROUS
MOURNING

CHAPTER ONE

___

"Good morning, Monk," Runcorn said with satisfaction spreading over his strong, narrow features. His wing collar was a trifle askew and apparently pinched him now and again. "Go over to Queen Anne Street. Sir Basil Moidore." He said the name as though it were long familiar to him, and watched Monk's face to see if he registered ignorance. He saw nothing, and continued rather more waspishly. "Sir Basil's widowed daughter, Octavia Haslett, was found stabbed to death. Looks like a burglar was rifling her jewelry and she woke and caught him." His smile tightened. "You're supposed to be the best detective we've got—go and see if you can do better with this than you did with the Grey case!"

Monk knew precisely what he meant. Don't upset the family; they are quality, and we are very definitely not. Be properly respectful, not only in what you say, how you stand, or whether you meet their eyes, but more importantly in what you discover.

Since he had no choice, Monk accepted with a look of bland unconcern, as if he had not understood the implications.

"Yes sir. What number in Queen Anne Street?"

"Number Ten. Take Evan with you. I daresay by the time you get there, there'll be some medical opinion as to the time of her death and kind of weapon used. Well, don't stand there, man! Get on with it!"

Monk turned on his heel without allowing time for Runcorn to add any more, and strode out, saying "Yes sir" almost under his breath. He closed the door with a sharpness very close to a slam.

Evan was coming up the stairs towards him, his sensitive, mobile face expectant.

"Murder in Queen Anne Street." Monk's irritation eased away.

He liked Evan more than anyone else he could remember, and since his memory extended only as far back as the morning he had woken in the hospital four months ago, mistaking it at first for the poorhouse, that friendship was unusually precious to him. He also trusted Evan, one of only two people who knew the utter blank of his life. The other person, Hester Latterly, he could hardly think of as a friend. She was a brave, intelligent, opinionated and profoundly irritating woman who had been of great assistance in the Grey case. Her father had been one of the victims, and she had returned from her nursing post in the Crimea, although the war was actually over at that point, in order to sustain her family in its grief. It was hardly likely Monk would meet her again, except perhaps when they both came to testify at the trial of Menard Grey, which suited Monk. He found her abrasive and not femininely pleasing, nothing like her sister-in-law, whose face still returned to his mind with such elusive sweetness.

Evan turned and fell into step behind him as they went down the stairs, through the duty room and out into the street. It was late November and a bright, blustery day. The wind caught at the wide skirts of the women, and a man ducked sideways and held on to his top hat with difficulty as a carriage bowled past him and he avoided the mud and ordure thrown up by its wheels. Evan hailed a hansom cab, a new invention nine years ago, and much more convenient than the old-fashioned coaches.

"Queen Anne Street," he ordered the driver, and as soon as he and Monk were seated the cab sped forward, across Tottenham Court Road, and east to Portland Place, Langham Place and then a dogleg into Chandos Street and Queen Anne Street. On the journey Monk told Evan what Runcorn had said.

"Who is Sir Basil Moidore?" Evan asked innocently.

"No idea," Monk admitted. "He didn't tell me." He grunted. "Either he doesn't know himself or he's leaving us to find out, probably by making a mistake."

Evan smiled. He was quite aware of the ill feeling between Monk and his superior, and of most of the reasons behind it. Monk was not easy to work with; he was opinionated, ambitious, intuitive, quick-tongued and acerbic of wit. On the other hand, he cared passionately about real injustice, as he saw it, and minded little whom he offended in order to set it right. He tolerated fools ungraciously, and fools, in his view, included Runcorn, an opinion of which he had made little secret in the past.

Runcorn was also ambitious, but his goals were different; he wanted social acceptability, praise from his superiors, and above all safety. His few victories over Monk were sweet to him, and to be savored.

They were in Queen Anne Street, elegant and discreet houses with gracious facades, high windows and imposing entrances. They alighted, Evan paid the cabby, and they presented themselves at the servants' door of Number 10. It rankled to go climbing down the areaway steps rather than up and in through the front portico, but it was far less humiliating than going to the front and being turned away by a liveried footman, looking down his nose, and dispatched to the back to ask again.

"Yes?" the bootboy said soberly, his face pasty white and his apron crooked.

"Inspector Monk and Sergeant Evan, to see Lord Moidore," Monk replied quietly. Whatever his feeling for Runcorn, or his general intolerance of fools, he had a deep pity for bereavement and the confusion and shock of sudden death.

"Oh—" The bootboy looked startled, as if their presence had turned a nightmare into truth. "Oh—yes. Yer'd better come in." He pulled the door wide and stepped back, turning into the kitchen to call for help, his voice plaintive and desperate. "Mr. Phillips! Mr. Phillips—the p'lice is 'ere!"

The butler appeared from the far end of the huge kitchen. He was lean and a trifle stooped, but he had the autocratic face of a man used to command—and receiving obedience without question. He regarded Monk with both anxiety and distaste, and some surprise at Monk's well-cut suit, carefully laundered shirt, and polished, fine leather boots. Monk's appearance did not coincide with his idea of a policeman's social position, which was beneath that of a peddler or a costermonger. Then he looked at Evan, with his long, curved nose and imaginative eyes and mouth, and felt no better. It made him uncomfortable when people did not fit into their prescribed niches in the order of things. It was confusing.

"Sir Basil will see you in the library," he said stiffly. "If you will come this way." And without waiting to see if they did, he walked very uprightly out of the kitchen, ignoring the cook seated in a wooden rocking chair. They continued into the passageway beyond, past the cellar door, his own pantry, the still room, the outer door to the laundry, the housekeeper's sitting room, and then through the green baize door into the main house.

The hall floor was wood parquet, scattered with magnificent Persian carpets, and the walls were half paneled and hung with excellent landscapes. Monk had a flicker of memory from some distant time, perhaps a burglary detail, and the word *Flemish* came to mind. There was still so much that was closed in that part of him before the accident, and only flashes came back, like movement caught out of the corner of the eye, when one turns just too late to see.

But now he must follow the butler, and train all his attention on learning the facts of this case. He must succeed, and without allowing anyone else to realize how much he was stumbling, guessing, piecing together from fragments out of what they thought was his store of knowledge. They must not guess he was working with the underworld connections any good detective has. His reputation was high; people expected brilliance from him. He could see that in their eyes, hear it in their words, the casual praise given as if they were merely remarking the obvious. He also knew he had made too many enemies to afford mistakes. He heard it between the words and in the inflections of a comment, the barb and then the nervousness, the look away. Only gradually was he discovering what he had done in the years before to earn their fear, their envy or their dislike. A piece at a time he found evidence of his own extraordinary skill, the instinct, the relentless pursuit of truth, the long hours, the driving ambition, the intolerance of laziness, weakness in others, failure in himself. And of course, in spite of all his disadvantages since the accident, he had solved the extremely difficult Grey case.

They were at the library. Phillips opened the door and announced them, then stepped back to allow them in.

The room was traditional, lined with shelves. One large bay window let in the light, and green carpet and furnishings made it restful, almost gave an impression of a garden.

But there was no time now to examine it. Basil Moidore stood in the center of the floor. He was a tall man, loose boned, unathletic, but not yet running to fat, and he held himself very erect. He could never have been handsome; his features were too mobile, his mouth too large, the lines around it deeply etched and reflecting appetite and temper more than wit. His eyes were startlingly dark, not fine, but very penetrating and highly intelligent. His thick, straight hair was thickly peppered with gray.

Now he was both angry and extremely distressed. His skin was pale and he clenched and unclenched his hands nervously.

"Good morning, sir." Monk introduced himself and Evan. He hated speaking to the newly bereaved—and there was something peculiarly appalling about seeing one's child dead—but he was used to it. No loss of memory wiped out the familiarity of pain, and seeing it naked in others.

"Good morning, Inspector," Moidore said automatically. "I'm damned if I know what you can do, but I suppose you'd better try. Some ruffian broke in during the night and murdered my daughter. I don't know what else we can tell you."

"May we see the room where it happened, sir?" Monk asked quietly. "Has the doctor come yet?"

Sir Basil's heavy eyebrows rose in surprise. "Yes—but I don't know what damned good the man can do now."

"He can establish the time and manner of death, sir."

"She was stabbed some time during the night. It won't require a doctor to tell you that." Sir Basil drew in a deep breath and let it out slowly. His gaze wandered around the room, unable to sustain any interest in Monk. The inspector and Evan were only functionaries incidental to the tragedy, and he was too shocked for his mind to concentrate on a single thought. Little things intruded, silly things; a picture crooked on the wall, the sun on the title of a book, the vase of late chrysanthemums on the small table. Monk saw it in his face and understood.

"One of the servants will show us." Monk excused himself and Evan and turned to leave.

"Oh . . . yes. And anything else you need," Basil acknowledged.

"I suppose you didn't hear anything in the night, sir?" Evan asked from the doorway.

Sir Basil frowned. "What? No, of course not, or I'd have mentioned it." And even before Evan turned away the man's attention had left them and was on the leaves wind whipped against the window.

In the hall, Phillips the butler was waiting for them. He led them silently up the wide, curved staircase to the landing, carpeted in reds and blues and set with several tables around the walls. It stretched to right and left fifty feet or more to oriel windows at either end. They were led to the left and stopped outside the third door.

"In there, sir, is Miss Octavia's room," Phillips said very quietly. "Ring if you require anything."

Monk opened the door and went in, Evan close behind him. The room had a high, ornately plastered ceiling with pendant chandeliers. The floral curtains were drawn to let in the light. There were three well-upholstered chairs, a dressing table with a three-mirror looking glass, and a large four-poster bed draped in the same pink-and-green floral print as the curtains. Across the bed lay the body of a young woman, wearing only an ivory silk nightgown, a dark crimson stain slashing down from the middle of her chest almost to her knees. Her arms were thrown wide and her heavy brown hair was loose over her shoulders.

Monk was surprised to see beside her a slender man of just average height whose clever face was now very grave and pinched in thought. The sun through the window caught his fair hair, thickly curled and sprinkled with white.

"Police?" he asked, looking Monk up and down. "Dr. Faverell," he said as introduction. "The duty constable called me when the footman called him—about eight o'clock."

"Monk," Monk replied. "And Sergeant Evan. What can you tell us?"

Evan shut the door behind them and moved closer to the bed, his young face twisted with pity.

"She died some time during the night," Faverell replied bleakly. "From the stiffness of the body I should say at least seven hours ago." He took his watch out of his pocket and glanced at it. "It's now ten past nine. That makes it well before, say, three A.M. at the very outside. One deep, rather ragged wound, very deep. Poor creature must have lost consciousness immediately and died within two or three minutes."

"Are you the family physician?" Monk asked.

"No. I live 'round the corner in Harley Street. Local constable knew my address."

Monk moved closer to the bed, and Faverell stepped aside for him. The inspector leaned over and looked at the body. Her face had a slightly surprised look, as if the reality of death had been unexpected, but even through the pallor there was a kind of loveliness left. The bones were broad across the brow and cheek, the eye sockets were large with delicately marked brows, the lips full. It was a face of deep emotion, and yet femininely soft, a woman he might have liked. There was something in the curve of her lips that reminded him for a moment of someone else, but he could not recall who.

His eyes moved down and saw under the torn fabric of her nightgown the scratches on her throat and shoulder with smears of blood on them. There was another long rent in the silk from hem to groin, although it was folded over, as if to preserve decency. He looked at her hands, lifting them gently, but her nails were perfect and there was no skin or blood under them. If she had fought, she had not marked her attacker.

He looked more carefully for bruises. There should be some purpling of the skin, even if she had died only a few moments after being hurt. He searched her arms first, the most natural place for injury in a struggle, but there was nothing. He could find no mark on the legs or body either.

"She's been moved," he said after a few moments, seeing the pattern of the stains to the end of her garments, and only smears on the sheets beneath her where there should have been a deep pool. "Did you move her?"

"No." Faverell shook his head. "I only opened the curtain." He looked around the floor. There were dark roses on the carpet. "There." He pointed. "That might be blood, and there's a tear on that chair. I suppose the poor woman put up a fight."

Monk looked around also. Several things on the dressing table were crooked, but it was hard to tell what would have been the natural design. However a cut glass dish was broken, and there were dried rose leaves scattered over the carpet underneath it. He had not noticed them before in the pattern of the flowers woven in.

Evan walked towards the window.

"It's unlatched," he said, moving it experimentally.

"I closed it," the doctor put in. "It was open when I came, and damned cold. Took it into account for the rigor, though, so don't bother to ask me. Maid said it was open when she came with Mrs. Haslett's morning tray, but she didn't sleep with it open normally. I asked that too."

"Thank you," Monk said dryly.

Evan pushed the window all the way up and looked outside.

"There's creeper of some sort here, sir; and it's broken in several places where it looks as if someone put his weight on it, some pieces crushed and leaves gone." He leaned out a little farther. "And there's a good ledge goes along as far as the drainpipe down. An agile man could climb it without too much difficulty."

Monk went over and stood beside him. "Wonder why not the next room?" he said aloud. "That's closer to the drainpipe, easier, and less chance of being seen."

"Maybe it's a man's room?" Evan suggested. "No jewelry—or at least not much—a few silver-backed brushes, maybe, and studs, but nothing like a woman's."

Monk was annoyed with himself for not having thought of the same thing. He pulled his head back in and turned to the doctor.

"Is there anything else you can tell us?"

"Not a thing, sorry." He looked harassed and unhappy. "I'll write it out for you, if you want. But now I've got live patients to see. Must be going. Good day to you."

"Good day." Monk came back to the landing door with him. "Evan, go and see the maid that found her, and get her ladies' maid and go over the room to see if anything's missing, jewelry in particular. We can try the pawnbrokers and fences. I'm going to speak to some of the family who sleep on this floor."

The next room turned out to be that of Cyprian Moidore, the dead woman's elder brother, and Monk saw him in the morning room. It was overfurnished, but agreeably warm; presumably the downstairs maids had cleaned the grate, sanded and swept the carpets and lit the fires long before quarter to eight, when the upstairs maids had gone to waken the family.

Cyprian Moidore resembled his father in build and stance. His features were similar—the short, powerful nose, the broad mouth with the extraordinary mobility which might so easily become loose in a weaker man. His eyes were softer and his hair still dark.

Now he looked profoundly shaken.

"Good morning, sir," Monk said as he came into the room and closed the door.

Cyprian did not reply.

"May I ask you, sir, is it correct that you occupy the bedroom next to Mrs. Haslett's?"

"Yes." Cyprian met his eyes squarely; there was no belligerence in them, only shock.

"What time did you retire, Mr. Moidore?"

Cyprian frowned. "About eleven, or a few minutes after. I didn't hear anything, if that is what you are going to ask."

"And were you in your room all night, sir?" Monk tried to phrase it without being offensive, but it was impossible.

Cyprian smiled very faintly.

"I was last night. My wife's room is next to mine, the first as you leave the stair head." He put his hands into his pockets. "My son has the room opposite, and my daughters the one next to that. But I thought we had established that whoever it was broke into Octavia's room through the window."

"It looks most likely, sir," Monk agreed. "But it may not be the only room they tried. And of course it is possible they came in else-where and went *out* through her window. We know only that the creeper was broken. Was Mrs. Haslett a light sleeper?"

"No—" At first he was absolutely certain, then doubt flickered in his face. He took his hands out of his pockets. "At least I think not. But what difference does it make now? Isn't this really rather a waste of time?" He moved a step closer to the fire. "It is indisputable some-one broke in and she discovered him, and instead of simply running, the wretch stabbed her." His face darkened. "You should be out there looking for him, not in here asking irrelevant questions! Perhaps she was awake anyway. People do sometimes waken in the night."

Monk bit back the reply that rose instinctively.

"I was hoping to establish the time," he continued levelly. "It would help when we come to question the closest constable on the beat, and any other people who might have been around at that hour. And of course it would help when we catch anyone, if he could prove he was elsewhere."

"If he was elsewhere, then you wouldn't have the right person, would you!" Cyprian said acidly.

"If we didn't know the relevant time, sir, we might think we had!" Monk replied immediately. "I'm sure you don't want the wrong man hanged!"

Cyprian did not bother to answer.

The three women of the immediate family were waiting together in the withdrawing room, all close to the fire: Lady Moidore stiff-backed, white-faced on the sofa; her surviving daughter, Araminta, in one of the large chairs to her right, hollow-eyed as if she had not slept in days; and her daughter-in-law, Romola, standing behind her, her face reflecting horror and confusion.

"Good morning, ma'am." Monk inclined his head to Lady Moidore, then acknowledged the others.

None of them replied. Perhaps they did not consider it necessary to observe such niceties in the circumstances.

"I am deeply sorry to have to disturb you at such a tragic time," he said with difficulty. He hated having to express condolences to someone whose grief was so new and devastating. He was a stranger intruding into their home, and all he could offer were words, stilted and predictable. But to have said nothing would be grossly uncaring.

"I offer you my deepest sympathy, ma'am."

Lady Moidore moved her head very slightly in indication that she had heard him, but she did not speak.

He knew who the two younger women were because one of them shared the remarkable hair of her mother, a vivid shade of golden red which in the dark room seemed almost as alive as the flames of the fire. Cyprian's wife, on the other hand, was much darker, her eyes brown and her hair almost black. He turned to address her.

"Mrs. Moidore?"

"Yes?" She stared at him in alarm.

"Your bedroom window is between Mrs. Haslett's and the main drainpipe, which it seems the intruder climbed. Did you hear any unaccustomed sounds during the night, any disturbances at all?"

She looked very pale. Obviously the thought of the murderer passing her window had not occurred to her before. Her hands gripped the back of Araminta's chair.

"No—nothing. I do not customarily sleep well, but last night I did." She closed her eyes. "How fearful!"

Araminta was of a harder mettle. She sat rigid and slender, almost bony under the light fabric of her morning gown—no one had thought of changing into black yet. Her face was thin, wide-eyed, her mouth curiously asymmetrical. She would have been beautiful but for a certain sharpness, something brittle beneath the surface.

"We cannot help you, Inspector." She addressed him with candor, neither avoiding his eyes nor making any apology. "We saw Octavia before she retired last night, at about eleven o'clock, or a few minutes before. I saw her on the landing, then she went to my mother's room to wish her good-night, and then to her own room. We went to ours. My husband will tell you the same. We were awoken this morning by the maid, Annie, crying and calling out that something terrible had happened. I was the first to open the door after Annie. I saw straight away that Octavia was dead and we could not help her. I took Annie out and sent her to Mrs. Willis; she is the housekeeper. The poor child was looking very sick. Then I found my father, who was about to assemble the servants for morning prayers, and told him what had happened. He sent one of the footmen for the police. There really isn't anything more to say."

"Thank you, ma'am." Monk looked at Lady Moidore. She had the broad brow and short, strong nose her son had inherited, but a far more delicate face, and a sensitive, almost ascetic mouth. When she spoke, even drained by grief as she was, there was a beauty of vitality and imagination in her.

"I can add nothing, Inspector," she said very quietly. "My room is in the other wing of the house, and I was unaware of any tragedy or intrusion until my maid, Mary, woke me and then my son told me what had . . . happened."

"Thank you, my lady. I hope it will not be necessary to disturb you again." He had not expected to learn anything; it was really only a formality that he asked, but to overlook it would have been careless. He excused himself and went to find Evan back in the servants' quarters.

However Evan had discovered nothing of moment either, except a list of the missing jewelry compiled by the ladies' maid: two rings, a necklace and a bracelet, and, oddly, a small silver vase.

A little before noon they left the Moidore house, now with its blinds drawn and black crepe on the door. Already, out of respect for the dead, the grooms were spreading straw on the roadway to deaden the sharp sound of horses' hooves.

"What now?" Evan asked as they stepped out into the footpath. "The bootboy said there was a party at the east end, on the corner of

Chandos Street. One of the coachmen or footmen may have seen something." He raised his eyebrows hopefully.

"And there'll be a duty constable somewhere around," Monk added. "I'll find him, you take the party. Corner house, you said?"

"Yes sir—people called Bentley."

"Report back to the station when you've finished."

"Yes sir." And Evan turned on his heel and walked rapidly away, more gracefully than his lean, rather bony body would have led one to expect.

Monk took a hansom back to the station to find the home address of the constable who would have been patrolling the area during the night.

An hour later he was sitting in the small, chilly front parlor in a house off Euston Road, sipping a mug of tea opposite a sleepy, unshaven constable who was very ill at ease. It was some five minutes into the conversation before Monk began to realize that the man had known him before and that his anxiety was not based on any omission or failure of duty last night but on something that had occurred in their previous meeting, of which Monk had no memory at all.

He found himself searching the man's face, trying without success to bring any feature of it back to recollection, and twice he missed what was said.

"I'm sorry, Miller; what was that?" he apologized the second time.

Miller looked embarrassed, uncertain whether this was an acknowledgment of inattention or some implied criticism that his statement was unbelievable.

"I said I passed by Queen Anne Street on the west side, down Wimpole Street an' up again along 'Arley Street, every twenty minutes last night, sir. I never missed, 'cause there wasn't no disturbances and I didn't 'ave ter stop fer anythin'."

Monk frowned. "You didn't see anybody about? No one at all?"

"Oh I saw plenty o' people—but no one as there shouldn't 'a bin," Miller replied. "There was a big party up the other corner o' Chandos Street where it turns inter Cavendish Square. Coachmen and footmen an' all sorts 'angin' around till past three in the mornin', but they wasn't making no nuisance an' they certainly wasn't climbing up no drainpipes to get in no winders." He screwed up his face as if he were about to add something, then changed his mind.

"Yes?" Monk pressed.

But Miller would not be drawn. Again Monk wondered if it was because of their past association, and if Miller would have spoken for someone else. There was so much he did not know! Ignorance about police procedures, underworld connections, the vast store of knowledge a good detective kept. Not knowing was hampering him at every turn, making it necessary for him to work twice as hard in order to hide his vulnerability; but it did not end the deep fear caused by ignorance about himself. What manner of man was the self that stretched for years behind him, to that boy who had left Northumberland full of an ambition so consuming he had not written regularly to his only relative, his younger sister who had loved him so loyally in spite of his silence? He had found her letters in his rooms—sweet, gentle letters full of references to what should have been familiar.

Now he sat here in this small, neat house and tried to get answers from a man who was obviously frightened of him. Why? It was impossible to ask.

"Anyone else?" he said hopefully.

"Yes sir," Miller said straightaway, eager to please and beginning to master his nervousness. "There was a doctor paid a call near the corner of 'Arley Street and Queen Anne Street. I saw 'im leave, but I din't see 'im get there."

"Do you know his name?"

"No sir." Miller bristled, his body tightening again as if to defend himself. "But I saw 'im leave an' the front door was open an' the master o' the 'ouse was seein' 'im out. 'Alf the lights was on, and 'e weren't there uninvited!"

Monk considered apologizing for the unintended slight, then changed his mind. It would be more productive for Miller to be kept up to the mark.

"Do you remember which house?"

"About the third or fourth one along, on the south side of 'Arley Street, sir."

"Thank you. I'll ask them; they may have seen something." Then he wondered why he had offered an explanation; it was not necessary. He stood up and thanked Miller and left, walking back towards the main street where there would be cabs. He should have left this to Evan, who knew his underworld contacts, but it was too late now. He behaved from instinct and intelligence, forgetting how much of his memory was trapped in that shadowy world before the night his carriage had turned over, breaking his ribs and arm, and blotting out his identity and everything that bonded him to the past.

Who else might have been out in the night around Queen Anne Street? A year ago he would have known where to find the footpads, the cracksmen, the lookouts, but now he had nothing but guesswork and plodding deduction, which would betray him to Runcorn, who was so obviously waiting for every chance to trap him. Enough mistakes, and Runcorn would work out the incredible, delicious truth, and find the excuses he had sought for years to fire Monk and feel safe at last; no more hard, ambitious lieutenant dangerously close on his heels.

Finding the doctor was not difficult, merely a matter of returning to Harley Street and calling at the houses along the south side until he came to the right one, and then asking.

"Indeed," he was told in some surprise when he was received somewhat coolly by the master of the house, looking tired and harassed. "Although what interest it can be to the police I cannot imagine."

"A young woman was murdered in Queen Anne Street last night," Monk replied. The evening paper would carry it and it would be common knowledge in an hour or two. "The doctor may have seen someone loitering."

"He would hardly know by sight the sort of person who murders young women in the street!"

"Not in the street, sir, in Sir Basil Moidore's house," Monk corrected, although the difference was immaterial. "It is a matter of learning the time, and perhaps which direction he was going, although you're right, that is of little help."

"I suppose you know your business," the man said doubtfully, too weary and engaged in his own concerns to care. "But servants keep some funny company these days. I'd look to someone she let in herself, some disreputable follower."

"The victim was Sir Basil's daughter, Mrs. Haslett," Monk said with bitter satisfaction.

"Good God! How appalling!" The man's expression changed instantly. In a single sentence the danger had moved from affecting someone distant, not part of his world, to being a close and alarming threat. The chill hand of violence had touched his own class and in so doing had become real. "This is dreadful!" The blood fled from his tired face and his voice cracked for an instant. "What are you doing about it? We need more police in the streets, more patrols! Where did the man come from? What is he doing here?"

Monk smiled sourly to see the alteration in him. If the victim was a servant, she had brought it upon herself by keeping loose company; but now it was a lady, then police patrols must be doubled and the criminal caught forthwith.

"Well?" the man demanded, seeing what to him was a sneer on Monk's face.

"As soon as we find him, we will discover what he was doing," Monk replied smoothly. "In the meantime, if you will give me your physician's name, I will question him to see if he observed anything as he came or went."

The man wrote the name on a piece of paper and handed it to him.

"Thank you, sir. Good day."

But the doctor had seen nothing, being intent upon his own art, and could offer no help. He had not even noticed Miller on his beat. All he could do was confirm his own time of arrival and departure with an exactitude.

By mid-afternoon Monk was back in the police station, where Evan was waiting for him with the news that it would have been quite impossible for anyone at all to have passed by the west end of Queen Anne Street and not have been seen by several of the servants waiting for their masters outside the house where the party was being held. There had been a sufficient number of guests, including late arrivals and early departures, to fill the mews at the back with carriages and overflow into the street at the front.

"With that many footmen and coachmen around, would an extra person be noticed?" Monk queried.

"Yes." Evan had no doubts at all. "Apart from the fact that a lot of them know each other, they were all in livery. Anyone dressed differently would have been as obvious as a horse in a field of cows."

Monk smiled at Evan's rural imagery. Evan was the son of a country parson, and every now and again some memory or mannerism showed through. It was one of the many things Monk found pleasing in him.

"None of them?" he said doubtfully. He sat down behind his desk.

Evan shook his head. "Too much conversation going on, and a

lot of horseplay, chatting to the maids, flirting, carriage lamps all over the place. If anyone had shinned up a drainpipe to go over the roofs he'd have been seen in a trice. And no one walked off up the road alone, they're sure of that."

Monk did not press it any further. He did not believe it was a chance burglary by some footman which had gone wrong. Footmen were chosen for their height and elegance, and were superbly dressed. They were not equipped to climb drainpipes and cling to the sides of buildings two and three floors up, balancing along ledges in the dark. That was a practiced art which one came dressed to indulge.

"Must have come the other way," he concluded. "From the Wimpole Street end, in between Miller's going down that way and coming back up Harley Street. What about the back, from Harley Mews?"

"No way over the roof, sir," Evan replied. "I had a good look there. And a pretty good chance of waking the Moidores' coachman and grooms who sleep over the stables. Not a good burglar who disturbs horses, either. No sir, much better chance coming in the front, the way the drainpipe is and the broken creeper, which seems to be the way he did come. He must have nipped between Miller's rounds, as you say. Easy enough to watch for him."

Monk hesitated. He loathed betraying his vulnerability, even though he knew Evan was perfectly aware of it, and if he had been tempted to let it slip to Runcorn, he would have done it weeks ago during the Grey case, when he was confused, frightened and at his wit's end, terrified of the apparitions his intelligence conjured out of the scraps of recollection which recurred like nightmare forms. Evan and Hester Latterly were the two people in the world he could trust absolutely. And Hester he would prefer not to think about. She was not an appealing woman. Again Imogen Latterly's face came sweet to his mind, eyes soft and frightened as she had been when she asked him for help, her voice low, her skirts rustling like leaves as she walked past him. But she was Hester's brother's wife, and might as well have been a princess for anything she could be to Monk.

"Shall I ask a few questions at the Grinning Rat?" Evan interrupted his thoughts. "If anyone tries to get rid of the necklace and earrings they'll turn up with a fence, but word of a murder gets out pretty quickly, especially one the police won't let rest. The regular cracksmen will want to be well out of this."

"Yes—" Monk grasped at it quickly. "I'll try the fences and pawn-

brokers, you go to the Grinning Rat and see what you can pick up.''
He fished in his pocket and brought out his very handsome gold watch.
He must have saved a long time for this particular vanity, but he
could not remember either the going without or the exultancy of the
purchase. Now his fingers played over its smooth surface, and he felt
an emptiness that all its flavor and memory were gone for him. He
opened it with a flick.

"It's a good time to do that. I'll see you here tomorrow morning."

Evan went home and changed his clothes before assaying on the
journey to find his hard-won contacts on the fringes of the criminal
underworld. His present rather respectable, trim-fitting coat and clean
shirt might be taken for the garb of a confidence trickster, but far
more likely the genuine clothes of a socially aspiring clerk or minor
tradesman.

When he left his lodgings an hour after speaking to Monk, he
looked entirely different. His fair brown hair with its wide wave was
pulled through with grease and a little dirt, his face was similarly
marred, he wore an old shirt without a collar and a jacket that hung
off his lean shoulders. He also had for the occasion a pair of boots he
had salvaged from a beggar who had found better. They rubbed his
feet, but an extra pair of socks made them adequate for walking in,
and thus attired he set off for the Grinning Rat in Pudding Lane, and
an evening of cider, eel pie and listening.

There was an enormous variety of public houses in London, from
the large, highly respectable ones which catered banquets for the well-
bred and well-financed; through the comfortable, less ostentatious ones
which served as meeting and business places for all manner of profes-
sions from lawyers and medical students, actors and would-be politi-
cians; down through those that were embryo music halls, gathering
spots for reformers and agitators and pamphleteers, street corner phi-
losophers and working men's movements; right down to those that
were filled with gamblers, opportunists, drunkards and the fringes of
the criminal world. The Grinning Rat belonged to the last order,
which was why Evan had chosen it several years ago; and he was now,
if not liked there, at least tolerated.

From outside in the street he could see the lights gleaming through
the windows across the dirty pavement and the gutter. Half a dozen
men and several women lounged around outside the doorway, all
dressed in colors so dark and drab with wear they seemed only a

variation of densities in the barred light filtering out. Even when someone opened the door in a gale of laughter and a man and woman staggered down the steps, arm in arm, nothing showed but browns and duns and a flicker of dull red. The man backed away, and a woman half sitting in the gutter shouted something lewd after them. They ignored her and disappeared up Pudding Lane towards East Cheap.

Evan ignored her likewise and went inside to the warmth and the babble and the smell of ale and sawdust and smoke. He jostled his way past a group of men playing dice and another boasting the merits of fighting dogs, a temperance believer crying his creed in vain, and an ex-pugilist, his battered face good-natured and bleary-eyed.

" 'Evening, Tom," he said pleasantly.

" 'Evenin'," the pugilist said benignly, knowing the face was familiar but unable to recall a name for it.

"Seen Willie Durkins?" Evan asked casually. He saw the man's nearly empty mug. "I'm having a pint of cider—can I get you one?"

Tom did not hesitate but nodded cheerfully and drank the last of his ale so his mug was suitably empty.

Evan took it, made his way to the bar and purchased two ciders, passing the time of evening with the bartender who fetched him his mug from among the many swinging on hooks above his head. Each regular customer had his own mug. Evan returned to where Tom was waiting hopefully and passed him his cider, and when Tom had drunk half of it, with a huge thirst, Evan began his unobtrusive inquiry.

"Seen Willie?" he said again.

"Not tonight, sir." Tom added the "sir" by way of acknowledging the pint. He still could not think of a name. "Wot was yer wantin' 'im fer? Mebbe I can 'elp?"

"Want to warn him," Evan lied, not watching Tom's face but looking down into his mug.

"Wot abaht?"

"Bad business up west," Evan answered. "Got to find somebody for it, and I know Willie." He looked up suddenly and smiled, a lovely dazzling gesture, full of innocence and good humor. "I don't want him put away—I'd miss him."

Tom gurgled his appreciation. He was not absolutely sure, but he rather thought this agreeable young fellow might be either a rozzer or someone who fed the rozzers judicious bits of information. He would not be above doing that himself, if he had any—for a reasonable con-

sideration, of course. Nothing about ordinary thievery, which was a
way of life, but about strangers on the patch, or nasty things that were
likely to bring a lot of unwelcome police attention, like murders, or
arson, or major forgery, which always upset important gents up in the
City. It made things hard for the small business of local burglary, street
robbery, petty forgery of money and legal letters or papers. It was
difficult to fence stolen goods with too many police about, or sell
illegal liquors. Small-time smuggling up the river suffered—and gambling, card sharping, petty fraud and confidence tricks connected with
sport, bare knuckle pugilism, and of course prostitution. Had Evan
asked about any of these Tom would have been affronted and told
him so. The underworld conducted these types of business all the
time, and no one expected to root them out.

But there were things one did not do. It was foolish, and very
inconsiderate to those who had their living to make with as little
disturbance as possible.

"Wot bad business is that, sir?"

"Murder," Evan replied seriously. "Very important man's daughter, stabbed in her own bedroom, by a burglar. Stupid—"

"I never 'eard." Tom was indignant. "W'en was that, then?
Nobody said!"

"Last night," Evan answered, drinking more of his cider. Somewhere over to their left there was a roar of laughter and someone
shouted the odds against a certain horse winning a race.

"I never 'eard," Tom repeated dolefully. "Wot 'e want ter go an'
do that fer? Stupid, I calls it. W'y kill a lady? Knock 'er one, if yer
'ave ter, like if she wakes up and starts ter 'oller. But it's a daft geezer
wot makes enough row ter wake people anyway."

"And stabbing." Evan shook his head. "Why couldn't he hit her,
as you said. Needn't have killed her. Now half the top police in the
West End will be all over the place!" A total exaggeration, at least
so far, but it served his purpose. "More cider?"

Again Tom indicated his reply by shoving his mug over word-
lessly, and Evan rose to oblige.

"Willie wouldn't do anything like that," Tom said when Evan
returned. " 'E in't stupid."

"If I thought he had I wouldn't want to warn him," Evan answered. "I'd let him swing."

"Yeah," Tom agreed gloomily. "But w'en, eh? Not before the

crushers 'as bin all over the place, an' everybody's bin upset and business ruined for all sorts!"

"Exactly." Evan hid his face in his mug. "So where's Willie?"

This time Tom did not equivocate. "Mincing Lane," he said dourly. "If'n yer wait there an hour or so 'e'll come by the pie stand there some time ternight. An' I daresay if'n yer tells 'im abaht this 'e'll be grateful, like." He knew Evan, whoever he was, would want something in return. That was the way of life.

"Thank you." Evan left his mug half empty; Tom would be only too pleased to finish it for him. "I daresay I'll try that. G'night."

"G'night." Tom appropriated the half mug before any overzealous barman could remove it.

Evan went out into the rapidly chilling evening and walked briskly, collar turned up, looking neither to right nor left, until he turned into Mincing Lane and past the groups of idlers huddled in doorways. He found the eel pie seller with his barrow, a thin man with a stovepipe hat askew on his head, an apron around his waist, and a delicious smell issuing from the inside of containers balanced in front of him.

Evan bought a pie and ate it with enjoyment, the hot pastry crunching and flaking and the eel flesh delicate on his tongue.

"Seen Willie Durkins?" he said presently.

"Not ternight." The man was careful: it did not do to give information for nothing, and without knowing to whom.

Evan had no idea whether to believe him or not, but he had no better plan, and he settled back in the shadows, chilly and bored, and waited. A street patterer came by, singing a ballad about a current scandal involving a clergyman who had seduced a schoolmistress and then abandoned her and her child. Evan recalled the case in the sensational press a few months ago, but this version was much more colorful, and in less than fifteen minutes the patterer, and the eel stand, had collected a dozen or more customers, all of whom bought pies and stood around to listen. For which service the patterer got his supper free—and a good audience.

A narrow man with a cheerful face came out of the gloom to the south and bought himself a pie, which he ate with evident enjoyment, then bought a second and treated a scruffy child to it with evident pleasure.

"Good night then, Tosher?" the pie man asked knowingly.

"Best this month," Tosher replied. "Found a gold watch! Don't get many o' them."

The pie man laughed. "Some flash gent'll be cursin' 'is luck!" He grinned. "Shame—eh?"

"Oh, terrible shame," Tosher agreed with a chuckle.

Evan knew enough of street life to understand. "Tosher" was the name for men who searched the sewers for lost articles. As far as he was concerned, they, and the mudlarks along the river, were more than welcome to what they found; it was hard won enough.

Other people came and went: costers, off duty at last; a cab driver; a couple of boatmen up from the river steps; a prostitute; and then, when Evan was stiff with cold and lack of movement and about to give up, Willie Durkins.

He recognized Evan after only a brief glance, and his round face became careful.

" 'Allo, Mr. Evan. Wot you want, then? This in't your patch."

Evan did not bother to lie; it would serve no purpose and evidence bad faith.

"Last night's murder up west, in Queen Anne Street."

"Wot murder was that?" Willie was confused, and it showed in his guarded expression, narrowed eyes, a trifle squinting in the street-light over the pie stall.

"Sir Basil Moidore's daughter, stabbed in her own bedroom—by a burglar."

"Go on—Basil Moidore, eh?" Willie looked dubious. " 'E must be worth a mint, but 'is 'ouse'd be crawlin' with servants! Wot cracks-man'd do that? It's fair stupid! Damn fool!"

"Best get it sorted." Evan pushed out his lip and shook his head a little.

"Dunno nuffin'," Willie denied out of habit.

"Maybe. But you know the house thieves who work that area," Evan argued.

"It wouldn't be one o' them," Willie said quickly.

Evan pulled a face. "And of course they wouldn't know a stranger on the patch," he said sarcastically.

Willie squinted at him, considering. Evan looked gullible; his was a dreamer's face; it should have belonged to a gentleman, not a ser-geant in the rozzers. Nothing like Monk; now there was someone not to mess about with, an ambitious man with a devious mind and a hard tongue. You knew from the set of his bones and the gray eyes that never wavered that it would be dangerous to play games with him.

"Sir Basil Moidore's daughter," Evan said almost to himself. "They'll hang someone—have to. Shake up a lot of people before they find the right man—if it becomes necessary."

"O'right!" Willie said grudgingly. "O'right! Chinese Paddy was up there last night. 'E din't do nothin'—din't 'ave the chance, so yer can't bust 'im. Clean as a w'istle, 'e is. But ask 'im. If 'e can't 'elp yer, then no one can. Now let me be—yer'll gimme a bad name, 'anging 'round 'ere wi' the likes o' you."

"Where do I find Chinese Paddy?" Evan caught hold of the man's arm, fingers hard till Willie squeaked.

"Leggo o' me! Wanna break me arm?"

Evan tightened his grip.

"Dark 'Ouse Lane, Billingsgate—termorrer mornin', w'en the market opens. Yer'll know 'im easy, 'e's got black 'air like a chimney brush, an' eyes like a Chinaman. Now le' go o' me!"

Evan obliged, and in a minute Willie disappeared down Mincing Lane towards the river and the ferry steps.

Evan went straight home to his rooms, washed off the worst surface dirt in a bowl of tepid water, and slipped into bed.

At five in the morning he rose again, put on the same clothes and crept out of the house and took a series of public omnibuses to Billingsgate, and by quarter past six in the dawn light he was in the crush of costers' barrows, fishmongers' high carts and dray wagons at the entrance to Dark House Lane itself. It was so narrow that the houses reared up like cliff walls on either side, the advertisement boards for fresh ice actually stretching across from one side to the other. Along both sides were stacked mountains of fresh, wet, slithering fish of every description, piled on benches, and behind them stood the salesmen crying their wares, white aprons gleaming like the fish bellies, and white hats pale against the dark stones behind them.

A fish porter with a basket full of haddock on his head could barely squeeze past the double row of shoppers crowding the thin passageway down the middle. At the far end Evan could just see the tangled rigging of oyster boats on the water and the occasional red worsted cap of a sailor.

The smell was overpowering; red herrings, every kind of white fish from sprats to turbot, lobsters, whelks, and over all a salty, seaweedy odor as if one were actually on a beach. It brought back a sudden jolt of childhood excursions to the sea, the coldness of the water and the sight of a crab running sideways across the sand.

But this was utterly different. All around him was not the soft slurp of the waves but the cacophony of a hundred voices: "Ye-o-o! Ye-o-o! 'Ere's yer fine Yarmouth bloaters! Whiting! Turbot—all alive! Beautiful lobsters! Fine cock crabs—alive O! Splendid skate—alive— all cheap! Best in the market! Fresh 'addock! Nice glass o' peppermint this cold morning! Ha'penny a glass! 'Ere yer are, sir! Currant and meat puddings, a ha'penny each! 'Ere ma'am! Smelt! Finny 'addock! Plaice—all alive O. Whelks—mussels—now or never! Shrimps! Eels! Flounder! Winkles! Waterproof capes—a shilling apiece! Keep out the wet!"

And a news vendor cried out: "I sell food for the mind! Come an' read all abaht it! Terrible murder in Queen Anne Street! Lord's daughter stabbed ter death in 'er bed!"

Evan pushed his way slowly through the crowd of costers, fish-mongers and housewives till he saw a brawny fish seller with a distinctly Oriental appearance.

"Are you Chinese Paddy?" he asked as discreetly as he could above the babble and still be heard.

"Sure I am. Will you be wantin' some nice fresh cod, now? Best in the market!"

"I want some information. It'll cost you nothing, and I'm prepared to pay for it—if it's right," Evan replied, standing very upright and looking at the fish as if he were considering buying it.

"And why would I be selling information at a fish market, mister? What is it you want to know—times o' the tides, is it?" Chinese Paddy raised his straight black eyebrows sarcastically. "I don't know you—"

"Metropolitan police," Evan said quietly. "Your name was given me by a very reliable fellow I know—down in Pudding Lane. Now do I have to do this in an unpleasant fashion, or can we trade like gentlemen, and you can stay here selling your fish when I leave and go about my business?" He said it courteously, but just once he looked up and met Chinese Paddy's eyes in a hard, straight stare.

Paddy hesitated.

"The alternative is I arrest you and take you to Mr. Monk and he can ask you again." Evan knew Monk's reputation, even though Monk himself was still learning it.

Paddy made his decision.

"What is it you're wanting to know?"

"The murder in Queen Anne Street. You were up there last night—"

" 'Ere—fresh fish—fine cod!" Paddy called out. "So I was," he went on in a quiet, hard tone. "But I never stole nuffin', an' I sure as death and the bailiffs never killed that woman!" Ignoring Evan for a moment, he sold three large cod to a woman and took a shilling and sixpence.

"I know that," Evan agreed. "But I want to know what you saw!"

"A bleedin' rozzer goin' up 'Arley Street an' down Wimpole Street every twenty minutes reg'lar," Paddy replied, looking one moment at his fish, and the next at the crowd as it passed. "You're ruinin' me trade, mister! People is wonderin' why you don't buy!"

"What else?" Evan pressed. "The sooner you tell me, the sooner I'll buy a fish and be gone."

"A quack coming to the third 'ouse up on 'Arley Street, an' a maid out on the tiles with 'er follower. The place was like bleedin' Piccadilly! I never got a chance to do anything."

"Which house did you come for?" Evan asked, picking up a fish and examining it.

"Corner o' Queen Anne Street and Wimpole Street, southwest corner."

"And where were you waiting, exactly?" Evan felt a curious prickle of apprehension, a kind of excitement and horror at once. "And what time?"

" 'Alf the ruddy night!" Paddy said indignantly. "From ten o'clock till near four. Welbeck Street end o' Queen Anne Street. That way I could see the 'ole length o' Queen Anne Street right down to Chandos Street. Bit of a party goin' on t'other end—footmen all over the place."

"Why didn't you pack up and go somewhere else? Why stick around there all night if it was so busy?"

" 'Ere, fresh cod—all alive—best in the market!" Paddy called over Evan's head. 'Ere missus! Right it is—that'll be one and eight pence—there y'are." His voice dropped again. "Because I 'ad the layout of a good place, o' course—an' I don't go in unprepared. I in't a bleedin' amacher. I kept thinkin' they'd go. But that perishin' maid was 'alf the night in the areaway like a damn cat. No morals at all."

"So who came and went up Queen Anne Street?" Evan could hardly keep the anticipation out of his voice. Whoever killed Octavia Haslett had not passed the footmen and coachmen at the other end, nor climbed over from the mews—he must have come this way, and if Chinese Paddy was telling the truth, he must have seen him. A thin shiver of excitement rippled through Evan.

"No one passed me, 'cept the quack an' the maid," Paddy repeated with irritation. "I 'ad me eyes peeled all bleedin' night—just waitin' me chance—an' it never came. The 'ouse where the quack went 'ad all its lights on an' the door open and closed, open and closed—I didn't dare go past. Then the ruddy girl with 'er man. No one went past me—I'd swear to that on me life, I would. An' Mr. Monk can do any damn thing 'e can think of—it won't change it. 'Oever scragged that poor woman, 'e was already in the 'ouse, that's for certain positive. An' good luck to you findin' 'im, 'cos I can't 'elp yer. Now take one o' them fish and pay me twice wot it's worth, and get out of 'ere. You're holdin' up trade terrible, you are."

Evan took the fish and handed over three shillings. Chinese Paddy was a contact worth keeping favor with.

"Already in the house." The words rang in his head. Of course he would have to check with the courting maid as well, but if she could be persuaded, on pain of his telling her mistress if she was reluctant, then Chinese Paddy was right—whoever killed Octavia Haslett was someone who already lived there, no stranger caught in the act of burglary but a premeditated murderer who disguised his act afterwards.

Evan turned sideways to push his way between a high fishmonger's cart and a coster's barrow and out into the street.

He could imagine Monk's face when he learned—and Runcorn's. This was a completely different thing, a very dangerous and very ugly thing.

CHAPTER
TWO

—

Hester Latterly straightened up from the fire she had been sweeping and stoking and looked at the long, cramped ward of the infirmary. The narrow beds were a few feet apart from each other and set down both sides of the dim room with its high, smoke-darkened ceiling and sparse windows. Adults and children lay huddled under the gray blankets in all conditions of illness and distress.

At least there was enough coal and she could keep the place tolerably warm, even though the dust and fine ash from it seemed to get into everything. The women in the beds closest to the fire were too hot, and kept complaining about the grit getting into their bandages, and Hester was forever dusting the table in the center of the room and the few wooden chairs where patients well enough occasionally sat. This was Dr. Pomeroy's ward, and he was a surgeon, so all the cases were either awaiting operations or recovering from them—or, in over half the instances, not recovering but in some stage of hospital fever or gangrene.

At the far end a child began to cry again. He was only five and had a tubercular abscess in the joint of his shoulder. He had been there three months already, waiting to have it operated on, and each time he had been taken along to the theater, his legs shaking, his teeth gritted, his young face white with fear, he had sat in the anteroom for over two hours, only to be told some other case had been treated today and he was to return to his bed.

To Hester's fury, Dr. Pomeroy had never explained either to the child or to her why this had been done. But then Pomeroy regarded nurses in the same light as most other doctors did: they were necessary only to do the menial tasks—washing, sweeping, scrubbing, disposing of soiled bandages, and rolling, storing and passing out new ones. The most senior were also to keep discipline, particularly moral discipline, among the patients well enough to misbehave or become disorderly.

Hester straightened her skirt and smoothed her apron, more from habit than for any purpose, and hurried down to the child. She could not ease his pain—he had already been given all he should have for that, she had seen to it—but she could at least offer him the comfort of arms around him and a gentle word.

He was curled up on his left side with his aching right shoulder high, crying softly into the pillow. It was a desolate, hopeless sound as if he expected nothing, simply could not contain his misery any longer.

She sat down on the bed and very carefully, not to jolt the shoulder, gathered him up in her arms. He was thin and light and not difficult to support. She laid his head against her and stroked his hair. It was not what she was there for; she was a skilled nurse with battlefield experience in horrific wounds and emergency surgery and care of men suffering from cholera, typhus and gangrene. She had returned home after the war hoping to help reform the backward and tradition-bound hospitals in England, as had so many other of the women who had nursed in the Crimea; but it had proved far more difficult than she expected even to find a post, let alone to exert any influence.

Of course Florence Nightingale was a national heroine. The popular press was full of praise for her, and the public adored her. She was perhaps the only person to emerge from the whole sorry campaign covered with glory. There were stories of the hectic, insane, misdirected charge of the Light Brigade right into the mouths of the Russian guns, and scarcely a military family in the country had not lost either a son or a friend in the carnage that followed. Hester herself had watched it helplessly from the heights above. She could still see in her mind's eye Lord Raglan sitting ramrod stiff on his horse as if he had been riding in some English park, and indeed he had said afterwards that his mind had been on his wife at home. It certainly could not have been on the matter at hand, or he could never have given such a suicidal command, however it was worded—and there had been enough argument about it afterwards. Lord Raglan had said one thing—Lieutenant Nolan had conveyed another to Lords Lucan and Cardigan. Nolan was killed, torn to pieces by a splinter from a Russian shell as he dashed in front of Cardigan waving his sword and shouting. Perhaps he had intended to tell Cardigan he was charging the manned guns—not the abandoned position the order intended. No one would ever know.

Hundreds were crippled or slain, the flower of the cavalry a scatter of mangled corpses in Balaclava. For courage and supreme sacrifice to duty the charge had been a high-water mark of history—militarily it was useless.

And there had been the glory of the thin red line at the Alma, the Heavy Brigade who had stood on foot, their scarlet uniforms a wavering line holding back the enemy, clearly visible even from the far distance where the women waited. As one man fell, another took his place, and the line never gave. The heroism would be remembered as long as stories of war and courage were told, but who even now remembered the maimed and the dead, except those who were bereaved, or caring for them?

She held the child a little closer. He was no longer crying, and it comforted her in some deep, wordless place in her own spirit. The sheer, blinding incompetence of the campaign had infuriated her, the conditions in the hospital in Scutari were so appalling she thought if she survived that, kept her sanity and some remnant of humor, then she would find anything in England a relief and encouragement. At least here there would be no cartloads of wounded, no raging epidemic fevers, no men brought in with frostbitten limbs to be amputated, or bodies frozen to death on the heights above Sebastopol. There would be ordinary dirt, lice and vermin, but nothing like the armies of rats that had hung on the walls and fallen like rotting fruit, the sounds of the fat bodies plopping on beds and floors sickening her dreams even now. And there would be the normal waste to clean, but not hospital floors running with pools of excrement and blood from hundreds of men too ill to move, and rats, but not by the thousands.

But that horror had brought out the strength in her, as it had in so many other women. It was the endless pomposity, rule-bound, paper-shuffling self-importance, and refusal to change that crippled her spirit now. The authorities regarded initiative as both arrogant and dangerous, and in women it was so totally misplaced as to be against nature.

The Queen might turn out to greet Florence Nightingale, but the medical establishment was not about to welcome young women with ideas of reform, and Hester had found this out through numerous infuriating, doomed confrontations.

It was all the more distressing because surgery had made such giant steps forward. It was ten years, to the month, since ether had been used successfully in America to anesthetize a patient during an operation. It was a marvelous discovery. Now all sorts of things could be done which had been impossible before. Of course a brilliant surgeon could amputate a limb; saw through flesh, arteries, muscle and bone; cauterize the stump and sew as necessary in a matter of forty or fifty seconds. Indeed Robert Liston, one of the fastest, had been known to saw through a thigh bone and amputate the leg, two of his assistant's fingers, and the tail of an onlooker's coat in twenty-nine seconds.

But the shock to the patient in such operations was appalling, and internal operations were out of the question because no one, with all the thongs and ropes in the world, could tie someone down securely enough for the knife to be wielded with any accuracy. Surgery had never been regarded as a calling of dignity or status. In fact, surgeons were coupled with barbers, more renowned for strong hands and speed of movement than for great knowledge.

Now, with anesthetic, all sorts of more complicated operations could be assayed, such as the removal of infected organs from patients diseased rather than wounded, frostbitten or gangrened; like this child she held in her arms, now close to sleep at last, his face flushed, his body curled around but eased to lie still.

She was holding him, rocking very gently, when Dr. Pomeroy came in. He was dressed for operating, in dark trousers, well worn and stained with blood, a shirt with a torn collar, and his usual waistcoat and old jacket, also badly soiled. It made little sense to ruin good clothes; any other surgeon would have worn much the same.

"Good morning, Dr. Pomeroy," Hester said quickly. She caught his attention because she wished to press him to operate on this child within the next day or two, best of all this afternoon. She knew his chances of recovery were only very moderate—forty percent of surgical patients died of postoperative infection—but he would get no better as he was, and his pain was becoming worse, and therefore his condition weaker. She endeavored to be civil, which was difficult because although she knew his skill with the knife was high, she despised him personally.

"Good morning, Miss—er—eh—" He still managed to look surprised, in spite of the fact that she had been there a month and they had conversed frequently, most often with opposing views. They were not exchanges he was likely to forget. But he did not approve of nurses who spoke before they were addressed, and it caught him awry every time.

"Latterly," she supplied, and forbore from adding "I have not changed it since yesterday—nor indeed at all," which was on the edge of her tongue. She cared more about the child.

"Yes, Miss Latterly, what is it?" He did not look at her, but at the old woman on the bed opposite, who was lying on her back with her mouth open.

"John Airdrie is in considerable pain, and his condition is not improving," she said with careful civility, keeping her voice much softer than the feeling inside her. Unconsciously she held the child closer to her. "I believe if you will operate quickly it will be his best chance."

"John Airdrie?" He turned back to look at her, a frown between his brows. He was a small man with gingery hair and a very neatly trimmed beard.

"The child," she said with gritted teeth. "He has a tubercular abscess in the joint of his shoulder. You are to excise it."

"Indeed?" he said coldly. "And where did you take your medical degree, Miss Latterly? You are very free with your advice to me. I have had occasion to remark on it a number of times!"

"In the Crimea, sir," she said immediately and without lowering her eyes.

"Oh yes?" He pushed his hands into his trouser pockets. "Did you treat many children with tubercular shoulders there, Miss Latterly? I know it was a hard campaign, but were we really reduced to drafting sickly five-year-olds to do our fighting for us?" His smile was thin and pleased with itself. He spoiled his barb by adding to it. "If they were also reduced to permitting young women to study medicine, it was a far harder time than we here in England were led to believe."

"I think you in England were led to believe quite a lot that was not true," she retorted, remembering all the comfortable lies and concealments that the press had printed to save the faces of government and army command. "They were actually very glad of us, as has been well demonstrated since." She was referring to Florence Nightingale again, and they both knew it; names were not necessary.

He winced. He resented all this fuss and adulation for one woman by common and uninformed people who knew no better. Medicine was a matter of skill, judgment and intelligence, not of wandering around interfering with established knowledge and practice.

"Nevertheless, Miss Latterly, Miss Nightingale and all her helpers, including you, are amateurs and will remain so. There is no medical school in this country which admits women, or is ever likely to. Good heavens! The best universities do not even admit religious nonconformists! Females would be unimaginable. And who, pray, would allow them to practice? Now will you keep your opinions to yourself and attend to the duties for which we pay you? Take off Mrs. Warburton's bandages and dispose of them—" His face creased with anger as she did not move. "And put that child down! If you wish for children to hold, then get married and have some, but do not sit here like a wet nurse. Bring me clean bandages so I can redress Mrs. Warburton's wound. Then you may see if she will take a little ice. She looks feverish."

Hester was so furious she was rooted to the spot. His statements were monstrously irrelevant, patronizing and complacent, and she had no weapons she dared use against him. She could tell him all the incompetent, self-preserving, inadequate things she thought he was, but it would only defeat her purposes and make an even more bitter enemy of him than he was now. And perhaps John Airdrie would suffer.

With a monumental effort she bit back the scalding contempt and the words remained inside her.

"When are you going to operate on the child?" she repeated, staring at him.

He colored very faintly. There was something in her eyes that discomfited him.

"I had already decided to operate this afternoon, Miss Latterly. Your comments were quite unnecessary," he lied—and she knew it, but kept it from her face.

"I am sure your judgment is excellent," she lied back.

"Well what are you waiting for?" he demanded, taking his hands out of his pockets. "Put that child down and get on with it! Do you not know how to do what I asked? Surely your competence stretches that far?" He indulged in sarcasm again; he still had a great deal of status to recoup. "The bandages are in the cupboard at the end of the ward, and no doubt you have the key."

Hester was too angry to speak. She laid the child down gently, rose to her feet.

"Is that not it, hanging at your waist?" he demanded.

She strode past him, swinging the keys so wide and hard they clipped his coattails as she passed, and marched along the length of the ward to fetch the bandages.

Hester had been on duty since dawn, and by four o'clock in the afternoon she was emotionally exhausted. Physically, her back ached, her legs were stiff, her feet hurt and her boots felt tight. And the pins in her hair were digging into her head. She was in no mood to continue her running battle with the matron over the type of woman who should be recruited into nursing. She wished particularly to see it become a profession which was respected and remunerated accordingly, so women of character and intelligence would be attracted. Mrs. Stansfield had grown up with the rough-and-ready women who expected to do no more than scrub, sweep, stoke fires and carry coals, launder, clean out slops and waste, and pass bandages. Senior nurses like herself kept discipline rigid and spirits high. She had no desire, as Hester had, to exercise medical judgment, change dressings herself and give medicines when the surgeon was absent, and certainly not to assist in operations. She considered these young women who had come back from the Crimea to overrate themselves greatly and be a disruptive and highly unwelcome influence, and she said so.

This evening Hester simply wished her good-night and walked out, leaving her surprised, and the lecture on morals and duty pent up unspoken inside her. It was very unsatisfying. It would be different tomorrow.

It was not a long journey from the infirmary to the lodging house where Hester had taken rooms. Previously she had lived with her brother, Charles, and his wife, Imogen, but since the financial ruin and death of their parents, it would be quite unfair to expect Charles to support her for longer than the first few months after she returned from the Crimea early in order to be with the family in its time of bereavement and distress. After the resolution of the Grey case she had accepted the help of Lady Callandra Daviot to obtain the post at the infirmary, where she could earn sufficient to maintain herself and could exercise the talents she possessed in administration and nursing.

During the war she had also learned a good deal about war correspondence from her friend Alan Russell, and when he died in the hospital in Scutari, she had sent his last dispatch to his newspaper in London. Later, when his death had not been realized in the thousands of others, she did not amend the error but wrote the letters herself, and was deeply satisfied when they were printed. She could no longer use his name now she was home again, but she wrote now and then, and signed herself simply as one of Miss Nightingale's volunteers. It paid only a few shillings, but money was not her primary motive; it was the desire to express the opinions she held with such intensity, and to move people to press for reform.

When she reached her lodgings, her landlady, a spare, hardworking woman with a sick husband and too many children, greeted her with the news that she had a visitor awaiting her in the parlor.

"A visitor?" Hester was surprised, and too weary to be pleased, even if it was Imogen, who was the only person she could think of. "Who is it, Mrs. Horne?"

"A Mrs. Daviot," the landlady replied without interest. She was too busy to be bothered with anything beyond her duties. "Said she'd wait for you."

"Thank you." Hester felt an unexpected lift, both because she liked Callandra Daviot as well as anyone she knew, and because characteristically she had omitted to use her title, a modesty exercised by very few.

Callandra was sitting in the small, well-worn parlor by the meager fire, but she had not kept on her coat, even though the room was chill. Her interesting, individual face lit up when Hester came in. Her hair was as wild as always, and she was dressed with more regard for comfort than style.

"Hester, my dear, you look appallingly tired. Come and sit down. I'm sure you need a cup of tea. So do I. I asked that woman, poor creature—what is her name?—if she would bring one."

"Mrs. Horne." Hester sat down and unbuttoned her boots. She slipped them off under her skirt with an exquisite relief and adjusted the worst of the pins in her hair.

Callandra smiled. She was the widow of an army surgeon, now very much past her later middle years, and she had known Hester some time before the Grey case had caused their paths to cross again. She had been born Callandra Grey, the daughter of the late Lord Shelburne, and was the aunt of the present Lord Shelburne and of his younger brother.

Hester knew she would not have come simply to visit, not at the end of a hard day when she was aware Hester would be tired and not in the best frame of mind for company. It was too late for genteel afternoon calling, and far too early for dinner. Hester waited expectantly.

"Menard Grey comes to trial the day after tomorrow," Callandra said quietly. "We must testify on his behalf—I presume you are still willing?"

"Of course!" There was not even a second's doubt.

"Then we had better go and meet with the lawyer I have employed to conduct his defense. He will have some counsel for us concerning our testimony. I have arranged to see him in his rooms this evening. I am sorry it is so hasty, but he is extremely busy and had no other opportunity. We may have dinner first, or later, as you please. My carriage will return in half an hour; I thought it unsuitable to leave it outside." She smiled wryly; explanation was not necessary.

"Of course." Hester sank deeper into her chair and thought of Mrs. Horne's cup of tea. She would have that well before she thought of changing her clothes, putting her boots on again, and traipsing out to see some lawyer.

But Oliver Rathbone was not "some lawyer"; he was the most brilliant advocate practicing at the bar, and he knew it. He was a lean man of no more than average height, neatly but unremarkably dressed, until one looked closely and saw the quality of the fabric and, after a little while, the excellence of the cut, which fitted him perfectly and seemed always to hang without strain or crease. His hair was fair and his face narrow with a long nose and a sensitive, beautifully shaped mouth. But the overriding impression was one of controlled emotion and brilliant, all-pervading intelligence.

His rooms were quiet and full of light from the chandelier which hung from the center of an ornately plastered ceiling. In the daylight they would have been equally well illuminated by three large sash windows, curtained in dark green velvet and bound by simple cords. The desk was mahogany and the chairs appeared extremely comfortable.

He ushered them in and bade them be seated. At first Hester was unimpressed, finding him a little too concerned for their ease than for the purpose of their visit, but this misapprehension vanished as soon as he addressed the matter of the trial. His voice was pleasing enough, but the preciseness of his diction made it memorable so that even his exact intonation remained with her long afterwards.

"Now, Miss Latterly," he said, "we must discuss the testimony you are to give. You understand it will not simply be a matter of reciting what you know and then being permitted to leave?"

She had not considered it, and when she did now, that was precisely what she had assumed. She was about to deny it, and saw in his face that he had read her thoughts, so she changed them.

"I was awaiting your instructions, Mr. Rathbone. I had not judged the matter one way or the other."

He smiled, a delicate, charming movement of the lips.

"Quite so." He leaned against the edge of his desk and regarded her gravely. "I will question you first. You are my witness, you understand? I shall ask you to tell the events of your family's tragedy, simply, from your own point of view. I do not wish you to tell me anything that you did not experience yourself. If you do, the judge will instruct the jury to disregard it, and every time he stops you and disallows what you say, the less credence the jury will give to what remains. They may easily forget which is which."

"I understand," she assured him. "I will say only what I know for myself."

"You may easily be tempted, Miss Latterly. It is a matter in which your feelings must be very deep." He looked at her with brilliant, humorous eyes. "It will not be as simple as you may expect."

"What chance is there that Menard Grey will not be hanged?" she asked gravely. She chose deliberately the harshest words. Rathbone was not a man with whom to use euphemisms.

"We will do the best we can," he replied, the light fading from his face. "But I am not at all sure that we will succeed."

"And what would be success, Mr. Rathbone?"

"Success? Success would be transportation to Australia, where he would have some chance to make a new life for himself—in time. But they stopped most transportation three years ago, except for cases warranting sentences over fourteen years—" He paused.

"And failure?" she said almost under her breath. "Hanging?"

"No," he said, leaning forward a little. "The rest of his life somewhere like the Coldbath Fields. I'd rather be hanged, myself."

She sat silent; there was nothing to say to such a reality, and trite words would be so crass as to be painful. Callandra, sitting in the corner of the room, remained motionless.

"What can we do that will be best?" Hester said after a moment or two. "Please advise me, Mr. Rathbone."

"Answer only what I ask you, Miss Latterly," he replied. "Do not offer anything, even if you believe it will be helpful. We will discuss everything now, and I will judge what will suit our case and what, in the jury's minds, may damage it. They did not live through the events; many things that are perfectly clear to you may be obscure to them." He smiled with a bleak, personal humor that lit his eyes and curved the corners of his abstemious mouth. "And their knowledge of the war may be very different from yours. They may well consider all officers, especially wounded ones, to be heroes. And if we try too clumsily to persuade them otherwise, they may resent the destruction of far more of their dreams than we are aware of. Like Lady Fabia Grey, they may need to believe as they do."

Hester had a sudden sharp recollection of sitting in the bedroom at Shelburne Hall with Fabia Grey, her crumpled face aged in a single blow as half a lifetime's treasures withered and died in front of her.

"With loss very often comes hatred." Rathbone spoke as if he had felt her thoughts as vividly as she had herself. "We need someone to blame when we cannot cope with the pain except through anger, which is so much easier, at least to begin with."

Instinctively she looked up and met his gaze, and was startled by its penetration. It was both assuring and discomfiting. He was not a man to whom she could ever lie. Thank heaven it would not be necessary!

"You do not need to explain to me, Mr. Rathbone," she said with a faint answering smile. "I have been home long enough to be quite aware that a great many people require their illusions more than the bits and pieces of truth I can tell them. The ugliness needs to have the real heroism along with it to become bearable—the day after day of suffering without complaint, the dedication to duty when all purpose seems gone, the laughter when you feel like weeping. I don't think it can be told—only felt by those who were there."

His smile was sudden and like a flash of light.

"You have more wisdom than I had been led to suppose, Miss Latterly. I begin to hope."

She found herself blushing and was furious. Afterwards she must confront Callandra and ask what she had said of her that he had such an opinion. But then more likely it was that miserable policeman, Monk, who had given Rathbone this impression. For all their cooperation at the end, and their few blazing moments of complete understanding, they had quarreled most of the time, and he had certainly made no secret of the fact that he considered her opinionated, meddlesome and thoroughly unappealing.

Not that she had not expressed her views of his conduct and character very forthrightly first!

Rathbone discussed all that he would ask her, the arguments the prosecuting counsel would raise, and the issues with which he would be most likely to attempt to trap her. He warned her against appearing to have any emotional involvement which would give him the opportunity to suggest she was biased or unreliable.

By the time he showed them out into the street at quarter to eight she was so tired her mind was dazed, and she was suddenly aware again of the ache in her back and the pinching of her boots. The idea of testifying for Menard Grey was no longer the simple and unfearful thing it had seemed when she had promised with such fierce commitment to do it.

"A little daunting, is he not?" Callandra said when they were seated in her carriage and beginning the journey back to dinner.

"Let us hope he daunts them as much," Hester replied, wriggling her feet uncomfortably. "I cannot imagine his being easily deceived." This was such an understatement she felt self-conscious making it, and turned away so Callandra would not see more than the outline of her face against the light of the carriage lamps.

Callandra laughed, a deep, rich sound full of amusement.

"My dear, you are not the first young woman not to know how to express your opinion of Oliver Rathbone."

"Perspicacity and an authoritative manner will not be enough to save Menard Grey!" Hester said with more sharpness than she had intended. Perhaps Callandra would recognize that Hester spoke from a great deal of apprehension for the day after tomorrow, and a growing fear that they would not succeed.

It was the following day that she read in the newspapers of the murder of Octavia Haslett in Queen Anne Street, but since the name of the police officer investigating was not considered of any public interest, and therefore was not mentioned, it did not bring Monk to her mind any more than he already was each time she remembered the tragedy of the Greys—and of her own family.

Dr. Pomeroy was in two minds as to how to treat her request for leave in order to testify. At her insistence he had operated on John Airdrie, and the child seemed to be recovering well; a little longer and he might not have—he had been weaker than Pomeroy realized. Nevertheless he resented her absence, and yet since he had frequently told her that she was eminently dispensable, he could hardly make too much of an issue of the inconvenience it would cause. His dilemma gave her some much needed amusement, even if it was bitterly flavored.

The trial of Menard Grey was held in the Central Criminal Court at the Old Bailey, and since the case had been sensational, involving the brutal death of an ex-officer of the Crimean War, the public seats were crowded and every newspaper distributed within a hundred miles had sent its reporters. Outside, the streets were crammed with newsboys waving the latest editions, cabbies depositing passengers, costers' barrows piled high with all manner of goods, pie and sandwich sellers crying their wares, and hot pea soup carts. Running patterers recounted the whole case, with much detail added, for the benefit of the ignorant—or any who simply wished to hear it all again. More people pressed in up Ludgate Hill, along Old Bailey itself, and along Newgate. Had they not been witnesses, Hester and Callandra would have found it impossible to gain entry.

Inside the court the atmosphere was different, darker and with an inexorable formality that forced one to be aware that this was the majesty of the law, that here all individual whim was ironed out and blind, impersonal justice ruled.

Police in dark uniform, top hat, shining buttons and belt; clerks in striped trousers; lawyers wigged and gowned, and bailiffs scurrying to shepherd people here and there. Hester and Callandra were shown into the room where they were to wait until they were called. They were not permitted into the courtroom in case they overheard evidence which might affect their own.

Hester sat silently, acutely uncomfortable. A dozen times she drew breath to speak, then knew that what she was going to say was pointless, and only to break the tension. Half an hour had gone by in stiff awkwardness when the outer door opened, and even before he entered she recognized the outline of the man's shoulders as he stood with his back to them, talking to someone beyond in the corridor. She felt a prickle of awareness, not quite apprehension, and certainly not excitement.

"Good morning, Lady Callandra, Miss Latterly." The man turned at last and came in, closing the door behind him.

"Good morning, Mr. Monk," Callandra replied, inclining her head politely.

"Good morning, Mr. Monk," Hester echoed, with exactly the same gesture. Seeing his smooth-boned face again with its hard, level gray eyes, broad aquiline nose and mouth with its faint scar, brought back all the memories of the Grey case: the anger, confusion, intense pity and fear, the brief moments of understanding each other more vividly than she had ever experienced with anyone else, and sharing a purpose with an intensity that was consuming.

Now they were merely two people who irritated each other and were brought together by their desire to save Menard Grey from further pain—and perhaps a sense of responsibility in some vague way because they had been the ones who had discovered the truth.

"Pray sit down, Mr. Monk," she instructed rather than offered. "Please be comfortable."

He remained standing.

For several moments there was silence. Deliberately she filled her mind with thoughts of how she would testify, the questions Rathbone had warned her the prosecution's lawyer would ask, and how to avoid damaging answers and being led to say more than she intended.

"Has Mr. Rathbone advised you?" she said without thinking.

His eyebrows rose. "I have testified in court before, Miss Latterly." His voice was heavy with sarcasm. "Even occasionally in cases of considerable importance. I am aware of the procedure."

She was annoyed with herself for having left herself open to such a remark, and with him for making it. Instinctively she dealt back the hardest blow that she could.

"I see a great deal of your recollection must have returned since we last met. I had not realized, or of course I should not have commented. I was endeavoring to be helpful, but it seems you do not require it."

The color drained from his face leaving two bright spots of pink on his cheekbones. His mind was racing for an equal barb to return.

"I have forgotten much, Miss Latterly, but that still leaves me with an advantage over those who never knew anything in the beginning!" he said tartly, turning away.

Callandra smiled and did not interfere.

"It was not my assistance I was suggesting, Mr. Monk," Hester snapped back. "It was Mr. Rathbone's. But if you believe you know better than he does, I can only hope you are right and indeed you do—not for your sake, which is immaterial, but for Menard Grey's. I trust you have not lost sight of our purpose in being here?"

She had won that exchange, and she knew it.

"Of course I haven't," he said coldly, standing with his back to her, hands in his pockets. "I have left my present investigation to Sergeant Evan and come early in case Mr. Rathbone wished to see me, but I have no intention of disturbing him if he does not."

"He may not know you are here to be seen," she argued.

He turned around to face her. "Miss Latterly, can you not for one moment refrain from meddling in other people's affairs and assume we are capable of managing without your direction? I informed his clerk as I came in."

"Then all civility required you do was say so when I asked you!" she replied, stung by the charge of interfering, which was totally unjust—or anyway largely—or to some extent! "But you do not seem to be capable of ordinary civility."

"You are not an ordinary person, Miss Latterly." His eyes were very wide, his face tight. "You are overbearing, dictatorial, and seem bent to treat everyone as if they were incapable of managing without your instruction. You combine the worst elements of a governess with the ruthlessness of a workhouse matron. You should have stayed in the army—you are eminently suited for it."

That was the perfect thrust; he knew how she despised the army command for its sheer arrogant incompetence, which had driven so many men to needless and appalling deaths. She was so furious she choked for words.

"I am not," she gasped. "The army is made up of men—and those in command of it are mostly stubborn and stupid—like you. They haven't the faintest idea what they are doing, but they would rather blunder along, no matter who is killed by it, than admit their ignorance and accept help." She drew breath again and went on. "They would rather die than take counsel from a woman—which in itself wouldn't matter a toss. It's their letting other people die that is unforgivable."

He was prevented from having to think of a reply by the bailiff coming to the door and requesting Hester to prepare herself to enter the courtroom. She rose with great dignity and swept out past him, catching her skirt in the doorway and having to stop and tweak it out, which was most irksome. She flashed a smile at Callandra over her other shoulder, then with fluttering stomach followed the bailiff along the passageway and into the court.

The chamber was large, high ceilinged, paneled in wood and so crowded with people they seemed to press in on her from every side. She could feel a heat from their bodies as they jostled and craned to see her come in, and there was a rustle and hiss of breath and a shuffle of feet as people fought to maintain balance. In the press benches pencils flew, scratching notes on paper, making outlines of faces and hats.

She stared straight ahead and walked up the cleared way to the witness box, angry that her legs were trembling. She stumbled on the step, and the bailiff put out his hand to steady her. She looked around for Oliver Rathbone, and saw him immediately, but with his white lawyer's wig on he looked different, very remote. He regarded her with the distant politeness he would a stranger, and it was surprisingly chilling.

She could hardly feel worse. There was nothing to be lost by reminding herself why she was here. She allowed her eyes to meet Menard Grey's in the dock. He was pale, all the fresh color gone from his skin. He looked white, tired and very frightened. It was enough to give her all the courage she needed. What was her brief, rather childish moment of loneliness in comparison?

She was passed the Bible and swore to her name and that she would tell the truth, her voice firm and positive.

Rathbone came towards her a couple of steps and began quietly.

"Miss Latterly, I believe you were one of the several well-born young women who answered the call of Miss Florence Nightingale, and left your home and family and sailed to the Crimea to nurse our soldiers out there, in the conflict?"

The judge, a very elderly man with a broad, fragile tempered face, leaned forward.

"I am sure Miss Latterly is an admirable young lady, Mr. Rathbone, but is her nursing experience of any relevance to this case? The accused did not serve in the Crimea, nor did the crime occur over there."

"Miss Latterly knew the victim in the hospital in Scutari, my lord. The roots of the crime begin there, and on the battlefields of Balaclava and Sebastopol."

"Do they indeed? I had rather thought from the prosecution that they began in the nursery at Shelburne Hall. Still—continue, please." He leaned back again in his high seat and stared gloomily at Rathbone.

"Miss Latterly," Rathbone prompted briskly.

Carefully, measuring each word to begin with, then gradually gathering confidence as the emotion of memory overtook her, she told the court about the hospital in which she had served, and the men she had come to know slightly, but as well as their injuries made possible. And as she spoke she became aware of a cessation of the jostling among the crowd. More faces were quickened in interest; even Menard Grey had raised his head and was staring at her.

Rathbone came out from behind his table and paced back and forth across the floor, not waving his arms or moving quickly to distract attention from her, but rather prowling, keeping the jury from becoming too involved in the story and forgetting it all had to do with a crime here in London, and a man on trial for his life.

He had been through her receipt of her brother's heartbroken letter recounting her parents' death, and her return home to the shame and the despair, and the financial restriction. He elicited the details without ever allowing her to repeat herself or sound self-pitying. She followed his direction with more and more appreciation for the skill with which he was building a picture of mounting and inevitable tragedy. Already the faces of the men in the jury were becoming strained with pity, and she knew how their anger would explode when the last piece was fitted into the picture and they understood the truth.

She did not dare to look at Fabia Grey in the front row, still dressed in black, or at her son Lovel and his wife, Rosamond, beside her. Each time her eyes roamed unintentionally towards them she averted them sharply, and looked either at Rathbone himself or at any anonymous face in the crowd beyond him.

In answer to his careful questions she told him of her visit to Callandra at Shelburne Hall, of her first meeting with Monk, and of all that had ensued. She made some slips, had to be corrected, but never once did she offer anything beyond a simple answer.

By the time he had come to the tragic and terrible conclusion, the faces of the jury were stunned with amazement and anger, and for the first time they were able to look at Menard Grey, because they understood what he had done, and why. Perhaps some even felt they might, had fortune been so cruel to them, have done the same.

When at last Rathbone stepped back and thanked her with a sudden, dazzling smile, she found her body was aching with the tension of clenched muscles and her hands were sore where her nails had unconsciously dug into the palms.

The counsel for the prosecution rose to his feet and smiled bleakly. "Please remain where you are, Miss Latterly. You will not mind if we put to the test this extremely moving story of yours?" It was a rhetorical question; he had no intention whatsoever of permitting such a testimony as hers had been to stand, and she felt the sweat break out on her skin as she looked at his face. At this moment he was losing, and such a thing was not only a shock to him in this instance, but of a pain so deep as to be almost physical.

"Now Miss Latterly, you admit you were—indeed still are—a woman rather past her first youth, without significant background, and in drastically impoverished circumstances—and you accepted an invitation to visit Shelburne Hall, the country home of the Grey family?"

"I accepted an invitation to visit Lady Callandra Daviot," Hester corrected.

"At Shelburne Hall," he said sharply. "Yes?"

"Yes."

"Thank you. And during that visit you spent some time with the accused, Menard Grey?"

She drew breath to say "Not alone," and just in time caught Rathbone's eye, and let out her breath again. She smiled at the prosecutor as if the implication had missed her.

"Of course. It is impossible to stay with a family and not meet all the members who are in residence, and to spend time with them." She was sorely tempted to add that perhaps he did not know such things, and forebore carefully. It would be a cheap laugh, and perhaps bought very dearly. This was an adversary to whom she could give no ground.

"I believe you now have a position in one of the London infirmaries, is that so?"

"Yes."

"Obtained for you by the same Lady Callandra Daviot?"

"Obtained with her recommendation, but I believe on my own merit."

"Be that as it may—with her influence? No; please do not look to Mr. Rathbone for guidance. Just answer me, Miss Latterly."

"I do not require Mr. Rathbone's assistance," she said, swallowing hard. "I cannot answer you, with or without it. I do not know what passed between Lady Callandra and the governors of the infirmary. She suggested I apply there, and when I did, they were satisfied with my references, which are considerable, and they employed me. Not many of Miss Nightingale's nurses find it difficult to obtain a position, should they desire it."

"No indeed, Miss Latterly." He smiled thinly. "But not many of them do desire it, as you do—do they? In fact, Miss Nightingale herself comes from an excellent family who could provide for her for the rest of her life."

"That my family could not, and that my parents are both dead, is the foundation of the case that brings us here, sir," she said with a hard note of victory in her voice. Whatever he thought or felt, she knew the jury understood that, and it was they who decided, after all each counsel could say.

"Indeed," he said with a flicker of irritation. Then he proceeded to ask her again how well she had known the victim, and to imply very subtly but unmistakably that she had fallen in love with him, succumbed to his now well established charm, and because he had rejected her, wished to blacken his name. Indeed he skirted close to suggesting she might have collaborated to conceal the crime, and now to defend Menard Grey.

She was horrified and embarrassed, but when the temptation to explode in fury came too close, she looked across at Menard Grey's face and remembered what was truly important.

"No, that is untrue," she said quietly. She thought of accusing him of sordidness, but caught Rathbone's eye again and refrained.

Only once did she see Monk. She felt a tingle of pleasure, even sweetness, to recognize the outrage in his expression as he glared at the counsel for the prosecution.

When the prosecution suddenly changed his mind and gave up, she was permitted to remain in the courtroom, since she was no longer of importance, and she found room to sit and listen while Callandra testified. She too was first questioned by Rathbone and then, with more politeness than he had used before, by the counsel for the prosecution. He judged the jury rightly that they would not view with sympathy any attempt to bully or insult an army surgeon's widow—and a lady. Hester did not watch Callandra, she had no fear for her; she concentrated on the faces of the jurymen. She saw the emotions flicker and change: anger, pity, confusion, respect, contempt.

Next Monk was called and sworn. She had not noticed in the waiting room how well he was dressed. His jacket was of excellent cut, and only the best woolen broadcloth hung in quite that way. What vanity. How, on police pay, did he manage such a thing? Then she thought with a flicker of pity that probably he did not know himself—not now. Had he wondered? Had he perhaps been afraid of the vanity or the ruthlessness the answer might reveal? How terrible it must be to look at the bare evidence of yourself, the completed acts, and know none of the reasons that made them human, explainable in terms of fear and hopes, things misunderstood, small sacrifices made, wounds compensated for—always to see only what resulted, never what was meant. This extravagant coat might be pure vanity, money grasped for—or it might be the mark of achievement after long years of saving and working, putting in extra duty when others were relaxing at home or laughing in some music hall or public house.

Rathbone began to question him, talking smoothly, knowing the words were powerful enough and emotion from him would heap the impact too high, too soon. He had called his witnesses in this order so he might build his story as it had happened, first the Crimea, then Hester's parents' death, then the crime. Detail by detail he drew from Monk the description of the flat in Mecklenburg Square, the marks of struggle and death, his own slow discovery piece by piece of the truth.

Most of the time Rathbone had his back to her, facing either Monk or the jury, but she found his voice compelling, every word as clear as a cut stone, insistent in the mind, unfolding an irresistible tragedy.

And she watched Monk and saw the respect and once or twice the momentary flicker of dislike cross his face as he answered. Rathbone was not treating him as a favored witness, rather as someone half an enemy. His phrases had a sharp turn to them, an element of antagonism. Only watching the jury did she understand why. They were utterly absorbed. Even a woman shrieking in the crowd and being revived by a neighbor did not break their attention. Monk's sympathy for Menard Grey appeared to be dragged from him reluctantly, although Hester knew it was acutely real. She could remember how Monk had looked at the time, the anger in him, the twisting pain of pity, and the helplessness to alter anything. It had been in that moment she had liked him with absolute completeness, an inner peace that shared, without reservation, and a knowledge that the communication was total.

When the court rose at the end of the afternoon, Hester went with the crowd that pushed and shoved on every side, onlookers rushing home in the jam of carts, wagons and carriages in the streets, newspaper writers hurrying to get the copy in before the presses started to roll for the first editions in the morning, running patterers to compose the next verse of their songs and pass the news along the streets.

She was outside on the steps in the sharp evening wind and the bright gas lamps looking for Callandra, from whom she had become separated, when she saw Monk. She hesitated, uncertain whether to speak to him or not. Hearing the evidence over again, recounting it herself, she had felt all the turmoil of emotions renewed, and her anger with him had been swept away.

But perhaps he still felt just as contemptuous of her? She stood, unable to decide whether to commit herself and unwilling to leave.

He took the matter out of her hands by walking over, a slight pucker between his brows.

"Well, Miss Latterly, do you believe your friend Mr. Rathbone is equal to the task?"

She looked at his eyes and saw the anxiety in him. The sharp retort died away, the irrelevancies as to whether Rathbone was her friend or not. Sarcasm was only a defense against the fear that they would hang Menard Grey.

"I think so," she said quietly. "I was watching the jurors' faces while you were testifying. Of course I do not know what is yet to come, but up until now, I believe they were more deeply horrified by the injustices of what happened, and our helplessness to prevent it, than by the murder itself. If Mr. Rathbone can keep this mood until they go to consider their verdict, it may be favorable. At least—" She stopped, realizing that no matter what the jurors believed in blame, the fact remained undeniable. They could not return a verdict of not guilty, regardless of any provocation on earth. The weighing lay with the judge, not with them.

Monk had perceived it before her. The bleak understanding was in his eyes.

"Let us trust he is equally successful with his lordship," he said dryly. "Life in Coldbath Fields would be worse than the rope."

"Will you come again tomorrow?" she asked him.

"Yes—in the afternoon. The verdict will not be in till then. Will you?"

"Yes—" She thought what Pomeroy would have to say. "But I will not come until late either, if you really do not believe the verdict will come in early. I do not wish to ask for time from the infirmary without good reason."

"And will they consider your desire to hear the verdict to be a good reason?" he said dryly.

She pulled a small face, not quite a smile. "No. I shall not phrase my request in quite those terms."

"Is it what you wished—the infirmary?" Again he was as frank and direct as she recalled, and his understanding as comfortable.

"No—" She did not think of prevaricating. "It is full of incompetence, unnecessary suffering, ridiculous ways of doing things which could so easily be reorganized, if only they would give up their petty self-importances and think of the end and not the means." She warmed to the subject and his interest. "A great deal of the trouble lies with their whole belief of nursing and the nature of people who should work in it. They pay only six shillings a week, and some of that is given in small beer. Many of the nurses are drunk half the time. But now the hospital provides their food, which is better than their eating the patients' food, which they used to. You may imagine what type of men and women it attracts! Most of them can neither read nor write." She shrugged expressively. "They sleep just off the wards, there are far too few basins or towels for them, and nothing more than a little Conde's fluid and now and again soap to wash themselves—even their hands after cleaning up waste."

His smile became wider and thinner, but there was a gleam of sympathy in his eyes.

"And you?" she asked. "Are you still working for Mr. Runcorn?" She did not ask if he had remembered more about himself, that was too sensitive and she would not probe. The subject of Runcorn was raw enough.

"Yes." He pulled a face.

"And with Sergeant Evan?" She found herself smiling.

"Yes, Evan too." He hesitated. He seemed about to add something when Oliver Rathbone came down the steps dressed for the street and without his wig and robes. He looked very trim and well pleased.

Monk's eyes narrowed, but he refused to comment.

"Do you think we may be hopeful, Mr. Rathbone?" Hester asked eagerly.

"Hopeful, Miss Latterly," he replied guardedly. "But still far from certain."

"Don't forget it is the judge you are playing to, Rathbone," Monk said tartly, buttoning his jacket higher. "And not Miss Latterly, or the gallery—or even the jury. Your performance before them may be brilliant, but it is dressing and not substance." And before Rathbone could reply he bowed fractionally to Hester, turned on his heel, and strode off down the darkening street.

"A man somewhat lacking in charm," Rathbone said sourly. "But I suppose his calling requires little enough. May I take you somewhere in my carriage, Miss Latterly?"

"I think charm is a very dubious quality," she said with deliberation. "The Grey case is surely the finest example of excessive charm we are likely ever to see!"

"I can well believe that you do not rate it highly, Miss Latterly," he retorted, his eyes perfectly steady but gleaming with laughter.

"Oh—" She longed to be equally barbed, as subtly rude, and could think of nothing whatsoever to say. She was completely unsure whether the amusement in him was at her, at himself, or at Monk— or even whether it contained unkindness or not. "No—" She fumbled for words. "No. I find it unworthy of trust, a spurious quality, all show and no substance, glitter without warmth. No thank you; I am returning with Lady Callandra—but it is most courteous of you to offer. Good day, Mr. Rathbone."

"Good day, Miss Latterly." He bowed, still smiling.

CHAPTER
THREE

Sir Basil Moidore stared at Monk across the carpeted expanse of the morning room floor. His face was pale but there was no vacillation in it, no lack of composure, only amazement and disbelief.

"I beg your pardon?" he said coldly.

"No one broke into your house on Monday night, sir," Monk repeated. "The street was well observed all night long, at both ends—"

"By whom?" Moidore's dark eyebrows rose, making his eyes the more startlingly sharp.

Monk could feel his temper prickling already. He resented being disbelieved more than almost anything else. It suggested he was incompetent. He controlled his voice with considerable effort.

"By the policeman on the beat, Sir Basil, a householder who was up half the night with a sick wife, the doctor who visited him." He did not mention Chinese Paddy; he did not think Moidore would be inclined to take his evidence well. "And by a large number of liveried footmen and coachmen waiting on their employers to leave a party at the corner of Chandos Street."

"Then obviously the man came from the mews," Basil responded irritably.

"Your own groom and coachmen sleep above your stables, sir," Monk pointed out. "And anyone climbing over there would be highly unlikely to get across that roof without disturbing at least the horses. Then he would have to get right over the house roof and down the other side. Almost impossible to do, unless he was a mountaineer with ropes and climbing equipment, and—"

"There is no call to be sarcastic," Basil snapped. "I take your point. Then he must have come in the front some time between your

51

policeman's patrols. There is no other answer. He certainly was not hiding in the house all evening! And neither did he leave after the servants were up."

Monk was forced to mention Chinese Paddy.

"I am sorry, but that is not so. We also found a housebreaker who was watching the Harley Street end all night, hoping to get a chance to break in farther along. He got no opportunity because there were people about who would have observed him if he had. But he was watching all night from eleven until four—which covers the relevant time. I am sorry."

Sir Basil swung around from the table he had been facing, his eyes black, his mouth drawn down in anger. "Then why in God's name haven't you arrested him? He must be the one! On his own admission he is a housebreaker. What more do you want?" He glared at Monk. "He broke in here and poor Octavia heard him—and he killed her. What is the matter with you, standing here like a fool?"

Monk felt his body tighten with fury, the more biting because it was impotent. He needed to succeed in his profession, and he would fail completely if he were as rude as he wished, and were thrown out. How Runcorn would love that! It would be not only professional disgrace but social as well.

"Because his story is true," he replied with a level, harsh voice. "Substantiated by Mr. Bentley, his doctor and a maid who has no interest in the matter and no idea what her testimony means." He did not meet Sir Basil's eyes because he dared not let him see the anger in them, and he hated the submission of it. "The housebreaker did not pass along the street," he went on. "He did not rob anyone, because he did not have the chance, and he can prove it. I wish it were so simple; we should be very pleased to solve the case as neatly—sir."

Basil leaned forward across the table.

"Then if no one broke in, and no one was concealed here, you have created an impossible situation—unless you are suggesting—" He stopped, the color drained out of his face and slowly a very real horror replaced the irritation and impatience. He stood stock-still. "Are you?" he said very quietly.

"Yes, Sir Basil," Monk answered him.

"That's—" Basil stopped. For several seconds he remained in absolute silence, his thoughts apparently inward, racing, ideas grasped and rejected. Finally he came to some realization he could not cast aside. "I see," he said at last. "I cannot think of any imaginable reason, but we must face the inevitable. It seems preposterous, and I still believe that you will find some flaw in your reasoning, or that your evidence is faulty. But until then we must proceed on your assumption." He frowned very slightly. "What do you require next? I assure you we have no violent quarrels or conflicts in the house and no one has behaved in any way out of their usual custom." He regarded Monk with something between dislike and a bitter humor. "And we do not have personal relationships with our servants, let alone of the sort which would occasion this." He put his hands in his pockets. "It is absurd—but I do not wish to obstruct you."

"I agree a quarrel seems unlikely." Monk measured his words, both to keep his own dignity and to show Basil there was some sense to the argument. "Especially in the middle of the night when all the household was in bed. But it is not impossible Mrs. Haslett was privy to some secret, albeit unintentionally, that someone feared she might expose—" It was not only possible, it excluded her from all blame. He saw Basil's face lose some of its anxiety, and a flicker of hope appeared in his eyes. His shoulder eased as he breathed out and let his arms drop.

"Poor Octavia." He looked at one of the soft landscape paintings on the wall. "That does sound possible. I apologize. I spoke hastily. You had better pursue your inquiries. What do you wish to do first?"

Monk respected him for his ability to admit both haste and discourtesy. It was more than he had expected, and something he would have found hard himself. The measure of the man was larger than he thought,

"I would like to speak to the family first, sir. They may have observed something, or Mrs. Haslett may have confided in one of them."

"The family?" Basil's mouth twitched, but whether it was from fear or a dark, inward humor Monk could not even guess. "Very well." He reached for the bell pull and tugged it. When the butler appeared he sent him to bring Cyprian Moidore to the morning room.

Monk waited in silence until he came.

Cyprian closed the door behind him and looked at his father. Seeing them almost side by side the resemblance was striking: the same shape of head; the dark, almost black eyes; and the broad mouth with its extraordinary mobility. And yet the expressions were so different the whole bearing was altered. Basil was more aware of his own power and was quicker tempered, the flash of humor more deeply covered. Cyprian was less certain, as if his strength was untried and he feared it might not prove adequate. Was the softer side of him compassion, or simply caution because he was still vulnerable and he knew it?

"The police have discerned that no one broke in to kill Octavia," Basil explained briefly and without preamble. He did not watch his son's face; apparently he was not concerned how the news affected him, nor did he explain Monk's reasoning of possible motive. "The only solution left seems to be that it was someone already living here. Obviously not the family—therefore, we must presume, one of the servants. Inspector Monk wishes to speak to all of us to see what we observed—if indeed we observed anything."

Cyprian stared at his father, then swung around to look at Monk as if he had been some monster brought in from a foreign land.

"I am sorry, sir." Monk put in the apology Basil had omitted. "I am aware that it must be distressing, but if you could tell me what you did on Monday, and what you can recall of anything Mrs. Haslett may have said, especially if at any time she confided a concern to you, or some matter she may have discovered that could be seen as dangerous to anyone else."

Cyprian frowned, concentration coming slowly to his face as thought took over from astonishment. He turned his back on his father.

"You think Octavia was killed because she knew someone's secret about—" He shrugged. "What? What could one of our servants have done that—" He stopped. It was apparent from his eyes that his question was answered in his imagination and he preferred not to speak it. "Tavie said nothing to me. But then I was out most of the day. I wrote a few letters in the morning, then about eleven I went to my club in Piccadilly for luncheon and spent the afternoon with Lord Ainslie, talking about cattle, mostly. He has some stock, and I considered buying some. We keep a large estate in Hertfordshire."

Monk had a rapid impression that Cyprian was lying, not about the meeting but about the subject of it.

"Damned Owenite politician!" Basil said with a flash of temper. "Have us all living in communities like farm animals."

"Not at all!" Cyprian retorted. "His thoughts are—"

"You were here at dinner," Basil overrode him curtly before he could form his argument. "Didn't you see Octavia then?"

"Only at table," Cyprian said with an edge to his voice. "And if you recall, Tavie barely spoke—to me, or to anyone else."

Basil turned from the fireplace and looked at Monk.

"My daughter was not always in the best of health. I think on that occasion she was feeling unwell. She certainly was extremely quiet and seemed in some distress." He put his hands back in his pockets. "I assumed at the time she had a headache, but looking back now, perhaps she was aware of some ugly secret and it consumed her thoughts. Although she can hardly have realized the danger it represented."

"I wish to God she had told someone," Cyprian said with sudden passion. There was no need to add all the tumult of feelings that lay behind it, the regret and the sense of having failed. It lay heavy in his voice and in the strain in his features.

Before the elder Moidore replied there was a knock on the door.

"Come in!" he said, raising his head sharply, irked by the intrusion.

Monk wondered for a moment who the woman was, then as Cyprian's expression changed, he remembered meeting her in the withdrawing room the first morning: Romola Moidore. This time she looked less drained with shock; her skin had a bloom to it and her complexion was flawless. Her features were regular, her eyes wide and her hair thick. The only thing which prevented her from being a beauty was a suggestion of sulkiness about the mouth, a feeling that her good temper was not to be relied on. She looked at Monk with surprise. Obviously she did not remember him.

"Inspector Monk," Cyprian supplied. Then, when her face did not clear: "Of the police." He glanced at Monk, and for a moment there was a bright intelligence in his eyes. He was leaving Monk to make whatever impact he chose.

Basil immediately spoiled it by explaining.

"Whoever killed Octavia is someone who lives in this house. That means one of the servants." His eyes were on her face, his voice careful. "The only reason that makes any sense is if one of them has a secret so shameful they would rather commit murder than have it revealed. Either Octavia knew this secret or they believed she did."

Romola sat down sharply, the color fading from her cheeks, and she put her hand to her mouth, but her eyes did not leave Basil's face. Never once did she look to her husband.

Cyprian glared at his father, who looked back at him boldly—and with something that Monk thought might well be dislike. He wished he could remember his own father, but rack his memory as he might, nothing came back but a faint blur, an impression of size and the smell of salt and tobacco, and the touch of beard, and skin softer than he expected. Nothing returned of the man, his voice, his words, a face. Monk had no real idea, only a few sentences from his sister, and a smile as if there were something familiar and precious.

Romola was speaking, her voice scratchy with fear.

"Here in the house?" She looked at Monk, although she was speaking to Cyprian. "One of the servants?"

"There doesn't seem to be any other explanation," Cyprian replied. "Did Tavie say anything to you—think carefully—anything about any of the servants?"

"No," she said almost immediately. "This is terrible. The very thought of it makes me feel ill."

A shadow passed over Cyprian's face, and for a moment it seemed as if he were about to speak, but he was aware of his father's eyes on him.

"Did Octavia speak to you alone that day?" Basil asked her without change of tone.

"No—no," she denied quickly. "I interviewed governesses all morning. None of them seemed suitable. I don't know what I'm going to do."

"See some more!" Basil snapped. "If you pay a requisite salary you will find someone who will do."

She shot him a look of repressed dislike, guarded enough that to a casual eye it could have been anxiety.

"I was at home all day." She turned back to Monk, her hands still clenched. "I received friends in the afternoon, but Tavie went out. I have no idea where; she said nothing when she came in. In fact she passed by me in the hall as if she had not seen me there at all."

"Was she distressed?" Cyprian asked quickly. "Did she seem frightened, or upset about anything?"

Basil watched them, waiting.

"Yes," Romola said with a moment's thought. "Yes she did. I

assumed she had had an unpleasant afternoon, perhaps friends who were disagreeable, but maybe it was more than that?"

"What did she say?" Cyprian pursued.

"Nothing. I told you, she barely seemed aware she had passed me. If you remember, she said very little at dinner, and we presumed she was not well."

They all looked at Monk, waiting for him to resolve some answer from the facts.

"Perhaps she confided in her sister?" he suggested.

"Unlikely," Basil said tersely. "But Minta is an observant woman." He turned to Romola. "Thank you, my dear. You may return to your tasks. Do not forget what I have counseled you. Perhaps you would be good enough to ask Araminta to join us here."

"Yes, Papa-in-law," she said obediently, and left without looking at Cyprian or Monk again.

Araminta Kellard was not a woman Monk could have forgotten as he had her sister-in-law. From her vivid fire-gold hair, her curiously asymmetrical features, to her slender, stiff body, she was unique. When she came into the room she looked first at her father, ignored Cyprian and faced Monk with guarded interest, then turned back to her father.

"Papa?"

"Did Tavie say anything to you about learning something shocking or distressing recently?" Basil asked her. "Particularly the day before she died?"

Araminta sat down and considered very carefully for several moments, without looking at anyone else in the room. "No," she said at last. She regarded Monk with steady, amber-hazel eyes. "Nothing specific. But I was aware that she was extremely concerned about something which she learned that afternoon. I am sorry, I have no idea what it was. Do you believe that is why she was killed?"

Monk looked at her with more interest than he had for anyone else he had yet seen in this house. There was an almost mesmeric intensity in her, and yet she was utterly composed. Her thin hands were tight in her lap, but her gaze was unwavering and penetratingly intelligent. Monk had no idea what wounds tore at the fabric of her emotions beneath, and he did not imagine he would easily frame any questions, no matter how subtle, which would cause her to betray them.

"It is possible, Mrs. Kellard," he answered. "But if you can think of any other motive anyone might have to wish her harm, or fear her, please let me know. It is only a matter of deduction. There is no evidence as yet, except that no one broke in."

"From which you conclude that it was someone already here," she said very quietly. "Someone who lives in this house."

"It seems inescapable."

"I suppose it does."

"What kind of a woman was your sister, Mrs. Kellard? Was she inquisitive, interested in other people's problems? Was she observant? An astute judge of character?"

She smiled, a twisted gesture with half her face.

"Not more than most women, Mr. Monk. In fact I think rather less. If she did discover anything, it will have been by chance, not because she went seeking it. You ask what kind of woman she was. The kind who walks into events, whose emotions lead her and she follows without regard to the price. She was the kind of woman who lurches into disaster without having foreseen it or understanding it once she is there."

Monk looked across at Basil and saw the intense concentration in his face, his eyes fixed on Araminta. There was no reflection in his expression of any other emotion, no grief, no curiosity.

Monk turned to Cyprian. In him was the terrible hurt of memory and the knowledge of loss. His face was hard etched with pain, the realization of all the words that could not now be said, the affections unexpressed.

"Thank you, Mrs. Kellard," Monk said slowly. "If you think of anything else I should be obliged if you would tell me. How did you spend Monday?"

"At home in the morning," she answered. "I went calling in the afternoon, and I dined at home with the family. I spoke to Octavia several times during the evening, but I did not attach any particular importance to anything we said. It seemed totally trivial at the time."

"Thank you, ma'am."

She rose to her feet, inclined her head very slightly, and walked out without looking behind her.

"Do you wish to see Mr. Kellard?" Basil asked with raised eyebrows, an air of contempt in his stance.

The very fact that Basil questioned it made Monk accept.

"If you please."

Basil's face tightened, but he did not argue. He summoned Phillips and dispatched him to fetch Myles Kellard.

"Octavia would not have confided in Myles," Cyprian said to Monk.

"Why not?" Monk asked.

A look of distaste flickered across Basil's face at the intrusive indelicacy of such a question, and he answered before Cyprian could. "Because they did not care for each other," he replied tersely. "They were civil, of course." His dark eyes regarded Monk quickly to make sure he understood that people of quality did not squabble like riffraff. "It seems most probable the poor girl spoke to no one about whatever she learned so disastrously, and we may never learn what it was."

"And whoever killed her will go unpunished," Cyprian challenged. "That is monstrous."

"Of course not!" Basil was furious; his eyes blazed and the deep lines in his face altered to become harsh. "Do you imagine I am going to live the rest of my life in this house with someone who murdered my daughter? What is the matter with you? Good God, don't you know me better than that?"

Cyprian looked as if he had been struck, and Monk felt a sharp, unexpected twinge of embarrassment. This was a scene he should not have witnessed, these were emotions that had nothing to do with Octavia Haslett's death; a viciousness between father and son stemming from no sudden act but years of resentment and failure to understand.

"If Monk—" Basil jerked his head towards the policeman—"is incapable of finding him, whoever it is, I shall have the commissioner send someone else." He moved restlessly from the ornate mantel back to the center of the floor. "Where the hell is Myles? This morning at least, he should make himself available when I send for him!"

At that moment the door opened, without a prefacing knock, and Myles Kellard answered his summons. He was tall and slender, but in every other respect the opposite of the Moidores. His hair was brown with streaks in it and waved in a sweep back from his forehead. His face was long and narrow with an aristocratic nose and a sensuous, moody mouth. It was at once the face of a dreamer and a libertine.

Monk hesitated from politeness, and before he could speak Basil asked Myles the questions that Monk would have, but without explanation as to their purpose or the need for them. He was correct in his assumption; Myles could tell them nothing of use. He had risen late and gone out in the morning for luncheon, where he did not say, and spent the afternoon at the merchant bank where he was a director. He too had dined at home, but had not seen Octavia, except at table in the company of everyone else. He had noticed nothing remarkable.

When he had left Monk asked if there was anyone else, apart from Lady Moidore, to whom he should speak.

"Aunt Fenella and Uncle Septimus." Cyprian answered this time, cutting his father off. "We would be obliged if you could keep your questions to Mama as brief as possible. In fact it would be better if we could ask her and relay her answers to you, if they are of any relevance."

Basil looked at his son coldly, but whether for the suggestion or simply because Cyprian stole his prerogative by making it first, Monk did not know: he guessed the latter. At this point it was an easy concession to make; there would be time enough later to see Lady Moidore, when he had something better than routine and very general questions to ask her.

"Certainly," he allowed. "But perhaps your aunt and uncle? One sometimes confides in aunts especially, when no one else seems as appropriate."

Basil let out his breath in a sharp round of contempt and turned away towards the window.

"Not Aunt Fenella." Cyprian half sat on the back of one of the leather-upholstered chairs. "But she is very observant—and inquisitive. She may have noticed something the rest of us did not—if she hasn't forgotten it."

"Has she a short memory?" Monk inquired.

"Erratic," Cyprian replied with an oblique smile. He reached for the bell, but when the butler arrived it was Basil who instructed him to fetch first Mrs. Sandeman, and then Mr. Thirsk.

Fenella Sandeman bore an extraordinary resemblance to Basil. She had the same dark eyes and short, straight nose, her mouth was similarly wide and mobile, but her whole head was narrower and the lines were smoothed out. In her youth she must have had an exotic charm close to real beauty, now it was merely extraordinary. Monk did not need to ask the relationship; it was too plain to miss. She was of approximately the same age as Basil, perhaps nearer sixty than fifty, but she fought against time with every artifice imagination could conceive. Monk did not know enough of women to realize precisely what tricks they were, but he knew their presence. If he had ever understood them it was forgotten, with so much else. But he saw an artificiality in her face: the color of the skin was unnatural, the line of her brows harsh, her hair stiff and too dark.

She looked at Monk with great interest and refused Basil's invitation to sit down.

"How do you do," she said with a charming husky voice, just a fraction blurred at the edges.

"Fenella, he's a policeman, not a social acquaintance," Basil snapped. "He is investigating Octavia's death. It seems she was killed by someone here in the house, presumably one of the servants."

"One of the servants?" Fenella's black-painted eyebrows rose startlingly. "My dear, how appalling." She did not look in the least alarmed; in fact, if it were not absurd, Monk would have thought she found a kind of excitement in it.

Basil caught the inflection also.

"Remember your conduct!" he said tartly. "You are here because it begins to appear that Octavia may have discovered some secret, albeit accidentally, for which she was killed. Inspector Monk wonders if she may have confided such a thing to you. Did she?"

"Oh my goodness." She did not even glance at her brother; her eyes were intent on Monk. Had it not been socially ridiculous, and she at the very least twenty years his senior, he would have thought she considered flirting with him. "I shall have to think about it," she said softly. "I'm sure I cannot recall all that she said over the last few days. Poor child. Her life was full of tragedy. Losing her husband in the war, so soon after her marriage. How awful that she should be murdered over some wretched secret." She shivered and hunched her shoulders. "Whatever could it be?" Her eyes widened dramatically. "An illegitimate child, do you think? No—yes! It would lose a servant her position—but could it really have been a woman? Surely not?" She came a step closer to Monk. "Anyway, none of our servants has had a child—we would all know about it." She made a sound deep in her throat, almost a giggle. "One can hardly keep such a thing secret, can one? A crime of passion—that's it. There has been a fateful passion, which no one else knows about, and Tavie stumbled on it by chance—and they killed her—poor child. How can we help, Inspector?"

"Please be careful, Mrs. Sandeman," Monk replied with a grim face. He was very uncertain how seriously to regard her, but he felt compelled to warn her against jeopardizing her own safety. "You may discover the secret yourself, or allow the person concerned to fear you may. You would be wise to observe in silence."

She took a step backward, drew in her breath, and her eyes grew even wider. For the first time he wondered, even though it was mid-morning, if she were entirely sober.

Basil must have had the same thought. He extended his hand perfunctorily and guided her to the door.

"Just think about it, Fenella, and if you remember anything, tell me, and I will call Mr. Monk. Now go and have breakfast, or write letters or something."

For an instant the glamour and excitement vanished from her face and she looked at him with intense dislike; then as quickly it was gone, and she accepted his dismissal, closing the door behind her softly.

Basil looked at Monk, searching to judge his perception, but Monk left his face blank and polite.

The last person to come in had an equally apparent relationship to the family. He had the same wide blue eyes as Lady Moidore, and although his hair was now gray, his skin was fair with the pinkness that would have been natural with light auburn hair, and his features echoed the sensitivity and fine bones of hers. However he was obviously older than she, and the years had treated him harshly. His shoulders were stooped and there was an indelible weariness in him as of the flavor of many defeats, small perhaps, but sharp.

"Septimus Thirsk." He announced himself with a remnant of military precision, as if an old memory had unaccountably slipped through and prompted him. "What can I do for you, sir?" He ignored his brother-in-law, in whose house he apparently lived, and Cyprian, who had retreated to the window embrasure.

"Were you at home on Monday, the day before Mrs. Haslett was killed, sir?" Monk asked politely.

"I was out, sir, in the morning and for luncheon," Septimus answered, still standing almost to attention. "I spent the afternoon here, in my quarters most of the time. Dined out." A shadow of concern crossed his face. "Why does that interest you, sir? I neither saw nor heard any intruder, or I should have reported it."

"Mrs. Haslett was killed by someone already in the house, Uncle Septimus," Cyprian explained. "We thought Tavie might have said something to you which would give us some idea why. We're asking everyone."

"Said something?" Septimus blinked.

Basil's face darkened with irritation. "For heaven's sake, man, the question is simple enough! Did Octavia say or do anything that led you to suppose she had stumbled on a secret unpleasant enough to cause someone to fear her! It's hardly likely, but it is necessary to ask!"

"Yes she did!" Septimus said instantly, two spots of color burning on his pale cheeks. "When she came in in the late afternoon she said a whole world had been opened up to her and it was quite hideous. She said she had one more thing to discover to prove it finally. I asked her what it was, but she refused to say."

Basil was stunned and Cyprian stood paralyzed on the spot.

"Where had she been, Mr. Thirsk?" Monk asked quietly. "You said she was coming in."

"I have no idea," Septimus replied with the grief replacing anger in his eyes. "I asked her, but she would not tell me, except that one day I would understand, better than anyone else. That was all she would say."

"Ask the coachman," Cyprian said immediately. "He'll know."

"She didn't go in our coaches." Septimus caught Basil's eye. "I mean your coaches," he corrected pointedly. "She walked in. I presume she either walked all the way or found a hansom."

Cyprian swore under his breath. Basil looked confused, and yet his shoulders eased under the black cloth of his jacket and he stared beyond them all out of the window. He spoke with his back to Monk.

"It seems, Inspector, as if the poor girl did hear something that day. It will be your task to discover what it was—and if you cannot do that, to deduce in some other way who it was who killed her. It is possible we may never discover why, and it hardly matters." He hesitated, for a moment more absorbed in his own thoughts. No one intruded.

"If there is any further help the family can give you, we shall of course do so," he continued. "Now it is past midday and I can think of no purpose in which we can assist you at present. Either you or your juniors are free to question the servants at any time you wish, without disturbing the family. I shall instruct Phillips to that effect. Thank you for your courtesy so far. I trust it will continue. You may report any progress you make to me, or if I am not present, to my son. I would prefer you did not distress Lady Moidore."

"Yes, Sir Basil." He turned to Cyprian. "Thank you for your assistance, Mr. Moidore." Monk excused himself, and was shown out, not by the butler this time but by a very striking footman with bold eyes and a face whose handsomeness was spoiled only by a small, clever mouth.

In the hallway he saw Lady Moidore and had every intention of passing her with no more than a polite acknowledgment, but she came towards him, dismissing the footman with a wave of her hand, and he had no option but to stop and speak with her.

"Good day, Lady Moidore."

It was hard to tell how much the pallor of her face was natural, an accompaniment to her remarkable hair, but the wide eyes and the nervous movements were unmistakable.

"Good morning, Mr. Monk. My sister-in-law tells me you believe there was no intruder in the house. Is that so?"

He could save her nothing by lying. The news would be no easier coming from someone else, and the mere fact that he had lied would make it impossible for her to believe him in future. It would add another confusion to those already inevitable.

"Yes ma'am. I am sorry."

She stood motionless. He could not even see the slight motion of her breathing.

"Then it was one of us who killed Tavie," she said. She surprised him by not flinching from it or dressing it in evasive words. She was the only one in the family to make no pretense that it must have been one of the servants, and he admired her intensely for the courage that must have cost.

"Did you see Mrs. Haslett after she came in that afternoon, ma'am?" he asked more gently.

"Yes. Why?"

"It seems she learned something while she was out which distressed her, and according to Mr. Thirsk, she intended to pursue it and discover a final proof of the matter. Did she confide anything of it to you?"

"No." Her eyes were so wide she seemed to stare at something so close to her she could not blink. "No. She was very quiet during dinner, and there was some slight unpleasantness with—" She frowned. "With both Cyprian and her father. But I assumed she had one of her headaches again. People are occasionally unpleasant with each other, especially when they live in the same house day in and day out. She did come and say good-night to me immediately before she went to bed. Her dressing robe was torn. I offered to mend it for her—she was never very good with a needle—" Her voice broke for just a moment. Memory must have been unbearably sharp, and so very close. Her child was dead. The loss was not yet wholly grasped. Life had only just slipped into the past.

He hated having to press her, but he had to know.

"What did she say to you, ma'am? Even a word may help."

"Nothing but 'good night,' " she said quietly. "She was very gentle, I remember that, very gentle indeed, and she kissed me. It was almost as if she knew we should not meet again." She put her hands up to her face, pushing the long, slender fingers till they held the skin tight across her cheekbones. He had the powerful impression it was not grief which shook her most but the realization that it was someone in her own family who had committed murder.

She was a remarkable woman, possessed of an honesty which he greatly respected. It cut his emotion, and his pride, that he was socially so inferior he could offer her no comfort at all, only a stiff courtesy that was devoid of any individual expression.

"You have my deep sympathy, ma'am," he said awkwardly. "I wish it were not necessary to pursue it—" He did not add the rest. She understood without tedious explanation.

She withdrew her hands.

"Of course," she said almost under her breath.

"Good day, ma'am."

"Good day, Mr. Monk. Percival, please see Mr. Monk to the door."

The footman reappeared, and to Monk's surprise he was shown out of the front door and down the steps into Queen Anne Street, feeling a mixture of pity, intellectual stimulation, and growing involvement which was familiar, and yet he could remember no individual occasion. He must have done this a hundred times before, begun with a crime, then learned experience by experience to know the people and their lives, their tragedies.

How many of them had marked him, touched him deeply enough to change anything inside him? Whom had he loved—or pitied? What had made him angry?

He had been shown out of the front door, so it was necessary to go around to the back areaway to find Evan, whom he had detailed to speak to the servants and to make at least some search for the knife. Since the murderer was still in the house, and had not left it that night, the weapon must be there too, unless he had disposed of it since. But there would be many knives in any ordinary kitchen of such a size, and several of them used for cutting meat. It would be a simple thing to have wiped it and replaced it. Even blood found in the joint of the handle would mean little.

He saw Evan coming up the steps. Perhaps word had reached him of Monk's departure, and he had left at the same time intentionally. Monk looked at Evan's face as he ran up, feet light, head high.

"Well?"

"I had P.C. Lawley help me. We went right through the house, especially servants' quarters, but didn't find the missing jewelry. Not that I really expected to."

Monk had not expected it either. He had never thought robbery the motive. The jewelry was probably flushed down the drain, and the silver vase merely mislaid. "What about the knife?"

"Kitchen full of knives," Evan said, falling into step beside him. "Wicked-looking things. Cook says there's nothing missing. If it was one of them, it was replaced. Couldn't find anything else. Do you think it was one of the servants? Why?" He screwed up his face doubtfully. "A jealous ladies' maid? A footman with amorous notions?"

Monk snorted. "More likely a secret of some sort that she discovered." And he told Evan what he had learned so far.

Monk was at the Old Bailey by half past three, and it took him another half hour and the exertion of considerable bribery and veiled threats to get inside the courtroom where the trial of Menard Grey was winding to its conclusion. Rathbone was making his final speech. It was not an impassioned oration as Monk had expected—after all he could see that the man was an exhibitionist, vain, pedantic and above all an actor. Instead Rathbone spoke quite quietly, his words precise, his logic exact. He made no attempt to dazzle the jurors or to appeal to their emotions. Either he had given up or he had at last realized that there could be only one verdict and it was the judge to whom he must look for any compassion.

The victim had been a gentleman of high breeding and noble heritage. But so was Menard Grey. He had struggled long with his burden of knowledge and terrible, continuing injustice which would afflict more and more innocent people if he did not act.

Monk saw the jury's faces and knew they would ask for clemency. But would that be enough?

Without realizing it he was searching the crowd for Hester Latterly. She had said she would be there. He could never think of the Grey case, or any part of it, without remembering her. She should be here now to see its close.

Callandra Daviot was here, sitting in the first row behind the lawyers, next to her sister-in-law, Fabia Grey, the dowager Lady Shelburne. Lovel Grey was beside his mother at the farther end, pale, composed, not afraid to look at his brother in the dock. The tragedy seemed to have added a stature to him, a certainty of his own convictions he had lacked before. He was not more than a yard away from his mother, and yet the distance between them was a gulf which he never once looked at her to cross.

Fabia sat like stone, white, cold and relentless. The wound of disillusion had destroyed her. There was nothing left now but hatred. The delicate face which had once been beautiful was sharpened by the violence of her emotions, and the lines around her mouth were ugly, her chin pointed, her neck thin and ropey. If she had not destroyed so many others with her dreams, Monk would have pitied her, but as it was all he could feel was a chill of fear. She had lost the son she idolized to a shocking death. With him had gone all the excitement and glamour from her life. It was Joscelin who had made her laugh, flattered her, told her she was lovely and charming and gay. It was hard enough that he should have had to go to war in the Crimea and return wounded, but when he had been battered to death in his flat in Mecklenburg Square it was more than she could bear. Neither Lovel nor Menard could take his place, and she would not let them try—or accept from them such love or warmth as they would have given.

Monk's bitter solution of the case had crushed her totally, and it was something she would never forgive.

Rosamond, Lovel's wife, sat to her mother-in-law's left, composed and solitary.

The judge spoke his brief summation and the jury retired. The crowd remained in its seats, fearful lest they lose their places and miss the climax of the drama.

Monk wondered how often before he had attended the trial of someone he had arrested. The case notes he had searched so painstakingly to discover himself had stopped short with the unmasking of the criminal. They had shown him a careful man who left no detail to chance, an intuitive man who could leap from bare evidence to complicated structures of motive and opportunity, sometimes brilliantly, leaving others plodding behind, mystified. It also showed relentless ambition, a career built step by step, both by dedicated work and hard hours and by maneuvering others so he was in the place, at the time, when he could seize the advantage over less able colleagues. He made very few mistakes and forgave none in others. He had many admirers, but no one apart from Evan seemed to like him. And looking at the man who emerged from the pages he was not surprised. He did not like him himself.

Evan had met him only after the accident. The Grey case had been their first together.

He stood waiting for another fifteen minutes, thinking about the shreds he knew of himself, trying to picture the rest, and unsure whether he would find it familiar, easy to understand, therefore to forgive—or a nature he neither liked nor respected. Of the man before, or apart from his work, there was nothing, not a letter or memento that had meaning.

The jury was returning, their faces tense, eyes anxious. The buzz of voices ceased, there was no sound but the rustle of fabric and squeak of boots.

The judge asked if they had reached a verdict, and if it had been the verdict of them all.

They answered that they had. He asked the foreman what it was, and he replied: "Guilty—but we plead for clemency, my lord. Most sincerely, we ask that you give all the mercy allowed you, within the law—sir."

Monk found himself standing to attention, breathing very slowly as if the very sound of it in his ears might lose him some fraction of what was said. Beside him someone coughed, and he could have hit the man for his intrusion.

Was Hester here? Was she waiting as he was?

He looked at Menard Grey, who had risen to his feet and appeared, for all the crowd around him, as alone as a man could be. Every person in this entire paneled and vaulted hall was here to see judgment upon him, his life, or death. Beside him Rathbone, slimmer, and at least three inches shorter, put out a hand to steady him, or perhaps simply to let him feel a touch and know someone else was at least aware.

"Menard Grey," the judge said very slowly, his face creased with sadness and something that looked like both pity and frustration. "You have been found guilty of murder by this court. Indeed, you have wisely not pleaded otherwise. That is to your credit. Your counsel has made much of the provocation offered you, and the emotional distress you suffered at the hands of the victim. The court cannot regard that as an excuse. If every man who felt himself ill used were to resort to violence our civilization would end."

There was a ripple of anger around the room, a letting out of breath in a soft hiss.

"However," the judge said sharply, "the fact that great wrongs were done, and you sought ways to prevent them, and could not find them within the law, and therefore committed this crime to prevent the continuation of these wrongs to other innocent persons, has been taken into account when considering sentence. You are a misguided man, but it is my judgment that you are not a wicked one. I sentence you to be transported to the land of Australia, where you will remain for a period of twenty-five years in Her Majesty's colony of Western Australia." He picked up his gavel to signal the end of the matter, but the sound of it was drowned in the cheering and stamping of feet and the scramble as the press charged to report the decision.

Monk did not find a chance to speak to Hester, but he did see her once, over the heads of a score of people. Her eyes were shining, and the tiredness suggested by her severe hairstyle, and the plain stuff of her dress, was wiped away by the glow of triumph—and utter relief. In that instant she was almost beautiful. Their eyes met and the moment was shared. Then she was carried along and he lost sight of her.

He also saw Fabia Grey as she was leaving, her body stiff, her face bleak and white with hatred. She walked alone, refusing to allow her daughter-in-law to help her, and her eldest and only remaining son chose to walk behind, head erect, a faint, tiny smile touching his mouth. Callandra Daviot would be with Rathbone. It was she, not Menard's own family, who had employed him, and she who would settle the account.

He did not see Rathbone, but he could imagine his triumph, and although it was what Monk also wanted most and had worked for, he found himself resenting Rathbone's success, the smugness he could so clearly envision in the lawyer's face and the gleam of another victory in his eyes.

He went straight from the Old Bailey back to the police station and up to Runcorn's office to report his progress to date in the Queen Anne Street case.

Runcorn looked at Monk's extremely smart jacket and his eyes narrowed and a flick of temper twitched in his high, narrow cheeks.

"I've been waiting for you for two days," he said as soon as Monk was through the door. "I assume you are working hard, but I require to be informed of precisely what you have learned—if anything! Have you seen the newspapers? Sir Basil Moidore is an extremely influential man. You don't seem to realize who we are dealing with, and he has friends in very high circles—cabinet ministers, foreign ambassadors, even princes."

"He also has enemies within his own house," Monk replied with more flippancy than was wise, but he knew the case was going to become uglier and far more difficult than it was already. Runcorn would hate it. He was terrified of offending authority, or people he thought of as socially important, and the Home Office would press for a quick solution because the public was outraged. At the same time he would be sick with fear lest he offend Moidore. Monk would be caught in the middle, and Runcorn would be only too delighted, if the results at last gave him the opportunity, to crush Monk's pretensions and make his failure public.

Monk could see it all ahead, and it infuriated him that even fore-knowledge could not help him escape.

"I am not amused by riddles," Runcorn snapped. "If you have discovered nothing and the case is too difficult for you, say so, and I shall put someone else on it."

Monk smiled, showing his teeth. "An excellent idea—sir," he answered. "Thank you."

"Don't be impertinent!" Runcorn was thoroughly out of countenance. It was the last response he had expected. "If you are giving me your resignation, do it properly, man, not with a casual word like this. Are you resigning?" For a brief moment hope gleamed in his round eyes.

"No sir." Monk could not keep the lift in his voice. The victory was only a single thrust; the whole battle was already lost. "I thought you were offering to replace me on the Moidore case."

"No I am not. Why?" Runcorn's short, straight eyebrows rose. "Is it too much for your skills? You used to be the best detective on the force—at least that was what you told everyone!" His voice grated with sour satisfaction. "But you've certainly lost your sharpness since your accident. You didn't do badly with the Grey case, but it took you long enough. I expect they'll hang Grey." He looked at Monk with satisfaction. He was sharp enough to have read Monk's feelings correctly, his sympathy for Menard.

"No they won't," Monk retorted. "They brought in the verdict this afternoon. Deportation for twenty-five years." He smiled, letting his triumph show. "He could make quite a decent life for himself in Australia."

"If he doesn't die of fever," Runcorn said spitefully. "Or get killed in a riot, or starve."

"That could happen in London." Monk kept his face expressionless.

"Well, don't stand there like a fool." Runcorn sat down behind his desk. "Why are you afraid of the Moidore case? You think it is beyond your ability?"

"It was someone in the house," Monk answered.

"Of course it was someone in the house." Runcorn glared at him. "What's the matter with you, Monk? Have you lost your wits? She was killed in the bedroom—someone broke in. No one suggested she was dragged out into the street."

Monk took malicious pleasure in disabusing him.

"They were suggesting a burglar broke in," he said, framing each word carefully and precisely, as if to someone slow of understanding. He leaned a little forward. "I am saying that no one broke in and whoever murdered Sir Basil's daughter, he—or she—was in the house already—and is still in the house. Social tact supposes one of the servants; common sense says it is far more probably one of the family."

Runcorn stared at him aghast, the blood draining from his long face as the full implication came home to him. He saw the satisfaction in Monk's eyes.

"Preposterous," he said with a dry throat, the sound robbed of its force by his tongue sticking to the roof of his mouth. "What's the matter with you, Monk? Do you have some personal hatred against the aristocracy that you keep on accusing them of such monstrosity? Wasn't the Grey case enough for you? Have you finally taken leave of your senses?"

"The evidence is incontrovertible." Monk's pleasure was only in seeing the horror in Runcorn. The inspector would immeasurably rather have looked for an intruder turned violent, acutely difficult as it would be to trace such a one in the labyrinths of petty crime and poverty in the rookeries, as the worst slum tenements were known, whole areas where the police dared not intrude, still less maintain any rule of law. Even so it would be less fraught with personal danger than accusing, even by implication, a member of a family like the Moidores.

Runcorn opened his mouth, then closed it again.

"Yes sir?" Monk prompted, his eyes wide.

A succession of emotions chased each other over Runcorn's face: terror of the political repercussions if Monk offended people, behaved clumsily, could not back up with proof every single allegation he made; and then the double-edged hope that Monk might precipitate some disaster great enough to ruin him, and rid Runcorn of his footsteps forever at his heels.

"Get out," Runcorn said between his teeth. "And God help you if you make a mistake in this. You can be certain I shan't!"

"I never imagined you would—*sir*." And Monk stood at attention for a second—in mockery, not respect—then turned for the door.

He despaired Runcorn, and it was not until he was almost back to his rooms in Grafton Street that it occurred to him to wonder what Runcorn had been like when they first met, before Monk had threatened him with his ambition, his greater agility of mind, his quick, cruel wit. It was an unpleasant thought, and it took the warmth out of his feeling of superiority. He had almost certainly contributed to what the man had become. That Runcorn had always been weak, vain, less able, was a thin excuse, and any honesty at all evaporated it. The more flawed a man was, the shoddier it was to take advantage of his inadequacies to destroy him. If the strong were irresponsible and self-serving, what could the weak hope for?

Monk went to bed early and lay awake staring at the ceiling, disgusted with himself.

The funeral of Octavia Haslett was attended by half the aristocracy in London. The carriages stretched up and down Langham Place, stopping the normal traffic, black horses whenever possible, black plumes tossing, coachmen and footmen in livery, black crepe fluttering, harnesses polished like mirrors, but not a single piece that jingled or made a sound. An ambitious person might have recognized the crests of many noble families, not only of Britain but of France and the states of Germany as well. The mourners wore black, immaculate, devastatingly fashionable, enormous skirts hooped and petticoated, ribboned bonnets, gleaming top hats and polished boots.

Everything was done in silence, muffled hooves, well-oiled heels, whispering voices. The few passersby slowed down and bowed their heads in respect.

From his position like a waiting servant on the steps of All Saints Church, Monk saw the family arrive, first Sir Basil Moidore with his remaining daughter, Araminta, not even a black veil able to hide the blazing color of her hair or the whiteness of her face. They climbed the steps together, she holding his arm, although she seemed to support him as much as he her.

Next came Beatrice Moidore, very definitely upheld by Cyprian. She walked uprightly, but was so heavily veiled no expression was visible, but her back and shoulders were stiff and twice she stumbled and he helped her gently, speaking with his head close to hers.

Some distance behind, having come in a separate carriage, Myles Kellard and Romola Moidore came side by side, but not seeming to offer each other anything more than a formal accompaniment. Romola moved as if she was tired; her step was heavy and her shoulders a little bowed. She too wore a veil so her face was invisible. A few feet to her right Myles Kellard looked bleak, or perhaps it was boredom. He climbed the steps slowly, almost absently, and only when they reached the top did he offer her a hand at her elbow, more as a courtesy than a support.

Lastly came Fenella Sandeman in overdramatic black, a hat with too much decoration on it for a funeral, but undoubtedly handsome. Her waist was nipped in so she looked fragile, at a few yards' distance giving an impression of girlishness, then as she came closer one saw the too-dark hair and the faint withering of the skin. Monk did not know whether to pity her ridiculousness or admire her bravado.

Close behind her, and murmuring to her every now and again, was Septimus Thirsk. The hard gray daylight showed the weariness in his face and his sense of having been beaten, finding his moments of happiness in very small victories, the great ones having long ago been abandoned.

Monk did not go inside the church yet, but waited while the reverent, the grieving and the envious made their way past him. He overheard snatches of conversation, expressions of pity, but far more of outrage. What was the world coming to? Where was the much vaunted new Metropolitan Police Force while all this was going on? What was the purpose in paying to have them if people like the Moidores could be murdered in their own beds? One must speak to the Home Secretary and demand something be done!

Monk could imagine the outrage, the fear and the excuses that would take place over the next days or weeks. Whitehall would be spurred by complaints. Explanations would be offered, polite refusals given, and then when their lordships had left, Runcorn would be sent for and reports requested with icy disfavor hiding a hot panic.

And Runcorn would break out in a sweat of humiliation and anxiety. He hated failure and had no idea how to stand his ground. And he in turn would pass on his fears, disguised as official anger, to Monk.

Basil Moidore would be at the beginning of the chain—and at the end, when Monk returned to his house to tear apart the comfort and safe beliefs of his family, all their assumptions about one another and the dead woman they were burying with such a fashionable funeral now.

A newsboy strolled past as Monk turned to go inside.

" 'Orrible murder!" the boy shouted out, regardless of standing beside the church steps. "Police baffled! Read all about it!"

The service was very formal, sonorous voices intoning all the well-known words, organ music swelling somberly, everything jewel colors of stained glass, gray masses of stone, light on a hundred textures of black, the shuffle of feet and rustle of fabric. Someone sniffed. Footsteps were loud as ushers moved down the aisles. Boots squeaked.

Monk waited at the back, and as they left to go after the coffin to the family vault he followed as closely as he dared.

During the interment he stood behind them, next to a large man with a bald head, his few strands of hair fluttering in the sharpening November wind.

Beatrice Moidore was immediately in front of him, close to her husband now.

"Did you see that policeman here?" she asked him very quietly. "Standing at the back behind the Lewises."

"Of course," he replied. "Thank God at least he is discreet and he looks like a mourner."

"His suit is beautifully cut," she said with a lift of surprise in her voice. "They must pay them more than I thought. He almost looks like a gentleman."

"He does not," Basil said sharply. "Don't be ridiculous, Beatrice."

"He'll be back, you know." She ignored his criticism.

"Of course he'll be back," he said between his teeth. "He'll be back every day until he gives up—or discovers who it was."

"Why did you say 'give up' first?" she asked. "Don't you think he will find out?"

"I've no idea."

"Basil?"

"What?"

"What will we do if he doesn't?"

His voice was resigned. "Nothing. There is nothing to do."

"I don't think I can live the rest of my life not knowing."

He lifted his shoulders fractionally. "You will have to, my dear. There will be no alternative. Many cases are unsolved. We shall have to remember her as she was, grieve for her, and then continue our lives."

"Are you being willfully deaf to me, Basil?" Her voice shook only at the last word.

"I have heard every word you said, Beatrice—and replied to it," he said impatiently. Both of them remained looking ahead all the time, as if their full attention were on the interment. Opposite them Fenella was leaning heavily on Septimus. He propped her up automatically, his mind obviously elsewhere. From the look of sadness not only in his face but in the whole attitude of his body, he was thinking of Octavia.

"It was not an intruder," Beatrice went on with quiet anger. "Every day we shall look 'round at faces, listen to inflections of voices and hear double meanings in everything that is said, and wonder if it was that person, or if not, if they know who it was."

"You are being hysterical," Basil snapped, his voice hard in spite of its very quietness. "If it will help you to keep control of yourself, I'll dismiss all the servants and we'll hire a new staff. Now for God's sake pay attention to the service!"

"Dismiss the servants." Her words were strangled in her throat. "Oh, Basil! How will that help?"

He stood still, his body rigid under the black broadcloth, his shoulders high.

"Are you saying you think it was one of the family?" he said at last, all expression ironed out of his voice.

She lifted her head a little higher. "Wasn't it?"

"Do you know something, Beatrice?"

"Only what we all know—and what common sense tells me." Unconsciously she turned her head a fraction towards Myles Kellard on the far side of the crypt.

Beside him Araminta was staring back at her mother. She could not possibly have heard anything of what had passed between her parents, but her hands tightened in front of her, holding a small handkerchief and tearing it apart.

The interment was over. The vicar intoned the last amen, and the company turned to depart. Cyprian and his wife, Araminta with several feet between herself and her husband, Septimus militarily upright and Fenella staggering a trifle, lastly Sir Basil and Lady Moidore side by side.

Monk watched them go with pity, anger and a growing sense of darkness.

CHAPTER
FOUR

"Do you want me to keep on looking for the jewelry?" Evan asked, his face puckered with doubt. Obviously he believed there was no purpose to it at all.

Monk agreed with him. In all probability it had been thrown away, or even destroyed. Whatever the motive had been for the death of Octavia Haslett, he was sure it was not robbery, not even a greedy servant sneaking into her room to steal. It would be too stupid to do it at the one time he, or she, could be absolutely sure Octavia would be there, when there was all day to do such a thing undisturbed.

"No," he said decisively. "Much better use your time questioning the servants." He smiled, baring his teeth, and Evan made a grimace back again. He had already been twice to the Moidore house, each time asking the same things and receiving much the same brief, nervous answers. He could not deduce guilt from their fear. Nearly all servants were afraid of the police; the sheer embarrassment of it was enough to shadow their reputations, let alone suspicion of having any knowledge of a murder. "Someone in that house killed her," he added.

Evan raised his eyebrows. "One of the servants?" He kept most of the surprise out of his voice, but there was still a lift of doubt there, and the innocence of his gaze only added to it.

"A far more comfortable thought," Monk replied. "We shall certainly find more favor with the powers in the land if we can arrest someone below stairs. But I think that is a gift we cannot reasonably look for. No, I was hoping that by talking with the servants enough we might learn something about the family. Servants notice a great deal, and although they're trained not to repeat any of it, they might unintentionally, if their own lives are in jeopardy." They were standing in Monk's office, smaller and darker than Runcorn's, even in this bright, sharp, late autumn morning. The plain wooden table was piled with papers, the old carpet worn in a track from door to chair. "You've seen most of them," he went on. "Any impressions so far?"

"Usual sort of complement," Evan said slowly. "Maids are mostly young—on the surface they look flighty, given to giggles and triviality." The sunlight came through the dusty window and picked out the fine lines on his face, throwing his expression into sharp relief. "And yet they earn their livings in a rigid world, full of obedience and among people who care little for them personally. They know a kind of reality that is harsher than mine. Some of the girls are only children." He looked up at Monk. "In another year or two I'll be old enough to be their father." The thought seemed to startle him, and he frowned. "The between-stairs maid is only twelve. I haven't discovered yet if they know anything of use, but I can't believe it was one of them."

"Maids?" Monk tried to clarify.

"Yes—older ones I suppose are possible." Evan looked dubious. "Can't think why they would, though."

"Men?"

"Can't imagine the butler." Evan smiled with a little twist. "He's a dry old stick, very formal, very military. If a person ever stirred passion of any sort in him I think it was so long ago even the memory of it has gone now. And why on earth would an excruciatingly respectable butler stab his mistress's daughter in her bedroom? What could he possibly be doing there in the middle of the night anyway?"

Monk smiled in spite of himself. "You don't read enough of the more lurid press, Evan. Listen to the running patterers some time."

"Rubbish," Evan said heartily. "Not Phillips."

"Footmen—grooms—bootboy?" Monk pressed. "And what about the older women?"

Evan was half leaning, half sitting on the windowsill.

"Grooms are in the stables and the back door is locked at night," Evan replied. "Bootboy possibly, but he's only fourteen. Can't think of a motive for him. Older women—I suppose it is imaginable, some jealous or slight perhaps, but it would have to be a very violent one to provoke murder. None of them looks raving mad, or has ever shown the remotest inclination to violence. And they'd have to be mad to do such a thing. Anyway, passions in servants are far more often against each other. They are used to being spoken to in all manner of ways by the family." He looked at Monk with gravity beneath the wry amusement. "It's each other they take exception to. There's a rigid hierarchy, and there's been blood spilled before now over what job is whose."

He saw Monk's expression.

"Oh—not murder. Just a few hard bruises and the occasional broken head," he explained. "But I think downstairs emotions concern others downstairs."

"What about if Mrs. Haslett knew something about them, some past sin of thieving or immorality?" Monk suggested. "That would lose them a very comfortable position. Without references they'd not get another—and a servant who can't get a place has nowhere to go but the sweatshops or the street."

"Could be," Evan agreed. "Or the footmen. There are two— Harold and Percival. Both seem fairly ordinary so far. I should say Percival is the more intelligent, and perhaps ambitious."

"What does a footman aspire to be?" Monk said a little waspishly.

"A butler, I imagine," Evan replied with a faint smile. "Don't look like that, sir. Butler is a comfortable, responsible and very respected position. Butlers consider themselves socially far superior to the police. They live in fine houses, eat the best, and drink it. I've seen butlers who drink better claret than their masters—"

"Do their masters know that?"

"Some masters don't have the palate to know claret from cooking wine." Evan shrugged. "All the same, it's a little kingdom that many men would find most attractive."

Monk raised his eyebrows sarcastically. "And how would knifing the master's daughter get him any closer to this enjoyable position?"

"It wouldn't—unless she knew something about him that would get him dismissed without a reference."

That was plausible, and Monk knew it.

"Then you had better go back and see what you can learn," he directed. "I'm going to speak to the family again, which I still think, unfortunately, is far more likely. I want to see them alone, away from Sir Basil." His face tightened. "He orchestrated the last time as if I had hardly been there."

"Master in his house." Evan hitched himself off the windowsill. "You can hardly be surprised."

"That is why I intend to see them away from Queen Anne Street, if I can," Monk replied tersely. "I daresay it will take me all week."

Evan rolled his eyes upward briefly, and without speaking again went out; Monk heard his footsteps down the stairs.

It did take Monk most of the week. He began straightaway with great success, almost immediately finding Romola Moidore walking in a leisurely fashion in Green Park. She started along the grass parallel with Constitution Row, gazing at the trees beyond by Buckingham Palace. The footman Percival had informed Monk she would be there, having ridden in the carriage with Mr. Cyprian, who was taking luncheon at his club in nearby Piccadilly.

She was expecting to meet a Mrs. Ketteridge, but Monk caught up with her while she was still alone. She was dressed entirely in black, as befitted a woman whose family was in mourning, but she still looked extremely smart. Her wide skirts were tiered and trimmed with velvet, the pergola sleeves of her dress were lined with black silk, her bonnet was small and worn low on the back of the head, and her hair was in the very fashionable style turned under at the ears into a lowset knot.

She was startled to see him, and not at all pleased. However there was nowhere for her to go to avoid him without being obvious, and perhaps she bore in mind her father-in-law's strictures that they were all to be helpful. He had not said so in so many words in Monk's hearing, but his implication was obvious.

"Good morning, Mr. Monk," she said coolly, standing quite still and facing him as if he were a stray dog that had approached too close and should be warded off with the fringed umbrella which she held firmly in her right hand, its point a little above the ground, ready to jab at him.

"Good morning, Mrs. Moidore," he replied, inclining his head a little in politeness.

"I really don't know anything of use to you." She tried to avoid the issue even now, as if he might go away. "I have no idea at all what can have happened. I still think you must have made a mistake—or been misled—"

"Were you fond of your sister-in-law, Mrs. Moidore?" he asked conversationally.

She tried to remain facing him, then decided she might as well walk, since it seemed he was determined to. She resented promenading with a policeman, as though he were a social acquaintance, and it showed in her face; although no one else would have known his station, certainly his clothes were almost as well cut and as fashionable as hers, and his bearing every bit as assured.

"Of course I was," she retorted hotly. "If I knew anything, I should not defend her attacker for an instant. I simply do not know."

"I do not doubt your honesty—or your indignation, ma'am," he said, although it was not entirely true. He trusted no one so far. "I was thinking that if you were fond of her, then you will have known her well. What kind of person was she?"

Romola was taken by surprise; the question was not what she had been expecting.

"I—well—it is very hard to say," she protested. "Really, that is a most unfair question. Poor Octavia is dead. It is most indecent to speak of the dead in anything but the kindest of terms, especially when they have died so terribly."

"I commend your delicacy, Mrs. Moidore," he replied with forced patience, measuring his step to hers. "But I believe at the moment truth, however tasteless, would serve her better. And since it seems an unavoidable conclusion that whoever murdered her is still in your house, you could be excused for placing your own safety, and that of your children, to the forefront of your thoughts."

That stopped her as if she had walked straight into one of the trees along the border. She drew in her breath sharply and almost cried out, then remembered the other passersby just in time and bit her knuckles instead.

"What kind of person was Mrs. Haslett?" Monk asked again.

She resumed her slow pace along the path, her face very pale, her skirts brushing the gravel.

"She was very emotional, very impulsive," she replied after only the briefest thought. "When she fell in love with Harry Haslett her family disapproved, but she was absolutely determined. She refused to consider anyone else. I have always been surprised that Sir Basil permitted it, but I suppose it was a perfectly acceptable match, and Lady Moidore approved. His family was excellent, and he had reasonable prospects for the future—" She shrugged. "Somewhat distant, but Octavia was a younger daughter, who could reasonably expect to have to wait."

"Had he an unfortunate reputation?" Monk asked.

"Not that I ever heard."

"Then why was Sir Basil so against the match? If he was of good family and had expectations, surely he would be agreeable?"

"I think it was a matter of personality. I know Sir Basil had been at school with his father and did not care for him. He was a year or two older, and a most successful person." She shrugged very slightly. "Sir Basil never said so, of course, but perhaps he cheated? Or in some other way that a gentleman would not mention, behaved dishonorably?" She looked straight ahead of her. A party of ladies and gentlemen was approaching and she nodded at them but did not make any sign of welcome. She was annoyed by the circumstance. Monk saw the color rise in her cheeks and guessed her dilemma. She did not wish them to speculate as to who he was that Romola walked alone with him in the park, and yet still less did she wish to introduce a policeman to her acquaintances.

He smiled sourly, a touch of mockery at himself, because it stung him, as well as at her. He despised her that appearances mattered so much, and himself because it caught him with a raw smart too, and for the same reasons.

"He was uncouth, brash?" he prompted with a trace of asperity.

"Not at all," she replied with satisfaction at contradicting him. "He was charming, friendly, full of good humor, but like Octavia, determined to have his own way."

"Not easily governed," he said wryly, liking Harry Haslett more with each discovery.

"No—" There was a touch of envy in her now, and a real sadness that came through the polite, expected grief. "He was always kind for one's comfort, but he never pretended to an opinion he did not have."

"He sounds a most excellent man."

"He was. Octavia was devastated when he was killed—in the Crimea, you know. I can remember the day the news came. I thought she would never recover—" She tightened her lips and blinked hard, as if tears threatened to rob her of composure. "I am not sure she ever did," she added very quietly. "She loved him very much. I believe no one else in the family realized quite how much until then."

They had been gradually slowing their pace; now conscious again of the cold wind, they quickened.

"I am very sorry," he said, and meant it.

They were passed by a nurserymaid wheeling a perambulator—a

brand-new invention which was much better than the old pulling carts, and which was causing something of a stir—and accompanied by a small, self-conscious boy with a hoop.

"She never even considered remarrying," Romola went on without being asked, and having regarded the perambulator with due interest. "Of course it was only a little over two years, but Sir Basil did approach the subject. She was a young woman, and still without children. It would not be unseemly."

Monk remembered the dead face he had seen that first morning. Even through the stiffness and the pallor he had imagined something of what she must have been like: the emotions, the hungers and the dreams. It was a face of passion and will.

"She was very comely?" He made it a question, although there was no doubt in his mind.

Romola hesitated, but there was no meanness in it, only a genuine doubt.

"She was handsome," she said slowly. "But her chief quality was her vividness, and her complete individuality. After Harry died she became very moody and suffered"—she avoided his eyes—"suffered a lot of poor health. When she was well she was quite delightful, everyone found her so. But when she was . . ." Again she stopped momentarily and searched for the word. "When she was poorly she spoke little—and made no effort to charm."

Monk had a brief vision of what it must be like to be a woman on her own, obliged to work at pleasing people because your acceptance, perhaps even your financial survival, depended upon it. There must be hundreds—thousands—of petty accommodations, suppressions of your own beliefs and opinions because they would not be what someone else wished to hear. What a constant humiliation, like a burning blister on the heel which hurt with every step.

And on the other hand, what a desperate loneliness for a man if he ever realized he was always being told not what she really thought or felt but what she believed he wanted to hear. Would he then ever trust anything as real, or of value?

"Mr. Monk."

She was speaking, and his concentration had left her totally.

"Yes ma'am—I apologize—"

"You asked me about Octavia. I was endeavoring to tell you." She was irritated that he was so inattentive. "She was most appealing, at her best, and many men had called upon her, but she gave none of them the slightest encouragement. Whoever it was who killed her, I do not think you will find the slightest clue to their identity along that line of inquiry."

"No, I imagine you are right. And Mr. Haslett died in the Crimea?"

"Captain Haslett. Yes." She hesitated, looking away from him again. "Mr. Monk."

"Yes ma'am?"

"It occurs to me that some people—some men—have strange ideas about women who are widowed—" She was obviously most uncomfortable about what it was she was attempting to say.

"Indeed," he said encouragingly.

The wind caught at her bonnet, pulling it a little sideways, but she disregarded it. He wondered if she was trying to find a way to say what Sir Basil had prompted, and if the words would be his or her own.

Two little girls in frilled dresses passed by with their governess, walking very stiffly, eyes ahead as if unaware of the soldier coming the other way.

"It is not impossible that one of the servants, one of the men, entertained such—such ludicrous ideas—and became overfamiliar."

They had almost stopped. Romola poked at the ground with the ferrule of her umbrella.

"If—if that happened, and she rebuffed him soundly—possibly he became angry—incensed—I mean . . ." She tailed off miserably, still avoiding looking at him.

"In the middle of the night?" he said dubiously. "He was certainly extremely bold to go to her bedroom and try such a thing."

The color burned up her cheeks.

"Someone did," she pointed out with a catch in her voice, still staring at the ground. "I know it seems preposterous. Were she not dead, I should laugh at it myself."

"You are right," he said reluctantly. "Or it may be that she discovered some secret that could have ruined a servant had she told it, and they killed her to prevent that."

She looked up at him, her eyes wide. "Oh—yes, I suppose that sounds . . . possible. What kind of a secret? You mean dishonesty—immorality? But how would Tavie have learned of it?"

"I don't know. Have you no idea where she went that afternoon?" He began to walk again, and she accompanied him.

"No, none at all. She barely spoke to us that evening, except a silly argument over dinner, but nothing new was said."

"What was the argument about?"

"Nothing in particular—just frayed tempers." She looked straight ahead of her. "It was certainly nothing about where she went that afternoon, and nothing about any secret."

"Thank you, Mrs. Moidore. You have been very courteous." He stopped and she stopped also, relaxing a little as she sensed he was leaving.

"I wish I could help, Mr. Monk," she said with her face suddenly pinched and sad. For a moment grief overtook anxiety for herself and fear for the future. "If I recall anything—"

"Tell me—or Mr. Evan. Good day, ma'am."

"Good day." And she turned and walked away, but when she had gone ten or fifteen yards she looked back again, not to say anything, simply to watch him leave the path and go back towards Piccadilly.

Monk knew that Cyprian Moidore was at his club, but he did not wish to ask for entry and interview him there because he felt it highly likely that he would be refused, and the humiliation would burn. Instead he waited outside on the pavement, kicking his heels, turning over in his mind what he would ask Cyprian when he finally came out.

Monk had been waiting about a quarter of an hour when two men passed him walking up towards Half Moon Street. There was something in the gait of one of them that struck a sharp chord in his memory, so vivid that he started forward to accost him. He had actually gone half a dozen steps before he realized that he had no idea who the man was, simply that for a moment he had seemed intimately familiar, and that there was both hope and sadness in him in that instant—and a terrible foreboding of pain to come.

He stood for another thirty minutes in the wind and fitful sun trying to bring back the face that had flashed on his recollection so briefly: a handsome, aristocratic face of a man at least sixty. And he knew the voice was light, very civilized, even a little affected—and knew it had been a major force in his life and the realization of ambition. He had copied him, his dress, his manner, even his inflection, in trying to lose his own unsophisticated Northumberland accent.

But all he recaptured were fragments, gone as soon as they were there, a feeling of success which was empty of flavor, a recurring pain as of some loss and some responsibility unfulfilled.

He was still standing undecided when Cyprian Moidore came down the steps of his club and along the street, only noticing Monk when he all but bumped into him.

"Oh—Monk." He stopped short. "Are you looking for me?"

Monk recalled himself to the present with a jolt.

"Yes—if you please, sir."

Cyprian looked anxious. "Have you—have you learned something?"

"No sir, I merely wanted to ask you more about your family."

"Oh." Cyprian started to walk again and Monk fell in beside him, back towards the park. Cyprian was dressed extremely fashionably, his concession to mourning in his dark coat over the jacket above the modern short waistcoat with its shawl collar, and his top hat was tall and straight sided. "Couldn't it have waited until I got home?" he asked with a frown.

"I just spoke to Mrs. Moidore, sir; in Green Park."

Cyprian seemed surprised, even a trifle discomfited. "I doubt she can tell you much. What exactly is it you wish to ask?"

Monk was obliged to walk smartly to keep up with him. "How long has your aunt, Mrs. Sandeman, lived in your father's house, sir?"

Cyprian winced very slightly, only a shadow across his face.

"Since shortly after her husband died," he replied brusquely.

Monk lengthened his own stride to match, avoiding bumping into the people moving less rapidly or passing in the opposite direction.

"Are she and your father very close?" He knew they were not; he had not forgotten the look on Fenella's face as she had left the morning room in Queen Anne Street.

Cyprian hesitated, then decided the lie would be transparent, if not now, then later.

"No. Aunt Fenella found herself in very reduced circumstances." His face was tight; he hated exposing such vulnerability. "Papa offered her a home. It is a natural family responsibility."

Monk tried to imagine it, the personal sense of obligation, the

duty of gratitude, the implicit requirement of certain forms of obedience. He would like to know what affection there was beneath the
duties, but he knew Cyprian would respond little to an open inquiry.

A carriage passed them too close to the curb, and its wheels sent
up a spray of muddy water. Monk leaped inwards to preserve his trousers.

"It must have been very distressing for her to find herself suddenly
thrown upon the resources of others," he said sympathetically. It was
not feigned. He could imagine Fenella's shock—and profound resentment.

"Most," Cyprian agreed taciturnly. "But death frequently leaves
widows in altered circumstances. One must expect it."

"Did she expect it?" Monk absently brushed the water off his
coat.

Cyprian smiled, possibly at Monk's unconscious vanity.

"I have no idea, Mr. Monk. I did not ask her. It would have been
both impertinent and intrusive. It was not my place, nor is it yours.
It happened many years ago, twelve to be precise, and has no bearing
on our present tragedy."

"Is Mr. Thirsk in the same unfortunate position?" Monk kept
exactly level with him along the pavement, brushing past three fashionable ladies taking the air and a couple dallying in polite flirtation
in spite of the cold.

"He resides with us because of misfortune," Cyprian snapped. "If
that is what you mean. Obviously he was not widowed." He smiled
briefly in a sarcasm that had more bitterness than amusement.

"How long has he lived in Queen Anne Street?"

"About ten years, as far as I recall."

"And he is your mother's brother?"

"You are already aware of that." He dodged a group of gentlemen
ambling along deep in conversation and oblivious of the obstruction
they caused. "Really, if this is a sample of your attempts at detection,
I am surprised you maintain employment. Uncle Septimus occasionally drinks a little more than you may consider prudent, and he is
certainly not wealthy, but he is a kind and decent man whose misfortune has nothing whatever to do with my sister's death, and you will
learn nothing useful by prying into it!"

Monk admired him for his defense, true or not. And he determined to discover what the misfortune was, and if Octavia had learned something about him that might have robbed him of this double-edged but much needed hospitality had she told her father.

"Does he gamble, sir?" he said aloud.

"What?" But there was a flush of color on Cyprian's cheeks, and he knocked against an elderly gentleman in his path and was obliged to apologize.

A coster's cart came by, its owner crying his wares in a loud, singsong voice.

"I wondered if Mr. Thirsk gambled," Monk repeated. "It is a pastime many gentlemen indulge in, especially if their lives offer little other change or excitement—and any extra finance would be welcome."

Cyprian's face remained carefully expressionless, but the color in his cheeks did not fade, and Monk guessed he had touched a nerve, whether on Septimus's account or Cyprian's own.

"Does he belong to the same club as you do, sir?" Monk turned and faced him.

"No," Cyprian replied, resuming walking after only a momentary hesitation. "No, Uncle Septimus has his own club."

"Not to his taste?" Monk made it sound very casual.

"No," Cyprian agreed quickly. "He prefers more men his own age—and experience, I suppose."

They crossed Hamilton Place, hesitating for a carriage and dodging a hansom.

"What would that be?" Monk asked when they were on the pavement again.

Cyprian said nothing.

"Is Sir Basil aware that Mr. Thirsk gambles from time to time?" Monk pursued.

Cyprian drew in his breath, then let it out slowly before answering. Monk knew he had considered denying it, then put loyalty to Septimus before loyalty to his father. It was another judgment Monk approved.

"Probably not," Cyprian said. "I would appreciate it if you did not find it necessary to inform him."

"I can think of no circumstance in which it would be necessary," Monk agreed. He made an educated guess, based on the nature of the club from which Cyprian had emerged. "Similarly your own gambling, sir."

Cyprian stopped and swiveled to face him, his eyes wide. Then he saw Monk's expression and relaxed, a faint smile on his lips, before resuming his stride.

"Was Mrs. Haslett aware of this?" Monk asked him. "Could that be what she meant when she said Mr. Thirsk would understand what she had discovered?"

"I have no idea." Cyprian looked miserable.

"What else have they particularly in common?" Monk went on. "What interests or experiences that would make his sympathy the sharper? Is Mr. Thirsk a widower?"

"No—no, he never married."

"And yet he did not always live in Queen Anne Street. Where did he live before that?"

Cyprian walked in silence. They crossed Hyde Park Corner, taking several minutes to avoid carriages, hansoms, a dray with four fine Clydesdales drawing it, several costers' carts and a crossing sweeper darting in and out like a minnow trying to clear a path and catch his odd penny rewards at the same time. Monk was pleased to see Cyprian toss him a coin, and added another to it himself.

On the far side they went past the beginning of Rotten Row and strolled across the grass towards the Serpentine. A troop of gentlemen in immaculate habits rode along the Row, their horses' hooves thudding on the damp earth. Two of them laughed loudly and broke into a canter, harness jingling. Ahead of them three women turned back to look.

Cyprian made up his mind at last.

"Uncle Septimus was in the army. He was cashiered. That is why he has no means. Father took him in. He was a younger son so he inherited nothing. There was nowhere else for him."

"How distressing." Monk meant it. He could imagine quite sharply the sudden reduction from the finance, power and status of an officer to the ignominy and poverty, and the utter friendlessness, of being cashiered, stripped of everything—and to your friends, ceasing to exist.

"It wasn't dishonesty or cowardice," Cyprian went on, now that he was started, his voice urgent, concerned that Monk should know the truth. "He fell in love, and his love was very much returned. He says he did nothing about it—no affair, but that hardly makes it any better—"

Monk was startled. There was no sense in it. Officers were permitted to marry, and many did.

Cyprian's face was full of pity—and wry, deprecating humor.

"I see you don't understand. You will. She was the colonel's wife."

"Oh—" There was nothing more to add. It was an offense that would be inexcusable. Honor was touched, and even more, vanity. A colonel so mortified would have no retaliation except to use his office. "I see."

"Yes. Poor Septimus. He never loved anyone else. He was well in his forties at that time, a major with an excellent record." He stopped speaking and they passed a man and a woman, apparently acquaintances from their polite nods. He tipped his hat and resumed only when they were out of earshot. "He could have been a colonel himself, if his family could have afforded it—but commissions aren't cheap these days. And the higher you go—" He shrugged. "Anyway, that was the end of it. Septimus found himself middle-aged, despised and penniless. Naturally he appealed to Mama, and then came to live with us. If he gambles now and then, who's to blame him? There's little enough pleasure in his life."

"But your father would not approve?"

"No he would not." Cyprian's face took on a sudden anger. "Especially since Uncle Septimus usually wins!"

Monk took a blind guess. "Whereas you more usually lose?"

"Not always, and nothing I can't afford. Sometimes I win."

"Did Mrs. Haslett know this—of either of you?"

"I never discussed it with her—but I think she probably knew, or guessed about Uncle Septimus. He used to bring her presents when he won." His face looked suddenly bleak again. "He was very fond of her. She was easy to like, very—" He looked for the word and could not find it. "She had weaknesses that made her comfortable to talk to. She was hurt easily, but for other people, not a matter of her taking offense—Tavie never took offense."

The pain deepened in his face and he looked intensely vulnerable. He stared straight ahead into the cold wind. "She laughed when things were funny. Nobody could tell her who to like and who not to; she made up her own mind. She cried when she was upset, but she never sulked. Lately she drank a little more than was becoming to a lady—" His mouth twisted as he self-consciously used such a euphemism. "And she was disastrously honest." He fell silent, staring across at the wind ripples whipping the water of the Serpentine. Had it not been totally impossible that a gentleman should weep in a public place, Monk thought at that moment Cyprian might have. Whatever Cyprian knew or guessed about her death, he grieved acutely for his sister.

Monk did not intrude.

Another couple walked past them, the man in the uniform of the Hussars, the woman's skirt fashionably fringed and fussy.

Finally Cyprian regained his self-control.

"It would have been something despicable," he continued. "And probably still a danger to someone before Tavie would have told another person's secret, Inspector." He spoke with conviction. "If some servant had had an illegitimate child, or a passionate affair, Tavie was the last person who would have betrayed them to Papa—or anyone else. I don't honestly think she would have reported a theft, unless it had been something of immense value."

"So the secret she discovered that afternoon was no trivial one, but something of profound ugliness," Monk said in reply.

Cyprian's face closed. "It would seem so. I'm sorry I cannot help you any further, but I really have no idea what such a thing could be, or about whom."

"You have made the picture much clearer with your candor. Thank you, sir." Monk bowed very slightly, and after Cyprian's acknowledgment, took his leave. He walked back along the Serpentine to Hyde Park Corner, but this time going briskly up Constitution Hill towards Buckingham Palace and St. James's.

It was the middle of the afternoon when he met Sir Basil, who was coming across the Horse Guards Parade from Whitehall. He looked startled to see Monk.

"Have you something to report?" he said rather abruptly. He was dressed in dark city trousers and a frock coat seamed at the waist as was the latest cut. His top hat was tall and straight sided, and worn elegantly a little to one side on his head.

"Not yet, sir," Monk answered, wondering what he had expected so soon. "I have a few questions to ask."

Basil frowned. "That could not have waited until I was at home? I do not appreciate being accosted in the street, Inspector."

Monk made no apology. "Some information about the servants which I cannot obtain from the butler."

"There is none," Basil said frostily. "It is the butler's job to employ the servants and to interview them and evaluate their references. If I did not believe he was competent to do it, I should replace him."

"Indeed." Already Monk was stung by his tone of voice and the sharp, chilly look in his eyes, as if Monk's ignorance were no more than he expected. "But were there any disciplining to do, would you not be made aware of it?"

"I doubt it, unless it concerned a member of the family—which, I presume, is what you are suggesting?" Basil replied. "Mere impertinences or tardiness would be dealt with by Phillips, or in the female servants' case, by the housekeeper, or the cook. Dishonesty or moral laxity would incur dismissal, and Phillips would engage a replacement. I would know about that. But surely you did not follow me to Westminster to ask me such paltry things, which you could have asked the butler—or anyone else in the house!"

"I cannot expect the same degree of truth from anyone else in the house, sir," Monk snapped back tartly. "Since one of them is responsible for Mrs. Haslett's death, they may be somewhat partisan in the matter."

Basil glared at him, the wind catching at the tails of his jacket and sending them flapping. He took his high hat off to save the indignity of having it blown askew.

"What do you imagine they would lie about to you and have the remotest chance of getting by with it?" he said with an edge of sarcasm.

Monk ignored the question.

"Any personal relationships between your staff, sir?" he asked instead. "Footmen and maids, for example? The butler and one of the ladies' maids—bootboy and scullery maid?"

Basil's black eyes widened in disbelief.

"Good God! Do you imagine I have the slightest idea—or any interest in the romantic daydreams of my servants, Inspector? You seem to live in a quite different world from the one I inhabit—or men like me."

Monk was furious and he did not even attempt to curb his tongue.

"Do I take it, Sir Basil, that you would have no concern if your male and female servants have liaisons with each other," he said sarcastically. "In twos—or threes—or whatever? You are quite right—it *is* a different world. The middle classes are obsessed with preventing such a thing."

The insolence was palpable, and for a moment Sir Basil's temper flashed close to violence, but he was apparently aware that he had invited such a comment, because he moderated his reply uncharacteristically. It was merely contemptuous.

"I find it hard to believe you can maintain your position, such as it is, and be as stupid as you pretend. Of course I should forbid anything of the sort, and dismiss any staff so involved instantly and without reference."

"And if there were such an involvement, presumably it is possible Mrs. Haslett might have become aware of it?" Monk asked blandly, aware of their mutual dislike and both their reasons for masking it.

He was surprised how quickly Basil's expression lightened, something almost like a smile coming to his lips.

"I suppose she might," he agreed, grasping the idea. "Yes, women are observant of such things. They notice inflections we are inclined to miss. Romance and its intrigue form a much greater part in their lives than they do of ours. It would be natural."

Monk appeared as innocent as he was capable.

"What do you suppose she might have discovered on her trip in the afternoon that affected her so deeply she spoke to Mr. Thirsk of it?" he asked. "Was there a servant for whom she had a particular regard?"

Basil was temporarily confused. He struggled for an answer that would fit all the facts they knew.

"Her ladies' maid, I imagine. That is usual. Otherwise I am aware of no special regard," he said carefully. "And it seems she did not tell anyone where she went."

"What time off do the servants have?" Monk pursued. "Away from the house."

"Half a day every other week," Basil replied immediately. "That is customary."

"Not a great deal for indulging in romance," Monk observed. "It would seem more probable that whatever it was took place in Queen Anne Street."

Sir Basil's black eyes were hard, and he slapped at his fluttering coattails irritably.

"If you are trying to say that there was something very serious taking place in my house, of which I was unaware, indeed still am unaware, Inspector, then you have succeeded. Now if you can be as efficient in doing what you are paid for—and discover what it was— we shall all be most obliged. If there is nothing further, good day to you!"

Monk smiled. He had alarmed him, which was what he intended. Now Basil would go home and start demanding a lot of pertinent and inconvenient answers.

"Good day, Sir Basil." Monk tipped his hat very slightly, and turning on his heel, marched on towards Horse Guards Parade, leaving Basil standing on the grass with a face heavy with anger and hardening resolution.

Monk attempted to see Myles Kellard at the merchant bank where he held a position, but he had already left for the day. And he had no desire to see any of the household in Queen Anne Street, where he would be most unlikely to be uninterrupted by Sir Basil or Cyprian.

Instead he made a few inquiries of the doorman of Cyprian's club and learned almost nothing, except that he visited it frequently, and certainly gentlemen did have a flutter on cards or horses from time to time. He really could not say how much; it was hardly anyone else's concern. Gentlemen always settled their debts of honor, or they would be blackballed instantly, not only here but in all probability by every other club in town as well. No, he did not know Mr. Septimus Thirsk; indeed he had not heard that gentleman's name before.

Monk found Evan back at the police station and they compared the results of their day. Evan was tired, and although he had expected to learn little he was still discouraged that that was what had happened. There was a bubble of hope in him that always regarded the best of possibilities.

"Nothing you would call a romance," he said dispiritedly, sitting on the broad ledge of the windowsill in Monk's office. "I gather from one of the laundrymaids, Lizzie, that she thinks the bootboy had a yearning toward Dinah, the parlormaid, who is tall and fair with skin like cream and a waist you could put your hands 'round." His eyes widened as he visualized her in his memory. "And she's not yet had so much attention paid her that she's full of airs. But then that seems hardly worthy of comment. Both footmen and both grooms also admire her very heartily. I must admit, so did I." He smiled, robbing the remark of any seriousness. "Dinah is as yet unmoved in return. General opinion is that she will set her cap a good deal higher."

"Is that all?" Monk asked with a wry expression. "You spent all day below stairs to learn that? Nothing about the family?"

"Not yet," Evan apologized. "But I am still trying. The other laundrymaid, Rose, is a pretty thing, very small and dark with eyes like cornflowers—and an excellent mimic, by the way. She has a dislike for the footman Percival, which sounds to me as if it may be rooted in having once been something much warmer—"

"Evan!"

Evan opened his eyes wide in innocence. "Based on much observation by the upstairs maid Maggie and the ladies' maid Mary, who has a high regard for other people's romances, moving them along wherever she can. And the other upstairs maid, Annie, has a sharp dislike for poor Percival, although she wouldn't say why."

"Very enlightening," Monk said sarcastically. "Get an instant conviction before any jury with that."

"Don't dismiss it too lightly, sir," Evan said quite seriously, hitching himself off the sill. "Young girls like that, with little else to occupy their minds, can be very observant. A lot of it is superficial, but underneath the giggles they see a great deal."

"I suppose so," Monk said dubiously. "But we'll need to do much better than that to satisfy either Runcorn or the law."

Evan shrugged. "I'll go back tomorrow, but I don't know what else to ask anyone."

Monk found Septimus the following lunchtime in the public house which he frequented regularly. It was a small, cheerful place just off the Strand, known for its patronage by actors and law students. Groups of young men stood around talking eagerly, gesticulating, flinging arms in the air and poking fingers at an imaginary audience, but whether it was envisioned in a theater or a courtroom was impossible even to guess. There was a smell of sawdust and ale, and at this time of the day, a pleasant steam of vegetables, gravy and thick pastry.

He had been there only a few minutes, with a glass of cider, when he saw Septimus alone on a leather-upholstered seat in the corner, drinking. He walked over and sat down opposite him.

"Good day, Inspector." Septimus put down his mug, and it was a moment before Monk realized how he had seen him while he was still drinking. The mug's bottom was glass, an old-fashioned custom so a drinker might not be taken by surprise in the days when men carried swords and coaching inn brawls were not uncommon.

"Good day, Mr. Thirsk," Monk replied, and he admired the mug with Septimus's name engraved on it.

"I cannot tell you anything more," Septimus said with a sad little smile. "If I knew who killed Tavie, or had the faintest idea why, I would have come to you without your bothering to follow me here."

Monk sipped his cider.

"I came because I thought it would be easier to speak without interruption here than it would in Queen Anne Street."

Septimus's faded blue eyes lit with a moment's humor. "You mean without Basil's reminding me of my obligation, my duty to be discreet and behave like a gentleman, even if I cannot afford to be one, except now and again, by his grace and favor."

Monk did not insult him by evasion. "Something like that," he agreed. He glanced sideways as a young man with a fair face, not unlike Evan, lurched close to them in mock despair, clutching his heart, then began a dramatic monologue directed at his fellows at a neighboring table. Even after a full minute or two, Monk was not sure whether he was an aspiring actor or a would-be lawyer defending a client. He thought briefly and satirically of Oliver Rathbone, and pictured him as a callow youth at some public house like this.

"I see no military men," he remarked, looking back at Septimus.

Septimus smiled down into his ale. "Someone has told you my story."

"Mr. Cyprian," Monk admitted. "With great sympathy."

"He would." Septimus pulled a face. "Now if you had asked Myles you would have had quite a different tale, meaner, grubbier, less flattering to women. And dear Fenella . . ." He took another deep draft of his ale. "Hers would have been more lurid, far more dramatic; the tragedy would have become grotesque, the love a frenzied passion, the whole thing rather gaudy; the real feeling, and the real pain, lost in effect—like the colored lights of a stage."

"And yet you like to come to a public house full of actors of one sort or another," Monk pointed out.

Septimus looked across the tables and his eye fell on a man of perhaps thirty-five, lean and oddly dressed, his face animated, but under the mask a weariness of disappointed hopes.

"I like it here," he said gently. "I like the people. They have imagination to take them out of the commonplace, to forget the defeats of reality and feed on the triumphs of dreams." His face was softened, its tired lines lifted by tolerance and affection. "They can evoke any mood they want into their faces and make themselves believe it for an hour or two. That takes courage, Mr. Monk; it takes a rare inner strength. The world, people like Basil, find it ridiculous—but I find it very heartening."

There was a roar of laughter from one of the other tables, and for a moment he glanced towards it before turning back to Monk again. "If we can still surmount what is natural and believe what we wish to believe, in spite of the force of evidence, then for a while at least we are masters of our fate, and we can paint the world we want. I had rather do it with actors than with too much wine or a pipe full of opium."

Someone climbed on a chair and began an oration to a few catcalls and a smattering of applause.

"And I like their humor," Septimus went on. "They know how to laugh at themselves and each other—they like to laugh, they don't see any sin in it, or any danger to their dignity. They like to argue. They don't feel it a mortal wound if anyone queries what they say, indeed they expect to be questioned." He smiled ruefully. "And if they are forced to a new idea, they turn it over like a child with a toy. They may be vain, Mr. Monk; indeed they assuredly are vain, like a garden full of peacocks forever fanning their tails and squawking." He looked at Monk without perception or double meaning. "And they are ambitious, self-absorbed, quarrelsome and often supremely trivial."

Monk felt a pang of guilt, as if an arrow had brushed by his cheek and missed its mark.

"But they amuse me," Septimus said gently. "And they listen to me without condemnation, and never once has one of them tried to convince me I have some moral or social obligation to be different. No, Mr. Monk, I enjoy myself here. I feel comfortable."

"You have explained yourself excellently, sir." Monk smiled at him, for once without guile. "I understand why. Tell me something about Mr. Kellard."

The pleasure vanished out of Septimus's face. "Why? Do you think he had something to do with Tavie's death?"

"Is it likely, do you think?"

Septimus shrugged and set down his mug.

"I don't know. I don't like the man. My opinion is of no use to you."

"Why do you not like him, Mr. Thirsk?"

But the old military code of honor was too strong. Septimus smiled dryly, full of self-mockery. "A matter of instinct, Mr. Monk," he lied, and Monk knew he was lying. "We have nothing in common in our natures or our interests. He is a banker, I was a soldier, and now I am a time server, enjoying the company of young men who playact and tell stories about crime and passion and the criminal world. And I laugh at all the wrong things, and drink too much now and again. I ruined my life over the love of a woman." He turned the mug in his hand, fingers caressing it. "Myles despises that. I think it is absurd— but not contemptible. At least I was capable of such a feeling. There is something to be said for that."

"There is everything to be said for it." Monk surprised himself; he had no memory of ever having loved, let alone to such cost, and yet he knew without question that to care for any person or issue enough to sacrifice greatly for it was the surest sign of being wholly alive. What a waste of the essence of a man that he should never give enough of himself to any cause, that he should always hear that passive, cowardly voice uppermost which counts the cost and puts caution first. One would grow old and die with the power of one's soul untasted.

And yet there was something. Even as the thoughts passed through his mind a memory stirred of intense emotions, outrage and grief for someone else, a passion to fight at all costs, not for himself but for others—and for one in particular. He knew loyalty and gratitude, he simply could not force it back into his mind for whom.

Septimus was looking at him curiously.

Monk smiled. "Perhaps he envies you, Mr. Thirsk," he said spontaneously.

Septimus's eyebrows rose in amazement. He looked at Monk's face, seeking sarcasm, and found none.

Monk explained himself. "Without realizing it," he added. "Maybe Mr. Kellard lacks the depth, or the courage, to feel anything deeply enough to pay for it. To suspect yourself a coward is a very bitter thing indeed."

Very slowly Septimus smiled, with great sweetness.

"Thank you, Mr. Monk. That is the finest thing anyone has said to me in years." Then he bit his lip. "I am sorry. I still cannot tell you anything about Myles. All I know is suspicion, and it is not my wound to expose. Perhaps there is no wound at all, and he is merely a bored man with too much time on his hands and an imagination that works too hard."

Monk did not press him. He knew it would serve no purpose. Septimus was quite capable of keeping silence if he felt honor required it, and taking whatever consequences there were.

Monk finished his cider. "I'll go and see Mr. Kellard myself. But if you do think of anything that suggests what Mrs. Haslett had discovered that last day, what it was she thought you would understand better than others, please let me know. It may well be that this secret was what caused her death."

"I have thought," Septimus replied, screwing up his face. "I have gone over and over in my mind everything we have in common, or that she might have believed we had, and I have found very little. We neither of us cared for Myles—but that seems very trivial. He has never injured me in any way—nor her, that I am aware of. We were both financially dependent upon Basil—but then so is everyone else in the house!"

"Is Mr. Kellard not remunerated for his work at the bank?" Monk was surprised.

Septimus looked at him with mild scorn, not unkindly.

"Certainly. But not to the extent that will support him in the way to which he would like to be accustomed—and definitely not Araminta as well. Also there are social implications to be considered; there are benefits to being Basil Moidore's daughter which do not accrue to being merely Myles Kellard's wife, not least of them living in Queen Anne Street."

Monk had not expected to feel any sympathy for Myles Kellard, but that single sentence, with its wealth of implications, gave him a sudden very sharp change of perception.

"Perhaps you are not aware of the level of entertaining that is conducted there," Septimus continued, "when the house is not in mourning? We regularly dined diplomats and cabinet ministers, ambassadors and foreign princes, industrial moguls, patrons of the arts and sciences, and on occasion even minor members of our own royalty. Not a few duchesses and dozens of society called in the afternoons. And of course there were all the invitations in return. I should think there are few of the great houses that have not received the Moidores at one time or another."

"Did Mrs. Haslett feel the same way?" Monk asked.

Septimus smiled with a rueful turning down of the lips. "She had no choice. She and Haslett were to have moved into a house of their own, but he went into the army before it could be accomplished, and of course Tavie remained in Queen Anne Street. And then Harry, the poor beggar, was killed at Inkermann. One of the saddest things I know. He was the devil of a nice fellow." He stared into the bottom of his mug, not at the ale dregs but into old grief that still hurt. "Tavie never got over it. She loved him—more than the rest of the family ever understood."

"I'm sorry," Monk said gently. "You were very fond of Mrs. Haslett—"

Septimus looked up. "Yes, yes I was. She used to listen to me as if what I said mattered to her. She would let me ramble on—sometimes we drank a little too much together. She was kinder than Fenella—" He stopped, realizing he was on the verge of behaving like less than a gentleman. He stiffened his back painfully and lifted his chin. "If I can help, Inspector, you may be assured that I will."

"I am assured, Mr. Thirsk." Monk rose to his feet. "Thank you for your time."

"I have more of it than I need." Septimus smiled, but it did not reach his eyes. Then he tipped up his mug and drank the dregs, and Monk could see his face distorted through the glass bottom.

Monk found Fenella Sandeman the next day at the end of a long late-morning ride, standing by her horse at the Kensington Gardens end of Rotten Row. She was superbly dressed in a black riding habit with gleaming boots and immaculate black Mousquetaire hat. Only her high-necked blouse and stock were vivid white. Her dark hair was neatly arranged, and her face with its unnatural color and painted eyebrows looked rakish and artificial in the cool November daylight.

"Why, Mr. Monk," she said in amazement, looking him up and

down and evidently approving what she saw. "Whatever brings you walking in the park?" She gave a girlish giggle. "Shouldn't you be questioning the servants or something? How does one detect?"

She ignored her horse, leaving the rein loosely over her arm as if that were sufficient.

"In a large number of ways, ma'am." He tried to be courteous and at the same time not play to her mood of levity. "Before I speak to the servants I would like to gain a clearer impression from the family, so that when I do ask questions they are the right ones."

"So you've come to interrogate me." She shivered melodramatically. "Well, Inspector, ask me anything. I shall give you what answers I consider wisest." She was a small woman, and she looked up at him through half-closed lashes.

Surely she could not be drunk this early in the day? She must be amusing herself at his expense. He affected not to notice her flippancy and kept a perfectly sober face, as if they were engaged in a serious conversation which might yield important information.

"Thank you, Mrs. Sandeman. I am informed you have lived in Queen Anne Street since shortly after the death of your husband some eleven or twelve years ago—"

"You have been delving into my past!" Her voice was husky, and far from being annoyed, she sounded flattered by the thought.

"Into everyone's, ma'am," he said coldly. "If you have been there such a time, you will have had frequent opportunity to observe both the family and the staff. You must know them all quite well."

She swung the riding crop, startling the horse and narrowly missing its head. She seemed quite oblivious of the animal, and fortunately it was sufficiently well schooled. It remained close to her, measuring its pace obediently to hers as she moved very slowly along the path.

"Of course," she agreed jauntily. "Who do you wish to know about?" She shrugged her beautifully clothed shoulders. "Myles is fun, but quite worthless—but then some of the most attractive men are, don't you think?" She turned sideways to look at him. Her eyes must have been marvelous once, very large and dark. Now the rest of her face had so altered they were grotesque.

He smiled very slightly. "I think my interest in them is probably very different from yours, Mrs. Sandeman."

She laughed uproariously for several moments, causing half a dozen people within earshot to turn curiously to find the cause of such mirth. When she had regained her composure she was still openly amused.

Monk was discomfited. He disliked being stared at as a matter of ribaldry.

"Don't you find pious women very tedious, Mr. Monk?" She opened her eyes very wide. "Be honest with me."

"Are there pious women in your family, Mrs. Sandeman?" His voice was cooler than he intended, but if she was aware she gave no sign.

"It's full of them." She sighed. "Absolutely prickling like fleas on a hedgehog. My mother was one, may heaven rest her soul. My sister-in-law is another, may heaven preserve me—I live in her house. You have no idea how hard it is to have any privacy! Pious women are so good at minding other people's business—I suppose it is so much more interesting than their own." She laughed again with a rich, gurgling sound.

He was becoming increasingly aware that she found him attractive, and it made him intensely uncomfortable.

"And Araminta is worse, poor creature," she continued, walking with grace and swinging her stick. The horse plodded obediently at her heels, its rein trailing loosely over her arm. "I suppose she has to be, with Myles. I told you he was worthless, didn't I? Of course Tavie was all right." She looked straight ahead of her along the Row towards a fashionable group riding slowly in their direction. "She drank, you know?" She glanced at him, then away again. "All that tommyrot about ill health and headaches! She was drunk—or suffering the after-effects. She took it from the kitchen." She shrugged. "I daresay one of the servants gave it to her. They all liked her because she was generous. Took advantage, if you ask me. Treat servants above their station, and they forget who they are and take liberties."

Then she swung around and stared at him, her eyes exaggeratedly wide. "Oh, my goodness! Oh, my dear, how perfectly awful. Do you suppose that was what happened to her?" Her very small, elegantly gloved hand flew to her mouth. "She was overfamiliar with one of the servants? He ran away with the wrong idea—or, heaven help us, the right one," she said breathlessly. "And then she fought him off—and he killed her in the heat of his passion? Oh, how perfectly frightful. What a scandal!" She gulped. "Ha-ha-ha. Basil will never get over it. Just imagine what his friends will say."

Monk was unaccountably revolted, not by the thought, which was pedestrian enough, but by her excitement at it. He controlled his disgust with difficulty, unconsciously taking a step backwards.

"Do you think that is what happened, ma'am?"

She heard nothing in his tone to dampen her titillation.

"Oh, it is quite possible," she went on, painting the picture for herself, turning away and beginning to walk again. "I know just the man to have done it. Percival—one of the footmen. Fine-looking man—but then all footmen are, don't you think?" She glanced sideways, then away again. "No, perhaps you don't. I daresay you've never had much occasion. Not many footmen in your line of work." She laughed again and hunched her shoulders without looking at him. "Percival has that kind of face—far too intelligent to be a good servant. Ambitious. And such a marvelously cruel mouth. A man with a mouth like that could do anything." She shuddered, wriggling her body as if shedding some encumbrance—or feeling something delicious against her skin. It occurred to Monk to wonder if perhaps she herself had encouraged the young footman into a relationship above and outside his station. But looking at her immaculate, artificial face the thought was peculiarly repellent. As close as he was to her now, in the hard daylight, it was clear that she must be nearer sixty than fifty, and Percival not more than thirty at the very outside.

"Have you any grounds for that idea, Mrs. Sandeman, other than what you observe in his face?" he asked her.

"Oh—you are angry." She turned her limpid gaze up at him. "I have offended your sense of propriety. You are a trifle pious yourself, aren't you, Inspector?"

Was he? He had no idea. He knew his instinctive reaction now: the gentle, vulnerable faces like Imogen Latterly's that stirred his emotions; the passionate, intelligent ones like Hester's which both pleased and irritated him; the calculating, predatorily female ones like Fenella Sandeman's which he found alien and distasteful. But he had no memory of any actual relationship. Was he a prig, a cold man, selfish and incapable of commitment, even short-lived?

"No, Mrs. Sandeman, but I am offended by the idea of a footman who takes liberties with his mistress's daughter and then knifes her to death," he said ruthlessly. "Are you not?"

Still she was not angry. Her boredom cut him more deeply than any subtle insult or mere aloofness.

"Oh, how sordid. Yes of course I am. You do have a crass way with words, Inspector. One could not have you in the withdrawing room. Such a shame. You have a—" She regarded him with a frank appreciation which he found very unnerving. "An air of danger about you." Her eyes were very bright and she stared at him invitingly.

He knew what the euphemism stood for, and found himself backing away.

"Most people find police intrusive, ma'am; I am used to it. Thank you for your time, you have been most helpful." And he bowed very slightly and turned on his heel, leaving her standing beside her horse with her crop in one hand and the rein still over her arm. Before he had reached the edge of the grass she was speaking to a middle-aged gentleman who had just dismounted from a large gray and was flattering her shamelessly.

He found the idea of an amorous footman both unpleasant and unlikely, but it could not be dismissed. He had put off interviewing the servants himself for too long. He hailed a hansom along the Knightsbridge Road and directed it to take him to Queen Anne Street, where he paid the driver and went down the areaway steps to the back door.

Inside the kitchen was warm and busy and full of the odors of roasting meat, baking pastry and fresh apples. Coils of peel lay on the table, and Mrs. Boden, the cook, was up to her elbows in flour. Her face was red with exertion and heat, but she had an agreeable expression and was still a handsome woman, even though the veins were beginning to break on her skin and when she smiled her teeth were discolored and would not last much longer.

"If you're wanting your Mr. Evan, he's in the housekeeper's sitting room," she greeted Monk. "And if you're looking for a cup o' tea you're too soon. Come back in half an hour. And don't get under my feet. I've dinner to think of; even in mourning they've still got to eat—and so have all of us."

"Us" were the servants, and he noted the distinction immediately.

"Yes ma'am. Thank you, I'd like to speak to your footmen, if you please, privately."

"Would you now." She wiped her hands on her apron. "Sal. Put those potatoes down and go and get Harold—then when 'e's done, tell Percival to come. Well don't stand there, you great pudding. Go an' do as you're told!" She sighed and began to mix the pastry with water to the right consistency. "Girls these days! Eats enough for a working navvy, she does, and look at her. Moves like treacle in winter. Shoo. Get on with you, girl."

With a flash of temper the red-haired kitchen maid swung out of the room and along the corridor, her heels clicking on the uncarpeted floor.

"And don't you sonse out of here like that!" the cook called after her. "Cheeky piece. Eyes on the footman next door, that's 'er trouble. Lazy baggage." She turned back to Monk. "Now if you 'aven't anything more to ask me, you get out of my way too. You can talk to the footmen in Mr. Phillips's pantry. He's busy down in the cellar and won't be disturbing you."

Monk obeyed and was shown by Willie the bootboy into the pantry, the room where the butler kept all his keys, his accounts, and the silver that was used regularly, and also spent much of his time when not on duty. It was warm and extremely comfortably, if serviceably, furnished.

Harold, the junior footman, was a thickset, fair-haired young man, in no way a pair to Percival, except in height. He must possess some other virtue, less visible to the first glance, or Monk guessed his days here would be numbered. He questioned him, probably just as Evan had already done, and Harold produced his now well-practiced replies. Monk could not imagine him the philanderer Fenella Sandeman had thought up.

Percival was a different matter, more assured, more belligerent, and quite ready to defend himself. When Monk pressed him he sensed a personal danger, and he answered with bold eyes and a ready tongue.

"Yes sir, I know it was someone in the house who killed Mrs. Haslett. That doesn't mean it was one of us servants. Why should we? Nothing to gain, and everything to lose. Anyway, she was a very pleasant lady, no occasion to wish her anything but good."

"You liked her?"

Percival smiled. He had read Monk's implication long before he replied, but whether from uneasy conscience or astute sense it was impossible to say.

"I said she was pleasant enough, sir. I wasn't familiar, if that's what you mean!"

"You jumped to that very quickly," Monk retorted. "What made you think that was what I meant?"

"Because you are trying to accuse one of us below stairs so you don't have the embarrassment of accusing someone above," Percival said baldly. "Just because I wear livery and say 'yes sir, no ma'am' doesn't mean I'm stupid. You're a policeman, no better than I am—"

Monk winced.

"And you know what it'll cost you if you charge one of the family," Percival finished.

"I'll charge one of the family if I find any evidence against them," Monk replied tartly. "So far I haven't."

"Then maybe you're too careful where you look." Percival's contempt was plain. "You won't find it if you don't want to—and it surely wouldn't suit you, would it?"

"I'll look anywhere I think there's something to find," Monk said. "You're in the house all day and all night. You tell me where to look."

"Well, Mr. Thirsk steals from the cellar—taken half the best port wine over the last few years. Don't know how he isn't drunk half the time."

"Is that a reason to kill Mrs. Haslett?"

"Might be—if she knew and ratted on him to Sir Basil. Sir Basil would take it very hard. Might throw the old boy out into the street."

"Then why does he take it?"

Percival shrugged very slightly. It was not a servant's gesture.

"I don't know—but he does. Seen him sneaking down the steps many a time—and back up with a bottle under his coat."

"I'm not very impressed."

"Then look at Mrs. Sandeman." Percival's face tightened, a shadow of viciousness about his mouth. "Look at some of the company she keeps. I've been out in the carriage sometimes and taken her to some very odd places. Parading up and down that Rotten Row like a sixpenny whore, and reads stuff Sir Basil would burn if he saw it—scandal sheets, sensational press. Mr. Phillips would dismiss any of the maids if he caught them with that kind of thing."

"It's hardly relevant. Mr. Phillips cannot dismiss Mrs. Sandeman, no matter what she reads," Monk pointed out.

"Sir Basil could."

"But would he? She is his sister, not a servant."

Percival smiled. "She might just as well be. She has to come and go when he says, wear what he approves of, speak to whoever he likes and entertain his friends. Can't have her own here, unless he approves them—or she doesn't get her allowance. None of them do."

He was a young man with a malicious tongue and a great deal of personal knowledge of the family, Monk thought, very possibly a frightened young man. Perhaps his fear was justified. The Moidores would not easily allow one of their own to be charged if suspicion could be diverted to a servant. Percival knew that; maybe he was only the first person downstairs to see just how sharp the danger was. In time no doubt others would also; the tales would get uglier as the fear closed in.

"Thank you, Percival," Monk said wearily. "You can go—for now."

Percival opened his mouth to add something, then changed his mind and went out. He moved gracefully—well trained.

Monk returned to the kitchen and had the cup of tea Mrs. Boden had previously offered, but even listening carefully he learned nothing of further use, and he left by the same way he had arrived and took a hansom from Harley Street down to the City. This time he was more fortunate in finding Myles Kellard in his office at the bank.

"I can't think what to tell you." Myles looked at Monk curiously, his long face lit with a faint humor as if he found the whole meeting a trifle ridiculous. He sat elegantly on one of the Chippendale armchairs in his exquisitely carpeted room, crossing his legs with ease. "There are all sorts of family tensions, of course. There are in any family. But none of them seems a motive for murder to anyone, except a lunatic."

Monk waited.

"I would find it a lot easier to understand if Basil had been the victim," Myles went on, an edge of sharpness in his voice. "Cyprian could follow his own political interests instead of his father's, and pay all his debts, which would make life a great deal easier for him—and for the fair Romola. She finds living in someone else's house very hard to take. Ideas of being mistress of Queen Anne Street shine in her eyes rather often. But she'll be a dutiful daughter-in-law until that day comes. It's worth waiting for."

"And then you will also presumably move elsewhere?" Monk said quickly.

"Ah." Myles pulled a face. "How uncivil of you, Inspector. Yes, no doubt we shall. But old Basil looks healthy enough for another twenty years. Anyway, it was poor Tavie who was killed, so that line of thought leads you nowhere."

"Did Mrs. Haslett know of her brother's debts?"

Myles's eyebrows shot up, giving his face a quizzical look. "I shouldn't think so—but it's a possibility. She certainly knew she was interested in the philosophies of the appalling Mr. Owen and his notions of dismantling the family." He smiled with a raw, twisted humor. "I don't suppose you've read Owen, Inspector? No—very radical—believes the patriarchal system is responsible for all sorts of greed, oppression and abuse—an opinion which Basil is hardly likely to share."

"Hardly," Monk agreed. "Are these debts of Mr. Cyprian's generally known?"

"Certainly not!"

"But he confided in you?"

Myles lifted his shoulders a fraction.

"No—not exactly. I am a banker, Inspector. I learn various bits of information that are not public property." He colored faintly. "I told you that because you are investigating a murder in my family. It is not to be generally discussed. I hope you understand that."

He had breached a confidence. Monk perceived that readily enough. Fenella's words about him came back, and her arch look as she said them.

Myles hurried on. "I should think it was probably some stupid wrangle with a servant who got above himself." He was looking very directly at Monk. "Octavia was a widow, and young. She wouldn't get her excitement from scandal sheets like Aunt Fenella. I daresay one of the footmen admired her and she didn't put him in his place swiftly enough."

"Is that really what you think happened, Mr. Kellard?" Monk searched his face, the hazel eyes under their fair brows, the long, fluted nose and the mouth which could so easily be imaginative or slack, depending on his mood.

"It seems far more likely than Cyprian, whom she cared for, killing her because she might have told their father, of whom she was not fond, about his debts—or Fenella, in case Octavia told Basil about the company she keeps, which is pretty ragged."

"I gathered Mrs. Haslett was still missing her husband," Monk said slowly, hoping Myles would read the less delicate implication behind his words.

Myles laughed outright. "Good God, no. What a prude you are." He leaned back in his chair. "She mourned Haslett—but she's a woman. She'd have gone on making a parade of sorrow, of course. It's expected. But she's a woman like any other. I daresay Percival, at any rate, knows that. He'd take a little protestation of reluctance, a few smiles through the eyelashes and modest glances for what they were worth."

Monk felt the muscles in his neck and scalp tightening in anger, but he tried to keep his emotion out of his voice.

"Which, if you are right, was apparently a great deal. She meant exactly what she said."

"Oh—" Myles sighed and shrugged. "I daresay she changed her mind when she remembered he was a footman, by which time he had lost his head."

"Have you any reason for suggesting this, Mr. Kellard, other than your belief that it seems likely to you?"

"Observation," he said with a shadow of irritation across his face. "Percival is something of a ladies' man, had considerable flirtations with one or two of the maids. It's to be expected, you know." A look of obscure satisfaction flickered across his face. "Can't keep people together in a house day in, day out and not have something happen now and again. He's an ambitious little beggar. Go and look there, Inspector. Now if you'll excuse me, there really is nothing I can tell you, except to use your common sense and whatever knowledge of women you have. Now I wish you good-day."

Monk returned to Queen Anne Street with a sense of darkness inside. He should have been encouraged by his interview with Myles Kellard. He had given an acceptable motive for one of the servants to have killed Octavia Haslett, and that would surely be the least unpleasant answer. Runcorn would be delighted. Sir Basil would be satisfied. Monk would arrest the footman and claim a victory. The press would praise him for his rapid and successful solution, which would annoy Runcorn, but he would be immensely relieved that the danger of scandal was removed and a prominent case had been closed satisfactorily.

But his interview with Myles had left him with a vague feeling of depression. Myles had a contempt for both Octavia and the footman Percival. His suggestions were born of a kind of malice. There was no gentleness in him.

Monk pulled his coat collar a little higher against the cold rain blowing down the pavement as he turned into Leadenhall Street and walked up towards Cornhill. Was he anything like Myles Kellard? He had seen few signs of compassion in the records he had found of himself. His judgments were sharp. Were they equally cynical? It was a frightening thought. He would be an empty man inside if it were so. In the months since he had awoken in the hospital, he had found no one who cared for him deeply, no one who felt gratitude or love for him, except his sister, Beth, and her love was born of loyalty, memory rather than knowledge. Was there no one else? No woman? Where were his relationships, the debts and the dependencies, the trusts, the memories?

He hailed a hansom and told the driver to take him back to Queen Anne Street, then sat back and tried to put his own life out of his mind and think of the footman Percival—and the possibility of a stupid physical flirtation that had run out of control and ended in violence.

He arrived and entered by the kitchen door again, and asked to speak to Percival. He faced him in the housekeeper's sitting room this time. The footman was pale-faced now, feeling the net closing around him, cold and a great deal tighter. He stood stiffly, his muscles shaking a little under his livery, his hands knotted in front of him, a fine beading of sweat on his brow and lip. He stared at Monk with fixed eyes, waiting for the attack so he could parry it.

The moment Monk spoke, he knew he would find no way to frame a question that would be subtle. Percival had already guessed the line of his thought and leaped ahead.

"There's a great deal you don't know about this house," he said with a harsh, jittery voice. "Ask Mr. Kellard about his relationship with Mrs. Haslett."

"What was it, Percival?" Monk asked quietly. "All I have heard suggests they were not particularly agreeable."

"Not openly, no." There was a slight sneer in Percival's thin mouth. "She never did like him much, but he lusted after her—"

"Indeed?" Monk said with raised brows. "They seem to have hidden it remarkably well. Do you think Mr. Kellard tried to force his attentions on her, and when she refused, he became violent and killed her? There was no struggle."

Percival looked at him with withering disgust.

"No I don't. I think he lusted after her, and even if he never did anything about it at all, Mrs. Kellard still discovered it—and boiled with the kind of jealousy that only a spurned woman can. She hated her sister enough to kill her." He saw the widening of Monk's eyes and the tightening of his hands. He knew he had startled the policeman and at least for a time confused him.

A tiny smile touched the corner of Percival's mouth.

"Will that be all, sir?"

"Yes—yes it will," Monk said after a hesitation. "For the moment."

"Thank you, sir." And Percival turned and walked out, a lift in his step now and a slight swing in his shoulders.

CHAPTER FIVE

———

Hester did not find the infirmary any easier to bear as days went by. The outcome of the trial had given her a sense of bitter struggle and achievement. She had been brought face-to-face again with a dramatic adversarial conflict, and for all its darkness and the pain she knew accompanied it, she had been on the side which had won. She had seen Fabia Grey's terrible face as she left the courtroom, and she knew the hate that now shriveled her life. But she also had seen the new freedom in Lovel Grey, as if ghosts had faded forever, leaving a beginning of light. And she chose to believe that Menard would make a life for himself in Australia, a land about which she knew almost nothing, but insofar as it was not England, there would be hope for him; and it was the best for which they could have striven.

She was not sure whether she liked Oliver Rathbone or not, but he was unquestionably exhilarating. She had tasted battle again, and it had whetted her appetite for more. She found Pomeroy even harder to endure than previously, his insufferable complacency, the smug excuses with which he accepted losses as inevitable, when she was convinced that with greater effort and attention and more courage, better nurses, more initiative by juniors, they need not have been lost at all. But whether that was true or not—he should fight. To be beaten was one thing, to surrender was another—and intolerable.

At least John Airdrie had been operated on, and now as she stood in the ward on a dark, wet November morning she could see him asleep in his cot at the far end, breathing fitfully. She walked down closer to him to find if he was feverish. She straightened his blankets and moved her lamp to look at his face. It was flushed and, when she touched it, it was hot. This was to be expected after an operation, and yet it was what she dreaded. It might be just the normal reaction, or it might be the first stage of infection, for which they knew no cure. They could only hope the body's own strength would outlast the disease.

Hester had met French surgeons in the Crimea and learned of treatments practiced in the Napoleonic Wars a generation earlier. In 1640 the wife of the governor of Peru had been cured of fever by the administration of a distillation from tree bark, first known as Poudre de la Comtesse, then Poudre de Jesuites. Now it was known as loxa quinine. It was possible Pomeroy might prescribe such a thing for the child, but he might not; he was extremely conservative—and he was also not due to make his rounds for another five hours.

The child stirred again. She leaned over and touched him gently, to soothe as much as anything. But he did not regain his senses, rather he seemed on the border of falling into delirium.

She made up her mind without hesitation. This was a battle she would not surrender. Since the Crimea she had carried a few basic medicines herself, things she thought she would be unable to obtain readily in England. A mixture of theriac, loxa quinine and Hoffman's liquor was among them. She kept them in a small leather case with an excellent lock which she left with her cloak and bonnet in a small outer room provided for such a purpose.

Now, the decision made, she glanced around the ward one more time to make sure no one was in distress, and when all seemed well, she hurried out and along the passage to the outer room, and pulled her case from where it was half hidden under the folds of her cloak. She fished for the key on its chain from her pocket and put it in the lock. It turned easily and she opened the lid. Under the clean apron and two freshly laundered linen caps were the medicines. The theriac and quinine mixture was easy to see. She took it out and slipped it into her pocket, then closed and locked the case again, sliding it back under her cloak.

Back in the ward she found a bottle of the ale the nurses frequently drank. The mixer was supposed to be Bordeaux wine, but since she had none, this would have to serve. She poured a little into a cup and added a very small dose of the quinine, stirring it thoroughly. She knew the taste was extremely bitter.

She went over to the bed and lifted the child gently, resting his head against her. She gave him two teaspoonfuls, putting them gently between his lips. He seemed unaware of what was happening, and swallowed only in reaction. She wiped his mouth with a napkin and laid him back again, smoothing the hair off his brow and covering him with the sheet.

Two hours later she gave him two more teaspoonfuls, and then a third time just before Pomeroy came.

"Very pleasing," he said, looking closely at the boy, his freckled face full of satisfaction. "He seems to be doing remarkably well, Miss Latterly. You see I was quite right to leave the operation till I did. There was no such urgency as you supposed." He looked at her with a tight smile. "You panic too easily." And he straightened up and went to the next bed.

Hester refrained from comment with difficulty. But if she told him of the fever the boy had been sinking into only five hours ago, she would also have to tell him of the medication she had given. His reaction to that she could only guess at, but it would not be agreeable. She would tell him, if she had to, when the child was recovered. Perhaps discretion would be best.

However circumstances did not permit her such latitude. By the middle of the week John Airdrie was sitting up with no hectic color in his cheeks and taking with pleasure a little light food. But the woman three beds along who had had an operation on her abdomen was sinking rapidly, and Pomeroy was looking at her with grave anxiety and recommending ice and frequent cool baths. There was no hope in his voice, only resignation and pity.

Hester could not keep silent. She looked at the woman's pain-suffused face, and spoke.

"Dr. Pomeroy, have you considered the possibility of giving her loxa quinine in a mixture of wine, theriac and Hoffman's mineral liquor? It might ease her fever."

He looked at her with incredulity turning slowly into anger as he realized exactly what she had said, his face pink, his beard bristling.

"Miss Latterly, I have had occasion to speak to you before about your attempts to practice an art for which you have no training and no mandate. I will give Mrs. Begley what is best for her, and you will obey my instructions. Is that understood?"

Hester swallowed hard. "Is that your instruction, Dr. Pomeroy, that I give Mrs. Begley some loxa quinine to ease her fever?"

"No it is not!" he snapped. "That is for tropical fevers, not for the normal recovery from an operation. It would do no good. We will have none of that foreign rubbish here!"

Part of Hester's mind still struggled with the decision, but her tongue was already embarked on the course her conscience would inevitably choose.

"I have seen it given with success by a French surgeon, sir, for fever following amputation, and it is recorded as far back as the Napoleonic campaigns before Waterloo."

His face darkened with angry color. "I do not take my instructions from the French, Miss Latterly! They are a dirty and ignorant race who only a short time ago were bent on conquering these islands and subjecting them, along with the rest of Europe! And I would remind you, since you seem apt to forget it, that you take your instructions from me—and from me alone!" He turned to leave the unfortunate woman, and Hester stepped almost in front of him.

"She is delirious, Doctor! We cannot leave her! Please permit me to try a little quinine; it cannot harm and it may help. I will give only a teaspoonful at a time, every two or three hours, and if it does not ease her I will desist."

"And where do you propose I obtain such a medication, were I disposed to do as you say?"

She took a deep breath and only just avoided betraying herself.

"From the fever hospital, sir. We could send a hansom over. I will go myself, if you wish."

His face was bright pink.

"Miss Latterly! I thought I had already made myself clear on the subject—nurses keep patients clean and cool from excessive temperature, they administer ice at the doctor's directions and drinks as have been prescribed." His voice was rising and getting louder, and he stood on the balls of his feet, rocking a little. "They fetch and carry and pass bandages and instruments as required. They keep the ward clean and tidy; they stoke fires and serve food. They empty and dispose of waste and attend to the bodily requirements of patients."

He thrust his hands into his pockets and rocked on his feet a little more rapidly. "They keep order and lift the spirits. That is all! Do you understand me, Miss Latterly? They are unskilled in medicine, except of the most rudimentary sort. They do not in any circumstances whatever exercise their own judgment!"

"But if you are not present!" she protested.

"Then you wait!" His voice was getting increasingly shrill.

She could not swallow her anger. "But patients may die! Or at best become sufficiently worse that they cannot easily be saved!"

"Then you will send for me urgently! But you will do nothing beyond your remit, and when I come I will decide what is best to do. That is all."

"But if I know what to do—"

"You do not know!" His hands flew out of his pockets into the air. "For God's sake, woman, you are not medically trained! You know nothing but bits of gossip and practical experience you have picked up from foreigners in some campaign hospital in the Crimea! You are not a physician and never will be!"

"All medicine is only a matter of learning and observation!" Her voice was rising considerably now, and even the farther patients were beginning to take notice. "There are no rules except that if it works it is good, and if it does not then try something else." She was exasperated almost beyond endurance with his stubborn stupidity. "If we never experiment we will never discover anything better than we have now, and people will go on dying when perhaps we could have cured them!"

"And far more probably killed them with our ignorance!" he retaliated with finality. "You have no right to conduct experiments. You are an unskilled and willful woman, and if there is one more word of insubordination out of you, you will be dismissed. Do you understand me?"

She hesitated a moment, meeting his eyes. There was no uncertainty in them, no slightest flexibility in his determination. If she kept silence now there was just the possibility he might come back later, when she was off duty, and give Mrs. Begley the quinine.

"Yes, I understand." She forced the words out, her hands clenched in the folds of her apron and skirt at her sides.

But once again he could not leave well enough alone even after he had seemingly won.

"Quinine does not work for postoperative fever infections, Miss Latterly," he went on with mounting condescension. "It is for tropical fevers. And even then it is not always successful. You will dose the patient with ice and wash her regularly in cool water."

Hester breathed in and out very slowly. His complacency was insufferable.

"Do you hear me?" he demanded.

Before she could reply this time, one of the patients on the far side of the ward sat up, his face twisted in concentration.

"She gave something to that child at the end when he had a fever after his operation," he said clearly. "He was in a bad way, like to go into delirium. And after she did it four or five times he recovered. He's cool as you like now. She knows what she's doing—she's right."

There was a moment's awful silence. He had no idea what he had done.

Pomeroy was stunned.

"You gave loxa quinine to John Airdrie!" he accused, realization flooding into him. "You did it behind my back!" His voice rose, shrill with outrage and betrayal, not only by her but, even worse, by the patient.

Then a new thought struck him.

"Where did you get it from? Answer me, Miss Latterly! I demand you tell me where you obtained it! Did you have the audacity to send to the fever hospital in my name?"

"No, Dr. Pomeroy. I have some quinine of my own—a very small amount," she added hastily, "against fever. I gave him some of that."

He was trembling with rage. "You are dismissed, Miss Latterly. You have been a troublemaker since you arrived. You were employed on the recommendation of a lady who no doubt owed some favor to your family and had little knowledge of your irresponsible and willful nature. You will leave this establishment today! Whatever possessions you have here, take them with you. And there is no purpose in your asking for a recommendation. I can give you none!"

There was silence in the ward. Someone rustled bedclothes.

"But she cured the boy!" the patient protested. "She was right! 'E's alive because of 'er!" The man's voice was thick with distress, at last understanding what he had done. He looked at Pomeroy, then at Hester. "She was right!" he said again.

Hester could at last afford the luxury of ceasing to care in the slightest what Pomeroy thought of her. She had nothing to lose now.

"Of course I shall go," she acknowledged. "But don't let your pride prevent you from helping Mrs. Begley. She doesn't deserve to die to save your face because a nurse told you what to do." She took a deep breath. "And since everyone in this room is aware of it, you will find it difficult to excuse."

"Why you—you—!" Pomeroy spluttered, scarlet in the face but lost for words violent enough to satisfy his outrage and at the same time not expose his weakness. "You—"

Hester gave him one withering look, then turned away and went over to the patient who had defended her, now sitting with the bedclothes in a heap around him and a pale face full of shame.

"There is no need to blame yourself," she said to him very gently, but clearly enough for everyone else in the ward to hear her. He needed his excusing to be known. "It was bound to happen that one day I should fall out with Dr. Pomeroy sufficiently for this to happen. At least you have spoken up for what you know, and perhaps you will have saved Mrs. Begley a great deal of pain, maybe even her life. Please do not criticize yourself for it or feel you have done me a disfavor. You have done no more than choose the time for what was inevitable."

"Are you sure, miss? I feel that badly!" He looked at her anxiously, searching her face for belief.

"Of course I'm sure." She forced herself to smile at him. "Have you not watched me long enough to judge that for yourself? Dr. Pomeroy and I have been on a course that was destined for collision from the beginning. And it was never possible that I should have the better of it." She began to straighten the sheet around him. "Now take care of yourself—and may God heal you!" She took his hand briefly, then moved away again. "In spite of Pomeroy," she added under her breath.

When she had reached her rooms, and the heat of temper had worn off a little, she began to realize what she had done. She was not only without an occupation to fill her time, and financial means with which to support herself, she had also betrayed Callandra Daviot's confidence in her and the recommendation to which she had given her name.

She had a late-afternoon meal alone, eating only because she did not want to offend her landlady. It tasted of nothing. By five o'clock it was growing dark, and after the gas lamps were lit and the curtains were drawn the room seemed to narrow and close her in in enforced idleness and complete isolation. What should she do tomorrow? There was no infirmary, no patients to care for. She was completely unnecessary and without purpose to anyone. It was a wretched thought, and if pursued for long would undermine her to the point where she would wish to crawl into bed and remain there.

There was also the extremely sobering thought that after a week or two she would have no money and be obliged to leave here and return to beg her brother, Charles, to provide a roof over her head until she could—what? It would be extremely difficult, probably impossible to gain another position in nursing. Pomeroy would see to that.

She felt herself on the edge of tears, which she despised. She must do something. Anything was better than sitting here in this shabby room listening to the gas hissing in the silence and feeling sorry for herself. One unpleasant task to be done was explaining herself to Callandra. She owed her that, and it would be a great deal better done face-to-face than in a letter. Why not get that over with? It could hardly be worse than sitting here alone thinking about it and waiting for time to pass until she could find it reasonable to go to bed, and sleep would not be merely a running away.

She put on her best coat—she had only two, but one was definitely more flattering and less serviceable than the other—and a good hat, and went out into the street to find a hansom and give the driver Callandra Daviot's address.

She arrived a few minutes before seven, and was relieved to find that Callandra was at home and not entertaining company, a contingency which she had not even thought of when she set out. She asked if she might see Lady Callandra and was admitted without comment by the maid.

Callandra came down the stairs within a few minutes, dressed in what she no doubt considered fashionable, but which was actually two years out of date and not the most flattering of colors. Her hair was already beginning to come out of its pins, although she must have left her dressing room no more than a moment ago, but the whole effect was redeemed by the intelligence and vitality in her face—and her evident pleasure in seeing Hester, even at this hour, and unannounced. It did not take her more than one glance to realize that something was wrong.

"What is it, my dear?" she said on reaching the bottom stair. "What has happened?"

There was no purpose in being evasive, least of all with Callandra.

"I treated a child without the doctor's permission—he was not there. The child seems to be recovering nicely—but I have been dismissed." It was out. She searched Callandra's face.

"Indeed." Callandra's eyebrows rose only slightly. "And the child was ill, I presume?"

"Feverish and becoming delirious."

"With what did you treat it?"

"Loxa quinine, theriac, Hoffman's mineral liquor—and a little ale to make it palatable."

"Seems very reasonable." Callandra led the way to the withdrawing room. "But outside your authority, of course."

"Yes," Hester agreed quietly.

Callandra closed the door behind them. "And you are not sorry," she added. "I assume you would do the same again?"

"I—"

"Do not lie to me, my dear. I am quite sure you would. It is a great pity they do not permit women to study medicine. You would make a fine doctor. You have intelligence, judgment and courage without bravado. But you are a woman, and that is an end of it." She sat down on a large and extremely comfortable sofa and signaled Hester to do the same. "And what do you intend to do now?"

"I have no idea."

"I thought not. Well perhaps you should begin by coming with me to the theater. You have had an extremely trying day and something in the realm of fantasy will be a satisfactory contrast. Then we will discuss what you are to do next. Forgive me for such an indelicate question, but have you sufficient funds to settle your accommodation for another week or two?"

Hester found herself smiling at such mundane practicality, so far from the moral outrage and portent of social disaster she might have expected from anyone else.

"Yes—yes I have."

"I hope that is the truth." Callandra's wild eyebrows rose inquiringly. "Good. Then that gives us a little time. If not, you would be welcome to stay with me until you obtain something more suitable."

It was better to tell it all now.

"I exceeded my authority," Hester confessed. "Pomeroy was extremely angry and will not give me any kind of reference. In fact I would be surprised if he did not inform all his colleagues of my behavior."

"I imagine he will," Callandra agreed. "If he is asked. But so long as the child recovers and survives he will be unlikely to raise the subject if he does not have to." She regarded Hester critically. "Oh dear, you are not exactly dressed for an evening out, are you? Still, it is too late to do a great deal now; you must come as you are. Perhaps my maid could dress your hair? That at least would help. Go upstairs and tell her I request it."

Hester hesitated; it had all been so rapid.

"Well don't stand there!" Callandra encouraged. "Have you eaten? We can have some refreshment there, but it will not be a proper meal."

"Yes—yes I have. Thank you—"

"Then go and have your hair dressed—be quick!"

Hester obeyed because she had no better idea.

The theater was crowded with people bent on enjoying themselves, women fashionably dressed in crinoline skirts full of flounces and flowers, lace, velvet, fringes and ribbons and all manner of femininity. Hester felt outstandingly plain and not in the least like laughing, and the thought of flirting with some trivial and idiotic young man was enough to make her lose what little of her temper was left. It was only her debt, and her fondness for Callandra, that kept any curb on her tongue at all.

Since Callandra had a box there was no difficulty about seats, and they were not placed close to anyone else. The play was one of the dozens popular at the moment, concerning the fall from virtue of a young woman, tempted by the weakness of the flesh, seduced by a worthless man, and only in the end, when it was too late, desiring to return to her upright husband.

"Pompous, opinionated fool!" Hester said under her breath, her tolerance at last stretched beyond bearing. "I wonder if the police ever charged a man with boring a woman to death?"

"It is not a sin, my dear," Callandra whispered back. "Women are not supposed to be interested."

Hester used a word she had heard in the Crimea among the soldiers, and Callandra pretended not to have heard it, although she had in fact heard it many times, and even knew what it meant.

When the play was finished the curtain came down to enthusiastic applause. Callandra rose, and Hester, after a brief glance down at the audience, rose also and followed her out into the wide foyer, now rapidly filling with men and women chattering about the play, each other and any trivialities or gossip that came to mind.

Hester and Callandra stepped among them, and within a few minutes and half a dozen exchanges of polite words, they came face-to-face with Oliver Rathbone and a dark young woman with a demure expression on her extremely pretty face.

"Good evening, Lady Callandra." He bowed very slightly and then turned to Hester, smiling. "Miss Latterly. May I present Miss Newhouse?"

They exchanged formal greetings in the approved fashion.

"Wasn't it a delightful play?" Miss Newhouse said politely. "So moving, don't you think?"

"Very," Callandra agreed. "The theme seems to be most popular these days."

Hester said nothing. She was aware of Rathbone looking at her with the same inquisitive amusement he had at their first meeting, before the trial. She was not in the mood for small talk, but she was Callandra's guest and she must endure it with some grace.

"I could not but feel sorry for the heroine," Miss Newhouse continued. "In spite of her weaknesses." She looked down for a moment. "Oh, I know of course that she brought her ruin upon herself. That was the playwright's skill, was it not, that one deplored her behavior and yet wept for her at the same time?" She turned to Hester. "Do you not think so, Miss Latterly?"

"I fear I had rather more sympathy with her than was intended," Hester said with an apologetic smile.

"Oh?" Miss Newhouse looked confused.

Hester felt compelled to explain further. She was acutely aware of Rathbone watching her.

"I thought her husband so extremely tedious I could well understand why she . . . lost interest."

"That hardly excuses her betrayal of her vows." Miss Newhouse was shocked. "It shows how easily we women can be led astray by a few flattering words," she said earnestly. "We see a handsome face and a little surface glamour, instead of true worth!"

Hester spoke before thinking. The heroine had been very pretty, and it seemed the husband had bothered to learn very little else about her. "I do not need anyone to lead me astray! I am perfectly capable of going on my own!"

Miss Newhouse stared at her, nonplussed.

Callandra coughed hard into her handkerchief.

"But not as much fun, going astray alone, is it?" Rathbone said with brilliant eyes and lips barely refraining from a smile. "Hardly worth the journey!"

Hester swung around and met his gaze. "I may go alone, Mr. Rathbone, but I am perfectly sure I would not find the ground uninhabited when I got there!"

His smile broadened, showing surprisingly beautiful teeth. He held out his arm in invitation.

"May I? Just to your carriage," he said with an expressionless face.

She was unable to stop laughing, and the fact that Miss Newhouse obviously did not know what was funny only added to her enjoyment.

The following day Callandra sent her footman to the police station with a note requesting that Monk wait upon her at his earliest convenience. She gave no explanation for her desire to see him and she certainly did not offer any information that would be of interest or use.

Nevertheless in the late morning he presented himself at her door and was duly shown in. He had a deep regard for her, of which she was aware.

"Good morning, Mr. Monk," she said courteously. "Please be seated and make yourself comfortable. May I offer you refreshment of some kind? Perhaps a hot chocolate? The morning is seasonably unpleasant."

"Thank you," he accepted, his face rather evidently showing his puzzlement as to why he had been sent for.

She rang for the maid, and when she appeared, requested the hot chocolate. Then she turned to Monk with a charming smile.

"How is your case progressing?" She had no idea which case he was engaged on, but she had no doubt there would be one.

He hesitated just long enough to decide whether the question was a mere politeness until the chocolate should arrive or whether she really wished to know. He decided the latter.

"Little bits and pieces of evidence all over the place," he replied. "Which do not as yet seem to add up to anything."

"Is that frequent?"

A flash of humor crossed his face. "It is not unknown, but these seem unusually erratic. And with a family like Sir Basil Moidore's, one does not press as one might with less socially eminent people."

She had the information she needed.

"Of course not. It must be very difficult indeed. And the public, by way of the newspapers, and the authorities also, will naturally be pressing very hard for a solution."

The chocolate came and she served them both, permitting the maid to leave immediately. The beverage was hot, creamy and delicious, and she saw the satisfaction in Monk's face as soon as his lips touched it.

"And you are at a disadvantage that you can never observe them except under the most artificial of circumstances," she went on, seeing his rueful agreement. "How can you possibly ask them the questions you really wish, when they are so forewarned by your mere presence that all their answers are guarded and designed to protect? You can only hope their lies become so convoluted as to trap some truth."

"Are you acquainted with the Moidores?" He was seeking for her interest in the matter.

She waved a hand airily. "Only socially. London is very small, you know, and most good families are connected with each other. That is the purpose of a great many marriages. I have a cousin of sorts who is related to one of Beatrice's brothers. How is she taking the tragedy? It must be a most grievous time for her."

He set down his chocolate cup for a moment. "Very hard," he replied, concentrating on a memory which puzzled him. "To begin with she seemed to be bearing it very well, with great calm and inner strength. Now quite suddenly she has collapsed and withdrawn to her bedroom. I am told she is ill, but I have not seen her myself."

"Poor creature," Callandra sympathized. "But most unhelpful to your inquiries. Do you imagine she knows something?"

He looked at her acutely. He had remarkable eyes, very dark clear gray, with an undeviating gaze that would have quelled quite a few people, but Callandra could have outstared a basilisk.

"It occurs to me," he said carefully.

"What you need is someone inside the house whom the family and servants would consider of no importance," she said as if the idea had just occurred to her. "And of course quite unrelated to the investigation—someone who has an acute sense of people's behavior and could observe them without their giving any thought to it, and then recount to you what was said and done in private times, the nuances of tone and expression."

"A miracle," he said dryly.

"Not at all," she replied with equally straight-faced aridity. "A woman would suffice."

"We do not have women officers in the police." He picked up his cup again and looked at her over the rim. "And if we did, we could hardly place one in the house."

"Did you not say Lady Moidore had taken to her bed?"

"That is of some help?" He looked wide-eyed.

"Perhaps she would benefit from having a nurse in the house? She is quite naturally ill with distress at her daughter's death by murder. It seems very possible she has some realization of who was responsible. No wonder she is unwell, poor creature. Any woman would be. I think a nurse would be an excellent thing for her."

He stopped drinking his chocolate and stared at her.

With some difficulty she kept her face blank and perfectly innocent.

"Hester Latterly is at present without employment, and she is an excellent nurse, one of Miss Nightingale's young ladies. I can recommend her highly. And she would be perfectly prepared to undertake such an engagement, I believe. She is most observant, as you know, and not without personal courage. The fact that a murder has taken place in the house would not deter her."

"What about the infirmary?" he said slowly, a brilliant light coming into his eyes.

"She is no longer there." Her expression was blandly innocent.

He looked startled.

"A difference of opinion with the doctor," she explained.

"Oh!"

"Who is a fool," she added.

"Of course." His smile was very slight, but went all the way to his eyes.

"I am sure if you were to approach her," she went on, "with some tact she would be prepared to apply for a temporary position with Sir Basil Moidore, to care for Lady Moidore until such time as she is herself again. I will be most happy to supply a reference. I would not speak to the hospital, if I were you. And it might be desirable not to mention my name to Hester—unless it is necessary to avoid untruth."

Now his smile was quite open. "Quite so, Lady Callandra. An excellent idea. I am most obliged to you."

"Not at all," she said innocently. "Not at all. I shall also speak to my cousin Valentina, who will be pleased to suggest such a thing to Beatrice and at the same time recommend Miss Latterly."

Hester was so surprised to see Monk she did not even think to wonder how he knew her address.

"Good morning," she said in amazement. "Has something—" she stopped, not sure what it was she was asking.

He knew how to be circumspect when it was in his own interest. He had learned it with some difficulty, but his ambition overrode his temper, even his pride, and it had come in time.

"Good morning," he replied agreeably. "No, nothing alarming has happened. I have a favor I wish of you, if you are willing."

"Of me?" She was still astonished and half disbelieving.

"If you will? May I sit down?"

"Oh—of course." They were in Mrs. Horne's parlor, and she waved to the seat nearest the thin fire.

He accepted, and began on the purpose of his visit before trivial conversation should lead him into betraying Callandra Daviot.

"I am engaged in the Queen Anne Street case, the murder of Sir Basil Moidore's daughter."

"I wondered if you would be," she answered politely, her eyes bright with expectation. "The newspapers are still full of it. But I have never met any of the family, nor do I know anything about them. Have they any connection with the Crimea?"

"Only peripheral."

"Then what can I—" She stopped, waiting for him to answer.

"It was someone in the house who killed her," he said. "Very probably one of the family—"

"Oh—" Understanding began in her eyes, not of her own part in the case, but of the difficulties facing him. "How can you investigate that?"

"Carefully." He smiled with a downward turn of his lips. "Lady Moidore has taken to her bed. I am not sure how much of it is grief— she was very composed to begin with—and how much of it may be because she has learned something which points to one of the family and she cannot bear it."

"What can I do?" He had all her attention now.

"Would you consider taking a position as nurse to Lady Moidore, and observing the family, and if possible learning what she fears so much?"

She looked uncomfortable. "They may require better references than I could supply."

"Would not Miss Nightingale speak well of you?"

"Oh, certainly—but the infirmary would not."

"Indeed. Then we shall hope they do not ask them. I think the main thing will be if Lady Moidore finds you agreeable—"

"I imagine Lady Callandra would also speak for me."

He relaxed back into his chair. "That should surely be sufficient. Then you will do it?"

She laughed very slightly. "If they advertise for such a person, I shall surely apply—but I can hardly turn up at the door and inquire if they need a nurse!"

"Of course not. I shall do what I can to arrange it." He did not tell her of Callandra Daviot's cousin, and hurried on to avoid difficult explanations. "It will be done by word of mouth, as these things are in the best families. If you will permit yourself to be mentioned? Good—"

"Tell me something of the household."

"I think it would be better if I left you to discover it yourself— and certainly your opinions would be of more use to me." He frowned curiously. "What happened at the infirmary?"

Ruefully she told him.

Valentina Burke-Heppenstall was prevailed upon to call in person at Queen Anne Street to convey her sympathies, and when Beatrice did not receive her, she commiserated with her friend's distress and suggested to Araminta that perhaps a nurse would be helpful in the circumstances and be able to offer assistance a busy ladies' maid could not.

After a few moments' consideration, Araminta was disposed to agree. It would indeed remove from the rest of the household the responsibility for a task they were not really equipped to handle.

Valentina could suggest someone, if it would not be viewed as impertinent? Miss Nightingale's young ladies were the very best, and very rare indeed among nurses; they were well-bred, not at all the sort of person one would mind having in one's house.

Araminta was obliged. She would interview this person at the first opportunity.

Accordingly Hester put on her best uniform and rode in a hansom cab to Queen Anne Street, where she presented herself for Araminta's inspection.

"I have Lady Burke-Heppenstall's recommendation of your work," Araminta said gravely. She was dressed in black taffeta which rustled with every movement, and the enormous skirt kept touching table legs and corners of sofas and chairs as Araminta walked in the over-furnished room. The somberness of the gown and the black crepes set over pictures and doors in recognition of death made her hair by contrast seem like a pool of light, hotter and more vivid than gold.

She looked at Hester's gray stuff dress and severe appearance with satisfaction.

"Why are you currently seeking employment, Miss Latterly?" She made no attempt at courtesy. This was a business interview, not a social one.

Hester had already prepared her excuse, with Callandra's help. It was frequently the desire of an ambitious servant to work for someone of title. They were greater snobs than many of their mistresses, and the manners and grammar of other servants were of intense importance to them.

"Now that I am home in England, Mrs. Kellard, I should prefer nursing in a private house of well-bred people to working in a public hospital."

"That is quite understandable," Araminta accepted without a flicker. "My mother is not ill, Miss Latterly; she has had a bereavement under most distressing circumstances. We do not wish her to fall into a melancholy. It would be easy enough. She will require agreeable company—and care that she sleeps well and eats sufficiently to maintain her health. Is this a position you would be willing to fill, Miss Latterly?"

"Yes, Mrs. Kellard, I should be happy to, if you feel I would suit?" Hester forced herself to be appropriately humble only by remembering Monk's face—and her real purpose here.

"Very well, you may consider yourself engaged. You may bring such belongings as are necessary, and begin tomorrow. Good day to you."

"Good day, ma'am—thank you."

Accordingly, the following day Hester arrived at Queen Anne Street with her few belongings in a trunk and presented herself at the back door to be shown her room and her duties. It was an extraordinary position, rather more than a servant, but a great deal less than a guest. She was considered skilled, but she was not part of the ordinary staff, nor yet a professional person such as a doctor. She was a member of the household, therefore must come and go as she was ordered and conduct herself in all ways as was acceptable to her mistress. *Mistress*—the word set her teeth on edge.

But why should it? She had no possessions and no prospects, and since she took it upon herself to administer to John Airdrie without Pomeroy's permission, she had no other employment either. And of course there was not only caring for Lady Moidore to consider and do well, there was the subtler and more interesting and dangerous job to do for Monk.

She was given an agreeable room on the floor immediately above the main family bedrooms and with a connecting bell so she could come at a moment's notice should she be required. In her time off duty, if there should be any, she might read or write letters in the ladies' maids' sitting room. She was told quite unequivocally what her duties would be, and what would remain those of the ladies' maid, Mary, a dark, slender girl in her twenties with a face full of character and a ready tongue. She was also told the province of the upstairs maid, Annie, who was about sixteen and full of curiosity, quick-witted and far too opinionated for her own good.

She was shown the kitchen and introduced to the cook, Mrs. Boden, the kitchen maid Sal, the scullery maid May, the bootboy Willie, and then to the laundrymaids Lizzie and Rose, who would attend to her linens. The other ladies' maid, Gladys, she only saw on the landing; she looked after Mrs. Cyprian Moidore and Miss Araminta. Similarly the upstairs maid Maggie, the between maid Nellie, and the handsome parlormaid Dinah were outside her responsibility. The tiny, fierce housekeeper, Mrs. Willis, did not have jurisdiction over nurses, and that was a bad beginning to their relationship. She was used to power and resented a female servant who was not answerable to her. Her small, neat face showed it in instant disapproval. She reminded Hester of a particularly efficient hospital matron, and the comparison was not a fortunate one.

"You will eat in the servants' hall with everyone else," Mrs. Willis informed her tartly. "Unless your duties make that impossible. After breakfast at eight o'clock we all," she said the word pointedly, and looked Hester in the eye, "gather for Sir Basil to lead us in prayers. I assume, Miss Latterly, that you are a member of the Church of England?"

"Oh yes, Mrs. Willis," Hester said immediately, although by inclination she was no such thing, her nature was all nonconformist.

"Good." Mrs. Willis nodded. "Quite so. We take dinner between twelve and one, while the family takes luncheon. There will be supper at whatever time the evening suits. When there are large dinner parties that may be very late." Her eyebrows rose very high. "We give some of the largest dinner parties in London here, and very fine cuisine indeed. But since we are in mourning at present there will be no entertaining, and by the time we resume I imagine your duties will be long past. I expect you will have half a day off a fortnight, like everyone else. But if that does not suit her ladyship, then you won't."

Since it was not a permanent position Hester was not yet concerned with time off, so long as she had opportunity to see Monk when necessary, to report to him any knowledge she had gained.

"Yes, Mrs. Willis," she replied, since a reply seemed to be awaited.

"You will have little or no occasion to go into the withdrawing room, but if you do I presume you know better than to knock?" Her eyes were sharp on Hester's face. "It is extremely vulgar ever to knock on a withdrawing room door."

"Of course, Mrs. Willis," Hester said hastily. She had never given the matter any thought, but it would not do to admit it.

"The maid will care for your room, of course," the housekeeper went on, looking at Hester critically. "But you will iron your own aprons. The laundrymaids have enough to do, and the ladies' maids are certainly not waiting on you! If anyone sends you letters—you have a family?" This last was something in the nature of a challenge. People without families lacked respectability; they might be anyone.

"Yes, Mrs. Willis, I do," Hester said firmly. "Unfortunately my parents died recently, and one of my brothers was killed in the Crimea, but I have a surviving brother, and I am very fond both of him and of his wife."

Mrs. Willis was satisfied. "Good. I am sorry about your brother who died in the Crimea, but many fine young men were lost in that conflict. To die for one's Queen and country is an honorable thing and to be borne with such fortitude as one can. My own father was a soldier—a very fine man, a man to look up to. Family is very important, Miss Latterly. All the staff here are most respectable."

With great difficulty Hester bit her tongue and forbore from saying what she felt about the Crimean War and its political motives or the utter incompetence of its conduct. She controlled herself with merely lowering her eyes as if in modest consent.

"Mary will show you the female servants' staircase." Mrs. Willis had finished the subject of personal lives and was back to business.

"I beg your pardon?" Hester was momentarily confused.

"The female servants' staircase," Mrs. Willis said sharply. "You will have to go up and down stairs, girl! This is a decent household—you don't imagine you are going to use the male servants' stairs, do you? Whatever next? I hope you don't have any ideas of that sort."

"Certainly not, ma'am." Hester collected her wits quickly and invented an explanation. "I am just unused to such spaciousness. I am not long returned from the Crimea." This in case Mrs. Willis had heard only the reputation of nurses in England, which was far from savory. "We had no menservants where I was."

"Indeed." Mrs. Willis was totally ignorant in the matter, but unwilling to say so. "Well, we have five outside menservants here, whom you are unlikely to meet, and inside we have Mr. Phillips, the butler; Rhodes, Sir Basil's valet; Harold and Percival, the footmen; and Willie, the bootboy. You will have no occasion to have dealings with any of them."

"No ma'am."

Mrs. Willis sniffed. "Very well. You had best go and present yourself to Lady Moidore and see if there is anything you can do for her, poor creature." She smoothed her apron fiercely and her keys jangled. "As if it wasn't enough to be bereaved of a daughter, without police creeping all over the house and pestering people with questions. I don't know what the world is coming to! If they were doing their job in the first place all this would never have happened."

Since she was not supposed to know it, Hester refrained from saying it was a bit unreasonable to expect police, no matter how diligent, to prevent a domestic murder.

"Thank you, Mrs. Willis," she said in compromise, and turned to go upstairs and meet Beatrice Moidore.

She tapped on the bedroom door, and when there was no answer, went in anyway. It was a charming room, very feminine, full of flowered brocades, oval framed pictures and mirrors, and three light, comfortable dressing chairs set about to be both ornamental and useful. The curtains were wide open and the room full of cold sunlight.

Beatrice herself was lying on the bed in a satin peignoir, her ankles crossed and her arms behind her head, her eyes wide, staring at the ceiling. She took no notice when Hester came in.

Hester was an army nurse used to caring for men sorely wounded or desperately ill, but she had a small experience of the shock and then deep depression and fear following an amputation, and the feeling of utter helplessness that overwhelms every other emotion. What she thought she saw in Beatrice Moidore was fear, and the frozen attitude of an animal that dares not move in case it draws attention to itself and does not know which way to run.

"Lady Moidore," she said quietly.

Beatrice realized it was a voice she did not know, and an unaccustomed tone, firmer and not tentative like a maid's. She turned her head and stared.

"Lady Moidore, I am Hester Latterly. I am a nurse, and I have come to look after you until you feel better."

Beatrice sat up slowly on her elbows. "A nurse?" she said with a faint, slightly twisted smile. "I'm not—" Then she changed her mind and lay back again. "There has been a murder in my family—that is not an illness."

So Araminta had not even told her of the arrangements, let alone consulted her—unless, of course, she had forgotten?

"No," Hester agreed aloud. "I would consider it more in the nature of an injury. But I learned most of my nursing in the Crimea, so I am used to injury and the shock and distress it causes. One can take some time even to desire to recover."

"In the Crimea? How useful."

Hester was surprised. It was an odd comment to make. She looked more carefully at Beatrice's sensitive, intelligent face with its wide eyes, jutting nose and fine lips. She was far from a classic beauty, nor did she have the rather heavy, sulky look that was currently much admired. She appeared far too spirited to appeal to many men, who might care for something a great deal more domestic seeming. And yet today her aspect completely denied the nature implicit in her features.

"Yes," Hester agreed. "And now that my family are dead and were not able to leave me provided for, I require to remain useful."

Beatrice sat up again. "It must be very satisfying to be useful. My children are adult and married themselves. We do a great deal of entertaining—at least we did—but my daughter Araminta is highly skilled at preparing guest lists that will be interesting and amusing, my cook is the envy of half of London, and my butler knows where to hire any extra help we might need. All my staff are highly trained, and I have an extremely efficient housekeeper who does not appreciate my meddling in her affairs."

Hester smiled. "Yes, I can imagine. I have met her. Have you taken luncheon today?"

"I am not hungry."

"Then you should take a little soup, and some fruit. It can give you very unpleasant effects if you do not drink. Internal distress will not help you at all."

Beatrice looked as surprised as her indifference would allow. "You are very blunt."

"I do not wish to be misunderstood."

Beatrice smiled in spite of herself. "I doubt you very often are."

Hester kept her composure. She must not forget that her primary duty was to care for a woman suffering deeply.

"May I bring you a little soup, and some fruit tart, or a custard?"

"I imagine you will bring it anyway—and I daresay you are hungry yourself?"

Hester smiled, glanced around the room once more, and went to begin her duties in the kitchen.

It was that evening that Hester made her next acquaintance with Araminta. She had come downstairs to the library to fetch a book which she thought would interest Beatrice and possibly help her to sleep, and she was searching along the shelves past weighty histories, and even weightier philosophies, until she should come to poetries and novels. She was bent over on her knees with her skirts around her when Araminta came in.

"Have you mislaid something, Miss Latterly?" she asked with faint disapproval. It was an undignified position, and too much at home for someone who was more or less a servant.

Hester rose to her feet and straightened her clothes. They were much of a height and looked at each other across a small reading table. Araminta was dressed in black silk trimmed with velvet with tiny silk ribbons on the bodice and her hair was as vivid as marigolds in the sun. Hester was dressed in blue-gray with a white apron, and her hair was a very ordinary brown with faint touches of honey or auburn in it in the sun, but excessively dull compared with Araminta's.

"No, Mrs. Kellard," she replied gravely. "I came to find something for Lady Moidore to read before she retires, so it might help her to sleep."

"Indeed? I would think a little laudanum would serve better?"

"It is a last resort, ma'am," Hester said levelly. "It tends to form a dependency, and can make one feel unwell afterwards."

"I imagine you know that my sister was murdered in this house less than three weeks ago?" Araminta stood very straight, her eyes unwavering. Hester admired her moral courage to be so blunt on a subject many would consider too shocking to speak of at all.

"Yes I am," she said gravely. "It is not surprising that your mother is extremely distressed, especially since I understand the police are still here quite often asking questions. I thought a book might take her mind off present grief, at least long enough to fall asleep, without causing the heaviness of drugs. It will not serve her to evade the pain forever. I don't mean to sound harsh. I have lost my own parents and a brother; I am acquainted with bereavement."

"Presumably that is why Lady Burke-Heppenstall recommended you. I think it will be most beneficial if you can keep my mother's mind from dwelling upon Octavia, my sister, or upon who might have been responsible for her death." Araminta's eyes did not flinch or evade in the slightest. "I am glad you are not afraid to be in the house. You have no need to be." She raised her shoulders very slightly. It was a cold gesture. "It is highly possible it was some mistaken relationship which ended in tragedy. If you conduct yourself with propriety, and do not encourage any attentions whatever, nor give the appearance of meddling or being inquisitive—"

The door opened and Myles Kellard came in. Hester's first thought was that he was an extraordinarily handsome man with a quite individual air to him, a man who might laugh or sing, or tell wild and entertaining stories. If his mouth was a trifle self-indulgent, perhaps it was only that of a dreamer.

"—you will find no trouble at all." Araminta finished without turning to look at him or acknowledge his presence.

"Are you warning Miss Latterly about our intrusive and rather arrogant policeman?" Myles asked curiously. He turned and smiled at Hester, an easy and charming expression. "Ignore him, Miss Latterly. And if he is overpersistent, report him to me, and I shall be glad to dispatch him for you forthwith. Whomever else he suspects—" His eyes surveyed her with mild interest, and she felt a sudden pang of regret that she was so ungenerously endowed and dressed so very plainly. It would have been most agreeable to see a spark of interest light in such a man's eyes as he looked at her.

"He will not suspect Miss Latterly," Araminta said for him. "Principally because she was not here at the time."

"Of course not," he agreed, putting out his arm towards his wife. With a delicate, almost imperceptible gesture she moved away from him so he did not touch her.

He froze, changed direction and reached instead to straighten a picture which was sitting on the desk.

"Otherwise he might," Araminta continued coolly, stiffening her back. "He seems to suspect everyone else, even the family."

"Rubbish!" Myles attempted to sound impatient, but Hester thought he was more uncomfortable. There was a sudden pinkness to his skin and his eyes moved restlessly from one object to another, avoiding their faces. "That is absurd! None of us could have the slightest reason for such a fearful thing, nor would we if we had. Really, Minta, you will be frightening Miss Latterly."

"I did not say one of us had done it, Myles, merely that Inspector Monk believed it of us—I think it must have been something Percival said about you." She watched the color ebb from his skin, then turned away and continued deliberately. "He is most irresponsible. If I were quite sure I should have him dismissed." She spoke very clearly. Her tone suggested she was musing aloud, intent upon her thoughts for themselves, not for any effect upon others, but her body inside its beautiful gown was as stiff as a twig in the still air, and her voice was penetrating.

"I think it is the suspicion of what Percival said that has made Mama take to her bed. Perhaps if you were to avoid her, Myles, it might be better for her. She may be afraid of you—" She turned suddenly and smiled at him, dazzling and brittle. "Which is perfectly absurd, I know—but fear is at times irrational. We can have the wildest ideas about people, and no one can convince us they are unfounded."

She cocked her head a little to one side. "After all, whatever reason could you possibly have to have quarreled so violently with Octavia?" She hesitated. "And yet she is sure you have. I hope she does not tell Mr. Monk so, as it would be most distressing for us." She swiveled around to Hester. "Do see if you can help her to take a rather firmer hold on reality, Miss Latterly. We shall all be eternally grateful to you. Now I must go and see how poor Romola is. She has a headache, and Cyprian never knows what to do for her." She swept her skirts around her and walked out, graceful and rigid.

Hester found herself surprisingly embarrassed. It was perfectly clear that Araminta was aware she had frightened her husband, and that she took a calculated pleasure in it. Hester bent to the bookshelf again, not wishing Myles to see the knowledge in her eyes.

He moved to stand behind her, no more than a yard away, and she was acutely conscious of his presence.

"There is no need to be concerned, Miss Latterly," he said with a very slight huskiness in his voice. "Lady Moidore has rather an active imagination. Like a lot of ladies. She gets her facts muddled, and frequently does not mean what she says. I am sure you understand that?" His tone implied that Hester would be the same, and her words were to be taken lightly.

She rose to her feet and met his eyes, so close she could see the shadow of his remarkable eyelashes on his cheeks, but she refused to step backwards.

"No I do not understand it, Mr. Kellard." She chose her words carefully. "I very seldom say what I do not mean, and if I do, it is accidental, a misuse of words, not a confusion in my mind."

"Of course, Miss Latterly." He smiled. "I am sure you are at heart just like all women—"

"Perhaps if Mrs. Moidore has a headache, I should see if I can help her?" she said quickly, to prevent herself from giving the retort in her mind.

"I doubt you can," he replied, moving aside a step. "It is not your attention she wishes for. But by all means try, if you like. It should be a nice diversion."

She chose to misunderstand him. "If one is suffering a headache, surely whose attention it is is immaterial."

"Possibly," he conceded. "I've never had one—at least not of Romola's sort. Only women do."

Hester seized the first book to her hand, and holding it with its face towards her so its title was hidden, brushed her way past him.

"If you will excuse me, I must return to see how Lady Moidore is feeling."

"Of course," he murmured. "Although I doubt it will be much different from when you left her!"

It was during the day after that she came to realize more fully what Myles had meant about Romola's headache. She was coming in from the conservatory with a few flowers for Beatrice's room when she came upon Romola and Cyprian standing with their backs to her, and too engaged in their conversation to be aware of her presence.

"It would make me very happy if you would," Romola said with a note of pleading in her voice, but dragged out, a little plaintive, as though she had asked many times before.

Hester stopped and took a step backwards behind the curtain, from where she could see Romola's back and Cyprian's face. He looked tired and harassed, shadows under his eyes and a hunched attitude to his shoulders as though half waiting for a blow.

"You know that it would be fruitless at the moment," he replied with careful patience. "It would not make matters any better."

"Oh, Cyprian!" She turned very petulantly, her whole body expressing disappointment and disillusion. "I really think for my sake you should try. It would make all the difference in the world to me."

"I have already explained to you—" he began, then abandoned the attempt. "I know you wish it," he said sharply, exasperation breaking through. "And if I could persuade him I would."

"Would you? Sometimes I wonder how important my happiness is to you."

"Romola—I—"

At this point Hester could bear it no longer. She resented people who by moral pressure made others responsible for their happiness.

Perhaps because no one had ever taken responsibility for hers, but without knowing the circumstances, she was still utterly on Cyprian's side. She bumped noisily into the curtain, rattling the rings, let out a gasp of surprise and mock irritation, and then when they both turned to look at her, smiled apologetically and excused herself, sailing past them with a bunch of pink daisies in her hand. The gardener had called them something quite different, but *daisies* would do.

She settled in to Queen Anne Street with some difficulty. Physically it was extremely comfortable. It was always warm enough, except in the servants' rooms on the third and fourth floors, and the food was by far the best she had ever eaten—and the quantities were enormous. There was meat, river fish and sea fish, game, poultry, oysters, lobster, venison, jugged hare, pies, pastries, vegetables, fruit, cakes, tarts and flans, puddings and desserts. And the servants frequently ate what was returned from the dining room as well as what was cooked especially for them.

She learned the hierarchy of the servants' hall, exactly whose domain was where and who deferred to whom, which was extremely important. No one intruded upon anyone else's duties, which were either above them or beneath them, and they guarded their own with jealous exactitude. Heaven forbid a senior housemaid should be asked to do what was the under housemaid's job, or worse still, that a footman should take a liberty in the kitchen and offend the cook.

Rather more interestingly she learned where the fondnesses lay, and the rivalries, who had taken offense at whom, and quite often why.

Everyone was in awe of Mrs. Willis, and Mr. Phillips was considered more the master in any practical terms than Sir Basil, whom many of the staff never actually saw. There was a certain amount of joking and irreverence about his military mannerisms, and more than one reference to sergeant majors, but never within his hearing.

Mrs. Boden, the cook, ruled with a rod of iron in the kitchen, but it was more by skill, dazzling smiles and a very hot temper than by the sheer freezing awe of the housekeeper or the butler. Mrs. Boden was also fond of Cyprian and Romola's children, the fair-haired, eight-year-old Julia and her elder brother, Arthur, who was just ten. She was given to spoiling them with treats from the kitchen whenever opportunity arose, which was frequently, because although they ate in the nursery, Mrs. Boden oversaw the preparation of the tray that was sent up.

Dinah the parlormaid was a trifle superior, but it was in good part her position rather than her nature. Parlormaids were selected for their appearance and were required to sail in and out of the front reception rooms heads high, skirts swishing, to open the front door in the afternoons and carry visitors' cards in on a silver tray. Hester actually found her very approachable, and keen to talk about her family and how good they had been to her, providing her with every opportunity to better herself.

Sal, the kitchen maid, remarked that Dinah had never been seen to receive a letter from them, but she was ignored. And Dinah took all her permitted time off duty, and once a year returned to her home village, which was somewhere in Kent.

Lizzie, the senior laundrymaid, on the other hand, was very superior indeed, and ran the laundry with an unbending discipline. Rose, and the women who came in to do some of the heavy ironing, were never seen to disobey, whatever their private feelings. It was an entertaining observation of nature, but little of it seemed of value in learning who had murdered Octavia Haslett.

Of course the subject was discussed below stairs. One could not possibly have a murder in the house and expect people not to speak of it, most particularly when they were all suspected—and one of them had to be guilty.

Mrs. Boden refused even to think about it, or to permit anyone else to.

"Not in my kitchen," she said briskly, whisking half a dozen eggs so sharply they all but flew out of the bowl. "I'll not have gossip in here. You've got more than enough to do without wasting your time in silly chatter. Sal—you do them potatoes by the time I've finished this, or I'll know the reason why! May! May! What about the floor, then? I won't have a dirty floor in here."

Phillips stalked from one room to another, grand and grim. Mrs. Boden said the poor man had taken it very hard that such a thing should happen in his household. Since it was obviously not one of the family, to which no one replied, obviously it must be one of the servants—which automatically meant someone he had hired.

Mrs. Willis's icy look stopped any speculation she overheard. It was indecent and complete nonsense. The police were quite incompetent, or they would know perfectly well it couldn't be anyone in the house. To discuss such a thing would only frighten the younger girls and was quite irresponsible. Anyone overheard being so foolish would be disciplined appropriately.

Of course this stopped no one who was minded to indulge in a little gossip, which was all the maids, to the endless patronizing comments of the male staff, who had quite as much to say but were less candid about it. It reached a peak at tea time in the servants' hall.

"I think it was Mr. Thirsk, when 'e was drunk," Sal said with a toss of her head. "I know 'e takes port from the cellar, an' no good sayin' 'e doesn't!"

"Lot o' nonsense," Lizzie dismissed with scorn. "He's ever such a gentleman. And what would he do such a thing for, may I ask?"

"Sometimes I wonder where you grew up." Gladys glanced over her shoulder to make sure Mrs. Boden was nowhere in earshot. She leaned forward over the table, her cup of tea at her elbow. "Don't you know anything?"

"She works downstairs!" Mary hissed back at her. "Downstairs people never know half what upstairs people do."

"Go on then," Rose challenged. "Who do you think did it?"

"Mrs. Sandeman, in a fit o' jealous rage," Mary replied with conviction. "You should see some o' the outfits she wears—and d'you know where Harold says he takes her sometimes?"

They all stopped eating or drinking in breathless anticipation of the answer.

"Well?" Maggie demanded.

"You're too young." Mary shook her head.

"Oh, go on," Maggie pleaded. "Tell us!"

"She doesn't know 'erself," Sal said with a grin. "She's 'avin us on."

"I do so!" Mary retorted. "He takes her to streets where decent women don't go—down by the Haymarket."

"What—over some admirer?" Gladys savored the possibility. "Go on! Really?"

"You got a better idea, then?" Mary asked.

Willie the bootboy appeared from the kitchen doorway, where he had been keeping cavey in case Mrs. Boden should appear.

"Well I think it was Mr. Kellard!" he said with a backward glance over his shoulder. "May I have that piece o' cake? I'm starvin' 'ungry."

"That's only because you don't like 'im." Mary pushed the cake towards him, and he took it and bit into it ravenously.

"Pig," Sal said without rancor.

"I think it was Mrs. Moidore," May the scullery maid said suddenly.

"Why?" Gladys demanded with offended dignity. Romola was her charge, and she was personally offended by the suggestion.

"Go on with you!" Mary dismissed it. "You've never even seen Mrs. Moidore!"

"I 'ave too," May retorted. "She came down 'ere when young Miss Julia was sick that time! A good mother, she is. I reckon she's too good to be true—all that peaches-an'-cream skin and 'andsome face. She done married Mr. Cyprian for 'is money."

" 'E don't 'ave any," William said with his mouth full. " 'E's always borrowin' off folks. Least that's what Percival says."

"Then Percival's speakin' out of turn," Annie criticized. "Not that I'm saying Mrs. Moidore didn't do it. But I reckon it was more likely Mrs. Kellard. Sisters can hate something 'orrible."

"What about?" Maggie asked. "Why should Mrs. Kellard hate poor Miss Octavia?"

"Well Percival said Mr. Kellard fancied Miss Octavia something rotten," Annie explained. "Not that I take any notice of what Percival says. He's got a wicked tongue, that one."

At that moment Mrs. Boden came in.

"Enough gossiping," she said sharply. "And don't you talk with your mouth full, Annie Latimer. Get on about your business. Sal. There's carrots you 'aven't scraped yet, and cabbage for tonight's dinner. You 'aven't time to sit chatterin' over cups o' tea."

The last suggestion was the only one Hester thought suitable to report to Monk when he called and insisted on interviewing all the staff again, including the new nurse, even though it was pointed out to him that she had not been present at the time of the crime.

"Forget the kitchen gossip. What is your own opinion?" he asked her, his voice low so no servants passing beyond the housekeeper's sitting room door might overhear them. She frowned and hesitated, trying to find words to convey the extraordinary feeling of embarrassment and unease she had experienced in the library as Araminta swept out.

"Hester?"

"I am not sure," she said slowly. "Mr. Kellard was frightened, that I have no doubt of, but I could not even guess whether it was guilt over having murdered Octavia or simply having made some improper advance towards her—or even just fear because it was quite apparent that his wife took a certain pleasure in the whole possibility that he might be suspected quite gravely—even accused. She was—" She thought again before using the word, it was too melodramatic, then could find none more appropriate. "She was torturing him. Of course," she hurried on, "I do not know how she would react if you were to charge him. She might simply be doing this as some punishment for a private quarrel, and she may defend him to the death from outsiders."

"Do you think she believes him guilty?" He stood against the mantel shelf, hands in his pockets, face puckered with concentration.

She had thought hard about this ever since the incident, and her reply was ready on her lips.

"She is not afraid of him, of that I am certain. But there is a deep emotion there which has a bitterness to it, and I think he is more afraid of her—but I don't know if that has anything to do with Octavia's death or is simply that she has the power to hurt him."

She took a deep breath. "It must be extremely difficult for him, living in his father-in-law's house and in a very real way being under his jurisdiction and constantly obliged to please him or face very considerable unpleasantness. And Sir Basil does seem to rule with a heavy hand, from what I have seen." She sat sideways on the arm of one of the chairs, an attitude which would have sent Mrs. Willis into a rage, both for its unladylike pose and for the harm she was sure it would do to the chair.

"I have not seen much of Mr. Thirsk or Mrs. Sandeman yet. She leads quite a busy life, and perhaps I am maligning her, but I am sure she drinks. I have seen enough of it in the war to recognize the signs, even in highly unlikely people. I saw her yesterday morning with a fearful headache which, from the pattern of her recovery, was not any ordinary illness. But I may be hasty; I only met her on the landing as I was going in to Lady Moidore."

He smiled very slightly. "And what do you think of Lady Moidore?"

Every vestige of humor vanished from her face. "I think she is very frightened. She knows or believes something which is so appalling that she dare not confront it, yet neither can she put it from her mind—"

"That it was Myles Kellard who killed Octavia?" he asked, stepping forward a pace. "Hester—be careful!" He took her arm and held it hard, the pressure of his fingers so strong as to be almost painful. "Watch and listen as your opportunities allow, but do not ask anything! Do you hear me?"

She backed away, rubbing her arm. "Of course I hear you. You requested me to help—I am doing so. I have no intention of asking any questions—they would not answer them anyway but would dismiss me for being impertinent and intrusive. I am a servant here."

"What about the servants?" He did not move away but remained close to her. "Be careful of the menservants, Hester, particularly the footmen. It is quite likely one of them had amorous ideas about Octavia, and misunderstood"—he shrugged—"or even understood correctly, and she got tired of the affair—"

"Good heavens. You are no better than Myles Kellard," she snapped at him. "He all but implied Octavia was a trollop."

"It is only a possibility!" he hissed sharply. "Keep your voice down. For all we know there may be a row of eavesdroppers at the door. Does your bedroom have a lock?"

"No."

"Then put a chair behind the handle."

"I hardly think—" Then she remembered that Octavia Haslett had been murdered in her bedroom in the middle of the night, and she found she was shaking in spite of herself.

"It is someone in this house!" Monk repeated, watching her closely.

"Yes," she said obediently. "Yes, I know that. We all know that— that is what is so terrible."

CHAPTER
SIX

Hester left her interview with Monk considerably chastened. Seeing him again had reminded her that this was not an ordinary household, and the difference of opinion, the quarrels, which seemed a trivial nastiness, in one case had been so deep they had led to violent and treacherous death. One of those people she looked at across the meal table, or passed on the stairs, had stabbed Octavia in the night and left her to bleed.

It made her a little sick as she returned to Beatrice's bedroom and knocked on the door before entering. Beatrice was standing by the window staring out into the remains of the autumn garden and watching the gardener's boy sweeping up the fallen leaves and pulling a few last weeds from around the Michaelmas daisies. Arthur, his hair blowing in the wind, was helping with the solemnity of a ten-year-old. Beatrice turned as Hester came in, her face pale, her eyes wide and anxious.

"You look distressed," she said, staring at Hester. She walked over to the dressing chair but did not sit, as if the chair would imprison her and she desired the freedom to move suddenly. "Why did the police want to see you? You weren't here when—when Tavie was killed."

"No, Lady Moidore." Hester's mind raced for a reason which would be believed, and perhaps which might even prompt Beatrice to yield something of the fear Hester was sure so troubled her. "I am not entirely certain, but I believe he thought I might have observed something since I came. And I have no cause for prevaricating, insofar as I could not fear he might accuse me."

"Who do you think is lying?" Beatrice asked.

Hester hesitated very slightly and moved to tidy the bed, plump up the pillows and generally appear to be working. "I don't know, but it is quite certain that someone must be."

Beatrice looked startled, as though it were not an answer she had foreseen.

"You mean someone is protecting the murderer? Why? Who would do such a thing and why? What reason could they have?"

Hester tried to excuse herself. "I meant merely that since it is someone in the house, that person is lying to protect himself." Then she realized the opportunity she had very nearly lost. "Although when you mention it, you are quite right, it seems most unlikely that no one else has any idea who it is, or why. I daresay several people are evading the truth, one way or another." She glanced up from the bed at Beatrice. "Wouldn't you, Lady Moidore?"

Beatrice hesitated. "I fear so," she said very quietly.

"If you ask me who," Hester went on, disregarding the fact that no one had asked her, "I have formed very few opinions. I can easily imagine why some people would hide a truth they knew, or suspected, in order to protect someone they cared for—" She watched Beatrice's face and saw the muscles tighten as if pain had caught her unaware. "I would hesitate to say something," Hester continued, "which might cause an unjustified suspicion—and therefore a great deal of distress. For example, an affection that might have been misunderstood—"

Beatrice stared back at her, wide-eyed. "Did you say that to Mr. Monk?"

"Oh no," Hester replied demurely. "He might have thought I had someone in particular in mind."

Beatrice smiled very slightly. She walked back towards the bed and lay on it, weary not in body but in mind, and Hester gently pulled the covers over her, trying to hide her own impatience. She was convinced Beatrice knew something, and every day that passed in silence was adding to the danger that it might never be discovered but that the whole household would close in on itself in corroding suspicion and concealed accusations. And would her silence be enough to protect her indefinitely from the murderer?

"Are you comfortable?" she asked gently.

"Yes thank you," Beatrice said absently. "Hester?"

"Yes?"

"Were you frightened in the Crimea? It must have been dangerous at times. Did you not fear for yourself—and for those of whom you had grown fond?"

"Yes of course." Hester's mind flew back to the times when she had lain in her cot with horror creeping over her skin and the sick knowledge of what pain awaited the men she had seen so shortly before, the numbing cold in the heights above Sebastopol, the mutilation of wounds, the carnage of battle, bodies broken and so mangled as to be almost unrecognizable as human, only as bleeding flesh, once alive and capable of unimaginable pain. It was seldom herself for whom she had been frightened; only sometimes, when she was so tired she felt ill, did the sudden specter of typhoid or cholera so terrify her as to cause her stomach to lurch and the sweat to break out and stand cold on her body.

Beatrice was looking at her, for once her eyes sharp with real interest—there was nothing polite or feigned in it.

Hester smiled. "Yes I was afraid sometimes, but not often. Mostly I was too busy. When you can do something about even the smallest part of it, the overwhelming sick horror goes. You stop seeing the whole thing and see only the tiny part you are dealing with, and the fact that you can do something calms you. Even if all you accomplish is easing one person's distress or helping someone to endure with hope instead of despair. Sometimes it is just tidying up that helps, getting a kind of order out of the chaos."

Only when she had finished and saw the understanding in Beatrice's face did she realize the additional meanings of what she had said. If anyone had asked her earlier if she would have changed her life for Beatrice's, married and secure in status and well-being with family and friends, she would have accepted it as a woman's most ideal role, as if it were a stupid thing even to doubt.

Perhaps Beatrice would just as quickly have refused. Now they had both changed their views with a surprise which was still growing inside them. Beatrice was safe from material misfortune, but she was also withering inside with boredom and lack of accomplishment. Pain appalled her because she had no part in addressing it. She endured passively, without knowledge or weapon with which to fight it, either in herself or in those she loved or pitied. It was a kind of distress Hester had seen before, but never more than casually, and never with so sharp and wounding an understanding.

Now it would be clumsy to try to put into words what was far too subtle, and which they both needed time to face in their own perceptions. Hester wanted to say something that would offer comfort, but anything that came to her mind sounded patronizing and would have shattered the delicate empathy between them.

"What would you like for luncheon?" she asked.

"Does it matter?" Beatrice smiled and shrugged, sensing the subtlety of moving from one subject to another quite different, and painlessly trivial.

"Not in the least." Hester smiled ruefully. "But you might as well please yourself, rather than the cook."

"Well not egg custard or rice pudding!" Beatrice said with feeling. "It reminds me of the nursery. It is like being a child again."

Hester had only just returned with the tray with cold mutton, fresh pickle, and bread and butter and a large slice of fruit flan with cream, to Beatrice's obvious approval, when there was a sharp rap on the door and Basil came in. He walked past Hester as if he had not seen her and sat down in one of the dressing chairs close to the bed, crossing his legs and making himself comfortable.

Hester was uncertain whether to leave or not. She had few tasks to do here, and yet she was extremely curious to know more of the relationship between Beatrice and her husband, a relationship which left the woman with such a feeling of isolation that she retreated to her room instead of running towards him, either for him to protect her or the better to battle it together. After all the affliction must lie in the area of family, emotions; there must be in it grief, love, hate, probably jealousy—all surely a woman's province, the area in which her skills mattered and her strength could be used?

Now Beatrice sat propped up against her pillows and ate the cold mutton with pleasure.

Basil looked at it disapprovingly. "Is that not rather heavy for an invalid? Let me send for something better, my dear—" He reached for the bell without waiting for her answer.

"I like it," she said with a flash of anger. "There is nothing wrong with my digestion. Hester got it for me and it is not Mrs. Boden's fault. She'd have sent me more rice pudding if I had let her."

"Hester?" He frowned. "Oh—the nurse." He spoke as if she were not there, or could not hear him. "Well—I suppose if you wish it."

"I do." She ate a few more mouthfuls before speaking again. "I assume Mr. Monk is still coming?"

"Of course. But he seems to be accomplishing singularly little—indeed I have seen no signs that he has achieved anything at all. He keeps questioning the servants. We shall be fortunate if they do not all give notice when this is over." He rested his elbows on the arms of the chair and put his fingertips together. "I have no idea how he hopes to come to any resolution. I think, my dear, you may have to prepare yourself for facing the fact that we may never know who it was." He was watching her and saw the sudden tightening, the hunch of her shoulders and the knuckles white where she held the knife. "Of course I have certain ideas," he went on. "I cannot imagine it was any of the female staff—"

"Why not?" she asked. "Why not, Basil? It is perfectly possible for a woman to stab someone with a knife. It doesn't take a great deal of strength. And Octavia would be far less likely to fear a woman in her room in the middle of the night than a man."

A flicker of irritation crossed his face. "Really, Beatrice, don't you think it is time to accept a few truths about Octavia? She had been widowed nearly two years. She was a young woman in the prime of her life—"

"So she had an affair with the footman!" Beatrice said furiously, her eyes wide, her voice cutting in its scorn. "Is that what you think of your daughter, Basil? If anyone in this house is reduced to finding their pleasure with a servant, it is far more likely to be Fenella! Except that I doubt she would ever have inspired a passion which drove anyone to murder—unless it was to murder her. Nor would she have changed her mind and resisted at the last moment. I doubt Fenella ever declined anyone—" Her face twisted in distaste and incomprehension.

His expression mirrored an equal disgust, mixed with an anger that was no sudden flash but came from deep within him.

"Vulgarity is most unbecoming, Beatrice, and even this tragedy is no excuse for it. I shall admonish Fenella if I think the occasion warrants it. I take it you are not suggesting Fenella killed Octavia in a fit of jealousy over the attentions of the footman?"

It was obviously intended as sarcasm, but she took it literally.

"I was not suggesting it," she agreed. "But now that you raise the thought, it does not seem impossible. Percival is a good-looking young man, and I have observed Fenella regarding him with appreciation." Her face puckered and she shuddered very slightly. "I know it is revolting—" She stared beyond him to the dressing table with its cut glass containers and silver-topped bottles neatly arranged. "But there is a streak of viciousness in Fenella—"

He stood up and turned his back to her, looking out of the window, still apparently oblivious of Hester standing in the dressing room doorway with a peignoir over her arm and a clothes brush in her hand.

"You are a great deal more fastidious than most women, Beatrice," he said flatly. "I think sometimes you do not know the difference between restraint and abstemiousness."

"I know the difference between a footman and a gentleman," she said quietly, and then stopped and frowned, a curious little twitch of humor on her lips. "That's a lie—I have no idea at all. I have no familiarity with footmen whatsoever—"

He swung around, unaware of the slightest humor in her remark or in the situation, only anger and acute insult.

"This tragedy has unhinged your mind," he said coldly, his black eyes flat, seeming expressionless in the lamplight. "You have lost your sense of what is fitting and what is not. I think it will be better if you remain here until you can compose yourself. I suppose it is to be expected, you are not strong. Let Miss—what is her name—care for you. Araminta will see to the household until you are better. We shall not be entertaining, naturally. There is no need for you to concern yourself; we shall manage very well." And without saying anything further he walked out and closed the door very quietly behind him, letting the latch fall home with a thud.

Beatrice pushed her unfinished tray away from her and turned over, burying her face in the pillows, and Hester could see from the quivering of her shoulders that she was weeping, although she made no sound.

Hester took the tray and put it on the side table, then wrung out a cloth in warm water from the ewer and returned to the bed. Very gently she put her arms around the other woman and held her until she was quiet, then, with great care, smoothed the hair off her brow and wiped her eyes and cheeks with the cloth.

It was the beginning of the afternoon when she was returning from the laundry with her clean aprons that Hester half accidentally overheard an exchange between the footman Percival and the laundrymaid Rose. Rose was folding a pile of embroidered linen pillowcases and had just given Lizzie, who was her elder sister, the parlormaid's lace-edged aprons. She was standing very upright, her back rigid, her shoulders squared and her chin high. She was tiny, with a waist even Hester could almost have put her hands around, and small, square hands with amazing strength in them. Her cornflower-blue eyes were enormous in her pretty face, not spoiled by a rather long nose and overgenerous mouth.

"What do you want in here?" she asked, but her words were belied by her voice. It was phrased as a demand, but it sounded like an invitation.

"Mr. Kellard's shirts," Percival said noncommittally.

"I didn't know that was your job. You'll have Mr. Rhodes after you if you step out of your duties!"

"Rhodes asked me to do it for him," he replied.

"Though you'd like to be a valet, wouldn't you? Get to travel with Mr. Kellard when he goes to stay at these big houses for parties and the like—" Her voice caressed the idea, and listening, Hester could envision her eyes shining, her lips parted in anticipation, all the excitement and delights imagined, new people, an elegant servants' hall, food, music, late nights, wine, laughter and gossip.

"It'd be all right," Percival agreed, for the first time a lift of warmth in his voice also. "Although I get to some interesting places now." That was the tone of the braggart, and Hester knew it.

It seemed Rose did too. "But not inside," she pointed out. "You have to wait in the mews with the carriages."

"Oh no I don't." There was a note of sharpness in his voice, and Hester could imagine the glitter in his eyes and the little curl of his lips. She had seen it several times as he walked through the kitchen past the maids. "I quite often go inside."

"The kitchen," Rose said dismissively. "If you were a valet you'd get upstairs as well. Valet is better than a footman."

They were all acutely conscious of hierarchy.

"Butler's better still," he pointed out.

"But less fun. Look at poor old Mr. Phillips." She giggled. "He hasn't had any fun in twenty years—and he looks as if 'e's forgotten that."

"Don't think 'e ever wanted any of your sort o' fun." Percival sounded serious again, remote and a trifle pompous. Suddenly he was talking of men's business, and putting a woman in her place. "He had an ambition to be in the army, but they wouldn't take him because of 'is feet. Can't have been that good a footman either, with his legs. Never wear livery without padding his stocking."

Hester knew Percival did not have to add any artificial enhancement to his calves.

"His feet?" Rose was incredulous. "What's wrong with 'is feet?"

This time there was derision in Percival's voice. "Haven't you ever watched 'im walk? Like someone broke a glass on the floor and 'e was picking 'is way over it and treading on half of it. Corns, bunions, I don't know."

"Pity," she said dryly. "He'd 'ave made a great sergeant major—cut out for it, 'e was. Mind, I suppose butler's the next best thing—the way 'e does it. And he does have a wonderful turn for putting some visitors in their place. He can size up anyone coming to call at a glance. Dinah says he never makes a mistake, and you should see his face if he thinks someone is less than a gentleman—or a lady—or if they're mean with their little appreciations. He can be so rude, just with his eyebrows. Dinah says she's seen people ready to curl up and die with mortification. It's not every butler as can do that."

"Any good servant can tell quality from riffraff, or they're not worth their position," Percival said haughtily. "I'm sure I can—and I know how to keep people in their places. There's dozens of ways—you can affect not to hear the bell, you can forget to stoke the fire, you can simply look at them like they were something the wind blew in, and then greet the person behind them like they was royalty. I can do that just as well as Mr. Phillips."

Rose was unimpressed. She returned to her first subject. "Anyway, Percy, you'd be out from under him if you were a valet—"

Hester knew why she wanted him to change. Valets worked far more closely with laundrymaids, and Hester had watched Rose's cornflower eyes following Percival in the few days she had been here, and knew well enough what lay behind the innocence, the casual comments, the big bows on her apron waist and the extra flick of her skirts and wriggle of her shoulders. She had been attracted to men often enough herself and would have behaved just the same had she Rose's confidence and her feminine skill.

"Maybe." Percival was ostentatiously uninterested. "Not sure I want to stay in this house anyway."

Hester knew that was a calculated rebuff, but she did not dare peer around the corner in case the movement was noticed. She stood still, leaning back against the piles of sheets on the shelf behind her and holding her aprons tightly. She could imagine the sudden cold feeling inside Rose. She remembered something much the same in the hospital in Scutari. There had been a doctor whom she admired, no, more than that, about whom she indulged in daydreams, imagined foolishness. And one day he had shattered them all with a dismissive word. For weeks afterwards she had turned it over and over in her mind, trying to decide whether he had meant it, even done it on purpose, bruising her feelings. That thought had sent waves of hot shame over her. Or had he been quite unaware and simply betrayed a side of his nature which had been there all the time—and which was better seen before she had committed herself too far. She would never know, and now it hardly mattered.

Rose said nothing. Hester did not even hear an indrawn breath.

"After all," Percival went on, adding to it, justifying himself, "this isn't the best house right now—police coming and going, asking questions. All London knows there's been a murder. And what's more, someone here did it. They won't stop till they find them, you know."

"Well if they don't, they won't let you go—will they?" Rose said spitefully. "After all—it might be you."

That must have been a thrust which struck home. For several seconds Percival was silent, then when he did speak his voice was sharp with a distinct edge, a crack of nervousness.

"Don't be stupid! What would any of us do that for? It must have been one of the family. The police aren't that easily fooled. That's why they're still here."

"Oh yes? And questioning us?" Rose retorted. "If that's so, what do they think we're going to tell them?"

"It's just an excuse." The certainty was coming back now. "They have to pretend it's us. Can you imagine what Sir Basil would say if they let on they suspected the family?"

"Nothing 'e could say!" She was still angry. "Police can go anywhere they want."

"Of course it's one of the family." Now he was contemptuous. "And I've got a few ideas who—and why. I know a few things—but I'd best say nothing; the police'll find out one of these days. Now I've got work to do, and so 'ave you." And he pushed on past her and around the corner. Hester stepped into the doorway so she was not discovered overhearing.

"Oh yes," Mary said, her eyes flashing as she flipped out a pillowcase and folded it. "Rose has a rare fancy for Percival. Stupid girl." She reached for another pillow slip and examined the lace to make sure it was intact before folding it to iron and put away. "He's nice enough looking, but what's that worth? He'd make a terrible husband, vain as a cockerel and always looking to his own advantage. Like enough leave her after a year or two. Roving eye, that one, and spiteful. Now Harold's a much better man—but then he wouldn't look at Rose; he never sees anyone but Dinah. Been eating his heart out for her for the last year and a half, poor boy." She put the pillow slip away and started on a pile of lace-edged petticoats, wide enough to fall over the huge hoops that kept skirts in the ungainly but very flattering crinoline shape. At least that shape was considered charming by those who liked to look dainty and a little childlike. Personally Hester would have preferred something very much more practical, and more natural in shape. But she was out of step with fashion—not for the first time.

"And Dinah's got her eye on next door's footman," Mary went on, straightening the ruffles automatically. "Although I can't see anything in him, excepting he's tall, which is nice, seein' as Dinah's so tall herself. But height's no comfort on a cold night. It doesn't keep you warm, and it can't make you laugh. I expect you met some fine soldiers when you were in the army?"

Hester knew the question was kindly meant, and she answered it in the same manner.

"Oh several." She smiled. "Unfortunately they were a trifle incapacitated at the time."

"Oh." Mary laughed and shook her head as she came to the end of her mistress's clothes from this wash. "I suppose they would be. Never mind. If you work in houses like this, there's no telling who you might meet." And with that hopeful remark she picked up the bundle and carried it out, walking jauntily towards the stairs with a sway of her hips.

Hester smiled and finished her own task, then went to the kitchen to prepare a tisane for Beatrice. She was taking the tray back upstairs when she passed Septimus coming out of the cellar door, one arm folded rather awkwardly across his chest as though he were carrying something concealed inside his jacket.

"Good afternoon, Mr. Thirsk," Hester said cheerfully, as if he had every business in the cellar.

"Er—good afternoon, Miss—er—er . . ."

"Latterly," she supplied. "Lady Moidore's nurse."

"Oh yes—of course." He blinked his washed-out blue eyes. "I do beg your pardon. Good afternoon, Miss Latterly." He moved to get away from the cellar door, still looking extremely uncomfortable.

Annie, one of the upstairs maids, came past and gave Septimus a knowing look and smiled at Hester. She was tall and slender, like Dinah. She would have made a good parlormaid, but she was too young at the moment and raw at fifteen, and she might always be too opinionated. Hester had caught her and Maggie giggling together more than once in the maids' room on the first landing, where the morning tea was prepared, or in the linen cupboard bent double over a penny dreadful book, their eyes out like organ stops as they pored over the scenes of breathless romance and wild dangers. Heaven knew what was in their imaginations. Some of their speculations over the murder had been more colorful than credible.

"Nice child, that," Septimus said absently. "Her mother's a pastry cook over in Portman Square, but I don't think you'll ever make a cook out of her. Daydreamer." There was affection in his voice. "Likes to listen to stories about the army." He shrugged and nearly let slip the bottle under his arm. He blushed and grabbed at it.

Hester smiled at him. "I know. She's asked me lots of questions. Actually I think both she and Maggie would make good nurses. They're just the sort of girls we need, intelligent and quick, and with minds of their own."

Septimus looked taken aback, and Hester guessed he was used to the kind of army medical care that had prevailed before Florence Nightingale, and all these new ideas were outside his experience.

"Maggie's a good girl too," he said with a frown of puzzlement. "A lot more common sense. Her mother's a laundress somewhere in the country. Welsh, I think. Accounts for the temper. Very quick temper, that girl, but any amount of patience when it's needed. Sat up all night looking after the gardener's cat when it was sick, though, so I suppose you're right, she'd be a good enough nurse. But it seems a pity to put two decent girls into that trade." He wriggled discreetly to move the bottle under his jacket high enough for it not to be noticed, and knew that he had failed. He was totally unaware of having insulted her profession; he was speaking frankly from the reputation he knew and had not even thought of her as being part of it.

Hester was torn between saving him embarrassment and learning all she could. Saving him won. She looked away from the lump under his jacket and continued as if she had not observed it.

"Thank you. Perhaps I shall suggest it to them one day. Of course I had rather you did not mention my idea to the housekeeper."

His face twitched in half-mock, half-serious alarm.

"Believe me, Miss Latterly, I wouldn't dream of it. I am too old a soldier to mount an unnecessary charge."

"Quite," she agreed. "And I have cleared up after too many."

For an instant his face was perfectly sober, his blue eyes very clear, the lines of anxiety ironed out, and they shared a complete understanding. Both had seen the carnage of the battlefield and the long torture of wounds afterwards and the maimed lives. They knew the price of incompetence and bravado. It was an alien life from this house and its civilized routine and iron discipline of trivia, the maids rising at five to clean the fires, black the grates, throw damp tea leaves on the carpets and sweep them up, air the rooms, empty the slops, dust, sweep, polish, turn the beds, launder, iron dozens of yards of linens, petticoats, laces and ribbons, stitch, fetch and carry till at last they were excused at nine, ten or eleven in the evening.

"You tell them about nursing," he said at last, and quite openly took out the bottle and repositioned it more comfortably, then turned and left, walking with a lift in his step and a very slight swagger.

Upstairs Hester had just brought the tray for Beatrice and set it down, and was about to leave when Araminta came in.

"Good afternoon, Mama," she said briskly. "How are you feeling?" Like her father she seemed to find Hester invisible. She went and kissed her mother's cheek and then sat down on the nearest dressing chair, her skirts overflowing in mounds of darkest gray muslin with a lilac fichu, dainty and intensely flattering, and yet still just acceptable for mourning. Her hair was the same bright flame as always, her face its delicate, lean asymmetry.

"Exactly the same, thank you," Beatrice answered without real interest. She turned slightly to look at Araminta, a pucker of confusion around her mouth. There was no sense of affection between them, and Hester was uncertain whether she should leave or not. She had a curious sense that in some way she was not intruding because the tension between the two women, the lack of knowing what to say to each other, already excluded her. She was a servant, someone whose opinion was of no importance whatever, indeed someone not really of existence.

"Well I suppose it is to be expected." Araminta smiled, but the warmth did not reach her eyes. "I am afraid the police do not seem to be achieving anything. I have spoken to the sergeant—Evan, I think his name is—but he either knows nothing or he is determined not to tell me." She glanced absently at the frill of the chair arm. "Will you speak to them, if they wish to ask you anything?"

Beatrice looked up at the chandelier above the center of the room. It was unlit this early in the afternoon, but the last rays of the lowering sun caught one or two of its crystals.

"I can hardly refuse. It would seem as if I did not wish to help them."

"They would certainly think so," Araminta agreed, watching her mother intently. "And they could not be criticized for it." She hesitated, her voice hard-edged, slow and very quiet, every word distinct. "After all, we know it was someone in the house, and while it may be one of the servants—my own opinion is that it was probably Percival—"

"Percival?" Beatrice stiffened and turned to look at her daughter. "Why?"

Araminta did not meet her mother's eyes but stared somewhere an inch or two to the left. "Mama, this is hardly the time for comfortable pretenses. It is too late."

"I don't know what you mean," Beatrice answered miserably, hunching up her knees.

"Of course you do." Araminta was impatient. "Percival is an arrogant and presumptuous creature who has the normal appetites of a man and considerable delusions as to where he may exercise them. And you may choose not to see it, but Octavia was flattered by his admiration of her—and not above encouraging him now and then—"

Beatrice winced with revulsion. "Really, Minta."

"I know it is sordid," Araminta said more gently, assurance gathering in her voice. "But it seems that someone in this house killed her—which is very hard, Mama, but we won't alter it by pretending. It will only get worse, until the police find whoever it is."

Beatrice narrowed her shoulders and leaned forward, hugging her legs, staring straight ahead of her.

"Mama?" Araminta said very carefully. "Mama—do you know something?"

Beatrice said nothing, but held herself even more tightly. It was an attitude of absorption with inner pain which Hester had seen often before.

Araminta leaned closer. "Mama—are you trying to protect me . . . because of Myles?"

Slowly Beatrice looked up, stiff, silent, the back of her bright head towards Hester, so similar in color to her daughter's.

Araminta was ashen, her features set, her eyes bright and hard.

"Mama, I know he found Tavie attractive, and that he was not above"—she drew in her breath and let it out slowly—"above going to her room. I like to believe that because I am her sister, she refused him. But I don't know. It is possible he went again—and she rebuffed him. He doesn't take refusal well—as I know."

Beatrice stared at her daughter, slowly stretched out her hand in a gesture of shared pain. But Araminta moved no closer, and she let her hand fall. She said nothing. Perhaps there were no words for what she either knew or dreaded.

"Is that what you are hiding from, Mama?" Araminta asked relentlessly. "Are you afraid someone will ask you if that is what happened?"

Beatrice lay back and straightened the covers around herself before replying. Araminta made no move to help her. "It would be a waste of time to ask me. I don't know, and I certainly should not say anything of that sort." She looked up. "Please, Minta, surely you know that?"

At last Araminta leaned forward and touched her mother, putting her thin, strong hand over hers. "Mama, if it were Myles, then we cannot hide the truth. Please God it was not—and they will find it was someone else . . . soon—" She stopped, her face full of concern, hope struggling with fear, and a desperate concentration.

Beatrice tried to say something comforting, something to dismiss the horror on the edge of both their minds, but in the face of Araminta's courage and unyielding desire for truth, she failed, and remained wordless.

Araminta stood up, leaned over and kissed her very lightly, a mere brushing of the lips on her brow, and left the room.

Beatrice sat still for several minutes, then slowly sank farther down in the bed.

"You can take the tray away, Hester; I don't think I want any tea after all."

So she had not forgotten her nurse was there. Hester did not know whether to be grateful her status gave her such opportunity to observe or insulted that she was of such total unimportance that no one cared what she saw or heard. It was the first time in her life she had been so utterly disregarded, and it stung.

"Yes, Lady Moidore," she said coolly, and picked up the tray, leaving Beatrice alone with her thoughts.

That evening she had a little time to herself, and she spent it in the library. She had dined in the servants' hall. Actually it was one of the best meals she had ever eaten, far richer and more varied than she had experienced in her own home, even when her father's circumstances were very favorable. He had never served more than six courses, the heaviest usually either mutton or beef. Tonight there had been a choice of three meats, and eight courses in all.

She found a book on the peninsular campaigns of the Duke of Wellington, and was deeply engrossed in it when the door opened and Cyprian Moidore came in. He seemed surprised to see her, but not unpleasantly so.

"I am sorry to disturb you, Miss Latterly." He glanced at her book. "I am sure you have well deserved a little time to yourself, but I wanted you to tell me candidly what you think of my mother's health."

He looked concerned, his face marked with anxiety and his eyes unwavering.

She closed the book and he saw the title.

"Good heavens. Couldn't you find anything more interesting than that? We have plenty of novels, and some poetry—farther along to the right, I think."

"Yes I know, thank you. I chose this intentionally." She saw his doubt, then as he realized she was not joking, his puzzlement. "I think Lady Moidore is deeply concerned over the death of your sister," she hurried on. "And of course having the police in the house is unpleasant. But I don't think her health is in any danger of breakdown. Grief always takes a time to run its course. It is natural to be angry, and bewildered, especially when the loss is so unexpected. With an illness at least there is some time to prepare—"

He looked down at the table between them.

"Has she said anything about who she thinks to be responsible?"

"No—but I have not discussed the subject with her—except, of course, I should listen to anything she wished to tell me, if I thought it would relieve her anxiety."

He looked up, a sudden smile on his face. Given another place, away from his family and the oppressive atmosphere of suspicion and defense, and away from her position as a servant, she would have liked him. There was a humor in him, and an intelligence beneath the careful manners.

"You do not think we should call in a doctor?" he pressed.

"I don't believe a doctor could help," she said frankly. She debated whether to tell him the truth of what she believed, or if it would only cause him greater concern and betray that she remembered and weighed what she overheard.

"What is it?" He caught her indecision and knew there was something more. "Please, Miss Latterly?"

She found herself responding from instinct rather than judgment, and a liking for him that was far from a rational decision.

"I think she is afraid she may know who it is who killed Mrs. Haslett, and that it will bring great distress to Mrs. Kellard," she answered. "I think she would rather retreat and keep silent than risk speaking to the police and having them somehow detect what she is thinking." She waited, watching his face.

"Damn Myles!" he said furiously, standing up and turning away. His voice was filled with anger, but there was remarkably little surprise in it. "Papa should have thrown *him* out, not Harry Haslett!" He swung back to face her. "I'm sorry, Miss Latterly. I beg your pardon for my language. I—"

"Please, Mr. Moidore, do not feel the need to apologize," she said quickly. "The circumstances are enough to make anyone with any feeling lose his temper. The constant presence of the police and the interminable wondering, whether it is spoken or not, would be intensely trying to anyone but a fool who had no understanding."

"You are very kind." It was a simple enough word, and yet she knew he meant it as no easy compliment.

"I imagine the newspapers are still writing about it?" she went on, more to fill the silence than because it mattered.

He sat down on the arm of the chair near her. "Every day," he said ruefully. "The better ones are castigating the police, which is unfair; they are no doubt doing all they can. They can hardly subject us to a Spanish Inquisition and torture us until someone confesses—" He laughed jerkily, betraying all his raw pain. "And the press would be the first to complain if they did. In fact it seems they are caught either way in a situation like this. If they are harsh with us they will be accused of forgetting their place and victimizing the gentry, and if they are lenient they will be charged with indifference and incompetence." He drew in his breath and let it out in a sigh. "I should imagine the poor devil curses the day he was clever enough to prove it had to be someone in the house. But he doesn't look like a man who takes the easy path—"

"No, indeed," Hester agreed with more memory and heart than Cyprian could know.

"And the sensational ones are speculating on every sordid possibility they can think up," he went on with distaste puckering his mouth and bringing a look of hurt to his eyes.

Suddenly Hester caught a glimpse of how deeply the whole intrusion was affecting him, the ugliness of it all pervading his life like a foul smell. He was keeping the pain within, as he had been taught since the nursery. Little boys are expected to be brave, never to complain, and above all never, never to cry. That was effeminate and a sign of weakness to be despised.

"I'm so sorry," she said gently. She reached out her hand and put it over his, closing her fingers, before she remembered she was not a nurse comforting a wounded man in hospital, she was a servant and a woman, putting her hand over her employer's in the privacy of his own library.

But if she withdrew it and apologized now she would only draw attention to the act and make it necessary for him to respond. They would both be embarrassed, and it would rob the moment of its understanding and create of it a lie.

Instead she sat back slowly with a very slight smile.

She was prevented from having to think what to say next by the library door opening and Romola coming in. She glanced at them together and instantly her face darkened.

"Should you not be with Lady Moidore?" she said sharply.

Her tone stung Hester, who kept her temper with an effort. Had she been free to, she would have replied with equal acerbity.

"No, Mrs. Moidore, her ladyship said I might have the evening to do as I chose. She decided to retire early."

"Then she must be unwell," Romola returned immediately. "You should be where she can call you if she needs you. Perhaps you could read in your bedroom, or write letters. Don't you have friends or family who will be expecting to hear from you?"

Cyprian stood up. "I'm sure Miss Latterly is quite capable of organizing her own correspondence, Romola. And she cannot read without first coming to the library to choose a book."

Romola's eyebrows rose sarcastically. "Is that what you were doing, Miss Latterly? Forgive me, that was not what appearances suggested."

"I was answering Mr. Moidore's questions concerning his mother's health," Hester said very levelly.

"Indeed? Well if he is now satisfied you may return to your room and do whatever it is you wish."

Cyprian drew breath to reply, but his father came in, glanced at their faces, and looked inquiringly at his son.

"Miss Latterly believes that Mama is not seriously ill," Cyprian said with embarrassment, obviously fishing for a palatable excuse.

"Did anyone imagine she was?" Basil asked dryly, coming into the middle of the room.

"I did not," Romola said quickly. "She is suffering, of course— but so are we all. I know I haven't slept properly since it happened."

"Perhaps Miss Latterly would give you something that would help?" Cyprian suggested with a glance at Hester—and the shadow of a smile.

"Thank you, I shall manage by myself," Romola snapped. "And I intend to go and visit Lady Killin tomorrow afternoon."

"It is too soon," Basil said before Cyprian could speak. "I think you should remain at home for another month at least. By all means receive her if she calls here."

"She won't call," Romola said angrily. "She will certainly feel uncomfortable and uncertain what to say—and one can hardly blame her for that."

"That is not material." Basil had already dismissed the matter.

"Then I shall call on her," Romola repeated, watching her father-in-law, not her husband.

Cyprian turned to speak to her, remonstrate with her, but again Basil overrode him.

"You are tired," he said coldly. "You had better retire to your room—and spend a quiet day tomorrow." There was no mistaking that it was an order. Romola stood as if undecided for a moment, but there was never any doubt in the issue. She would do as she was told, both tonight and tomorrow. Cyprian and his opinions were irrelevant.

Hester was acutely embarrassed, not for Romola, who had behaved childishly and deserved to be reproved, but for Cyprian, who had been disregarded totally. She turned to Basil.

"If you will excuse me, sir, I will retire also. Mrs. Moidore made the suggestion that I should be in my room, in case Lady Moidore should need me." And with a brief nod at Cyprian, hardly meeting his eyes so she did not see his humiliation, and clutching her book, Hester went out across the hall and up the stairs.

Sunday was quite unlike any other day in the Moidore house, as indeed was the case the length and breadth of England. The ordinary duties of cleaning grates and lighting and stoking fires had to be done, and of course breakfast was served. Prayers were briefer than usual because all those who could would be going to church at least once in the day.

Beatrice chose not to be well enough, and no one argued with her, but she insisted that Hester should ride with the family and attend services. It was preferable to her going in the evening with the upper servants, when Beatrice might well need her.

Luncheon was a very sober affair with little conversation, according to Dinah's report, and the afternoon was spent in letter writing, or in Basil's case, he put on his smoking jacket and retired to the smoking room to think or perhaps to doze. Books and newspapers were forbidden as unfitting the sabbath, and the children were not allowed to play with their toys or to read, except Scripture, or to indulge in any games. Even musical practice was deemed inappropriate.

Supper was to be cold, to permit Mrs. Boden and the other upper servants to attend church. Afterwards the evening would be occupied by Bible reading, presided over by Sir Basil. It was a day in which no one seemed to find pleasure.

It brought childhood flooding back to Hester, although her father at his most pompous had never been so unrelievedly joyless. Since leaving home for the Crimea, although it was not so very long ago, she had forgotten how rigorously such rules were enforced. War did not allow such indulgences, and caring for the sick did not stop even for the darkness of night, let alone a set day of the week.

Hester spent the afternoon in the study writing letters. She would have been permitted to use the ladies' maids' sitting room, had she wished, but Beatrice did not need her, having decided to sleep, and it would be easier to write away from Mary's and Gladys's chatter.

She had written to Charles and Imogen, and to several of her friends from Crimean days, when Cyprian came in. He did not seem surprised to see her, and apologized only perfunctorily for the intrusion.

"You have a large family, Miss Latterly?" he said, noticing the pile of letters.

"Oh no, only a brother," she said. "The rest are to friends with whom I nursed during the war."

"You formed such friendships?" he asked curiously, interest quickening in his face. "Do you not find it difficult to settle back into life in England after such violent and disturbing experiences?"

She smiled, in mockery at herself rather than at him.

"Yes I do," she admitted candidly. "One had so much more responsibility; there was little time for artifice or standing upon ceremony. It was a time of so many things: terror, exhaustion, freedom, friendship that crossed all the normal barriers, honesty such as one cannot normally afford—''

He sat facing her, balancing on the arm of one of the easy chairs.

"I have read a little of the war in the newspapers," he said with a pucker between his brows. "But one never knows how accurate the accounts are. I fear they tell us very much what they wish us to believe. I don't suppose you have read any—no, of course not."

"Yes I have!" she contradicted immediately, forgetting in the heat of the discourse how improper it was for well-bred women to have access to anything but the social pages of a newspaper.

But he was not shocked, only the more interested.

"Indeed, one of the bravest and most admirable men I nursed was a war correspondent with one of London's best newspapers," she went on. "When he was too ill to write himself, he would dictate to me, and I sent his dispatches for him."

"Good gracious. You do impress me, Miss Latterly," he said sincerely. "If you can spare time, I should be most interested to hear some of your opinions upon what you saw. I have heard rumors of great incompetence and a terrible number of unnecessary deaths, but then others say such stories are spread by the disaffected and the troublemakers wishing to advance their own cause at the expense of others."

"Oh, there is some of that too," she agreed, setting her quill and paper aside. He seemed so genuinely concerned it gave her a distinct pleasure to recount to him both some of what she had seen and experienced and the conclusions she had drawn from it.

He listened with total attention, and his few questions were perceptive and made with both pity and a wry humor she found most attractive. Away from the influence of his family, and for an hour forgetting his sister's death and all the misery and suspicion it brought in its wake, he was a man of individual ideas, some quite innovative with regard to social conditions and the terms of agreement and service between the governed and the governing.

They were deep in discussion and the shadows outside were lengthening when Romola came in, and although they were both aware of her, it was several minutes before they let go of the topic of argument and acknowledged her presence.

"Papa wishes to speak to you," she said with a frown. "He is waiting in the withdrawing room."

Reluctantly Cyprian rose to his feet and excused himself from Hester as if she had been a much regarded friend, not a semiservant.

When he had gone Romola looked at Hester with perplexed concern in her smooth face. Her complexion really was very lovely and her features perfectly proportioned, all except her lower lip, which was a trifle full and drooped at the corners sometimes, giving her a discontented look in repose, especially when she was tired.

"Really, Miss Latterly, I don't know how to express myself without seeming critical, or how to offer advice where it may not be desired. But if you wish to obtain a husband, and surely all natural women must, then you will have to learn to master this intellectual and argumentative side of your nature. Men do not find it in the least attractive in a woman. It makes them uncomfortable. It is not restful and does not make a man feel at his ease or as if you give proper deference to his judgment. One does not wish to appear opinionated! That would be quite dreadful."

She moved a stray hair back into its pins with a skilled hand.

"I can remember my mama advising me when I was a girl—it is most unbecoming in a woman to be agitated about anything. Almost all men dislike agitation and anything that detracts from a woman's image as serene, dependable, innocent of all vulgarity or meanness, never critical of anything except slovenliness or unchastity, and above all never contradictory towards a man, even if you should think him mistaken. Learn how to run your household, how to eat elegantly, how to dress well and deport yourself with dignity and charm, the correct form of address for everyone in society, and a little painting or drawing, as much music as you can master, especially singing if you have any gift at all, some needlework, an elegant hand with a pen, and a pleasing turn of phrase for a letter—and above all how to be obedient and control your temper no matter how you may be provoked.

"If you do all these things, Miss Latterly, you will marry as well as your comeliness and your station in life allow, and you will make your husband happy. Therefore you also will be happy." She shook her head very slightly. "I fear you have quite a way to go."

Hester achieved the last of these admonitions instantly, and kept her temper in spite of monstrous provocation.

"Thank you, Mrs. Moidore," she said after taking a deep breath. "I fear perhaps I am destined to remain single, but I shall not forget your advice."

"Oh, I hope not," Romola said with deep sympathy. "It is a most unnatural state for a woman. Learn to bridle your tongue, Miss Latterly, and never give up hope."

Fortunately, upon that final piece of counsel she went back to the withdrawing room, leaving Hester boiling with words unsaid. And yet she was curiously perplexed, and her temper crippled by a sense of pity that did not yet know its object, only that there was confusion and unhappiness and she was sharply aware of it.

Hester took the opportunity to rise early the following day and find herself small tasks around the kitchen and laundry in the hope of improving her acquaintance with some of the other servants—and whatever knowledge they might have. Even if the pieces seemed to them to be meaningless, to Monk they might fit with other scraps to form a picture.

Annie and Maggie were chasing each other up the stairs and falling over in giggles, stuffing their aprons in their mouths to stop the sound from carrying along the landing.

"What's entertained you so early?" Hester asked with a smile.

They both looked at her, wide-eyed and shaking with laughter.

"Well?" Hester said, without criticism in her tone. "Can't you share it? I could use a joke myself."

"Mrs. Sandeman," Maggie volunteered, pushing her fair hair out of her eyes. "It's those papers she's got, miss. You never seen anything like it, honest, such tales as'd curdle your blood—and goings-on between men and women as'd make a street girl blush."

"Indeed?" Hester raised her eyebrows. "Mrs. Sandeman has some very colorful reading?"

"Mostly purple, I'd say." Annie grinned.

"Scarlet," Maggie corrected, and burst into giggles again.

"Where did you get this?" Hester asked her, holding the paper and trying to keep a sober face.

"Out of her room when we cleaned it," Annie replied with transparent innocence.

"At this time in the morning?" Hester said doubtfully. "It's only half past six. Don't tell me Mrs. Sandeman is up already?"

"Oh no. 'Course not. She doesn't get up till lunchtime," Maggie said quickly. "Sleeping it off, I shouldn't wonder."

"Sleeping what off?" Hester was not going to let it go. "She wasn't out yesterday evening."

"She gets tiddly in her room," Annie replied. "Mr. Thirsk brings it to her from the cellar. I dunno why; I never thought he liked her. But I suppose he must do, to pinch port wine for her—and the best stuff too."

"He takes it because he hates Sir Basil, stupid!" Maggie said sharply. "That's why he takes the best. One of these days Sir Basil's going to send Mr. Phillips for a bottle of old port, and there isn't going to be any left. Mrs. Sandeman's drunk it all."

"I still don't think he likes her," Annie insisted. "Have you seen the way his eyes are when he looks at her?"

"Perhaps he had a fancy for her?" Maggie said hopefully, a whole new vista of speculation opening up before her imagination. "And she turned him down, so now he hates her."

"No." Annie was quite sure. "No, I think he despises her. He used to be a pretty good soldier, you know—I mean something special—before he had a tragic love affair."

"How do you know?" Hester demanded. "I'm sure he didn't tell you."

" 'Course not. I heard 'er ladyship talking about it to Mr. Cyprian. I think he thinks she's disgusting—not like a lady should be at all." Her eyes grew wider. "What if she made an improper advance to him, and he was revolted and turned her down?"

"Then she should hate him," Hester pointed out.

"Oh, she does," Annie said instantly. "One of these days she'll tell Sir Basil about him taking the port, you'll see. Only maybe she'll be so squiffy by then he won't believe her."

Hester seized the opportunity, and was half ashamed of doing it. "Who do you think killed Mrs. Haslett?"

Their smiles vanished.

"Well, Mr. Cyprian's much too nice, an' why would he anyway?" Annie dismissed him. "Mrs. Moidore never takes that much notice of anyone else to hate them. Nor does Mrs. Sandeman—"

"Unless Mrs. Haslett knew something disgraceful about her?" Maggie offered. "That's probably it. I reckon Mrs. Sandeman would stick a knife into you if you threatened to split on her."

"True," Annie agreed. Then her face sobered and she lost all the imagination and the banter. "Honestly, miss, we think it's likely Percival, who has airs about himself in that department, and fancied Mrs. Haslett. Thinks he's one dickens of a fellow, he does."

"Thinks God made him as a special gift for women." Maggie sniffed with scorn. " 'Course there's some daft enough to let him. Then God doesn't know much about women, is all I can say."

"And Rose," Annie went on. "She's got a real thing for Percival. Really taken bad with him—the more fool her."

"Then why would she kill Mrs. Haslett?" Hester asked.

"Jealousy, of course." They both looked at her as if she were slow-witted.

Hester was surprised. "Did Percival really have that much of a fancy for Mrs. Haslett? But he's a footman, for goodness' sake."

"Tell him that," Annie said with deep disgust.

Nellie, the little tweeny maid, came scurrying up the stairs with a broom in one hand and a pail of cold tea leaves in the other, ready to scatter them on the carpets to lay the dust.

"Why aren't you sweeping?" she demanded, looking at the two older girls. "If Mrs. Willis catches me at eight and we 'aven't done this it'll be trouble. I don't want to go to bed without me tea."

The housekeeper's name was enough to galvanize both the girls into instant action, and they left Hester on the landing while they ran downstairs for their own brooms and dusters.

In the kitchen an hour later, Hester prepared a breakfast tray for Beatrice, just tea, toast, butter and apricot preserve. She was thanking the gardener for one of the very last of the late roses for the silver vase when she passed Sal, the red-haired kitchen maid, laughing loudly and nudging the footman from next door, who had sneaked over, ostensibly with a message from his cook for hers. The two of them were flirting with a lot of poking and slapping on the doorstep, and Sal's loud voice could be heard up the scullery steps and along the passage to the kitchen.

"That girl's no better than she should be," Mrs. Boden said with a shake of her head. "You mark my words—she's a trollop, if ever I saw one. Sal!" she shouted. "Come back in here and get on with your work!" She looked at Hester again. "She's an idle piece. It's a wonder how I put up with her. I don't know what the world's coming to." She picked up the meat knife and tested it with her finger. Hester looked at the blade and swallowed with a shiver when she thought that maybe it was the knife someone had held in his hands creeping up the stairs in the night to stab Octavia Haslett to death.

Mrs. Boden found the edge satisfactory and pulled over the slab of steak to begin slicing it ready for the pie.

"What with Miss Octavia's death, and now policemen creeping all over the house, everyone scared o' their own shadows, 'er ladyship took to 'er bed, and a good-for-nothing baggage like Sal in my kitchen—it's enough to make a decent woman give up."

"I'm sure you won't," Hester said, trying to soothe her. If she was going to be responsible for luring two housemaids away, she did not want to add to the domestic chaos by encouraging the cook to desert as well. "The police will go in time, the whole matter will be settled, her ladyship will recover, and you are quite capable of disciplining Sal. She cannot be the first wayward kitchen maid you've trained into being thoroughly competent—in time."

"Well now, you're right about that," Mrs. Boden agreed. "I 'ave a good 'and with girls, if I do say so myself. But I surely wish the police would find out who did it and arrest them. I don't sleep safe in my bed, wondering. I just can't believe anyone in the family would do such a thing. I've been in this house since before Mr. Cyprian was born, never mind Miss Octavia and Miss Araminta. I never did care a great deal for Mr. Kellard, but I expect he has his qualities, and he is a gentleman, after all."

"You think it as one of the servants?" Hester affected surprise, and considerable respect, as though Mrs. Boden's opinion on such matters weighed heavily with her.

"Stands to reason, don't it?" Mrs. Boden said quietly, slicing the steak with expert strokes, quick, light and extremely powerful. "And it wouldn't be any of the girls—apart from anything else, why would they?"

"Jealousy?" Hester suggested innocently.

"Nonsense." Mrs. Boden reached for the kidneys. "They wouldn't be so daft. Sal never goes upstairs. Lizzie is a bossy piece and wouldn't give a halfpenny to a blind man, but she knows right from wrong, and sticks by it whatever. Rose is a willful creature, always wants what she can't 'ave, and I wouldn't put it past her to do something wild, but not that." She shook her head. "Not murder. Too afraid of what'd happen to her, apart from anything else. Fond of 'er own skin, that one."

"And not the upstairs girls," Hester added instinctively, then wished she had waited for Mrs. Boden to speak.

"They can be silly bits of things," Mrs. Boden agreed. "But no harm in them, none at all. And Dinah's far too mild to do anything so passionate. Nice girl, but bland as a cup of tea. Comes from a nice family in the country somewhere. Too pretty maybe, but that's parlormaids for you. And Mary and Gladys—well, that Mary's got a temper, but it's all flash and no heat. She wouldn't harm anyone—and wouldn't have any call to. Very fond of Miss Octavia, she was, very fond—and Miss Octavia of her too. Gladys is a sourpuss, puts on airs—but that's ladies' maids. No viciousness in her, least not that much. Wouldn't 'ave the courage either."

"Harold?" Hester asked. She did not even bother to mention Mr. Phillips, not because he could not have done it, but because Mrs. Boden's natural loyalties to a servant she considered of her own seniority would prevent her from entertaining the possibility with any open-mindedness.

Mrs. Boden gave her an old-fashioned look. "And what for, may I ask? What would Harold be doing in Miss Octavia's room in the middle of the night? He can't see any girl but Dinah, the poor boy, not but it'll do him a ha'porth of good."

"Percival?" Hester said the inevitable.

"Must be." Mrs. Boden pushed away the last of the kidney and reached for the mixing bowl full of pastry dough. She tipped the dough out onto the board, floured it thoroughly and began to roll it out with the wooden pin, brisk, sharp strokes first one way, then turned it with a single movement and started in the other direction. "Always had ideas above himself, that one, but never thought it would go this far. Got a sight more money than I can account for," she added viciously. "Nasty streak in him. Seen it a few times. Now your kettle's boiling, don't let it fill my kitchen with steam."

"Thank you." Hester turned and went to the range, picking the kettle off the hob with a potholder and first scalding the teapot, then swilling it out and making the tea with the rest of the water.

Monk returned to Queen Anne Street because he and Evan had exhausted every other avenue of possible inquiry. They had not found the missing jewelry, nor had they expected to, but it was obligatory that they pursue it to the end, even if only to satisfy Runcorn. They had also taken the character references of every servant in the Moidore house and checked with all their previous employers, and found no blemish of character that was in the slightest way indicative of violence of emotion or action to come. There were no dark love affairs, no accusations of theft or immorality, nothing but very ordinary lives of domesticity and work.

Now there was nowhere to look except back in Queen Anne Street among the servants yet again. Monk stood in the housekeeper's sitting room waiting impatiently for Hester. He had again given Mrs. Willis no reason for asking to see the nurse, a woman who was not even present at the time of the crime. He was aware of her surprise and considerable criticism. He would have to think of some excuse before he saw her again.

There was a knock on the door.

"Come," he ordered.

Hester came in and closed the door behind her. She looked neat and professional, her hair tied back severely and her dress plain gray-blue stuff and undecorated, her apron crisp white. Her costume was both serviceable and more than a little prudish.

"Good morning," she said levelly.

"Good morning," he replied, and without preamble started to ask her about the days since he had last seen her, his manner more curt than he would have chosen, simply because she was so similar to her sister-in-law, Imogen, and yet so different, so lacking in mystery and feminine grace.

She was recounting her duties and all that she had seen or overheard.

"All of which tells me only that Percival is not particularly well liked," he said tartly. "Or simply that everyone is afraid and he seems the most likely scapegoat."

"Quite," she agreed briskly. "Have you a better idea?"

Her very reasonableness caught him on a raw nerve. He was

acutely aware of his failure to date, and that he had nowhere else to look but here.

"Yes!" he snapped back. "Take a better look at the family. Find out more about Fenella Sandeman, for one. Have you any idea where she goes to indulge her disreputable tastes, if they really are disreputable? She stands to lose a lot if Sir Basil throws her out. Octavia might have found out that afternoon. Maybe that was what she was referring to when she spoke to Septimus. And see if you can find out whether Myles Kellard really did have an affair with Octavia, or if it is just malicious gossip among servants with idle tongues and busy imaginations. It seems they don't lack for either."

"Don't give me orders, Mr. Monk." She looked at him frostily. "I am not your sergeant."

"Constable, ma'am," he corrected with a sour smile. "You have promoted yourself unwarrantably. You are not my constable."

She stiffened, her shoulders square, almost military, her face angry.

"Whatever the rank I do not hold, Mr. Monk, I think the main reason for suggesting that Percival may have killed Octavia is the belief that he either was having an affair with her or was attempting to."

"And he killed her for that?" He raised his eyebrows in sarcastic inquiry.

"No," she said patiently. "Because she grew tired of him, and they quarreled, I suppose. Or possibly the laundrymaid Rose did, in jealousy. She is in love with Percival—or perhaps *love* is not the right word—something rather cruder and more immediate, I think, would be more accurate. Although I don't know how you can prove it."

"Good. For a moment I was afraid you were about to instruct me."

"I would not presume—not until I am at least a sergeant." And with a swing of her skirt she turned and went out.

It was ridiculous. It was not the way he had intended the interview to go, but something about her so frequently annoyed him, an arbitrariness. A large part of his anger was because she was in some degree correct, and she knew it. He had no idea how to prove Percival's guilt—if indeed he was guilty.

Evan was busy talking to the grooms, not that he had anything else specific to ask them. Monk spoke to Phillips, learning nothing, then sent for Percival.

This time the footman looked far more nervous. Monk had seen the tense shoulders tight and a little high, the hands that were never quite still, the fine beading of sweat on the lips, and the wary eyes. It meant nothing, except that Percival had enough intelligence to know the circle was closing and he was not liked. They were all frightened for themselves, and the sooner someone was charged, the sooner life could begin to settle to normality again, and safety. The police would go, and the awful, sick suspicion would die away. They could look each other straight in the eye again.

"You're a handsome fellow." Monk looked him up and down with anything but approval. "I gather footmen are often picked for their looks."

Percival met his eyes boldly, but Monk could almost smell his fear.

"Yes sir."

"I imagine quite a few women are enamored of you, in one way or another. Women are often attracted by good looks."

A flicker of a smirk crossed Percival's dark face and died away.

"Yes sir, from time to time."

"You must have experienced it?"

Percival relaxed a fraction, his body easing under his livery jacket. "That's true."

"Is it ever an embarrassment?"

"Not often. You get used to it."

Conceited swine, Monk thought, but perhaps not without cause. He had a suppressed vitality and a sort of insolence Monk imagined many women might find exciting.

"You must have to be very discreet?" he said aloud.

"Yes sir." Percival was quite amused now, off his guard, pleased with himself as memories came to mind.

"Especially if it's a lady, not merely one of the maids?" Monk went on. "Must be awkward for you if a visiting lady is . . . interested?"

"Yes sir—have to be careful."

"I imagine men get jealous?"

Percival was puzzled; he had not forgotten why he was here. Monk could see the thoughts flicker across his face, and none of them provided explanation.

"I suppose they might," he said carefully.

"Might?" Monk raised his eyebrows. His voice was patronizing, sarcastic. "Come, Percival, if you were a gentleman, wouldn't you be jealous as the grave if your fine lady preferred the attentions of the footman to yours?"

This time the smirk was unmistakable, the thought was too sweet, the most delicious of all superiorities, better, closer to the essence of a man than even money or rank.

"Yes sir—I imagine I would be."

"Especially over a woman as comely as Mrs. Haslett?"

Now Percival was confused. "She was a widow, sir. Captain Haslett died in the war." He shifted his weight uncomfortably. "And she didn't have any admirers that were serious. She wouldn't look at anyone—still grieving over the captain."

"But she was a young woman, used to married life, and handsome," Monk pressed.

The light was back in Percival's face. "Oh yes," he agreed. "But she didn't want to marry again." He sobered quickly. "And anyway, nobody's threatened me—it was her that was killed. And there wasn't anyone close enough to be that jealous. Anyhow, even if there was, there wasn't anyone else in the house that night."

"But if there had been, would they have had cause to be jealous?" Monk screwed up his face as if the answer mattered and he had found some precious clue.

"Well—" Percival's lips curled in a satisfied smile. "Yes—I suppose they would." His eyes widened hopefully. "Was there someone here, sir?"

"No." Monk's expression changed and all the lightness vanished. "No. I simply wanted to know if you had had an affair with Mrs. Haslett."

Suddenly Percival understood and the blood fled from his skin, leaving him sickly pale. He struggled for words and could only make strangled sounds in his throat.

Monk knew the moment of victory and the instinct to kill; it was as familiar as pain, or rest, or the sudden shock of cold water, a memory in his flesh as well as his mind. And he despised himself for it. This was the old self surfacing through the cloud of forgetting since the accident; this was the man the records showed, who was admired and feared, who had no friends.

And yet this arrogant little footman might have murdered Octavia

Haslett in a fit of lust and male conceit. Monk could not afford to indulge his own conscience at the cost of letting him go.

"Did she change her mind?" he asked with all the old edge to his voice, a world of biting contempt. "Suddenly saw the ridiculous vulgarity of an amorous adventure with a footman?"

Percival called him something obscene under his breath, then his chin came up and his eyes blazed.

"Not at all," he said cockily, his terror mastered at least on the surface. His voice shook, but his speech was perfectly clear. "If it was anything to do with me, it'd be Rose, the laundrymaid. She's infatuated with me, and jealous as death. She might have gone upstairs in the night with a kitchen knife and killed Mrs. Haslett. She had reason to—I hadn't."

"You are a real gentleman." Monk curled his lip with disgust, but it was a possibility he could not ignore, and Percival knew it. The sweat of relief was glistening on the footman's brow.

"All right." Monk dismissed him. "You can go for now."

"Do you want me to send Rose in?" he asked at the door.

"No I don't. And if you want to survive here, you'll do well not to tell anyone of this conversation. Lovers who suggest their mistresses for murder are not well favored by other people."

Percival made no reply, but he did not look guilty, just relieved—and careful.

Swine, Monk thought, but he could not blame him entirely. The man was cornered, and too many other hands were turning against him, not necessarily because they thought he was guilty, but someone was, and that person was afraid.

At the end of another day of interviews, all except that with Percival proving fruitless, Monk started off towards the police station to report to Runcorn, not that he had anything conclusive to say, simply that Runcorn had demanded it.

He was walking the last mile in the crisp late-autumn afternoon, trying to formulate in his mind what he would say, when he passed a funeral going very slowly north up Tottenham Court Road towards the Euston Road. The hearse was drawn by four black horses with black plumes, and through the glass he could see the coffin was covered with flowers. There must have been pounds and pounds worth.

He could imagine the perfume of them, and the care that had gone into raising them in a hothouse at this time of the year.

Behind the hearse were three other carriages packed full with mourners, all in black, and again there was a sudden stab of familiarity. He knew why they were crammed elbow to elbow, and the harnesses so shiny, no crests on the carriage doors. It was a poor man's funeral; the carriages were hired, but no expense had been spared. There would be black horses, no browns or bays would do. There would be flowers from everyone, even if there was nothing to eat for the rest of the week and they sat by cold hearths in the evening. Death must have its due, and the neighborhood must not be let down by a poor show, a hint of meanness. Poverty must be concealed at all costs. They would mourn properly as a last tribute.

He stood on the pavement with his hat off and watched them go past with a feeling close to tears, not for the unknown corpse, or even for those who were bereaved, but for everyone who cared so desperately what others thought of them, and for the shadows and flickers of his own past that he saw in it. Whatever his dreams, he was part of these people, not of those in Queen Anne Street or their like. He had fine clothes now, ate well enough and owned no house and had no family, but his roots were in close streets where everyone knew each other, weddings and funerals involved them all, they knew every birth or sickness, the hopes and the losses, there was no privacy and no loneliness.

Who was it whose face had come so clearly for an instant as he waited outside the club Piccadilly, and why had he wanted so intensely to emulate him, not only his intellect, but even his accent of speech and his manner of dress and gait in walking?

He looked again at the mourners, seeking some sense of identity with them, and as the last carriage passed slowly by he caught a glimpse of a woman's face, very plain, nose too broad, mouth wide and eyebrows low and level, and it struck a familiarity in him so sharp it left him gasping, and another homely face came back to his mind and then was gone again, an ugly woman with tears on her cheeks and hands so lovely he never tired of looking at them, or lost his intense pleasure in their delicacy and grace. And he was wounded with an old guilt, and he had no idea why, or how long ago it had been.

CHAPTER
SEVEN

———

Araminta was very composed as she stood in front of Monk in the boudoir, that room of ease and comfort especially for the women of the house. It was ornately decorated with lush French Louis XVI furniture, all scrolls and curlicues, gilt and velvet. The curtains were brocade and the wallpaper pink embossed in gold. It was an almost oppressively feminine room, and Araminta looked out of place in it, not for her appearance, which was slender and delicately boned with a flame of hair, but for her stance. It was almost aggressive. There was nothing yielding in her, nothing soft to compliment all the sweetness of the pink room.

"I regret having to tell you this, Mr. Monk." She looked at him unflinchingly. "My sister's reputation is naturally dear to me, but in our present stress and tragedy I believe only the truth will serve. Those of us who are hurt by it will have to endure the best we may."

He opened his mouth to try to say something at once soothing and encouraging, but apparently she did not need any word from him. She continued, her face so controlled there was no apparent tension, no quiver to the lips or voice.

"My sister, Octavia, was a very charming person, and very affectionate." She was choosing her words with great care; this was a speech which had been rehearsed before he came. "Like most people who are pleasing to others, she enjoyed admiration, indeed she had a hunger for it. When her husband, Captain Haslett, was killed in the Crimea she was, of course, deeply grieved. But that was nearly two years ago, and that is a long time for a young woman of Octavia's nature to be alone."

This time he did not interrupt, but waited for her to continue, only showing his total attention by his unwavering gaze.

The only way her inner feelings showed was a curious stillness, as if something inside her dared not move.

"What I am endeavoring to say, Mr. Monk, much as it pains me, and all my family, is that Octavia from time to time would encourage from the footman an admiration that was personal, and of a more familiar nature than it should have been."

"Which footman, ma'am?" He would not put Percival's name in her mouth.

A flash of irritation tweaked her mouth. "Percival of course. Do not affect to be a fool with me, Mr. Monk. Does Harold look like a man to have airs above his station? Besides which, you have been in this house quite long enough to have observed that Harold is taken with the parlormaid and not likely to see anyone else in that light—for all the good it will do him." She jerked her shoulders sharply, as if to shrug off the distasteful idea. "Still, she is very likely not the charming creature he imagines, and he may well be better served by dreams than he would be by the disillusion of reality." For the first time she looked away from him. "I daresay she is very bland and tedious once you are tired of looking at her pretty face."

Had Araminta been a plain woman Monk might have suspected her of envy, but since she was in her own way quite remarkably fine it could not be so.

"Impossible dreams always end in awakening," he agreed. "But he may grow out of his obsession before he meets with any reality. Let us hope so."

"It is hardly important," she said, swinging back to face him and recall him to the subject that mattered. "I have come to inform you of my sister's relationship with Percival, not Harold's moonings after the parlormaid. Since it seems inescapable that someone in this house murdered Octavia, it is relevant that you should know she was over-familiar with the footman."

"Very relevant," he agreed quietly. "Why did you not mention it before, Mrs. Kellard?"

"Because I hoped it would not be necessary, of course," she replied immediately. "It is hardly a pleasant thing to have to admit—least of all to the police."

Whether that was because of the implication for crime, or the indignity of discussing it with someone of the social standing of the police, she did not say, but Monk thought from the lopsided suggestion of a sneer on her mouth that it was the latter.

"Thank you for mentioning it now." He ironed out the anger from his expression as well as he could, and was rewarded, and insulted, that she seemed to notice nothing at all. "I shall investigate the possibility," he concluded.

"Naturally." Her fine golden eyebrows rose. "I did not put myself to the discomfort of telling you for you merely to acknowledge it and do nothing."

He bit back any further comment and contented himself with opening the door for her and bidding her good-day.

He had no alternative but to face Percival, because he had already drawn from everyone else the fragments of knowledge, speculation and judgment of character on the subject. Nothing added now would be proof of anything, only the words of fear, opportunism or malice. And undoubtedly Percival was disliked by some of his fellow servants, for greater or lesser reason. He was arrogant and abrasive and he had played with at least one woman's affections, which produced volatile and unreliable testimony, at best.

When Percival appeared this time his attitude was different; the all-permeating fear was there, but far less powerfully. There was a return of the old confidence in the tilt of his head and the brash directness of his stare. Monk knew immediately there would be no point in even hoping to panic him into confession of anything.

"Sir?" Percival waited expectantly, bristlingly aware of tricks and verbal traps.

"Perhaps discretion kept you from saying so before." Monk did not bother to prevaricate. "But Mrs. Haslett was one of the ladies who had more than an employer's regard for you, was she not?" He smiled with bared teeth. "You need not permit modesty to direct your answer. It has come to me from another source."

Percival's mouth relaxed in something of a smirk, but he did not forget himself.

"Yes sir. Mrs. Haslett was . . . very appreciative."

Monk was suddenly infuriated by the man's complacence, his insufferable conceit. He thought of Octavia lying dead with the blood dark down her robe. She had seemed so vulnerable, so helpless to protect herself—which was ridiculous, since she was the one person in all of this tragedy who was now beyond pain or the petty fancies of dignity. But he bitterly resented this grubby little man's ease of reference to her, his self-satisfaction, even his thoughts.

"How gratifying for you," he said acidly. "If occasionally embarrassing."

"No sir," Percival said quickly, but there was a smugness to his face. "She was very discreet."

"But of course," Monk agreed, loathing Percival the more. "She was, after all, a lady, even if she occasionally forgot it."

Percival's narrow mouth twitched with irritation. Monk's contempt had reached him. He did not like being reminded that it was beneath a lady to admire a footman in that way.

"I don't expect you to understand," Percival said with a sneer. He looked Monk up and down and stood a little straighter himself, his opinion in his eyes.

Monk had no idea what ladies of whatever rank might similarly have admired him; his memory was blank but his temper burned.

"I can imagine," he replied viciously. "I've arrested a few whores from time to time."

Percival's cheeks flamed but he dared not say what came to his mind. He stared back with brilliant eyes.

"Indeed sir? I expect your job brings you into company of a great many people I have no experience of at all. Very regrettable." Now his eyes were perfectly level and hard. "But like cleaning the drains, someone has to do it."

"Precarious," Monk said with deliberate edge. "Being admired by a lady. Never know where you are. One minute you are the servant, dutiful and respectfully inferior, the next the lover, with hints of being stronger, masterful." He smiled with a sneer like Percival's own. "Then before you know where you are, back to being the footman again, 'Yes ma'am,' 'No ma'am,' and dismissed to your own room whenever my lady is bored or has had enough. Very difficult not to make a mistake—" He was watching Percival's face and the succession of emotions racing across it. "Very hard to keep your temper—"

There it was—the first shadow of real fear, the quick beading of sweat on the lip, the catching of breath.

"I didn't lose my temper," Percival said, his voice cracking and loathing in his eyes. "I don't know who killed her—but it wasn't me!"

"No?" Monk raised his eyebrows very high. "Who else had a

reason? She didn't 'admire' anyone else, did she? She didn't leave any money. We cannot find anything to suggest she knew something shameful about anyone. We can't find anyone who hated her—"

"Because you aren't very clever, are you." Percival's dark eyes were narrow and bright. "I already told you Rose hated her, because she was jealous as a cat over me. And what about Mr. Kellard? Or are you too well trained to dare accuse one of the gentry if you can pin it on a servant?"

"No doubt you would like me to ask why Mr. Kellard should kill Mrs. Haslett." Monk was equally angry, but would not reply to the jibe because that would be to admit it hurt. He would as soon have charged one of the family as a servant, but he knew what Runcorn would feel, and try to drive him to do, and his frustration was equally with him as with Percival. "And you will tell me whether I ask or not, to divert my attention from you."

That robbed Percival of a great deal of his satisfaction, which was what Monk had intended. Nevertheless he could not afford to remain silent.

"Because he had a fancy for Mrs. Haslett," Percival said in a hard, quiet voice. "And the more she declined him, the hotter it got—that's how it is."

"And so he killed her?" Monk said, baring his teeth in something less than a smile. "Seems an odd way of persuading her. Would put her out of his reach permanently, wouldn't it? Or are you supposing a touch of necrophilia?"

"What?"

"Gross relationship with the dead," Monk explained.

"Disgusting." Percival's lip curled.

"Or perhaps he was so infatuated he decided if he could not have her then no one should?" Monk suggested sarcastically. It was not the sort of passion either of them thought Myles Kellard capable of, and he knew it.

"You're playing the fool on purpose," Percival said through thin lips. "You may not be very bright—and the way you've gone about this case surely shows it—but you're not that stupid. Mr. Kellard wanted to lie with her, nothing more. But he's one that won't accept a refusal." He lifted one shoulder. "And if he fancied her and she said she'd tell everyone he'd have to kill her. He couldn't cover that up the way he did with poor Martha. It's one thing to rape a maid, no one cares—but you can't rape your wife's sister and get away with it. Her father won't hide that up for you!"

Monk stared at him. Percival had won his attention without shadow this time, and he knew it; the victory was shining in his narrowed eyes.

"Who is Martha?" Resent it as he might, Monk had no option but to ask.

Percival smiled slowly. He had small, even teeth.

"Was," he corrected. "God knows where she is now—workhouse, if she's alive at all."

"All right, who was she?"

He looked at Monk with a level, jubilant stare.

"Parlormaid before Dinah. Pretty thing, neat and slender, walked like a princess. He took a fancy to her, and wouldn't be told no. Didn't believe she meant it. Raped her."

"How do you know this?" Monk was skeptical, but not totally disbelieving. Percival was too sure of himself for it to be simply a malicious invention, nor was there the sweat of desperation on his skin. He stood easily, his body relaxed, almost excited.

"Servants are invisible," Percival replied, eyes wide. "Don't you know that? Part of the furniture. I overheard Sir Basil when he made some of the arrangements. Poor little bitch was dismissed for being of loose tongue and even looser morals. He got her out of the house before she could tell anyone else. She made the mistake of going to him about it, because she was afraid she was with child—which she was. Funny thing is he didn't even doubt her—he knew she was telling the truth. But he said she must have encouraged him—it was her fault. Threw her out without a reference." He shrugged. "God knows what happened to her."

Monk thought Percival's anger was outrage for his own class rather than pity for the girl, and was ashamed of himself for his judgment. It was harsh and without proof, and yet he did not change it.

"And you don't know where she is now?"

Percival snorted. "A maid without a position or a character, alone in London, and with child? What do you think? Sweatshops wouldn't have her with a child, whorehouses wouldn't either for the same reason. Workhouse, I should think—or the grave."

"What was her full name?"

"Martha Rivett."

"How old was she?"

"Seventeen."

Monk was not surprised, but he felt an almost uncontrollable rage and a ridiculous desire to weep. He did not know why; it was surely more than pity for this one girl whom he had not even met. He must have seen hundreds of others, simple, abused, thrown out without a twinge of guilt. He must have seen their defeated faces, the hope and the death of hope, and he must have seen their bodies dead of hunger, violence and disease.

Why did it hurt? Why was there no skin of callousness grown over it? Was there something, someone who had touched him more closely? Pity—guilt? Perhaps he would never know again. It was gone, like almost everything else.

"Who else knew about it?" he asked, his voice thick with emotion which could have been taken for any of a dozen feelings.

"Only Lady Moidore, so far as I know." A quick spark flashed in Percival's eyes. "But maybe that was what Mrs. Haslett found out." He lifted his shoulders a fraction. "And she threatened to tell Mrs. Kellard? And for that matter maybe she did tell her, that night. . . ." He left it hanging. He did not need to add that Araminta might have killed her sister in a fit of fury and shame to keep her from telling the whole household. The possibilities were many, and all ugly, and nothing to do with Percival or any of the other servants.

"And you told no one?" Monk said with grating unbelief. "You had this extraordinary piece of information, and you kept it the secret the family would wish? You were discreet and obedient. Why, for heaven's sake?" He allowed into his voice an exact mockery of Percival's own contempt for him a few moments earlier. "Knowledge like that is power—you expect me to believe you didn't use it?"

Percival was not discomfited. "I don't know what you mean, sir."

Monk knew he was lying.

"No reason to tell anyone," Percival went on. "Not in my interest." The sneer returned. "Sir Basil wouldn't like it, and then I might find myself in the workhouse. It's different now. This is a matter of duty that any other employer would understand. When it's a matter of concealing a crime—"

"So suddenly rape has become a crime?" Monk was disgusted. "When did that happen? When your own neck was in danger?"

If Percival was frightened or embarrassed there was no trace of it in his expression.

"Not rape, sir—murder. That has always been the crime." Again his shoulders lifted expressively. "If it's actually called murder, not justice, privilege, or some such thing."

"Like rape of a servant, for example." Monk for one instant agreed with him. He hated it. "All right, you can go."

"Shall I tell Sir Basil you want to see him?"

"If you want to keep your position, you'd better not put it like that."

Percival did not bother to reply, but went out, moving easily, even gracefully, his body relaxed.

Monk was too concerned, too angry at the appalling injustice and suffering, and apprehensive of his interview with Basil Moidore to spare any emotion for contempt of Percival.

It was nearly a quarter of an hour before Harold came back to tell him that Sir Basil would see him in the library.

"Good morning, Monk. You wanted to see me?" Basil stood near the window with the armchair and the table forcing a distance between them. He looked harassed and his face creased in lines of temper. Monk irritated him by his questions, his stance, the very shape of his face.

"Good morning, sir," Monk replied. "Yes, some new information has come to me this morning. I would like to ask you if it is true, and if it is, to tell me what you know of the matter."

Basil did not seem concerned, and was only moderately interested. He was still dressed in black, but elegant, self-consciously smart black. It was not the mourning of someone bowed down with grief.

"What matter is this, Inspector?"

"A maid that worked here two years ago, by the name of Martha Rivett."

Basil's face tightened, and he moved from the window and stood straighter.

"What can she possibly have to do with my daughter's death?"

"Was she raped, Sir Basil?"

Basil's eyes widened. Distaste registered sharply in his face, then another, more thoughtful expression. "I have no idea!"

Monk controlled himself with great difficulty. "Did she come to you and say that she had?"

A slight smile moved Basil's mouth, and his hand at his side curled and uncurled.

"Inspector, if you had ever kept a house with a large staff, many of them young, imaginative and excitable women, you would hear a great many stories of all sorts of entanglements, charges and counter-charges of wrongs. Certainly she came and said she had been molested—but I have no way of knowing whether she really had or whether she had got herself with child and was trying to lay the blame on someone else—and get us to look after her. Possibly one of the male servants forced his attentions—" His hands uncurled, and he shrugged very faintly.

Monk bit his tongue and stared at Basil with hard eyes.

"Is that what you believe, sir? You spoke with the girl. I believe she charged that it was Mr. Kellard who assaulted her. Presumably you also spoke with Mr. Kellard. Did he tell you he had never had anything to do with her?"

"Is that your business, Inspector?" Basil said coldly.

"If Mr. Kellard raped this girl, yes, Sir Basil, it is. It may well be the root of this present crime."

"Indeed? I fail to see how." But there was no conciliation in his voice, and no outrage.

"Then I will explain it," Monk said between his teeth. "If Mr. Kellard raped this unfortunate girl, the fact was concealed and the girl dismissed to whatever fate she could find, then that says a great deal about Mr. Kellard's nature and his belief that he is free to force his attentions upon women, regardless of their feelings. It seems highly probable that he admired Mrs. Haslett, and may have tried to force his attentions upon her also."

"And murdered her?" Basil was considering it. There was caution in his voice, the beginning of a new thought, but still heavily tinged with doubt. "Martha never suggested he threatened her with any weapon, and she perfectly obviously had not been injured—"

"You had her examined?" Monk asked baldly.

Temper flashed in Basil's face. "Of course I didn't. Whatever for? She made no claim of violence—I told you that."

"I daresay she considered it of no purpose—and she was right. She charged rape, and was dismissed without a character to live or die in the streets." As soon as he had said it he knew his words were the result of temper, not judgment.

Basil's cheeks darkened with anger. "Some chit of a maid gets with child and accuses my daughter's husband of raping her! For God's sake, man, do you expect me to keep her in the house? Or recommend her to the houses of my friends?" Still he remained at the far side of the room, glaring at Monk across the table and the chair. "I have a duty both to my family, especially my daughter and her happiness, and to my acquaintances. To give any recommendation to a young woman with a character that would charge such a thing of her employer would be completely irresponsible."

Monk wanted to ask him about his duty toward Martha Rivett, but knew that such an affront would very probably cause him just the sort of complaint that Runcorn would delight in, and would give Runcorn an excuse for censure, perhaps even removal from the case.

"You did not believe her, sir?" He was civil with difficulty. "Mr. Kellard denied having any relationship with her?"

"No he didn't," Basil said sharply. "He said she had led him on and was perfectly willing; it was only later when she discovered she was with child she made this charge to protect herself—and I daresay to try and force us to care for her, to stop her spreading about such a story. The girl was obviously of loose character and out to take a chance to profit from it if she could."

"So you put an end to it. I assume you believed Mr. Kellard's account?"

Basil looked at him coldly. "No, as a matter of fact I did not. I think it very probable he forced his attentions on the girl, but that is hardly important now. Men have natural appetites, always have had. I daresay she flirted with him and he mistook her. Are you suggesting he tried the same with my daughter Octavia?"

"It seems possible."

Basil frowned. "And if he did, why should that lead to murder, which is what you seem to be suggesting? If she had struck at him, that would be understandable, but why should he kill her?"

"If she intended telling people," Monk replied. "To rape a maid is apparently acceptable, but would you have viewed it with the same leniency had he raped your daughter? And would Mrs. Kellard, if she knew?"

Basil's face was scored with deep lines, now all dragged downward with distaste and anxiety.

"She does not know," he said slowly, meeting Monk's eyes. "I trust I make myself plain, Inspector? For her to be aware of Myles's indiscretion would distress her, and serve no purpose. He is her husband and will remain so. I don't know what women do in your walk of life, but in ours they bear their difficulties with dignity and silence. Do you understand me?"

"Of course I do," Monk said tartly. "If she does not know now, I shall not tell her unless it become necessary—by which time I imagine it will be common knowledge. Similarly may I ask you, sir, not to forewarn Mr. Kellard of my knowledge in the matter. I can hardly expect him to confess to anything, but I may learn quite a lot from his first reaction when I speak to him about it."

"You expect me to . . ." Basil began indignantly, then his voice faded away as he realized what he was saying.

"I do," Monk agreed with a downward turn of his mouth. "Apart from the ends of justice towards Mrs. Haslett, you and I both know that it was someone in this house. If you protect Mr. Kellard to save scandal—and Mrs. Kellard's feelings—you only prolong the investigation, the suspicion, Lady Moidore's distress—and it will still come down to someone in the house in the end."

For a moment their eyes met, and there was intense dislike—and complete understanding.

"If Mrs. Kellard needs to know, I will be the one to tell her," Basil stated.

"If you wish," Monk agreed. "Although I would not leave it too long. If I can learn of it, so may she—"

Basil jerked upward. "Who told you? It damned well wasn't Myles! Was it Lady Moidore?"

"No, I have not spoken to Lady Moidore."

"Well, don't stand there, man! Who was it?"

"I prefer not to say, sir."

"I don't give a damn what you prefer! Who was it?"

"If you force me, sir—I decline to say."

"You—you what?" He tried to outstare Monk, and then realized he could not intimidate him without a specific threat and that he was not prepared at this point to make one. He looked down again; he was not used to being defied, and he had no ready reaction. "Well pursue your investigation for the moment, but I will know in the end, I promise you."

Monk did not force his victory; it was too tenuous and the temper between them too volatile.

"Yes sir, very possibly. Since she is the only other person you are aware of having known of this, may I speak with Lady Moidore, please?"

"I doubt she can tell you anything. I dealt with the affair."

"I'm sure you did, sir. But she knew of it, and may have observed emotions in people that you did not. She would have opportunities not afforded you, domestic occasions; and women are more sensitive to such things, on the whole."

Basil hesitated.

Monk thought of several arguments: the quick ending of the case, some justice for Octavia—and then caution argued that Octavia was dead and Basil might well think that saving the reputations of those alive was more important. He could do nothing for Octavia now, but he could still protect Araminta from deep shame and hurt. Monk ended by saying nothing.

"Very well," Basil agreed reluctantly. "But have the nurse present, and if Lady Moidore is distressed, you will cease immediately. Is that understood?"

"Yes sir," Monk said instantly. To have Hester's impressions also was an advantage he had not thought to look for. "Thank you."

Again he was required to wait while Beatrice dressed appropriately for receiving the police, and some half an hour later it was Hester herself who came to the morning room to collect him and take him to the withdrawing room.

"Shut the door," he ordered as soon as she was inside.

She obeyed, watching him curiously. "Do you know something?" she asked, her tone guarded, as though whatever it was she would find it only partly welcome.

He waited until the latch was fast and she had returned to the center of the floor.

"There was a maid here about two years ago who charged that Myles Kellard raped her, and she was promptly dismissed without a character."

"Oh—" She looked startled. Obviously she had heard nothing of it from the servants. Then, as amazement dissolved, she was furiously angry, the hot color in her cheeks. "You mean they threw her out? What happened to Myles?"

"Nothing," he said dryly. "What did you expect?"

She stood stiffly, shoulders back, chin high, and stared at him. Then gradually she realized the inevitability of what he had said and that her first thought of justice and open judgment was never a reality.

"Who knows about it?" she asked instead.

"Only Sir Basil and Lady Moidore, so far as I am aware," he replied. "That is what Sir Basil believes, anyway."

"Who told you? Not Sir Basil, surely?"

He smiled with a hard, twisted grimace. "Percival, when he thought I was closing in on him. He certainly won't go docilely into the darkness for them, whatever poor Martha Rivett did. If Percival goes down, he'll do his best to take as many of the rest of them with him as he can."

"I don't like him," she said quietly, looking down. "But I can't blame him for fighting. I think I would. I might suffer injustice for someone I loved—but not for these people, who are only too willing to see him take the blame to get it away from them. What are you going to ask Lady Moidore? You know it's true—"

"I don't," he contradicted. "Myles Kellard says she was a trollop who invited it—Basil doesn't care whether that is true or not. She couldn't stay here after she'd accused Kellard—apart from the fact she was with child. All Basil cared about was clearing up the mess here and protecting Araminta."

The surprise was evident in her face. "She doesn't know?"

"You think she does?" he said quickly.

"She hates him for something. It may not be that—"

"Could be anything," he agreed. "Even so, I can't see how knowing that would be a reason for anyone to murder Octavia—even if the rape was what Octavia found out the day before she was killed."

"Neither do I," she admitted. "There's something very important we don't know yet."

"And I don't suppose I'll learn it from Lady Moidore. Still, I had better go and see her now. I don't want them to suspect we discuss them or they will not speak so freely in front of you. Come."

Obediently she opened the door again and led him across the wide hallway and into the withdrawing room. It was cold and windy outside, and the first drops of heavy rain were beating against the long windows. There was a roaring fire in the hearth, and its glow spread across the red Aubusson carpet and even touched the velvet of the curtains that hung from huge swathed pelmets in swags and rich falls to the fringed sashes, spreading their skirts on the floor.

Beatrice Moidore was seated in the largest chair, dressed in unrelieved black, as if to remind them of her bereaved state. She looked very pale, in spite of her marvelous hair, or perhaps because of it, but her eyes were bright and her manner attentive.

"Good morning, Mr. Monk. Please be seated. I understand you wish to ask me about something?"

"Good morning, Lady Moidore. Yes, if you please. Sir Basil asked that Miss Latterly should remain, in case you feel unwell and need any assistance." He sat down as he had been invited, opposite her in one of the other armchairs. Hester remained standing as suited her station.

A half smile touched Beatrice's lips, as though something he could not understand amused her.

"Most thoughtful," she said expressionlessly. "What is it you would like to ask? I know nothing that I did not know when we last spoke."

"But I do, ma'am."

"Indeed?" This time there was a flicker of fear in her, a shadow across the eyes, a tightness in the white hands in her lap.

Who was it she was frightened for? Not herself. Who else did she care about so much that even without knowing what he had learned she feared for them? Who would she protect? Her children, surely—no one else.

"Are you going to tell me, Mr. Monk?" Her voice was brittle, her eyes very clear.

"Yes ma'am. I apologize for raising what must be a most painful subject, but Sir Basil confirmed that about two years ago one of your maids, a girl called Martha Rivett, claimed that Mr. Kellard raped her." He watched her expression and saw the muscles tighten in her neck and across the high, delicate brows. Her lips pulled crooked in distaste.

"I don't see what that can have to do with my daughter's death. It happened two years ago, and it concerned her in no way at all. She did not even know of it."

"Is it true, ma'am? Did Mr. Kellard rape the parlormaid?"

"I don't know. My husband dismissed her, so I assume she was at least in great part to blame for whatever happened. It is quite possible." She took a deep breath and swallowed. He saw the constricted movement of her throat. "It is quite possible she had another relationship and became with child, and then lied to save herself by blaming one of the family—hoping that we should feel responsible and look after her. Such things, unfortunately, do happen."

"I expect they do," he agreed, keeping his voice noncommittal with a great effort. He was sharply aware of Hester standing behind the chair, and knowing what she would feel. "But if that is what she hoped in this instance, then she was sorely disappointed, wasn't she?"

Beatrice's face paled and her head moved fractionally backwards, as if she had been struck but elected to ignore the blow. "It is a terrible thing, Mr. Monk, to charge a person wrongfully with such a gross offense."

"Is it?" he asked sardonically. "It does not appear to have done Mr. Kellard any damage whatever."

She ignored his manner. "Only because we did not believe her!"

"Really?" he pursued. "I rather thought that Sir Basil did believe her, from what he said to me."

She swallowed hard and seemed to sit a little lower in the chair.

"What is it you want of me, Mr. Monk? Even if she was right, and Myles did assault her—in that way—what has it to do with my daughter's death?"

Now he was sorry he had asked her with so little gentleness. Her loss was deep, and she had answered him without evasion or antagonism.

"It would prove that Mr. Kellard has an appetite which he is prepared to satisfy," he explained quietly, "regardless of the personal cost to someone else, and that his past experience has shown him he can do it with impunity."

Now she was as pale as the cambric handkerchief between her clenched fingers.

"Are you suggesting that Myles tried to force himself upon Octavia?" The idea appalled her. Now the horror touched her other daughter as well. Monk felt a stab of guilt for forcing her to think of it—and yet he had no alternative that was honest.

"Is it impossible, ma'am? I believe she was most attractive, and that he had previously been known to admire her."

"But—but she was not—I mean . . ." Her voice died away; she was unable to bring herself to speak the words aloud.

"No. No, she was not molested in that way," he assured her. "But it is possible she had some forewarning he would come and was prepared to defend herself, and in the struggle it was she who was killed, and not he."

"That is—grotesque!" she protested, her eyes wide. "To assault a maid is one thing—to go deliberately and cold-bloodedly to your sister-in-law's bedroom at night, intent upon the same thing, against her will—is—is quite different, and appalling. It is quite wicked!"

"Is it such a great step from one to the other?" He leaned a little closer to her, his voice quiet and urgent. "Do you really believe that Martha Rivett was not equally unwilling? Just not as well prepared to defend herself—younger, more afraid, and more vulnerable since she was a servant in this house and could look for little protection."

She was so ashen now that it was not only Hester who was afraid she might collapse; Monk himself was concerned that he had been too brutal. Hester took a step forward, but remained silent, staring at Beatrice.

"That is terrible!" Beatrice's voice was dry, difficult to force from her throat. "You are saying that we do not care for our servants properly—that we offer them no—no decency—that we are immoral!"

He could not apologize. That was exactly what he had said.

"Not all of you, ma'am—only Mr. Kellard, and that perhaps to spare your daughter the shame and the distress of knowing what her husband had done, you concealed the offense from her—which effectively meant getting rid of the girl and allowing no one else to know of it either."

She put the hands up to her face and pushed them over her cheeks and upward till her fingers ran through her hair, disarranging its neatness. After a moment's painful silence she lowered them and stared at him.

"What would you have us do, Mr. Monk? If Araminta knew it would ruin her life. She could not live with him, and she could not divorce him—he has not deserted her. Adultery is no grounds for separation, unless it is the woman who commits it. If it is the man that means nothing at all. You must know that. All a woman can do is conceal it, so she is not publicly ruined and becomes a creature of pity for the kindly—and of contempt for the others. She is not to blame for any of it, and she is my child. Would you not protect your own child, Mr. Monk?"

He had no answer. He did not know the fierce, consuming love for a child, the tenderness and the bond, and the responsibility. He had no child—he had only a sister, Beth, and he could recall very little about her, only how she had followed him, her wide eyes full of admiration, and the white pinafore she wore, frilled on the edges, and how often she fell over as she tried to run after him, to keep up. He could remember holding her soft, damp little hand in his as they walked down on the shore together, he half lifting her over the rocks till they reached the smooth sand. A wave of feeling came back to him, a mixture of impatient exasperation and fierce, consuming protectiveness.

"Perhaps I would, ma'am. But then if I had a daughter she would more likely be a parlormaid like Martha Rivett," he said ruthlessly, leaving all that that meant hanging in the air between them, and watched the pain, and the guilt, in her face.

The door opened and Araminta came in, the evening's menu in her hand. She stopped, surprised to see Monk, then turned and looked at her mother's face. She ignored Hester as she would any other servant doing her duty.

"Mama, you look ill. What has happened?" She swung around to Monk, her eyes brilliant with accusation. "My mother is unwell, Inspector. Have you not the common courtesy to leave her alone? She can tell you nothing she has not already said. Miss Latterly will open the door for you and the footman will show you out." She turned to Hester, her voice tense with irritation. "Then, Miss Latterly, you had better fetch Mama a tisane and some smelling salts. I cannot think what possessed you to allow this. You should take your duties a great deal more seriously, or we shall be obliged to find someone else who will."

"I am here with Sir Basil's permission, Mrs. Kellard," Monk said tartly. "We are all quite aware the discussion is painful, but postponing it will only prolong the distress. There has been murder in this house, and Lady Moidore wishes to discover who was responsible as much as anyone."

"Mama?" Araminta challenged.

"Of course I do," Beatrice said very quietly. "I think—"

Araminta's eyes widened. "You think? Oh—" And suddenly some realization struck her with a force so obvious it was like a physical blow. She turned very slowly to Monk. "What were your questions about, Mr. Monk?"

Beatrice drew in her breath and held it, not daring to let it out until Monk should have spoken.

"Lady Moidore has already answered them," Monk replied. "Thank you for your offer, but it concerns a matter of which you have no knowledge."

"It was not an offer." Araminta did not look at her mother but kept her hard, straight gaze level at Monk's eyes. "I wished to be informed for my own sake."

"I apologize," Monk said with a thin thread of sarcasm. "I thought you were trying to assist."

"Are you refusing to tell me?"

He could no longer evade. "If you wish to phrase it so, ma'am, then yes, I am."

Very slowly a curious expression of pain, acceptance, almost a subtle pleasure, came into her eyes.

"Because it is to do with my husband." She turned fractionally towards Beatrice. This time the fear was palpable between them. "Are you trying to protect me, Mama? You know something which implicates Myles." The rage of emotions inside her was thick in her voice. Beatrice half reached towards her, then dropped her hands.

"I don't think it does," she said almost under her breath. "I see no reason to think of Myles. . . ." She trailed off, her disbelief heavy in the air.

Araminta swung back to Monk.

"And what do you think, Mr. Monk?" she said levelly. "That is what matters, isn't it?"

"I don't know yet, ma'am. It is impossible to say until I have learned more about it."

"But it does concern my husband?" she insisted.

"I am not going to discuss the matter until I know much more of the truth," he replied. "It would be unjust—and mischief making."

Her curious, asymmetrical smile was hard. She looked from him to her mother again. "Correct me if I am unjust, Mama." There was a cruel mimicry of Monk's tone in her voice. "But does this concern

Myles's attraction towards Octavia, and the thought that he might have forced his attentions upon her, and as a result of her refusal killed her?"

"You are unjust," Beatrice said in little more than a whisper. "You have no reason to think such a thing of him."

"But you have," Araminta said without hesitation, the words hard and slow, as if she were cutting her own flesh. "Mama, I do not deserve to be lied to."

Beatrice gave up; she had no heart left to go on trying to deceive. Her fear was too great; it could be felt like an electric presage of storm in the room. She sat unnaturally motionless, her eyes unfocused, her hands knotted together in her lap.

"Martha Rivett charged that Myles forced himself upon her," she said in a level voice, drained of passion. "That is why she left. Your father dismissed her. She was—" She stopped. To have added the child was an unnecessary blow. Araminta had never borne a child. Monk knew what Beatrice had been going to say as surely as if she had said it. "She was irresponsible," she finished lamely. "We could not keep her in the house saying things like that."

"I see." Araminta's face was ashen white with two high spots of color in her cheeks.

The door opened again and Romola came in, saw the frozen tableau in front of her, Beatrice sitting upright on the sofa, Araminta stiff as a twig, her face set and teeth clenched tight, Hester still standing behind the other large armchair, not knowing what to do, and Monk sitting uncomfortably leaning forward. She glanced at the menu in Araminta's hand, then ignored it. It was apparent even to her that she had interrupted something acutely painful, and dinner was of little importance.

"What is wrong?" she demanded, looking from one to another of them. "Do you know who killed Octavia?"

"No we don't!" Beatrice turned toward her and spoke surprisingly sharply. "We were discussing the parlormaid who was dismissed two years ago."

"Whatever for?" Romola's voice was heavy with disbelief. "Surely that can hardly matter now?"

"Probably not," Beatrice agreed.

"Then why are you wasting time discussing it?" Romola came over to the center of the room and sat down in one of the smaller chairs, arranging her skirts gracefully. "You all look as if it were fear-ful. Has something happened to her?"

"I have no idea," Beatrice snapped, her temper broken at last. "I should think it is not unlikely."

"Why should it?" Romola was confused and frightened; this was all too much for her. "Didn't you give her a character? Why did you dismiss her anyway?" She twisted around to look at Araminta, her eyebrows raised.

"No, I did not give her a character," Beatrice said flatly.

"Well why not?" Romola looked at Araminta and away again. "Was she dishonest? Did she steal something? No one told me!"

"It was none of your concern," Araminta said brusquely.

"It was if she was a thief! She might have taken something of mine!"

"Hardly. She charged that she had been raped!" Araminta glared at her.

"Raped?" Romola was amazed, her expression changed from fear to total incredulity. "You mean—*raped*? Good gracious!" Relief flooded her, the color returning to her beautiful skin. "Well if she was of loose morals of course you had to dismiss her. No one would argue with that. I daresay she took to the streets; women of that sort do. Why on earth are we concerned about it now? There is nothing we can do about it, and probably there never was."

Hester could contain herself no longer.

"She was raped, Mrs. Moidore—taken by force by someone heav-ier and stronger than herself. That does not stem from immorality. It could happen to any woman."

Romola stared at her as if she had grown horns. "Of course it stems from immorality! Decent women don't get violated—they don't lay themselves open to it—they don't invite it—or frequent such places in such company. I don't know what kind of society you come from that you could suggest such a thing." She shook her head a little. "I daresay your experiences as a nurse have robbed you of any finer feel-ings—I beg your pardon for saying such a thing, but you force the issue. Nurses have a reputation for loose conduct which is well known—and scarcely to be envied. Respectable women who behave moderately and dress with decorum do not excite the sort of passions you are speaking of, nor do they find themselves in situations where such a thing could occur. The very idea is quite preposterous—and repulsive."

"It is not preposterous," Hester contradicted flatly. "It is frightening, certainly. It would be very comfortable to suppose that if you behave discreetly you are in no danger of ever being assaulted or having unwelcome attentions forced upon you." She drew in her breath. "It would also be completely untrue, and a quite false sense of safety—and of being morally superior and detached from the pain and the humiliation of it. We would all like to think it could not happen to us, or anyone we know—but it would be wrong." She stopped, seeing Romola's incredulity turning to outrage, Beatrice's surprise and a first spark of respect, and Araminta's extraordinary interest and something that looked almost like a momentary flicker of warmth.

"You forget yourself!" Romola said. "And you forget who we are. Or perhaps you never knew? I am not aware what manner of person you nursed before you came here, but I assure you we do not associate with the sort of people who assault women."

"You are a fool," Araminta said witheringly. "Sometimes I wonder what world it is you live in."

"Minta," Beatrice warned, her voice on edge, her hands clenched together again. "I think we have discussed the matter enough. Mr. Monk will pursue whatever course he deems appropriate. There is nothing more we can offer at the moment. Hester, will you please help me upstairs? I wish to retire. I will not be down for dinner, nor do I wish to see anyone until I feel better."

"How convenient," Araminta said coldly. "But I am sure we shall manage. There is nothing you are needed for. I shall see to everything, and inform Papa." She swung around to Monk. "Good day, Mr. Monk. You must have enough to keep you busy for some time—although whether it will serve any purpose other than to make you appear diligent, I doubt. I don't see how you can prove anything, whatever you suspect."

"Suspect?" Romola looked first at Monk, then at her sister-in-law, her voice rising with fear again. "Suspect of what? What has this to do with Octavia?"

But Araminta ignored her and walked past her out of the door.

Monk stood up and excused himself to Beatrice, inclined his head to Hester, then held the door open for them as they left, Romola behind them, agitated and annoyed, but helpless to do anything about it.

As soon as Monk stepped inside the police station the sergeant looked up from the desk, his face sober, his eyes gleaming.

"Mr. Runcorn wants to see you, sir. Immediate, like."

"Does he," Monk replied dourly. "Well I doubt he'll get much joy of it, but I'll give him what there is."

"He's in his room, sir."

"Thank you," Monk said. "Mr. Evan in?"

"No sir. He came in, and then he went out again. Didn't say where."

Monk acknowledged the reply and went up the stairs to Runcorn's office. He knocked on the door and at the command went in. Runcorn was sitting behind his large, highly polished desk, two elegant envelopes and half a dozen sheets of fine notepaper written on and half folded lying next to them. The other surfaces were covered with four or five newspapers, some open, some folded.

He looked up, his face dark with anger and his eyes narrow and bright.

"Well. Have you seen the newspapers, eh? Have you seen what they are saying about us?" He held one up and Monk saw the black headlines halfway down the page: QUEEN ANNE STREET MURDERER STILL LOOSE. POLICE BAFFLED. And then the writer went on to question the usefulness of the new police force, and was it money well spent or now an unworkable idea.

"Well?" Runcorn demanded.

"I hadn't seen that one," Monk answered. "I haven't spent much time reading newspapers."

"I don't want you reading the newspapers, dammit," Runcorn exploded. "I want you doing something so they don't write rubbish like this. Or this." He snatched up the next one. "Or this." He threw them away, disregarding the mess as they slid on the polished surface and fell onto the floor in a rattling heap. He grasped one of the letters. "From the Home Office." His fingers closed on it, knuckles white. "I'm getting asked some very embarrassing questions, Monk, and I can't answer them. I'm not prepared to defend you indefinitely—I can't. What in hell's name are you doing, man? If someone in that house killed the wretched woman, then you haven't far to look, have you? Why can't you get this thing settled? For heaven's sake, how many suspects can you have? Four or five at the most. What's the matter with you that you can't finish it up?"

"Because four or five suspects is three or four too many—sir. Unless, of course, you can prove a conspiracy?" Monk said sarcastically.

Runcorn slammed his fist on the table. "Don't be impertinent, damn you! A smart tongue won't get you out of this. Who are your suspects? This footman, what's his name—Percival. Who else? As far as I can see, that's it. Why can't you settle it, Monk? You're beginning to look incompetent." His anger turned to a sneer. "You used to be the best detective we had, but you've certainly lost your touch lately. Why can't you arrest this damned footman?"

"Because I have no proof he did anything," Monk replied succinctly.

"Well who else could it be? Think clearly. You used to be the sharpest and most rational man we had." His lip curled. "Before that accident you were as logical as a piece of algebra—and about as charming—but you knew your job. Now I'm beginning to wonder."

Monk kept his temper with difficulty. "As well as Percival, sir," he said heavily, "it could be one of the laundrymaids—"

"What?" Runcorn's mouth opened in disbelief close to derision. "Did you say one of the laundrymaids? Don't be absurd. Whatever for? If that's the best you can do, I'd better put someone else on the case. Laundrymaid. What in heaven's name would make a laundrymaid get out of her bed in the middle of the night and creep down to her mistress's bedroom and stab her to death? Unless the girl is raving mad. Is she raving mad, Monk? Don't say you couldn't recognize a lunatic if you saw one."

"No, she is not raving mad; she is extremely jealous," Monk answered him.

"Jealous? Of her mistress? That's ludicrous. How can a laundrymaid compare herself with her mistress? That needs some explaining, Monk. You are reaching for straws."

"The laundrymaid is in love with the footman—not a particularly difficult circumstance to understand," Monk said with elaborate, hard-edged patience. "The footman has airs above his station and imagines the mistress admired him—which may or may not be true. Certainly he had allowed the laundrymaid to suppose so."

Runcorn frowned. "Then it was the laundrymaid? Can't you arrest her?"

"For what?"

Runcorn glared at him. "All right, who are your other suspects? You said four or five. So far you have only mentioned two."

"Myles Kellard, the other daughter's husband—"

"What for?" Runcorn was worried now. "You haven't made any accusations, have you?" The blood was pink in his narrow cheeks. "This is a very delicate situation. We can't go around charging people like Sir Basil Moidore and his family. For God's sake, where's your judgment?"

Monk looked at him with contempt.

"That is exactly why I am not charging anyone, sir," he said coldly. "Myles Kellard apparently was strongly attracted by his sister-in-law, which his wife knew about—"

"That's no reason for him to kill her," Runcorn protested. "If he'd killed his wife, maybe. For heaven's sake, think clearly, Monk!"

Monk refrained from telling him about Martha Rivett until he should find the girl, if he could, and hear her side of the story and make some judgment himself as to whom he could believe.

"If he forced his attentions on her," Monk said with continued patience, "and she defended herself, then there may have been a struggle, in which she was knifed—"

"With a carving knife?" Runcorn's eyebrows went up. "Which she just conveniently chanced to have in her bedroom?"

"I don't imagine it was chance," Monk bit back savagely. "If she had reason to think he was coming she probably took it there on purpose."

Runcorn grunted.

"Or it may have been Mrs. Kellard," Monk continued. "She would have good reason to hate her sister."

"Something of an immoral woman, this Mrs. Haslett." Runcorn's lips curled in distaste. "First the footman, now her sister's husband."

"There is no proof she encouraged the footman," Monk said crossly. "And she certainly did not encourage Kellard. Unless you think it's immoral to be beautiful, I don't see how you can find fault with her for either case."

"You always did have some strange ideas of right." Runcorn was disgusted—and confused. The ugly headlines in the newspapers threatened public opinion. The letters from the Home Office lay stiff and white on his desk, polite but cold, warning that it would be little appreciated if he did not find a way to end this case soon, and satisfactorily.

"Well don't stand there," he said to Monk. "Get about finding out which of your suspects is guilty. For heaven's sake, you've only got five; you know it has to be one of them. It's a matter of exclusion. You can stop thinking about Mrs. Kellard, to begin with. She might have a quarrel, but I doubt she'd knife her sister in the night. That's cold-blooded. She couldn't expect to get away with it."

"She couldn't know about Chinese Paddy in the street," Monk pointed out.

"What? Oh—well, neither could the footman. I'd look for a man in this—or the laundrymaid, I suppose. Either way, get on with it. Don't stand here in front of my fire talking."

"You sent for me."

"Yes—well now I'm sending you out again. Close the door as you go—it's cold in the passage."

Monk spent the next two and a half days searching the workhouses, riding in endless cabs through narrow streets, pavements gleaming in the lamplight and the rain, amid the rattle of carts and the noise of street cries, carriage wheels, and the clatter of hooves on the cobbles. He began to the east of Queen Anne Street with the Clerkenwell Workhouse in Farringdon Road, then Holborn Workhouse on the Grey's Inn Road. The second day he moved westward and tried the St. George's Workhouse on Mount Street, then the St. Marylebone Workhouse on Northumberland Street. On the third morning he came to the Westminster Workhouse on Poland Street, and he was beginning to get discouraged. The atmosphere depressed him more than any other place he knew. There was some deeply ingrained fear that touched him at the very name, and when he saw the flat, drab sides of the building rearing up he felt its misery enter into him, and a coldness that had nothing to do with the sharp November wind that whined along the street and rattled an old newspaper in the gutter.

He knocked at the door, and when it was opened by a thin man with lank dark hair and a lugubrious expression, he stated immediately who he was and his profession, so there should be no mistaking his purpose in being here. He would not allow them even for an instant to suppose he was seeking shelter, or the poor relief such places were built and maintained to give.

"You'd better come in. I'll ask if the master'll see yer," the man said without interest. "But if yer want 'elp, yer'd best not lie," he added as an afterthought.

Monk was about to snap at him that he did not, when he caught sight of one of the "outdoor poor" who did, who were reduced by circumstance to seeking charity to survive from one of these grim institutions which robbed them of decision, dignity, individuality, even of dress or personal appearance; which fed them bread and potatoes, separated families, men from women, children from parents, housed them in dormitories, clothed them in uniforms and worked them from dawn until dusk. A man had to be reduced to despair before he begged to be admitted to such a place. But who would willingly let his wife or his children perish?

Monk found the hot denial sticking in his throat. It would humiliate the man further, to no purpose. He contented himself with thanking the doorkeeper and following him obediently.

The workhouse master took nearly a quarter of an hour to come to the small room overlooking the labor yard where rows of men sat on the ground with hammers, chisels and piles of rocks.

He was a pallid man, his gray hair clipped close to his head, his eyes startlingly dark and ringed around with hollow circles as if he never slept.

"What's wrong, Inspector?" he said wearily. "Surely you don't think we harbor criminals here? He'd have to be desperate indeed to seek this asylum—and a very unsuccessful scoundrel."

"I'm looking for a woman who may have been the victim of rape," Monk replied, a dark, savage edge to his voice. "I want to hear her side of the story."

"You new to the job?" the workhouse master said doubtfully, looking him up and down, seeing the maturity in his face, the smooth lines and powerful nose, the confidence and the anger. "No." He answered his own question. "Then what good do you imagine that will do? You're not going to try and prosecute on the word of a pauper, are you?"

"No—it's just corroborative evidence."

"What?"

"Just to confirm what we already know—or suspect."

"What's her name?"

"Martha Rivett. Probably came about two years ago—with child. I daresay the child would be born about seven months later, if she didn't lose it."

"Martha Rivett—Martha Rivett. Would she be a tall girl with fairish hair, about nineteen or twenty?"

"Seventeen—and I'm afraid I don't know what she looked like—except she was a parlormaid, so I expect she was handsome, and possibly tall."

"We've got a Martha about that age, with a baby. Can't remember her other name, but I'll send for her. You can ask her," the master offered.

"Couldn't you take me to her?" Monk suggested. "Don't want to make her feel—" He stopped, uncertain what word to choose.

The workhouse master smiled wryly. "More likely she'll feel like talking away from the other women. But whatever you like."

Monk was happy to concede. He had no desire to see more of the workhouse than he had to. Already the smell of the place—overboiled cabbage, dust and blocked drains—was clinging in his nose, and the misery choked him.

"Yes—thank you. I don't doubt you're right."

The workhouse master disappeared and returned fifteen minutes later with a thin girl with stooped shoulders and a pale, waxen face. Her brown hair was thick but dull, and her wide blue eyes had no life in them. It was not hard to imagine that two years ago she might have been beautiful, but now she was apathetic and she stared at Monk with neither intelligence nor interest, her arms folded under the bib of her uniform apron, her gray stuff dress ill fitting and harsh.

"Yes sir?" she said obediently.

"Martha." Monk spoke very gently. The pity he felt was like a pain in his stomach, churning and sick. "Martha, did you work for Sir Basil Moidore about two years ago?"

"I didn't take anything." There was no protest in her voice, simply a statement of fact.

"No, I know you didn't," he said quickly. "What I want to know is did Mr. Kellard pay you any attention that was more than you wished?" What a mealymouthed way of expressing himself, but he was afraid of being misunderstood, of having her think he was accusing her of lying, troublemaking, raking up old and useless accusations no one would believe, and perhaps being further punished for slander. He watched her face closely, but he saw no deep emotion in it, only a flicker, too slight for him to know what it meant. "Did he, Martha?"

She was undecided, staring at him mutely. Misfortune and workhouse life had robbed her of any will to fight.

"Martha," he said very softly. "He may have forced himself on someone else, not a maid this time, but a lady. I need to know if you were willing or not—and I need to know if it was him or if it was really someone else?"

She looked at him silently, but this time there was a spark in her eyes, a little life.

He waited.

"Does she say that?" she said at last. "Does she say she weren't willing?"

"She doesn't say anything—she's dead."

Her eyes grew huge with horror—and dawning realization, as memory became sharp and focused again.

"He killed her?"

"I don't know," he said frankly. "Was he rough with you?"

She nodded, the memory of pain sharp in her face and fear rekindling as she thought of it again. "Yes."

"Did you tell anyone that?"

"What's the point? They didn't even believe me I was unwilling. They said I was loose-tongued, a troublemaker and no better than I should be. They dismissed me without a character. I couldn't get another position. No one would take me on with no character. An' I was with child—" Her eyes hazed over with tears, and suddenly there was life there again, passion and tenderness.

"Your child?" he asked, although he was afraid to know. He felt himself cringe inside as if waiting for the blow.

"She's here, with the other babes," she said quietly. "I get to see her now and again, but she's not strong. How could she be, born and raised here?"

Monk determined to speak to Callandra Daviot. Surely she could use another servant for something? Martha Rivett was one among tens of thousands, but even one saved from this was better than nothing.

"He was violent with you?" he repeated. "And you make it quite plain you didn't want his attentions?"

"He didn't believe me—he didn't think any woman meant it when she said no," she replied with a faint, twisted smile. "Even Miss Araminta. He said she liked to be took—but I don't believe that. I was there when she married him—an' she really loved him then. You should have seen her face, all shining and soft. Then after her wedding night she changed. She looked like a sparkling fire the night before, all dressed in cherry pink and bright as you like. The morning after she looked like cold ashes in the grate. I never saw that softness back in her as long as I was there."

"I see," Monk said very quietly. "Thank you, Martha. You have been a great help to me. I shall try to be as much help to you. Don't give up hope."

A fraction of her old dignity returned, but there was no life in her smile.

"There's nothing to hope for, sir. Nobody'd marry me. I never see anyone except people that haven't a farthing of their own, or they'd not be here. And nobody looks for servants in a workhouse, and I wouldn't leave Emmie anyway. And even if she doesn't live, no one takes on a maid without a character, and my looks have gone too."

"They'll come back. Just please—don't give up," he urged her.

"Thank you, sir, but you don't know what you're saying."

"Yes I do."

She smiled patiently at his ignorance and took her leave, going back to the labor yard to scrub and mend.

Monk thanked the workhouse master and left also, not to the police station to tell Runcorn he had a better suspect than Percival. That could wait. First he would go to Callandra Daviot.

CHAPTER
EIGHT

Monk's sense of elation was short-lived. When he returned to Queen Anne Street the next day he was greeted in the kitchen by Mrs. Boden, looking grim and anxious, her face very pink and her hair poking in wild angles out of her white cap.

"Good morning, Mr. Monk. I am glad you've come!"

"What is it, Mrs. Boden?" His heart sank, although he could think of nothing specific he feared. "What has happened?"

"One of my big kitchen carving knives is missing, Mr. Monk." She wiped her hands on her apron. "I could have sworn I had it last time we had a roast o' beef, but Sal says she thinks as it was the other one I used, the old one, an' now I reckon she must be right." She poked her hair back under her cap and wiped her face agitatedly. "No one else can remember, and May gets sick at the thought. I admit it fair turns my stomach when I think it could've been the one that stabbed poor Miss Octavia."

Monk was cautious. "When did this thought come to you, Mrs. Boden?" he asked guardedly.

"Yesterday, in the evening." She sniffed. "Miss Araminta sent down for a little thin-cut beef for Sir Basil. He'd come in late and wanted a bite to eat." Her voice was rising and there was a note of hysteria in it. "I went to get my best knife, an' it weren't there. That's when I started to look for it, thinking as it had been misplaced. And it in't here—not anywhere."

"And you haven't seen it since Mrs. Haslett's death?"

"I don't know, Mr. Monk!" Her hands jerked up in the air. "I thought I 'ad, but Sal and May tell me as they 'aven't, and when I last cut beef I did it with the old one. I was so upset I can't recall what I did, and that's the truth."

"Then I suppose we'd better see if we can find it," Monk agreed. "I'll get Sergeant Evan to organize a search. Who else knows about this?"

Her face was blank; she understood no implication.

"Who else, Mrs. Boden?" he repeated calmly.

"Well I don't know, Mr. Monk. I don't know who I might have asked. I looked for it, naturally, and asked everyone if they'd seen it."

"Who do you mean by 'everyone,' Mrs. Boden? Who else apart from the kitchen staff?"

"Well—I'm sure I can't think." She was beginning to panic because she could see the urgency in him and she did not understand. "Dinah. I asked Dinah because sometimes things get moved through to the pantry. And I may have mentioned it to 'Arold. Why? They don't know where it is, or they'd 'ave said."

"Someone wouldn't have," he pointed out.

It was several seconds before she grasped what he meant, then her hand flew to her mouth and she let out a stifled shriek.

"I had better inform Sir Basil." That was a euphemism for asking Sir Basil's permission for the search. Without a warrant he could not proceed, and it would probably cost him his job if he were to try against Sir Basil's wishes. He left Mrs. Boden in the kitchen sitting in the chair and May running for smelling salts—and almost certainly a strong nip of brandy.

He was surprised to find himself shown to the library and left barely five minutes before Basil came in looking tense, his face creased, his eyes very dark.

"What is it, Monk? Have you learned anything at last? My God, it is past time you did!"

"The cook reports one of her kitchen carving knives missing, sir. I would like your permission to search the house for it."

"Well of course search for it!" Basil said. "Do you expect me to look for it for you?"

"It was necessary to have your permission, Sir Basil," Monk said between his teeth. "I cannot go through your belongings without a warrant, unless you permit me to."

"My belongings." He was startled, his eyes wide with disbelief.

"Is not everything in the house yours, sir, apart from what is Mr. Cyprian's, or Mr. Kellard's—and perhaps Mr. Thirsk's?"

Basil smiled bleakly, merely a slight movement of the corner of the lips. "Mrs. Sandeman's personal belongings are her own, but otherwise, yes, they are mine. Of course you have my permission to search anywhere you please. You will need assistance, no doubt. You may send one of my grooms in the small carriage to fetch whomever you wish—your sergeant . . ." He shrugged, but his shoulders under the black barathea of his coat were tense. "Constables?"

"Thank you," Monk acknowledged. "That is most considerate. I shall do that immediately."

"Perhaps you should wait for them at the head of the male servants' staircase?" Basil raised his voice a little. "If whoever has the knife gets word of this they may be tempted to move it before you can begin your task. From there you can see the far end of the passage where the female servants' staircase emerges." He was explaining himself more than usual. It was the first real crack in his composure that Monk had seen. "That is the best position I can offer. I imagine there is little point in having any one of the servants stand guard—they must all be suspect." He watched Monk's face.

"Thank you," Monk said again. "That is most perceptive of you. May I also have one of the upstairs maids stay on the main landing? They would observe anyone coming or going on other than an ordinary duty—which they would be used to. Perhaps the laundrymaids and other domestic staff could remain downstairs until this is over—and the footmen of course?"

"By all means." Basil was regaining his command. "And the valet as well."

"Thank you, sir. That is most helpful of you."

Basil's eyebrows rose. "What on earth did you expect me to do, man? It was my daughter who was murdered." His control was complete again.

There was nothing Monk could reply to that, except to express a brief sympathy again and take his leave to go downstairs, write a note to Evan at the police station, and dispatch the groom to fetch him and another constable.

The search, begun forty-five minutes later, started with the rooms of the maids at the far end of the attic, small, cold garrets looking over the gray slates towards their own mews, and the roofs of Harley Mews beyond. They each contained an iron bedstead with mattress, pillow and covers, a wooden hard-backed chair, and a plain wood dresser with a glass on the wall above. No maid would be permitted to present herself for work untidy or in an ill-kept uniform. There was also a cupboard for clothes and a ewer and basin for washing. The rooms were distinguished one from another only by the patterns of the knotted rag rugs on the floor and by the few pictures that belonged to each inhabitant, a sketch of family, in one case a silhouette, a religious text or reproduction of a famous painting.

Neither Monk nor Evan found a knife. The constable, under detailed instructions, was searching the outside property, simply because it was the only other area to which the servants had access without leaving the premises, and thus their duty.

"Of course if it was a member of the family they've all been over half London by now," Evan observed with a crooked smile. "It could be at the bottom of the river, or in any of a million gutters or rubbish bins."

"I know that." Monk did not stop his work. "And Myles Kellard looks by far the most likely, at the moment. Or Araminta, if she knew. But can you think of a better thing to be doing?"

"No," Evan admitted glumly. "I've spent the last week and a half chasing my shadow around London looking for jewelry I'll lay any odds you like was destroyed the night it was taken—or trying to find out the past history of servants whose records are exemplary and deadly monotonous." He was busy turning out drawers of neat, serviceable feminine clothes as he spoke, his long fingers touching them carefully, his face pulled into an expression of distaste at his intrusion. "I begin to think employers don't see people at all, simply aprons and uniform stuff dresses and a lace cap," he went on. "Whose head it is on is all the same, providing the tea is hot, the table is laid, the fires are blacked and laid and stoked, the meal is cooked and served and cleared away, and every time the bell is rung, someone answers it to do whatever you want." He folded the clothes neatly and replaced them. "Oh—and of course the house is always clean and there are always clean clothes in the dresser. Who does it is largely immaterial."

"You are becoming cynical, Evan!"

Evan flashed a smile. "I'm learning, sir."

After the maids' rooms they came down the stairs to the second floor up from the main house. At one end of the landing were the rooms of the housekeeper and the cook and the ladies' maids, and now of course Hester; and at the other the rooms of the butler, the two footmen, the bootboy and the valet.

"Shall we begin with Percival?" Evan asked, looking at Monk apprehensively.

"We may as well take them in order," Monk answered. "The first is Harold."

But they found nothing beyond the private possessions of a very ordinary young man in service in a large house: one suit of clothes for the rare times off duty, letters from his family, several from his mother, a few mementoes of childhood, a picture of a pleasant-faced woman of middle years with the same fair hair and mild features as himself, presumably his mother, and a feminine handkerchief of inexpensive cambric, carefully pressed and placed in his Bible—perhaps Dinah's?

Percival's room was as different from Harold's as the one man was from the other. Here there were books, some poetry, some philosophy of social conditions and change, one or two novels. There were no letters, no sign of family or other ties. He had two suits of his own clothes in the cupboard for his times off duty, and some very smart boots, several neckties and handkerchiefs, and a surprising number of shirts and some extremely handsome cuff links and collar studs. He must have looked quite a dandy when he chose. Monk felt a stab of familiarity as he moved the personal belongings of this other young man who strove to dress and deport himself out of his station in life. Had he himself begun like this—living in someone else's house, aping their manners trying to improve himself? It was also a matter of some curiosity as to where Percival got the money for such things—they cost a great deal more than a footman's wages, even if carefully saved over several years.

"Sir!"

He jerked up and stared at Evan, who was standing white-faced, the whole drawer of the dresser on the floor at his feet, pulled out completely, and in his hand a long garment of ivory silk, stained brown in smears, and a thin, cruel blade poking through, patched and blotched with the rusty red of dried blood.

Monk stared at it, stunned. He had expected an exercise in futility, merely something to demonstrate that he was doing all he could—and now Evan held in his hand what was obviously the weapon, wrapped in a woman's peignoir, and it had been concealed in Percival's room. It was a conclusion so startling he found it hard to grasp.

"So much for Myles Kellard," Evan said, swallowing hard and

laying the knife and the silk down carefully on the end of the bed, withdrawing his hand quickly as if desiring to be away from it.

Monk replaced the things he had been looking through in the cupboard and stood up straight, hands in his pockets.

"But why would he leave it here?" he said slowly. "It's damning!"

Evan frowned. "Well, I suppose he didn't want to leave the knife in her room, and he couldn't risk carrying it openly, with blood on it, in case he met someone—"

"Who, for heaven's sake?"

Evan's fair face was intensely troubled, his eyes dark, his lips pulled in distaste that was far deeper than anything physical.

"I don't know! Anyone else on the landing in the night—"

"How would he explain his presence—with or without a knife?" Monk demanded.

"I don't know!" Evan shook his head. "What do footmen do? Maybe he'd say he heard a noise—intruders—the front door—I don't know. But it would be better if he didn't have a knife in his hands— especially a bloodstained one."

"Better still if he had left it there in her room," Monk argued.

"Perhaps he took it out without thinking." He looked up and met Monk's eyes. "Just had it in his hand and kept hold of it? Panicked? Then when he got outside and halfway along the corridor he didn't dare go back?"

"Then why the peignoir?" Monk said. "He wrapped it in that to take it, by the look of it. That's not the kind of panic you're talking about. Now why on earth should he want the knife? It doesn't make sense."

"Not to us," Evan agreed slowly, staring at the crumpled silk in his hand. "But it must have to him—there it is!"

"And he never had the opportunity to get rid of it between then and now?" Monk screwed up his face. "He couldn't possibly have forgotten it!"

"What other explanation is there?" Evan looked helpless. "It's here!"

"Yes—but was Percival the one who put it here? And why didn't we find it when we looked for the jewelry?"

Evan blushed. "Well I didn't pull out drawers and look under them for anything. I daresay the constable didn't either. Honestly I was pretty sure we wouldn't find it anyway—and the silver vase wouldn't have fitted." He looked uncomfortable.

Monk pulled a face. "Even if we had, it might not have been there then—I suppose. I don't know, Evan. It just seems so . . . stupid! And Percival is arrogant, abrasive, contemptuous of other people, especially women, and he's got a hell of a lot of money from somewhere, to judge from his wardrobe, but he's not stupid. Why should he leave something as damning as this hidden in his room?"

"Arrogance?" Evan suggested tentatively. "Maybe he just thinks we are not efficient enough for him to be afraid of? Up until today he was right."

"But he was afraid," Monk insisted, remembering Percival's white face and the sweat on his skin. "I had him in the housekeeper's room and I could see the fear in him, smell it! He fought to get out of it, spreading blame everywhere else he could—on the laundrymaid, and Kellard—even Araminta."

"I don't know!" Evan shook his head, his eyes puzzled. "But Mrs. Boden will tell us if this is her knife—and Mrs. Kellard will tell us if that is her sister's—what did you call it?"

"Peignoir," Monk replied. "Dressing robe."

"Right—peignoir. I suppose we had better tell Sir Basil we've found it!"

"Yes." Monk picked up the knife, folding the silk over the blade, and carried it out of the room, Evan coming after him.

"Are you going to arrest him?" Evan asked, coming down the stairs a step behind.

Monk hesitated. "I'm not happy it's enough," he said thoughtfully. "Anyone could have put these in his room—and only a fool would leave them there."

"They were fairly well hidden."

"But why keep them?" Monk insisted. "It's stupid—Percival's far too sly for that."

"Then what?" Evan was not argumentative so much as puzzled and disturbed by a series of ugly discoveries in which he saw no sense. "The laundrymaid? Is she really jealous enough to murder Octavia and hide the weapon and the gown in Percival's room?"

They had reached the main landing, where Maggie and Annie were standing together, wide-eyed, staring at them.

"All right girls, you've done a good job. Thank you," Monk said to them with a tight smile. "You can go about your own duties now."

"You've got something!" Annie stared at the silk in his hand, her face pale, and she looked frightened. Maggie stood very close to her, equal fear in her features.

There was no point in lying; they would find out soon enough.

"Yes," he admitted. "We've got the knife. Now get about your duties, or you'll have Mrs. Willis after you."

Mrs. Willis's name was enough to break the spell. They scuttled off to fetch carpet beaters and brushes, and he saw their long gray skirts whisk around the corner into the broom cupboard in a huddle together, whispering breathlessly.

Basil was waiting for the two police in his study, sitting at his desk. He admitted them immediately and looked up from the papers he had been writing on, his face angry, his brow dark.

"Yes?"

Monk closed the door behind him.

"We found a knife, sir; and a silk garment which I believe is a peignoir. Both are stained with blood."

Basil let out his breath slowly, his face barely changed, just a shadow as if some final reality had come home.

"I see. And where did you find these things?"

"Behind a drawer in the dresser in Percival's room," Monk answered, watching him closely.

If Basil was surprised it did not show in his expression. His heavy face with its short, broad nose and mouth wreathed in lines remained careful and tired. Perhaps one could not expect it of him. His family had endured bereavement and suspicion for weeks. That it should finally be ended and the burden lifted from his immediate family must be an overwhelming relief. He could not be blamed if that were paramount. However repugnant the thought, he cannot have helped wondering if his son-in-law might be responsible, and Monk had already seen that he and Araminta had a deeper affection than many a father and child. She was the only one who had his inner strength, his command and determination, his dignity and almost total self-control. Although that might be an unfair judgment, since Monk had never seen Octavia alive; but she had apparently been flawed by the weakness of drink and the vulnerability of loving her husband too much to recover from his death—if indeed that were a flaw. Perhaps it was to Basil and Araminta, who had disapproved of Harry Haslett in the first place.

"I assume you are going to arrest him." It was barely a question.

"Not yet," Monk said slowly. "The fact that they were found in his room does not prove it was he who put them there."

"What?" Basil's face darkened with angry color and he leaned forward over the desk. Another man might have risen to his feet, but he did not stand to servants, or police, who were in his mind the same. "For God's sake, man, what more do you want? The very knife that stabbed her, and her clothes found in his possession!"

"Found in his room, sir," Monk corrected. "The door was not locked; anyone in the house could have put them there."

"Don't be absurd!" Basil said savagely. "Who in the devil's name would put such things there?"

"Anyone wishing to implicate him—and thus remove suspicion from themselves," Monk replied. "A natural act of self-preservation."

"Who, for example?" Basil said with a sneer. "You have every evidence that it was Percival. He had the motive, heaven help us. Poor Octavia was weak in her choice of men. I was her father, but I can admit that. Percival is an arrogant and presumptuous creature. When she rebuffed him and threatened to have him thrown out, he panicked. He had gone too far." His voice was shaking, and deeply as he disliked him, Monk had a moment's pity for him. Octavia had been his daughter, whatever he had thought of her marriage, or tried to deny her; the thought of her violation must have wounded him inwardly more than he could show, especially in front of an inferior like Monk.

He mastered himself with difficulty and continued. "Or perhaps she took the knife with her," he said quietly, "fearing he might come, and when he did, she tried to defend herself, poor child." He swallowed. "And he overpowered her and it was she who was stabbed." At last he turned, leaving his back towards Monk. "He panicked," he went on. "And left, taking the knife with him, and then hid it because he had no opportunity to dispose of it." He moved away towards the window, hiding his face. He breathed in deeply and let it out in a sigh. "What an abominable tragedy. You will arrest him immediately and get him out of my house. I will tell my family that you have solved the crime of Octavia's death. I thank you for your diligence—and your discretion."

"No sir," Monk said levelly, part of him wishing he could agree. "I cannot arrest him on this evidence. It is not sufficient—unless he confesses. If he denies it, and says someone else put these things in his room—"

Basil swung around, his eyes hard and very black. "Who?"

"Possibly Rose," Monk replied.

Basil stared at him. "What?"

"The laundrymaid who is infatuated with him, and might have been jealous enough to kill Mrs. Haslett and then implicate Percival. That way she would be revenged upon them both."

Basil's eyebrows rose. "Are you suggesting, Inspector, that my daughter was in rivalry with a laundrymaid for the love of a footman? Do you imagine anyone at all will believe you?"

How easy it would be to do what they all wanted and arrest Percival. Runcorn would be torn between relief and frustration. Monk could leave Queen Anne Street and take a new case. Except that he did not believe this one was over—not yet.

"I am suggesting, Sir Basil, that the footman in question is something of a braggart," he said aloud. "And he may well have tried to make the laundrymaid jealous by telling her that that was the case. And she may have been gullible enough to believe him."

"Oh." Basil gave up. Suddenly the anger drained out of him. "Well it is your job to find out which is the truth. I don't much care. Either way, arrest the appropriate person and take them away. I will dismiss the other anyway—without a character. Just attend to it."

"Or, on the other hand," Monk said coldly, "it might have been Mr. Kellard. It now seems undeniable that he resorts to violence when his desire is refused."

Basil looked up. "Does it? I don't recall telling you anything of the sort. I said that she made some such charge and that my son-in-law denied it."

"I found the girl," Monk told him with a hard stare, all his dislike flooding back. The man was callous, almost brutal in his indifference. "I heard her account of the event, and I believe it." He did not mention what Martha Rivett had said about Araminta and her wedding night, but it explained very precisely the emotions Hester had seen in her and her continuous, underlying bitterness towards her husband. If Basil did not know, there was no purpose in telling him so private and painful a piece of information.

"Do you indeed?" Basil's face was bleak. "Well fortunately judgment does not rest with you. Nor will any court accept the unsubstantiated word of an immoral servant girl against that of a gentleman of unblemished reputation."

"And what anyone believes is irrelevant," Monk said stiffly. "I cannot prove that Percival is guilty—but more urgent than that, I do not yet know that he is."

"Then get out and find out!" Basil said, losing his temper at last. "For God's sake do your job!"

"Sir." Monk was too angry to add anything further. He swung on his heel and went out, shutting the door hard behind him. Evan was standing miserably in the hall, waiting, the peignoir and the knife in his hand.

"Well?" Monk demanded.

"It's the kitchen knife Mrs. Boden was missing," Evan answered. "I haven't asked anyone about this yet." He held up the peignoir, his face betraying the distress he felt for death, loneliness and indignity. "But I requested to see Mrs. Kellard."

"Good. I'll take it. Where is she?"

"I don't know. I asked Dinah and she told me to wait."

Monk swore. He hated being left in the hall like a mendicant, but he had no alternative. It was a further quarter of an hour before Dinah returned and conducted them to the boudoir, where Araminta was standing in the center of the floor, her face strained and grim but perfectly composed.

"What is it, Mr. Monk?" she said quietly, ignoring Evan, who waited silently by the door. "I believe you have found the knife—in one of the servants' bedrooms. Is that so?"

"Yes, Mrs. Kellard." He did not know how she would react to this visual and so tangible evidence of death. So far everything had been words, ideas—terrible, but all in the mind. This was real, her sister's clothes, her sister's blood. The iron resolution might break. He could not feel a warmth towards her, she was too distant, but he could feel both pity and admiration. "We also found a silk peignoir stained with blood. I am sorry to have to ask you to identify such a distressing thing, but we need to know if it belonged to your sister."

He had been holding it low, half behind him, and he knew she had not noticed it.

She seemed very tense, as if it were important rather than painful. He thought that perhaps it was her way of keeping her control.

"Indeed?" She swallowed. "You may show it to me, Mr. Monk. I am quite prepared and will do all I can."

He brought the peignoir forward and held it up, concealing as much of the blood as he could. It was only spatters, as if it had been open when she was stabbed; the stains had come largely from being wrapped around the blade.

She was very pale, but she did not flinch from looking at it.

"Yes," she said quietly and slowly. "That is Octavia's. She was wearing it the night she was killed. I spoke to her on the landing just before she went in to say good-night to Mama. I remember it very clearly—the lace lilies. I always admired it." She took a deep breath. "May I ask you where you found it?" Now she was as white as the silk in Monk's hand.

"Behind a drawer in Percival's bedroom," he answered.

She stood quite still. "Oh. I see."

He waited for her to continue, but she did not.

"I have not yet asked him for an explanation," he went on, watching her face.

"Explanation?" She swallowed again, so painfully hard he could see the constriction in her throat. "How could he possibly explain such a thing?" She looked confused, but there was no observable anger in her, no rage or revenge. Not yet. "Is not the only answer that he hid it there after he had killed her, and had not found an opportunity to dispose of it?"

Monk wished he could help her, but he could not.

"Knowing something of Percival, Mrs. Kellard, would you expect him to hide it in his own room, such a damning thing; or in some place less likely to incriminate him?" he asked.

The shadow of a smile crossed her face. Even now she could see a bitter humor in the suggestion. "In the middle of the night, Inspector, I should expect him to put it in the one place where his presence would arouse no suspicion—his own room. Perhaps he intended to put it somewhere else later, but never found the opportunity." She took a deep breath and her eyebrows arched high. "One requires to be quite certain of being unobserved for such an act, I should imagine?"

"Of course." He could not disagree.

"Then it is surely time you questioned him? Have you sufficient force with you, should he prove violent, or shall I send for one of the grooms to assist you?"

How practical.

"Thank you," he declined. "But I think Sergeant Evan and I can manage. Thank you for your assistance. I regret having to ask you such questions, or that you should need to see the peignoir." He would have added something less formal, but she was not a woman to whom one offered anything as close or gentle as pity. Respect, and an understanding of courage, was all she would accept.

"It was necessary, Inspector," she acknowledged with stiff grace.

"Ma'am." He inclined his head, excusing himself, and with Evan a step behind him, went to the butler's pantry to ask Phillips if he might see Percival.

"Of course," Phillips said gravely. "May I ask, sir, if you have discovered something in your search? One of the upstairs maids said that you had, but they are young, and inclined to be overimaginative."

"Yes we have," Monk replied. "We found Mrs. Boden's missing knife and a peignoir belonging to Mrs. Haslett. It appears to have been the knife used to kill her."

Phillips looked very white and Monk was afraid for a moment he was going to collapse, but he stood rigid like a soldier on parade.

"May I ask where you found it?" There was no "sir." Phillips was a butler, and considered himself socially very superior to a policeman. Even these desperate circumstances did not alter that.

"I think it would be better at the moment if that were a confidential matter," Monk replied coolly. "It is indicative of who hid them there, but not conclusive."

"I see." Phillips felt the rebuff; it was there in his pale face and rigid manner. He was in charge of the servants, used to command, and he resented a mere policeman intruding upon his field of responsibility. Everything beyond the green baize door was his preserve. "And what is it you wish of me? I shall be pleased to assist, of course." It was a formality; he had no choice, but he would keep up the charade.

"I'm obliged," Monk said, hiding his flash of humor. Phillips would not appreciate being laughed at. "I would like to see the menservants one at a time—beginning with Harold, and then Rhodes the valet, then Percival."

"Of course. You may use Mrs. Willis's sitting room if you wish to."

"Thank you, that would be convenient."

He had nothing to say to either Harold or Rhodes, but to keep up appearances he asked them about their whereabouts during the day and if their rooms were locked. Their answers told him nothing he did not already know.

When Percival came he already knew something was deeply wrong. He had far more intelligence than either of the other two, and perhaps something in Phillips's manner forewarned him, as did the knowledge that something had been found in the servants' rooms. He knew the family members were increasingly frightened. He saw them every day, heard the sharpened tempers, saw the suspicion in their eyes, the altered relationships, the crumbling belief. Indeed he had tried to turn Monk towards Myles Kellard himself. He must know they would be doing the same thing, feeding every scrap of information they could to turn the police to the servants' hall. He came in with the air of fear about him, his body tense, his eyes wide, a small nerve ticking in the side of his face.

Evan moved silently to stand between him and the door.

"Yes sir?" Percival said without waiting for Monk to speak, although his eyes flickered as he became aware of Evan's change of position—and its meaning.

Monk had been holding the silk and the knife behind him. Now he brought them forward and held them up, the knife in his left hand, the peignoir hanging, the spattered blood dark and ugly. He watched Percival's face minutely, every shade of expression. He saw surprise, a shadow of puzzlement as if it were confusing to him, but no blanching of new fear. In fact there was even a quick lift of hope, as if a moment of sun had shone through clouds. It was not the reaction he had expected from a guilty man. At that instant he believed Percival did not know where they had been found.

"Have you seen these before?" he said. The answer would be of little value to him, but he had to begin somewhere.

Percival was very pale, but more composed than when he came in. He thought he knew what the threat was now, and it disturbed him less than the unknown.

"Maybe. The knife looks like several in the kitchen. The silk could be any of those I've passed in the laundry. But I certainly haven't seen them like that. Is that what killed Mrs. Haslett?"

"It certainly looks like it, doesn't it?"

, "Yes sir."

"Don't you want to know where we found them?" Monk glanced past him to Evan and saw the doubt in his face also, an exact reflection of what he was feeling himself. If Percival knew they had found these things in his room, he was a superb actor and a man of self-control worthy of anyone's admiration—and an incredible fool not to have found some way of disposing of them before now.

Percival lifted his shoulders a fraction but said nothing.

"Behind the bottom drawer in the dresser in your bedroom."

This time Percival was horrified. There was no mistaking the sudden rush of blood from his skin, the dilation of his eyes and the sweat standing out on his lip and brow.

He drew breath to speak, and his voice failed him.

In that moment Monk had a sudden sick conviction that Percival had not killed Octavia Haslett. He was arrogant, selfish, and had probably misused her, and perhaps Rose, and he had money that would take some explaining, but he was not guilty of murder. Monk looked at Evan again and saw the same thoughts, even to the shock of unhappiness, mirrored in his eyes.

Monk looked back at Percival.

"I assume you cannot tell me how they got there?"

Percival swallowed convulsively. "No—no I can't."

"I thought not."

"I can't!" Percival's voice rose an octave to a squeak, cracking with fear. "Before God, I didn't kill her! I've never seen them before—not like that!" The muscles of his body were so knotted he was shaking. "Look—I exaggerated. I said she admired me—I was bragging. I never had an affair with her." He started to move agitatedly. "She was never interested in anyone but Captain Haslett. Look—I was polite to her, no more than that. And I never went to her room except to carry trays or flowers or messages, which is my job." His hands moved convulsively. "I don't know who killed her—but it wasn't me! Anyone could have put these things in my room—why would I keep them there?" His words were falling over each other. "I'm not a fool.

Why wouldn't I clean the knife and put it back in its place in the kitchen—and burn the silk? Why wouldn't I?" He swallowed hard and turned to Evan. "I wouldn't leave them there for you to find."

"No, I don't think you would," Monk agreed. "Unless you were so sure of yourself you thought we wouldn't search? You've tried to direct us to Rose, and to Mr. Kellard, or even Mrs. Kellard. Perhaps you thought you had succeeded—and you were keeping them to implicate someone else?"

Percival licked his dry lips. "Then why didn't I do that? I can go in and out of bedrooms easily enough; I've only got to get something from the laundry to carry and no one would question me. I wouldn't leave them in my own room, I'd have hidden them in someone else's— Mr. Kellard's—for you to find!"

"You didn't know we were going to search today," Monk pointed out, pushing the argument to the end, although he had no belief in it. "Perhaps you planned to do that—but we were too quick?"

"You've been here for weeks," Percival protested. "I'd have done it before now—and said something to you to make you search. It'd have been easy enough to say I'd seen something, or to get Mrs. Boden to check her knives to find one gone. Come on—don't you think I could do that?"

"Yes," Monk agreed. "I do."

Percival swallowed and choked. "Well?" he said when he regained his voice.

"You can go for now."

Percival stared wide-eyed for a long moment, then turned on his heel and went out, almost bumping into Evan and leaving the door open.

Monk looked at Evan.

"I don't think he did it," Evan said very quietly. "It doesn't make sense."

"No—neither do I," Monk agreed.

"Mightn't he run?" Evan asked anxiously.

Monk shook his head. "We'd know within an hour—and it'd send half the police in London after him. He knows that."

"Then who did it?" Evan asked. "Kellard?"

"Or did Rose believe that Percival really was having an affair, and she did it in jealousy?" Monk thought aloud.

"Or somebody we haven't even thought of?" Evan added with a downward little smile, devoid of humor. "I wonder what Miss Latterly thinks?"

Monk was prevented from answering by Harold putting his head around the door, his face pale, his blue eyes wide and anxious.

"Mr. Phillips says are you all right, sir?"

"Yes, thank you. Please tell Mr. Phillips we haven't reached any conclusion so far, and will you ask Miss Latterly to come here."

"The nurse, sir? Are you unwell, sir? Or are you going to . . ." He trailed off, his imagination ahead of propriety.

Monk smiled sourly. "No, I'm not going to say anything to make anyone faint. I merely want to ask her opinion about something. Will you send for her please?"

"Yes sir. I—yes sir." And he withdrew in haste, glad to be out of a situation beyond him.

"Sir Basil won't be pleased," Evan said dryly.

"No, I imagine not," Monk agreed. "Nor will anyone else. They all seemed keen that poor Percival should be arrested and the matter dealt with, and us out of the way."

"And someone who will be even angrier," Evan pulled a face, "will be Runcorn."

"Yes," Monk said slowly with some satisfaction. "Yes—he will, won't he!"

Evan sat down on the arm of one of Mrs. Willis's best chairs, swinging his legs a little. "I wonder if your not arresting Percival will prompt whoever it is to try something more dramatic?"

Monk grunted and smiled very slightly. "That's a very comfortable thought."

There was a knock on the door and as Evan opened it Hester came in, looking puzzled and curious.

Evan closed the door and leaned against it.

Monk told her briefly what had happened, adding his own feelings and Evan's in explanation.

"One of the family," she said quietly.

"What makes you say that?"

She lifted her shoulders very slightly, not quite a shrug, and her brow wrinkled in thought. "Lady Moidore is afraid of something, not something that has happened, but something she is afraid may yet happen. Arresting a footman wouldn't trouble her; it would be a relief." Her gray eyes were very direct. "Then you would go away, the public and the newspapers would forget about it, and they could begin to recover. They would stop suspecting one another and trying to pretend they are not."

"Myles Kellard?" he asked.

She frowned, finding words slowly. "If he did, I think it would be in panic. He doesn't seem to me to have the nerve to cover for himself as coolly as this. I mean keeping the knife and the peignoir and hiding it in Percival's room." She hesitated. "I think if he killed her, then someone else is hiding it for him—perhaps Araminta? Maybe that is why he is afraid of her—and I think he is."

"And Lady Moidore knows this—or suspects it?"

"Perhaps."

"Or Araminta killed her sister when she found her husband in her room?" Evan suggested suddenly. "That is something that might happen. Perhaps she went along in the night and found them together and killed her sister and left her husband to take the blame?"

Monk looked at him with considerable respect. It was a solution he had not yet thought of himself, and now it was there in words. "Eminently possible," he said aloud. "Far more likely than Percival going to her room, being rejected and knifing her. For one thing, he would hardly go for a seduction armed with a kitchen knife, and unless she was expecting him, neither would she." He leaned comfortably against one of Mrs. Willis's chairs. "And if she were expecting him," he went on, "surely there were better ways of defending herself, simply by informing her father that the footman had overstepped himself and should be dismissed. Basil had already proved himself more than willing to dismiss a servant who was innocently involved with one of the family, how much more easily one who was not innocent."

He saw their immediate comprehension.

"Are you going to tell Sir Basil?" Evan asked.

"I have no choice. He's expecting me to arrest Percival."

"And Runcorn?" Evan persisted.

"I'll have to tell him too. Sir Basil will—"

Evan smiled, but no answer was necessary.

Monk turned to Hester. "Be careful," he warned. "Whoever it is wants us to arrest Percival. They will be upset that we haven't and may do something rash."

"I will," she said quite calmly.

Her composure irritated him. "You don't appear to understand the risk." His voice was sharp. "There would be a physical danger to you."

"I am acquainted with physical danger." She met his eyes levelly with a glint of amusement. "I have seen a great deal more death than you have, and been closer to my own than I am ever likely to be in London."

His reply was futile, and he forbore from making it. This time she was perfectly right—he had forgotten. Dryly he excused himself and reported to the front of the house and an irate Sir Basil.

"In God's name, what more do you need?" he shouted, banging his fist on his desk and making the ornaments jump. "You find the weapon and my daughter's bloodstained clothes in the man's bedroom! Do you expect a confession?"

Monk explained with as much clarity and patience as he could exactly why he felt it was not yet sufficient evidence, but Basil was angry and dismissed him with less than courtesy, at the same time calling for Harold to attend him instantly and take a letter.

By the time Monk had returned to the kitchen and collected Evan, walked along to Regent Street and picked up a hansom to the police station to report to Runcorn, Harold, with Sir Basil's letter, was ahead of him.

"What in the devil's name are you doing, Monk?" Runcorn demanded, leaning across his desk, the paper clenched in his fist. "You've got enough evidence to hang the man twice over. What are you playing at, man, telling Sir Basil you aren't going to arrest him? Go back and do it right now!"

"I don't think he's guilty," Monk said flatly.

Runcorn was nonplussed. His long face fell into an expression of disbelief. "You what?"

"I don't think he's guilty," Monk repeated clearly and with a sharper edge to his voice.

The color rose in Runcorn's cheeks, beginning to mottle his skin. "Don't be ridiculous. Of course he's guilty!" he shouted. "Good God man, didn't you find the knife and her bloodstained clothes in his room? What more do you want? What innocent explanation could there possibly be?"

"That he didn't put them there." Monk kept his own voice low.

"Only a fool would have left things like that where they might be found."

"But you didn't find them, did you?" Runcorn said furiously, on his feet now. "Not until the cook told you her knife was missing. This damn footman can't have known she'd notice it after this time. He didn't know you'd search the place."

"We already searched it once for the missing jewelry," Monk pointed out.

"Well you didn't search it very well, did you?" Runcorn accused with satisfaction lacing through his words even now. "You didn't expect to find it, so you didn't make a proper job of it. Slipshod—think you're cleverer than anybody else and leap to conclusions." He leaned forward over the desk, his hands resting on the surface, splay fingered. "Well you were wrong this time, weren't you—in fact I'd say downright incompetent. If you'd done your job and searched properly in the beginning, you'd have found the knife and the clothes and spared the family a great deal of distress, and the police a lot of time and effort."

He waved the letter. "If I thought I could, I'd take all the rest of the police wages out of yours, to cover the hours wasted by your incompetence! You're losing your touch, Monk, losing your touch. Now try to make up for it in some degree by going back to Queen Anne Street, apologizing to Sir Basil, and arresting the damned footman."

"It wasn't there when we looked the first time," Monk repeated. He was not going to allow Evan to be blamed, and he believed that what he said was almost certainly true.

Runcorn blinked. "Well all that means is that he had it somewhere else then—and put it in the drawer afterwards." Runcorn's voice was getting louder in spite of himself. "Get back to Queen Anne Street and arrest that footman—do I make myself clear? I don't know what simpler words to put it in. Get out, Monk—arrest Percival for murder."

"No sir. I don't think he did it."

"Nobody gives a fig what you think, damn it! Just do as you are told." Runcorn's face was deepening in color and his hands were clenching on the desk top.

Monk forced himself to keep his temper sufficiently to argue the case. He would like simply to have told Runcorn he was a fool and left.

"It doesn't make sense," he began with an effort. "If he had the chance to get rid of the jewelry, why didn't he get rid of the knife and the peignoir at the same time?"

"He probably didn't get rid of the jewelry," Runcorn said with a sudden flash of satisfaction. "I expect it's still there, and if you searched properly you'd find it—stuffed inside an old boot, or sewn in a pocket or something. After all, you were looking for a knife this time; you wouldn't look anywhere too small to conceal one."

"We were looking for jewelry the first time," Monk pointed out with a touch of sarcasm he could not conceal. "We could hardly have missed a carving knife and a silk dressing robe."

"No you couldn't, if you'd been doing your job," Runcorn agreed. "Which means you weren't—doesn't it, Monk?"

"Either that or it wasn't there then," Monk agreed, staring back at him without a flicker. "Which is what I said before. Only a fool would keep things like that, when he could clean the knife and put it back in the kitchen without any difficulty at all. Nobody would be surprised to see a footman in the kitchen; they're in and out all the time on errands. And they are frequently the last to go to bed at night because they lock up."

Runcorn opened his mouth to argue, but Monk overrode him.

"Nobody would be surprised to see Percival about at midnight or later. He could explain his presence anywhere in the house, except someone else's bedroom, simply by saying he had heard a window rattle, or feared a door was unlocked. They would simply commend him for his diligence."

"A position you might well envy," Runcorn said. "Even your most fervent admirer could hardly recommend you for yours."

"And he could as easily have put the peignoir on the back of the kitchen range and closed the lid, and it would be burned without a trace," Monk went on, disregarding the interruption. "Now if it were the jewelry we found, that would make more sense. I could understand someone keeping that, in the hope that some time they would be able to sell it, or even give it away or trade it for something. But why keep a knife?"

"I don't know, Monk," Runcorn said between his teeth. "I don't have the mind of a homicidal footman. But he did keep it, didn't he, damn it. You found it."

"We found it, yes," Monk agreed with elaborate patience which brought the blood dark and heavy to Runcorn's cheeks. "But that is the point I am trying to make, sir. There is no proof that it was Percival who kept it—or that it was he who put it there. Anyone could have. His room is not locked."

Runcorn's eyebrows shot up.

"Oh indeed? You have just been at great pains to point out to me that no one would keep such a thing as a bloodstained knife! Now you say someone else did—but not Percival. You contradict yourself, Monk." He leaned even farther across the desk, staring at Monk's face. "You are talking like a fool. The knife was there, so someone did keep it—for all your convoluted arguments—and it was found in Percival's room. Get out and arrest him."

"Someone kept it deliberately to put it in Percival's room and make him seem guilty." Monk forgot his temper and began to raise his voice in exasperation, refusing to back away either physically or intellectually. "It only makes sense if it was kept to be used."

Runcorn blinked. "By whom, for God's sake? This laundrymaid of yours? You've no proof against her." He waved his hand, dismissing her. "None at all. What's the matter with you, Monk? Why are you so dead against arresting Percival? What's he done for you? Surely you can't be so damned perverse that you make trouble simply out of habit?" His eyes narrowed and his face was only a few feet from Monk's.

Monk still refused to step backward.

"Why are you so determined to try to blame one of the family?" Runcorn said between his teeth. "Good God, wasn't the Grey case enough for you, dragging the family into that? Have you got it into your mind that it was this Myles Kellard, simply because he took advantage of a parlormaid? Do you want to punish him for that—is that what this is about?"

"Raped," Monk corrected very distinctly. His diction became more perfect as Runcorn lost his control and slurred his words in rage.

"All right, raped, if you prefer—don't be pedantic," Runcorn shouted. "Forcing yourself on a parlormaid is not the next step before murdering your sister-in-law."

"Raping. Raping a seventeen-year-old maid who is a servant in your house, a dependent, who dare not say much to you, or defend herself, is not such a long way from going to your sister-in-law's room in the night with the intention of forcing yourself on her and, if need be, raping her." Monk used the word loudly and very clearly, giving each letter its value. "If she says no to you, and you think she really means yes, what is the difference between one woman and another on that point?"

"If you don't know the difference between a lady and a parlormaid, Monk, that says more about your ignorance than you would like." Runcorn's face was twisted with all the pent-up hatred and fear of their long relationship. "It shows that for all your arrogance and ambition, you're just the uncouth provincial clod you always were. Your fine clothes and your assumed accent don't make a gentleman of you—the boor is still underneath and it will always come out." His eyes shone with a kind of wild, bitter triumph. He had said at last what had been seething inside him for years, and there was an uncontrollable joy in its release.

"You've been trying to find the courage to say that ever since you first felt me treading on your heels, haven't you?" Monk sneered. "What a pity you haven't enough courage to face the newspapers and the gentlemen of the Home Office that scare the wits out of you. If you were man enough you'd tell them you won't arrest anyone, even a footman, until you have reasonable evidence that he's guilty. But you aren't, are you? You're a weakling. You'll turn the other way and pretend not to see what their lordships don't like. You'll arrest Percival because he's convenient. Nobody cares about him! Sir Basil will be satisfied and you can wrap it up without offending anyone who frightens you. You can present it to your superiors as a case closed—true or not, just or not—hang the poor bastard and close the file on it."

He stared at Runcorn with ineffable contempt. "The public will applaud you, and the gentlemen will say what a good and obedient servant you are. Good God, Percival may be a selfish and arrogant little swine, but he's not a craven lickspittle like you—and I will not arrest him until I think he's guilty."

Runcorn's face was blotched with purple and his fists were clenched on the desk. His whole body shook, his muscles so tight his shoulders strained against the fabric of his coat.

"I am not asking, Monk, I am ordering you. Go and arrest Percival—now!"

"No."

"No?" A strange light flickered in Runcorn's eyes: fear, disbelief and exultancy. "Are you refusing, Monk?"

Monk swallowed, knowing what he was doing.

"Yes. You are wrong, and I am refusing."

"You are dismissed!" He flung his arm out at the door. "You are no longer employed by the Metropolitan Police Force." He thrust out one heavy hand. "Give me your official identification. As of this moment you have no office, no position, do you understand me? You are dismissed! Now get out!"

Monk fished in his pocket and found his papers. His hands were stiff and he was furious that he fumbled. He threw them on the desk and turned on his heel and strode out, leaving the door open.

Out in the passage he almost pushed past two constables and a sergeant with a pile of papers, all standing together frozen in disbelief and a kind of awed excitement. They were witnessing history, the fall of a giant, and there was regret and triumph in their faces, and a kind of guilt because such vulnerability was unexpected. They felt both superior and afraid.

Monk passed them too quickly for them to pretend they had not been listening, but he was too wrapped in his own emotions to heed their embarrassment.

By the time he was downstairs the duty constable had composed himself and retired to his desk. He opened his mouth to say something, but Monk did not listen, and he was relieved of the necessity.

It was not until Monk was out in the street in the rain that he felt the first chill of realization that he had thrown away not only his career but his livelihood. Fifteen minutes ago he had been an admired and sometimes feared senior policeman, good at his job, secure in his reputation and his skill. Now he was a man without work, without position, and in a short while he would be without money. And over Percival.

No—over the hatred between Runcorn and himself over the years, the rivalry, the fear, the misunderstandings.

Or perhaps over innocence and guilt?

CHAPTER
NINE

Monk slept poorly and woke late and heavy-headed. He rose and was half dressed before he remembered that he had nowhere to go. Not only was he off the Queen Anne Street case, he was no longer a policeman. In fact he was nothing. His profession was what had given him purpose, position in the community, occupation for his time, and now suddenly desperately important, his income. He would be all right for a few weeks, at least for his lodgings and his food. There would be no other expenditures, no clothes, no meals out, no new books or rare, wonderful visits to theater or gallery in his steps towards being a gentleman.

But those things were trivial. The center of his life had fallen out. The ambition he had nourished and sacrificed for, disciplined himself towards for all the lifetime he could remember or piece together from records and other people's words, that was gone. He had no other relationships, nothing else he knew to do with his time, no one else who valued him, even if it was with admiration and fear, not love. He remembered sharply the faces of the men outside Runcorn's door. There was confusion in them, embarrassment, anxiety—but not sympathy. He had earned their respect, but not their affection.

He felt more bitterly alone, confused, and wretched than at any time since the climax of the Grey case. He had no appetite for the breakfast Mrs. Worley brought him and ate only a rasher of bacon and two slices of toast. He was still looking at the crumb-scattered plate when there was a sharp rap on the door and Evan came in without waiting to be invited. He stared at Monk and sat down astride the other hard-backed chair and said nothing, his face full of anxiety and something so painfully gentle it could only be called compassion.

"Don't look like that!" Monk said sharply. "I shall survive. There is life outside the police force, even for me."

Evan said nothing.

"Have you arrested Percival?" Monk asked him.

"No. He sent Tarrant."

Monk smiled sourly. "Perhaps he was afraid you wouldn't do it. Fool!"

Evan winced.

"I'm sorry," Monk apologized quickly. "But your resigning as well would hardly help—either Percival or me."

"I suppose not," Evan conceded ruefully, a shadow of guilt still lingering in his eyes. Monk seldom remembered how young he was, but now he looked every inch the country parson's son with his correct casual clothes and his slightly different manner concealing an inner certainty Monk himself would never have. Evan might be more sensitive, less arrogant or forceful in his judgment, but he would always have a kind of ease because he was born a minor gentleman, and he knew it, if not on the surface of his mind, then in the deeper layer from which instinct springs. "What are you going to do now, have you thought? The newspapers are full of it this morning."

"They would be," Monk acknowledged. "Rejoicing everywhere, I expect? The Home Office will be praising the police, the aristocracy will be congratulating itself it is not at fault—it may have hired a bad footman, but that kind of misjudgment is bound to happen from time to time." He heard the bitterness in his voice and despised it, but he could not remove it, it was too high in him. "Any honest gentleman can think too well of someone. Moidore's family is exonerated. And the public at large can sleep safe in its beds again."

"About right," Evan conceded, pulling a face. "There's a long editorial in the *Times* on the efficiency of the new police force, even in the most trying and sensitive of cases, to wit—in the very home of one of London's most eminent gentlemen. Runcorn is mentioned several times as being in charge of the investigation. You aren't mentioned at all." He shrugged. "Neither am I."

Monk smiled for the first time, at Evan's innocence.

"There's also a piece by someone regretting the rising arrogance of the working classes," Evan went on. "And predicting the downfall of the social order as we know it and the general decline of Christian morals."

"Naturally," Monk said tersely. "There always is. I think someone writes a pile of them and sends one in every time he thinks the occasion excuses it. What else? Does anyone speculate as to whether Percival is actually guilty or not?"

Evan looked very young. Monk could see the shadow of the boy in him so clearly behind the man, the vulnerability in the mouth, the innocence in the eyes.

"None that I saw. Everyone wants him hanged," Evan said miserably. "There seems to be general relief all 'round, and everyone is very happy to call the case closed and put an end to it. The running patterers have already started composing songs about it, and I passed one selling it by the yard on the Tottenham Court Road." His words were sophisticated, but his expression belied them. "Very lurid, and not much resemblance to the truth as we saw it—or thought we did. All twopenny dreadful stuff, innocent widow and lust in the pantry, going to bed with a carving knife to defend her virtue, and the evil footman afire with unholy passions creeping up the stairs to have his way with her." He looked up at Monk. "They want to bring back drawing and quartering. Bloodthirsty swine!"

"They've been frightened," Monk said without pity. "An ugly thing, fear."

Evan frowned. "Do you think that's what it was—in Queen Anne Street? Everyone afraid, and just wanted to put it onto someone, anyone, to get us out of the house, and to stop thinking about each other and learning more than they wanted to know?"

Monk leaned forward, pushing the plates away, and rested his elbows on the table wearily.

"Perhaps." He sighed. "God—I've made a mess of it! The worst thing is that Percival will hang. He's an arrogant and selfish sod, but he doesn't deserve to die for that. But nearly as bad is that whoever did kill him is still in that house, and is going to get away with it. And try as they might to ignore things, forget things, at least one of them has a fair idea who it is." He looked up. "Can you imagine it, Evan? Living the rest of your life with someone you know committed murder and let another man swing for it? Passing them on the stairs, sitting opposite them at the dinner table, watching them smile and tell jokes as if it had never happened?"

"What are you going to do?" Evan was watching him with intelligent, troubled eyes.

"What in hell's name can I do?" Monk exploded. "Runcorn's arrested Percival and will send him to trial. I haven't any evidence I've not already given him, and I'm not only off the case, I'm off the force. I don't even know how I'm going to keep a roof over my head, damn it. I'm the last person to help Percival—I can't even help myself."

"You're the only one who can help him," Evan said quietly. There was friendship in his face and understanding, but no moderation of the truth. "Except perhaps Miss Latterly," he added. "Anyway, apart from us, there's no one else who's going to try." He stood up from the chair, uncoiling his legs. "I'll go and tell her what happened. She'll know about Percival, of course, and the fact that it was Tarrant and not you will have told her something was wrong, but she won't know whether it's illness, another case, or what." He smiled with a wry twist of his lips. "Unless of course she knows you well enough to have guessed you lost your temper with Runcorn?"

Monk was about to deny that as ridiculous, then he remembered Hester and the doctor in the infirmary, and had a sudden blossoming of fellow-feeling, a warmth inside evaporating a little of the chill in him.

"She might," he conceded.

"I'll go to Queen Anne Street and tell her." Evan straightened his jacket, unconsciously elegant even now. "Before I'm thrown off the case too and I've no excuse to go back there."

Monk looked up at him. "Thank you—"

Evan made a little salute, with more courage in it than hope, and went out, leaving Monk alone with the remnants of his breakfast.

He stared at the table for several minutes longer, his mind half searching for something further, then suddenly a shaft of memory returned so vividly it stunned him. At some other time he had sat at a polished dining table in a room filled with gracious furniture and mirrors framed in gilt and a bowl of flowers. He had felt the same grief, and the overwhelming burden of guilt because he could not help.

It was the home of the mentor of whom he had been reminded so sharply on the pavement in Piccadilly outside Cyprian's club. There had been a financial disaster, a scandal in which he had been ruined. The woman in the funeral carriage whose ugly, grieving face had struck him so powerfully—it was his mentor's wife he had seen in her place, she whose beautiful hands he recalled; it was her distress he had ached to relieve, and been helpless. The whole tragedy had played itself out relentlessly, leaving the victims in its wake.

He remembered the passion and the impotence seething inside him as he had sat on that other table, and the resolve then to learn some skill that would give him weapons to fight injustice, uncover the dark frauds that seemed so inaccessible. That was when he had changed his mind from commerce and its rewards and chosen the police.

Police. He had been arrogant, dedicated, brilliant—and earned himself promotion—and dislike; and now he had nothing left, not even memory of his original skills.

"He what?" Hester demanded as she faced Evan in Mrs. Willis's sitting room. Its dark, Spartan furnishings and religious texts on the walls were sharply familiar to her now, but this news was a blow she could barely comprehend. "What did you say?"

"He refused to arrest Percival, and told Runcorn what he thought of him," Evan elaborated. "With the result, of course, that Runcorn threw him off the force."

"What is he going to do?" She was appalled. The sense of fear and helplessness was too close in her own memory to need imagination, and her position at Queen Anne Street was only temporary. Beatrice was not ill, and now that Percival had been arrested she would in all probability recover in a matter of days, as long as she believed he was guilty. Hester looked at Evan. "Where will he find employment? Has he any family?"

Evan looked at the floor, then up at her again.

"Not here in London, and I don't think he would go to them anyway. I don't know what he'll do," he said unhappily. "It's all he knows, and I think all he cares about. It's his natural skill."

"Does anybody employ detectives, apart from the police?" she asked.

He smiled, and there was a flash of hope in his eyes, then it faded. "But if he hired out his skills privately, he would need means to live until he developed a reputation—it would be too difficult."

"Perhaps," she said reluctantly, not yet prepared to consider the idea. "In the meantime, what can we do about Percival?"

"Can you meet Monk somewhere to discuss it? He can't come here now. Will Lady Moidore give you half an afternoon free?"

"I haven't had any time since I came here. I shall ask. If she permits me, where will he be?"

"It's cold outside." He glanced beyond her to the single, narrow window facing onto a small square of grass and two laurel bushes. "How about the chocolate house in Regent Street?"

"Excellent. I will go and ask Lady Moidore now."

"What will you say?" he asked quickly.

"I shall lie," she answered without hesitation. "I shall say a family emergency has arisen and I need to speak with them." She pulled a harsh, humorous face. "She should understand a family emergency, if anyone does!"

"A family emergency." Beatrice turned from staring out of the window at the sky and looked at Hester with consternation. "I'm sorry. Is it illness? I can recommend a doctor, if you do not already have one, but I imagine you do—you must have several."

"Thank you, that is most thoughtful." Hester felt distinctly guilty. "But as far as I know there is no ill health; it is a matter of losing a position, which may cause a considerable amount of hardship."

Beatrice was fully dressed for the first time in several days, but she had not yet ventured into the main rooms of the house, nor had she joined in the life of the household, except to spend a little time with her grandchildren, Julia and Arthur. She looked very pale and her features were drawn. If she felt any relief at Percival's arrest it did not show in her expression. Her body was tense and she stood awkwardly, ill at ease. She forced a smile, bright and unnatural.

"I am so sorry. I hope you will be able to help, even if it is only with comfort and good advice. Sometimes that is all we have for each other—don't you think?" She swung around and stared at Hester as if the answer were of intense importance to her. Then before Hester could reply she walked away and started fishing in one of her dressing table drawers searching for something.

"Of course you know the police arrested Percival and took him away last night. Mary said it wasn't Mr. Monk. I wonder why. Do you know, Hester?"

There was no possible way Hester could have known the truth except by being privy to police affairs that she could not share.

"I have no idea, your ladyship. Perhaps he has become involved in another matter, and someone else was delegated to do this. After all, the detection has been completed—I suppose."

Beatrice's fingers froze and she stood perfectly still.

"You suppose? You mean it might not? What else could they want? Percival is guilty, isn't he?"

"I don't know." Hester kept her voice quite light. "I assume they must believe so, or they would not have arrested him; though we cannot say beyond any possible doubt until he has been tried."

Beatrice drew more tightly into herself. "They'll hang him, won't they?"

Hester felt a trifle sick. "Yes," she agreed very quietly. Then she felt compelled to persist. "Does that distress you?"

"It shouldn't—should it?" Beatrice sounded surprised at herself. "He murdered my daughter."

"But it does?" Hester allowed nothing to slip by. "It is very final, isn't it? I mean—it allows for no mistakes, no time for second thoughts on anything."

Still Beatrice stood motionless on the spot, her hands plunged in the silks, chiffons and laces in the drawer.

"Second thoughts? What do you mean?"

Now Hester retreated. "I'm not sure. I suppose another way of looking at the evidence—perhaps if someone were lying—or remembered inaccurately—"

"You are saying that the murderer is still here—among us, Hester." There was no panic in Beatrice's voice, just cold pain. "And whoever it is, is calmly watching Percival go to his death on—on false evidence."

Hester swallowed hard and found her voice difficult to force into her throat.

"I suppose whoever it is must be very frightened. Perhaps it was an accident at first—I mean it was a struggle that was not meant to end in death. Don't you think?"

At last Beatrice turned around, her hands empty.

"You mean Myles?" she said slowly and distinctly. "You think it was Myles who went to her room and she fought with him and he took the knife from her and stabbed her, because by then he had too much to lose if she should speak against him and told everyone what had happened?" She leaned a little against the chest. "That is what they are saying happened with Percival, you know. Yes, of course you know. You are in the servants' hall more than I am. That's what Mary says."

She looked down at her hands. "And it is what Romola believes. She is terribly relieved, you know. She thinks it is all over now. We can stop suspecting one another. She thought it was Septimus, you know, that Tavie discovered something about him! Which is ridiculous—she always knew his story!" She tried to laugh at the idea, and failed. "Now she imagines we will forget it all and go on just as before. We'll forget everything we've learned about each other—and ourselves: the shallowness, the self-deception, how quick we are to blame someone else when we are afraid. Anything to protect ourselves. As if nothing would be different, except that Tavie won't be here." She smiled, a dazzling, nervous gesture without warmth. "Sometimes I think Romola is the stupidest woman I've ever met."

"It won't be the same," Hester agreed, torn between wanting to comfort her and the need to follow every shade or inflection of truth she could. "But in time we may at least forgive, and some things can be forgotten."

"Can they?" Beatrice looked not at her but out of the window again. "Will Minta ever forget that Myles raped that wretched girl? Whatever rape is. What is rape, Hester? If you do your duty within marriage, that is lawful and right. You would be condemned for doing anything less. How different is it outside marriage that it should be regarded as such a despicable crime?"

"Is it?" Hester allowed some of her anger to come through. "It seems to me very few people were upset about Mr. Kellard's rape of the maid, in fact they were angrier with her for speaking of it than they were with him for having done it. It all hangs upon who is involved."

"I suppose so. But that is small comfort if it is your husband. I can see the hurt of it in her face. Not often—but sometimes in repose, when she does not think of anyone looking at her, I see pain under the composure." She turned back, frowning, a slow troubled expression not intended for Hester. "And sometimes I think a terrible anger."

"But Mr. Kellard is unhurt," Hester said very gently, longing to be able to comfort her and knowing now beyond doubt that Percival's arrest was by no means the beginning of healing. "Surely if Mrs. Kellard were thinking any violence it would be him she would direct it against? It is only natural to be angry, but in time she may forget the sharpness of it, and even think of the fact less and less often." She nearly added that if Myles were to be tender enough with her, and generous, then it would eventually cease to matter. But thinking of Myles she could not believe it, and to speak such an ephemeral hope aloud might only add to the wound. Beatrice must see him at least as clearly as Hester, who knew him such a short while.

"Yes," Beatrice said without conviction. "Of course, you are right. And please, take what time you need this afternoon."

"Thank you."

As she turned to leave, Basil came in, having knocked so perfunctorily that neither of them heard him. He walked past Hester, barely noticing her, his eyes on Beatrice.

"Good," he said briskly. "I see you are dressed today. Naturally you are feeling much better."

"No—" Beatrice began, but he cut her off.

"Of course you are." His smile was businesslike. "I'm delighted, my dear. This fearful tragedy has naturally affected your health, but the worst of it is already over, and you will gain strength every day."

"Over." She faced him with incredulity. "Do you really believe it is over, Basil?"

"Of course it is." He did not look at her but walked around the room slowly, looking at the dressing table, then straightening one of the pictures. "There will be the trial, of course; but you do not need to attend."

"I wish to!"

"If it will help you to feel the matter is dealt with, I can understand it, although I think it would be better if you accepted my account."

"It is not over, Basil! Just because they have arrested Percival . . ."

He swung around to face her, impatience in his eyes and mouth.

"All of it is over that needs to concern you, Beatrice. If it will help you to see justice done, then go to the trial by all means, otherwise I advise you to remain at home. Either way, the investigation is closed and you may cease to think about it. You are much better, and I am delighted to see it." She accepted the futility of arguing and looked away, her hands fiddling with the lace handkerchief from her pocket.

"I have decided to help Cyprian to obtain a seat in Parliament," Basil went on, satisfied her concern was over. "He has been interested in politics for some time, and it would be an excellent thing for him to do. I have connections that will make a safe Tory seat available to him by the next general election."

"Tory?" Beatrice was surprised. "But his beliefs are radical!"

"Nonsense!" He dismissed it with a laugh. "He reads some very odd literature, I know; but he doesn't take it seriously."

"I think he does."

"Rubbish. You have to consider such stuff to know how to fight against it, that is all."

"Basil—I—"

"Absolute nonsense, my dear. It will do him excellently. You will see the change in him. Now I am due in Whitehall in half an hour. I will see you for dinner." And with a perfunctory kiss on her cheek he left, again walking past Hester as if she were invisible.

Hester walked into the chocolate house in Regent Street and saw Monk immediately, sitting at one of the small tables, leaning forward staring into the dregs of a glass cup, his face smooth and bleak. She had seen that expression before, when he had thought the Grey case catastrophic.

She sailed in with a swish of skirts, albeit only blue stuff and not satin, and sat down on the chair opposite him prepared to be angry even before he spoke. His defeatism reached her emotions the more easily because she had no idea how to fight any further herself.

He looked up, saw the accusation in her eyes, and instantly his face hardened.

"I see you have managed to escape the sickroom this afternoon," he said with a heavy trace of sarcasm. "I presume now that the 'illness' is at an end, her ladyship will recover rapidly?"

"Is the illness at an end?" she said with elaborate surprise. "I thought from Sergeant Evan that it was far from over; in fact it appears to have suffered a serious relapse, which may even prove fatal."

"For the footman, yes—but hardly her ladyship and her family," he said without trying to hide his bitterness.

"But for you." She regarded him without the sympathy she felt. He was in danger of sinking into self-pity, and she believed most people were far better bullied out of it than catered to. Real compassion should be reserved for the helplessly suffering, of whom she had seen immeasurably too many. "So you have apparently given up your career in the police—"

"I have not given it up," he contradicted angrily. "You speak as if I did it with deliberate intent. I refused to arrest a man I did not believe guilty, and Runcorn dismissed me for it."

"Very noble," she agreed tersely. "But totally foreseeable. You cannot have imagined for a second that he would do anything else."

"Then you will have an excellent fellow-feeling," he returned savagely. "Since you can hardly have supposed Dr. Pomeroy would permit you to remain at the infirmary after prescribing the dispensing medicine yourself!" He was apparently unaware of having raised his voice, or of the couple at the next table turning to stare at them. "Unfortunately I doubt you can find me private employment detecting as a free-lance, as you can with nursing," he finished.

"It was your suggestion to Callandra." Not that she was surprised; it was the only answer that made sense.

"Of course." His smile was without humor. "Perhaps you can go and ask her if she has any wealthy friends who need a little uncovering of secrets, or tracing of lost heirs?"

"Certainly—that is an excellent idea."

"Don't you dare!" He was furious, offended and patronized. "I forbid it!"

The waiter was standing at his elbow to accept their order, but Monk ignored him.

"I shall do as I please," Hester said instantly. "You will not dictate to me what I shall say to Callandra. I should like a cup of chocolate, if you would be so good."

The waiter opened his mouth, and then when no one took any notice of him, closed it again.

"You are an arrogant and opinionated woman," Monk said fiercely. "And quite the most overbearing I have ever met. And you will not start organizing my life as if you were some damned governess. I am not helpless nor lying in a hospital bed at your mercy."

"Not helpless?" Her eyebrows shot up and she looked at him with all the frustration and impotent anger boiling up inside her, the fury at the blindness, complacency, cowardice and petty malice that had conspired to have Percival arrested and Monk dismissed, and the rest of them unable to see any way to begin to redress the situation. "You have managed to find evidence to have the wretched footman taken away in manacles, but not enough to proceed any further. You are without employment or prospects of any, and have covered yourself with dislike. You are sitting in a chocolate house staring at the dregs of an empty cup. And you have the luxury to refuse help?"

Now the people at all the tables in the immediate vicinity had stopped eating or drinking and were staring at them.

"I refuse your condescending interference," he said. "You should marry some poor devil and concentrate your managerial skills on one man and leave the rest of us in peace."

She knew precisely what was hurting him, the fear of the future when he had not even the experience of the past to draw on, the specter of hunger and homelessness ahead, the sense of failure. She struck where it would wound the most surely, and perhaps eventually do the most good.

"Self-pity does not become you, nor does it serve any purpose," she said quietly, aware now of the people around them. "And please lower your voice. If you expect me to be sorry for you, you are wasting your time. Your situation is of your own making, and not markedly worse than mine—which was also of my own making, I am aware." She stopped, seeing the overwhelming fury in his face. She was afraid for a moment she had really gone too far.

"You—" he began. Then very slowly the rage died away and was replaced by a sharp humor, so hard as to be almost sweet, like a clean wind off the sea. "You have a genius for saying the worst possible thing in any given situation," he finished. "I should imagine a good many patients have taken up their beds and walked, simply to be free of your ministrations and go where they could suffer in peace."

"That is very cruel," she said a little huffily. "I have never been harsh to someone I believed to be genuinely in distress—"

"Oh." His eyebrows rose dramatically. "You think my predicament is not real?"

"Of course your predicament is real," she said. "But your anguish over it is unhelpful. You have talents, in spite of the Queen Anne

Street case. You must find a way to use them for remuneration." She warmed to the subject. "Surely there are cases the police cannot solve—either they are too difficult or they do not fall within their scope to handle? Are there not miscarriages of justice—" That thought brought her back to Percival again, and without waiting for his reply she hurried on. "What are we going to do about Percival? I am even more sure after speaking to Lady Moidore this morning that there is grave doubt as to whether he had anything to do with Octavia's death."

At last the waiter managed to intrude, and Monk ordered chocolate for her, insisting on paying for it, overriding her protest with more haste than courtesy.

"Continue to look for proof, I suppose," he said when the matter was settled and she began to sip at the steaming liquid. "Although if I knew where or what I should have looked already."

"I suppose it must be Myles," she said thoughtfully. "Or Araminta—if Octavia were not as reluctant as we have been led to suppose. She might have known they had an assignation and taken the kitchen knife along, deliberately meaning to kill her."

"Then presumably Myles Kellard would know it," Monk argued. "Or have a very strong suspicion. And from what you said he is more afraid of her than she of him."

She smiled. "If my wife had just killed my mistress with a carving knife I would be more than a trifle nervous, wouldn't you?" But she did not mean it, and she saw from his face that he knew it as well as she. "Or perhaps it was Fenella?" she went on. "I think she has the stomach for such a thing, if she had the motive."

"Well, not out of lust for the footman," Monk replied. "And I doubt Octavia knew anything about her so shocking that Basil would have thrown her out for it. Unless there is a whole avenue we have not explored."

Hester drank the last of her chocolate and set the glass down on its saucer. "Well I am still in Queen Anne Street, and Lady Moidore certainly does not seem recovered yet, or likely to be in the next few days. I shall have a little longer to observe. Is there anything you would like me to pursue?"

"No," he said sharply. Then he looked down at his own glass on the table in front of him. "It is possible that Percival is guilty; it is simply that I do not feel that what we have is proof. We should respect not only the facts but the law. If we do not, then we lay ourselves open to every man's judgment of what may be true or false; and a belief of guilt will become the same thing as proof. There must be something above individual judgment, however passionately felt, or we become barbarous again."

"Of course he may be guilty," she said very quietly. "I have always known that. But I shall not let it go by default as long as I can remain in Queen Anne Street and learn anything at all. If I do find anything, I shall have to write to you, because neither you nor Sergeant Evan will be there. Where may I send a letter, so that the rest of the household will not know it is to you?"

He looked puzzled for a moment.

"I do not post my own mail," she said with a flicker of impatience. "I seldom leave the house. I shall merely put it on the hall table and the footman or the bootboy will take it."

"Oh—of course. Send it to Mr.—" He hesitated, a shadow of a smile crossing his face. "Send it to Mr. Butler—let us move up a rung on the social ladder. At my address in Grafton Street. I shall be there for a few weeks yet."

She met his eyes for a moment of clear and total understanding, then rose and took her leave. She did not tell him she was going to make use of the rest of the afternoon to see Callandra Daviot. He might have thought she was going to ask for help for him, which was exactly what she intended to do, but not with his knowledge. He would refuse beforehand, out of pride; when it was a fait accompli he would be obliged to accept.

"He what?" Callandra was appalled, then she began to laugh in spite of her anger. "Not very practical—but I admire his sentiment, if not his judgment."

They were in her withdrawing room by the fire, the sharp winter sun streaming in through the windows. The new parlormaid, replacing the newly married Daisy, a thin waif of a girl with an amazing smile and apparently named Martha, had brought their tea and hot crumpets with butter. These were less ladylike than cucumber sandwiches, but far nicer on a cold day.

"What could he have accomplished if he had obeyed and arrested Percival?" Hester defended Monk quickly. "Mr. Runcorn would still consider the case closed, and Sir Basil would not permit him to ask any further questions or pursue any investigation. He could hardly even look for more evidence of Percival's guilt. Everyone else seems to consider the knife and the peignoir sufficient."

"Perhaps you are right," Callandra admitted. "But he is a hot-headed creature. First the Grey case, and now this. He seems to have little more sense than you have." She took another crumpet. "You have both taken matters into your own hands and lost your liveli-hoods. What does he propose to do next?"

"I don't know!" Hester threw her hands wide. "I don't know what I am to do myself when Lady Moidore is sufficiently well not to need me. I have no desire whatever to spend my time as a paid companion, fetching and carrying and pandering to imaginary illnesses and fits of the vapors." Suddenly she was overtaken by a profound sense of failure. "Callandra, what happened to me? I came home from the Crimea with such a zeal to work hard, to throw myself into reform and accomplish so much. I was going to see our hospitals cleaner—and of so much greater comfort for the sick." Those dreams seemed utterly out of reach now, part of a golden and lost realm. "I was going to teach people that nursing is a noble profession, fit for fine and dedicated women to serve in, women of sobriety and good character who wished to minister to the sick with skill—not just to keep a bare standard of removing the slops and fetching and carrying for the sur-geons. How did I throw all that away?"

"You didn't throw it away, my dear," Callandra said gently. "You came home afire with your accomplishments in wartime, and did not realize the monumental inertia of peace, and the English passion to keep things as they are, whatever they are. People speak of this as being an age of immense change, and so it is. We have never been so inventive, so wealthy, so free in our ideas good and bad." She shook her head. "But there is still an immeasurable amount that is deter-mined to stay the same, unless it is forced, screaming and fighting, to advance with the times. One of those things is the belief that women should learn amusing arts of pleasing a husband, bearing children, and if you cannot afford the servants to do it for you, of raising them, and of visiting the deserving poor at appropriate times and well accom-panied by your own kind."

A fleeting smile of wry pity touched her lips.

"Never, in any circumstance, should you raise your voice, or try

to assert your opinions in the hearing of gentlemen, and do not attempt to appear clever or strong-minded; it is dangerous, and makes
them extremely uncomfortable."

"You are laughing at me," Hester accused her.

"Only slightly, my dear. You will find another position nursing
privately, if we cannot find a hospital to take you. I shall write to
Miss Nightingale and see what she can advise." Her face darkened.
"In the meantime, I think Mr. Monk's situation is rather more pressing. Has he any skills other than those connected with detecting?"

Hester thought for a moment.

"I don't believe so."

"Then he will have to detect. In spite of this fiasco, I believe he
is gifted at it, and it is a crime for a person to spend his life without
using the talents God gave him." She pushed the crumpet plate towards Hester and Hester took another.

"If he cannot do it publicly in the police force, then he will have
to do it privately." She warmed to the subject. "He will have to
advertise in all the newspapers and periodicals. There must be people
who have lost relatives, I mean mislaid them. There are certainly
robberies the police do not solve satisfactorily—and in time he will
earn a reputation and perhaps be given cases where there has been
injustice or the police are baffled." Her face brightened conspicuously.
"Or perhaps cases where the police do not realize there has been a
crime, but someone does, and is desirous to have it proved. And re-
grettably there will be cases where an innocent person is accused and
wishes to clear his name."

"But how will he survive until he has sufficient of these cases to
earn himself a living?" Hester said anxiously, wiping her fingers on
the napkin to remove the butter.

Callandra thought hard for several moments, then came to some
inner decision which clearly pleased her.

"I have always wished to involve myself in something a trifle more
exciting than good works, however necessary or worthy. Visiting
friends and struggling for hospital, prison or workhouse reform is most
important, but we must have a little color from time to time. I shall
go into partnership with Mr. Monk." She took another crumpet. "I
will provide the money, to begin with, sufficient for his needs and for
the administration of such offices as he has to have. In return I shall
take some of the profits, when there are any. I shall do my best to

acquire contacts and clients—he will do the work. And I shall be told all that I care about what happens." She frowned ferociously. "Do you think he will be agreeable?"

Hester tried to keep a totally sober face, but inside she felt a wild upsurge of happiness.

"I imagine he will have very little choice. In his position I should leap at such a chance."

"Excellent. Now I shall call upon him and make him a proposition along these lines. Which does not answer the question of the Queen Anne Street case. What are we to do about that? It is all very unsatisfactory."

However it was another fortnight before Hester came to a conclusion as to what she was going to do. She had returned to Queen Anne Street, where Beatrice was still tense, one minute struggling to put everything to do with Octavia's death out of her mind, the next still concerned that she might yet discover some hideous secret not yet more than guessed at.

Other people seemed to have settled into patterns of life more closely approximating normal. Basil went into the City on most days, and did whatever it was he usually did. Hester asked Beatrice in a polite, rather vague way, but Beatrice knew very little about it. It was not considered necessary as part of her realm of interest, so Sir Basil had dismissed her past inquiries with a smile.

Romola was obliged to forgo her social activities, as were they all, because the house was in mourning. But she seemed to believe that the shadow of investigation had passed completely, and she was relentlessly cheerful about the house, when she was not in the schoolroom supervising the new governess. Only rarely did an underlying unhappiness and uncertainty show through, and it had to do with Cyprian, not any suspicion of murder. She was totally satisfied that Percival was the guilty one and no one else was implicated.

Cyprian spent more time speaking with Hester, asking her opinions or experiences in all manner of areas, and seemed most interested in her answers. She liked him, and found his attention flattering. She looked forward to her meetings with him on the few occasions when they were alone and might speak frankly, not in the customary platitudes.

Septimus looked anxious and continued to take port wine from Basil's cellar, and Fenella continued to drink it, make outrageous remarks, and absent herself from the house as often as she dared without incurring Basil's displeasure. Where she went to no one knew, although many guesses were hazarded, most of them unkind.

Araminta ran the house very efficiently, even with some flair, which in the circumstances of mourning was an achievement, but her attitude towards Myles was cold with suspicion, and his towards her was casually indifferent. Now that Percival was arrested, he had nothing to fear, and mere displeasure did not seem to concern him.

Below stairs the mood was somber and businesslike. No one spoke of Percival, except by accident, and then immediately fell silent or tried to cover the gaffe with more words.

In that time Hester received a letter from Monk, passed to her by the new footman, Robert, and she took it upstairs to her room to open it.

December 19th, 1856

Dear Hester,

I have received a most unexpected visit from Lady Callandra with a business proposition which was quite extraordinary. Were she a woman of less remarkable character I would suspect your hand in it. As it is I am still uncertain. She did not learn of my dismissal from the police force out of the newspapers; they do not concern themselves with such things. They are far too busy rejoicing in the solution of the Queen Anne Street case and calling for the rapid hanging of footmen with overweening ideas in general, and Percival in particular.

The Home Office is congratulating itself on such a fortunate solution, Sir Basil is the object of everyone's sympathy and respect, and Runcorn is poised for promotion. Only Percival languishes in Newgate awaiting trial. And maybe he is guilty? But I do not believe it.

Lady Callandra's proposition (in case you do not know!) is that I should become a private investigating detective, which she will finance, and promote as she can. In return for which I will work, and share such profits as there may be—? And all she requires of me is that I keep her informed as to

my cases, what I learn, and something of the process of detection. I hope she finds it as interesting as she expects!

I shall accept—I see no better alternative. I have done all
I can to explain to her the unlikelihood of there being much
financial return. Police are not paid on results, and private
agents would be—or at least if results were not satisfactory a
very large proportion of the time, they would cease to find
clients. Also the victims of injustice are very often not in a
position to pay anything at all. However she insists that she
has money beyond her needs, and this will be her form of
philanthropy—and she is convinced she will find it both more
satisfying than donating her means to museums or galleries or
homes for the deserving poor; and more entertaining. I shall
do all I can to prove her right.

You write that Lady Moidore is still deeply concerned, and
that Fenella is less than honest, but you are not certain yet
whether it is anything to do with Octavia's death. This is
interesting, but does not do more than increase our conviction
that the case is not yet solved. Please be careful in your pursuit, and above all, remember that if you do appear to be close
to discovering anything of significance, the murderer will then
turn his, or her, attention towards you.

I am still in touch with Evan and he informs me how the
police case is being prepared. They have not bothered to seek
anything further. He is as sure as he can be that there is more
to learn, but neither of us knows how to go about it. Even
Lady Callandra has no ideas on that subject.

Again, please take the utmost care,

I remain, yours sincerely,
William Monk

She closed it with her decision already made. There was nothing
else she could hope to learn in Queen Anne Street herself, and Monk
was effectively prevented from investigating anything to do with the
case. The trial was Percival's only hope. There was one person who
could perhaps give her advice on that—Oliver Rathbone. She could
not ask Callandra again; if she had been willing to do such a thing
she would have suggested it when they met previously and Hester told
her of the situation. Rathbone was for hire. There was no reason why

she should not go to his offices and purchase half an hour of his time, which was very probably all she could afford.

First she asked Beatrice for permission to take an afternoon off duty to attend to her family matter, which was granted with no difficulty. Then she wrote a brief letter to Oliver Rathbone explaining that she required legal counsel in a matter of some delicacy and that she had only Tuesday afternoon on which to present herself at his offices, if he would make that available to her. She had previously purchased several postage stamps so she could send the letter, and she asked the bootboy if he would put it in the mailbox for her, which he was pleased to do.

She received her answer the following noon, there being several deliveries of post each day, and tore it open as soon as she had a moment unobserved.

December 20th, 1856

Dear Miss Latterly,

I shall be pleased to receive you at my offices in Vere Street, which is just off Lincoln's Inn Fields, on the afternoon on Tuesday 23rd of December, at three in the afternoon. I hope at that time to be of assistance to you in whatever matter at present concerns you.

Until that time, I remain yours sincerely,

Oliver Rathbone

It was brief and to the point. It would have been absurd to expect more, and yet its very efficiency reminded her that she would be paying for each minute she was there and she must not incur a charge she could not meet. There must be no wasted words, no time for pleasantries or euphemisms.

She had no appealing clothes, no silk and velvet dresses like Araminta's or Romola's, no embroidered snoods or bonnets, and no lace gloves such as ladies habitually wore. They were not suitable for those in service, however skilled. Her only dresses, purchased since her family's financial ruin, were gray or blue, and made on modest and serviceable lines and of stuff fabric. Her bonnet was of a pleasing deep pink, but that was about the best that could be said for it. It also was not new.

Still, Rathbone would not be interested in her appearance; she was going to consult his legal ability, not enjoy a social occasion.

She regarded herself in the mirror without pleasure. She was too thin, and taller than she would have liked. Her hair was thick, but almost straight, and required more time and skill than she possessed to form it into fashionable ringlets. And although her eyes were dark blue-gray, and extremely well set, they had too level and plain a stare, it made people uncomfortable; and her features generally were too bold.

But there was nothing she, or anyone, could do about it, except make the best of a very indifferent job. She could at least endeavor to be charming, and that she would do. Her mother had frequently told her she would never be beautiful, but if she smiled she might make up for a great deal.

It was an overcast day with a hard, driving wind, and most unpleasant.

She took a hansom from Queen Anne Street to Vere Street, and alighted a few minutes before three. At three o'clock precisely she was sitting in the spare, elegant room outside Oliver Rathbone's office and becoming impatient to get the matter begun.

She was about to stand and make some inquiry when the door opened and Rathbone came out. He was as immaculately dressed as she remembered from last time, and immediately she was conscious of being shabby and unfeminine.

"Good afternoon, Mr. Rathbone." Her resolve to be charming was already a little thinner. "It is good of you to see me at such short notice."

"It is a pleasure, Miss Latterly." He smiled, a very sweet smile, showing excellent teeth, but his eyes were dark and she was aware only of their wit and intelligence. "Please come into my office and be comfortable." He held the door open for her, and she accepted rapidly, aware that from the moment he had greeted her, no doubt her half hour was ticking away.

The room was not large, but it was furnished very sparsely, in a fashion reminiscent more of William IV than of the present Queen, and the very leanness of it gave an impression of light and space. The colors were cool and the woodwork white. There was a picture on the farthest wall which reminded her of a Joshua Reynolds, a portrait of a gentleman in eighteenth-century dress against a romantic landscape.

All of which was irrelevant; she must address the matter in hand. She sat down on one of the easy chairs and left him to sit on the other and cross his legs after neatly hitching his trousers so as not to lose their line.

"Mr. Rathbone, I apologize for being so blunt, but to do otherwise would be dishonest. I can afford only half an hour's worth of your time. Please do not permit me to detain you longer than that." She saw the spark of humor in his eyes, but his reply was completely sober.

"I shall not, Miss Latterly. You may trust me to attend the clock. You may concentrate your mind on informing me how I may be of assistance to you."

"Thank you," she said. "It is concerning the murder in Queen Anne Street. Are you familiar with any of the circumstances?"

"I have read of it in the newspapers. Are you acquainted with the Moidore family?"

"No—at least not socially. Please do not interrupt me, Mr. Rathbone. If I digress, I shall not have sufficient time to tell you what is important."

"I apologize." Again there was that flash of amusement.

She suppressed her desire to be irritated and forgot to be charming.

"Sir Basil Moidore's daughter, Octavia Haslett, was found stabbed in her bedroom." She had practiced what she intended to say, and now she concentrated earnestly on remembering every word in the exact order she had rehearsed, for clarity and brevity. "At first it was presumed an intruder had disturbed her during the night and murdered her. Then it was proved by the police that no one could have entered, either by the front or from the back of the house, therefore she was killed by someone already there—either a servant or one of her own family."

He nodded and did not speak.

"Lady Moidore was very distressed by the whole affair and became ill. My connection with the family is as her nurse."

"I thought you were at the infirmary?" His eyes widened and his brows rose in surprise.

"I was," she said briskly. "I am not now."

"But you were so enthusiastic about hospital reform."

"Unfortunately they were not. Please, Mr. Rathbone, do not interrupt me! This is of the utmost importance, or a fearful injustice may be done."

"The wrong person has been charged," he said.

"Quite." She hid her surprise only because there was not time for it. "The footman, Percival, who is not an appealing character—he is vain, ambitious, selfish and something of a lothario—"

"Not appealing," he agreed, sitting a little farther back in his chair and regarding her steadily.

"The theory of the police," she continued, "is that he was en-amored of Mrs. Haslett, and with or without her encouragement, he went up to her bedroom in the night, tried to force his attentions upon her, and she, being forewarned and having taken a kitchen knife upstairs with her"—she ignored his look of amazement—"against just such an eventuality, attempted to save her virtue, and in the struggle it was she, not he, who was stabbed—fatally."

He looked at her thoughtfully, his fingertips together.

"How do you know all this, Miss Latterly? Or should I say, how do the police deduce it?"

"Because on hearing, some considerable time into the investiga-tion—in fact, several weeks—that the cook believed one of her kitchen knives to be missing," she explained, "they instituted a second and very thorough search of the house, and in the bedroom of the footman in question, stuffed behind the back of a drawer in his dresser, be-tween the drawer itself and the outer wooden casing, they found the knife, bloodstained, and a silk peignoir belonging to Mrs. Haslett, also bloodstained."

"Why do you not believe him guilty?" he asked with interest.

Put so bluntly it was hard to be succinct and lucid in reply.

"He may be, but I do not believe it has been proved," she began, now less certain. "There is no real evidence other than the knife and the peignoir, and anyone could have placed them there. Why would he keep such things instead of destroying them? He could very easily have wiped the knife clean and replaced it, and put the peignoir in the range. It would have burned completely."

"Some gloating in the crime?" Rathbone suggested, but there was no conviction in his voice.

"That would be stupid, and he is not stupid," she said immedi-ately. "The only reason for keeping them that makes sense is to use them to implicate someone else—"

"Then why did he not do so? Was it not known that the cook had discovered the loss of her knife, which must surely provoke a search?" He shook his head fractionally. "That would be a most unusual kitchen."

"Of course it was known," she said. "That is why whoever had them was able to hide them in Percival's room."

His brows furrowed and he looked puzzled, his interest more acutely engaged.

"What I find most pertinent," he said, looking at her over the tops of his fingers, "is why the police did not find these items in the first place. Surely they were not so remiss as not to have searched at the time of the crime—or at least when they deduced it was not an intruder but someone resident?"

"Those things were not in Percival's room then," she said eagerly. "They were placed there, without his knowledge, precisely so someone would find them—as they did."

"Yes, my dear Miss Latterly, that may well be so, but you have not taken my point. One presumes the police searched everywhere in the beginning, not merely the unfortunate Percival's room. Wherever they were, they should have been found."

"Oh!" Suddenly she saw what he meant. "You mean they were removed from the house, and then brought back. How unspeakably cold-blooded! They were preserved specifically to implicate someone, should the need arise."

"It would seem so. But one wonders why they chose that time, and not sooner. Or perhaps the cook was dilatory in noticing that her knife was gone. They may well have acted several days before her attention was drawn to it. It might be of interest to learn how she did observe it, whether it was a remark of someone else's, and if so, whose."

"I can endeavor to do that."

He smiled. "I presume that the servants do not get more than the usual time off, and that they do not leave the house during their hours of duty?"

"No. We—" How odd that word was in connection with servants. It rankled especially in front of Rathbone, but this was no time for self-indulgence. "We have half a day every second week, circumstances permitting."

"So the servants would have little or no opportunity to remove the knife and the peignoir immediately after the murder, and to fetch it from its hiding place and return it between the time the cook reported her knife missing and the police conducted their search," he concluded.

"You are right." It was a victory, small, but of great meaning. Hope soared inside her and she rose to her feet and walked quickly over to the mantel shelf and turned. "You are perfectly right. Runcorn never thought of that. When it is put to him he will have to reconsider—"

"I doubt it," Rathbone said gravely. "It is an excellent point of logic, but I would be pleasantly surprised if logic is now what is governing the police's procedure, if, as you say, they have already arrested and charged the wretched Percival. Is your friend Mr. Monk involved in the affair?"

"He was. He resigned rather than arrest Percival on what he believed to be inadequate evidence."

"Very noble," Rathbone said sourly. "If impractical."

"I believe it was temper," Hester said, then instantly felt a traitor. "Which I cannot afford to criticize. I was dismissed from the infirmary for taking matters into my own hands when I had no authority to do so."

"Indeed?" His eyebrows shot up and his face was alive with interest. "Please tell me what happened."

"I cannot afford your time, Mr. Rathbone." She smiled to soften her words—and because what she was about to say was impertinent. "If you wish to know sufficiently, then you may have half an hour of my time, and I shall tell you with pleasure."

"I should be delighted," he accepted. "Must it be here, or may I invite you to dine with me? What is your time worth?" His expression was wry and full of humor. "Perhaps I cannot afford it? Or shall we come to an accommodation? Half an hour of your time for an additional half an hour of mine? That way you may tell me the rest of the tale of Percival and the Moidores, and I shall give you what advice I can, and you shall then tell me the tale of the infirmary."

It was a singularly appealing offer, not only for Percival's sake but because she found Rathbone's company both stimulating and agreeable.

"If it can be within the time Lady Moidore permits me, I should be very pleased," she accepted, then felt unaccountably shy.

He rose to his feet in one graceful gesture.

"Excellent. We shall adjourn to the coaching house around the corner, where they will serve us at any hour. It will be less reputable than the house of a mutual friend, but since we have none, nor the time to make any, it will have to do. It will not mar your reputation beyond recall."

"I think I may already have done that in any sense that matters to me," she replied with a moment of self-mockery. "Dr. Pomeroy will see to it that I do not find employment in any hospital in London. He was very angry indeed."

· "Were you right in your treatment?" he asked, picking up his hat and opening the door for her.

"Yes, it seemed so."

"Then you are correct, it was unforgivable." He led the way out of the offices into the icy street. He walked on the outside of the pavement, guiding her along the street, across the corner, dodging the traffic and the crossing sweeper, and at the far side, into the entrance of a fine coaching inn built in the high day when post coaches were the only way of travel from one city to another, before the coming of the steam railway.

The inside was beautifully appointed, and she would have been interested to take greater notice of pictures, notices, the copper and pewter plates and the post horns, had there been more time. The patrons also caught her attention, well-to-do men of business, rosy faced, well clothed against the winter chill, and most of all in obvious good spirits.

But Rathbone was welcomed by the host the moment they were through the door, and was immediately offered a table advantageously placed in a good corner and advised as to the specialty dishes of the day.

He consulted Hester as to her preference, then ordered, and the host himself set about seeing that only the best was provided. Rathbone accepted it as if it were pleasing, but no more than was his custom. He was gracious in his manner, but kept the appropriate distance between gentleman and innkeeper.

Over the meal, which was neither luncheon nor dinner, but was excellent, she told him the rest of the case in Queen Anne Street, so far as she knew it, including Myles Kellard's attested rape of Martha Rivett and her subsequent dismissal, and more interestingly, her opinion of Beatrice's emotions, her fear, which was obviously not removed by Percival's arrest, and Septimus's remarks that Octavia had said she heard something the afternoon before her death which was shocking and distressing, but of which she still lacked any proof.

She also told him of John Airdrie, Dr. Pomeroy and the loxa quinine.

By that time she had used an hour and a half of his time and he had used twenty-five minutes of hers, but she forgot to count it until she woke in the night in her room in Queen Anne Street.

"What do you advise me?" she said seriously, leaning a little across the table. "What can be done to prevent Percival being convicted without proper proof?"

"You have not said who is to defend him," he replied with equal gravity.

"I don't know. He has no money."

"Naturally. If he had he would be suspect for that alone." He smiled with a harsh twist. "I do occasionally take cases without payment, Miss Latterly, in the public good." His smile broadened. "And recoup by charging exorbitantly next time I am employed by someone who can afford it. I will inquire into it and do what I can, give you my word."

"I am very obliged to you," she said, smiling in return. "Now would you be kind enough to tell me what I owe you for your counsel?"

"We agreed upon half a guinea, Miss Latterly."

She opened her reticule and produced a gold half guinea, the last she had left, and offered it to him.

He took it with courteous thanks and slid it into his pocket.

He rose, pulled her chair out for her, and she left the coaching inn with an intense feeling of satisfaction quite unwarranted by the circumstances, and sailed out into the street for him to hail her a hansom and direct it back to Queen Anne Street.

The trial of Percival Garrod commenced in mid-January 1857, and since Beatrice Moidore was still suffering occasional moods of deep distress and anxiety, Hester was not yet released from caring for her. She complied with this arrangement eagerly, because she had not yet found other means of earning her living, but more importantly because it meant she could remain in the house at Queen Anne Street and observe the Moidore family. Not that she was aware of having learned anything helpful, but she never lost hope.

The whole family attended the trial at the Old Bailey. Basil had wished the women to remain at home and give their evidence in writing, but Araminta refused to consider obedience to such an instruction, and on the rare occasions when she and Basil clashed, it was she who prevailed. Beatrice did not confront him on the issue; she simply dressed in quiet, unadorned black, heavily veiled, and gave Robert instructions to fetch her carriage. Hester offered to go with her as a matter of service, and was delighted when the offer was accepted.

Fenella Sandeman laughed at the very idea that she should forgo such a marvelously dramatic occasion, and swept out of the room, a little high on alcohol, wearing a long black silk kerchief and flinging it in the air with one white arm, delicately mittened in black lace.

Basil swore, but it was to no avail whatever. If she even heard him, it passed over her head harmlessly.

Romola refused to be the only one left at home, and no one bothered to argue with her.

The courtroom was crammed with spectators, and since this time Hester was not required to give any evidence, she was able to sit in the public gallery throughout.

The prosecution was conducted by a Mr. F. J. O'Hare, a flamboyant gentleman who had made his name in a few sensational cases— and many less publicized ones which had earned him a great deal of money. He was well respected by his professional peers and adored by the public, who were entertained and impressed by his quiet, intense manner and sudden explosions into drama. He was of average height but stocky build, short neck and fine silver hair, heavily waved. Had he permitted it to be longer it would have been a leonine mane, but he apparently preferred to appear sleek. He had a musical lilt to his voice which Hester could not place, and the slightest of lisps.

Percival was defended by Oliver Rathbone, and as soon as she saw him Hester felt a wild, singing hope inside her like a bird rising on the wind. It was not only that justice might be done after all, but that Rathbone had been prepared to fight, simply for the cause, not for its reward.

The first witness called was the upstairs maid, Annie, who had found Octavia Haslett's body. She looked very sober, dressed in her best off-duty blue stuff dress and a bonnet that hid her hair and made her look curiously younger, both aggressive and vulnerable at the same time.

Percival stood in the dock, upright and staring in front of him. He might lack humility, compassion or honor, but he was not without courage. He looked smaller than Hester remembered him, narrower across the shoulders and not as tall. But then he was motionless; the swagger that was part of him could not be used, nor the vitality. He was helpless to fight back. It was all in Rathbone's hands now.

The doctor was called next, and gave his evidence briefly. Octavia Haslett had been stabbed to death during the night, with not more than two blows to the lower chest, beneath the ribs.

The third witness was William Monk, and his evidence lasted the rest of the morning and all the afternoon. He was abrasive, sarcastic, and punctiliously accurate, refusing to draw even the most obvious conclusions from anything.

F. J. O'Hare was patient to begin with and scrupulously polite, waiting his chance to score a deciding thrust. It did not come until close to the end, when he was passed a note by his junior, apparently reminding him of the Grey case.

"It would seem to me, Mr. Monk—it is Mr. now, not Inspector, is that so?" His lisp was very slight indeed.

"It is so," Monk conceded without a flicker of expression.

"It would seem to me, Mr. Monk, that from your testimony you do not consider Percival Garrod to be guilty."

"Is that a question, Mr. O'Hare?"

"It is, Mr. Monk, indeed it is!"

"I do not consider it to be proved by the evidence to hand so far," Monk replied. "That is not the same thing."

"Is it materially different, Mr. Monk? Correct me if I am in error, but were you not sincerely unwilling to convict the offender in your last case as well? One Menard Grey, as I recall!"

"No," Monk instantly contradicted. "I was perfectly willing to convict him—in fact, I was eager to. I was unwilling to see him hanged."

"Oh, yes—mitigating circumstances," O'Hare agreed. "But you could find none in the case of Percival Garrod murdering his master's daughter—it would strain even your ingenuity, I imagine? So you maintain the proof of the murder weapon and the bloodstained garment of the victim hidden in his room, which you have told us you discovered, is not enough to satisfy you? What do you require, Mr. Monk, an eyewitness?"

"Only if I considered their veracity beyond question," Monk replied wolfishly and without humor. "I would prefer some evidence that made sense."

"For example, Mr. Monk?" O'Hare invited. He glanced at Rathbone to see if he would object. The judge frowned and waited also. Rathbone smiled benignly back and said nothing.

"A motive for Percival to have kept such—" Monk hesitated and avoided the word *damning*, catching O'Hare's eye and knowing a sudden victory, brief and pointless. "Such a useless and damaging piece of material," he said instead, "which he could so easily have destroyed, and a knife which he could simply have wiped and returned to the cook's rack."

"Perhaps he wished to incriminate someone else?" O'Hare raised his voice with a life of something close to humor, as if the idea were obvious.

"Then he was singularly unsuccessful," Monk replied. "And he had the opportunity. He should have gone upstairs and put it where he wished as soon as he knew the cook had missed the knife."

"Perhaps he intended to, but did not have the chance? What an agony of impotence for him. Can you imagine it?" O'Hare turned to the jury and raised his hands, palms upward. "What a rich irony! It was a man hoist with his own petard! And who would so richly deserve it?"

This time Rathbone rose and objected.

"My lord, Mr. O'Hare is assuming something which has yet to be proved. Even with all his well-vaunted gifts of persuasion, he has not so far shown us anything to indicate who put those objects in Percival's room. He is arguing his conclusion from his premise, and his premise from his conclusion!"

"You will have to do better, Mr. O'Hare," the judge cautioned.

"Oh, I will, my lord," O'Hare promised. "You may be assured, I will!"

The second day O'Hare began with the physical evidence so dramatically discovered. He called Mrs. Boden, who took the stand looking homely and flustered, very much out of her element. She was used to being able to exercise her judgment and her prodigious physical skills. Her art spoke for her. Now she was faced with standing motionless, every exchange to be verbal, and she was ill at ease.

When it was shown her, she looked at the knife with revulsion, but agreed that it was hers, from her kitchen. She recognized various nicks and scratches on the handle, and an irregularity in the blade. She knew the tools of her art. However she became severely rattled when Rathbone pressed her closely about exactly when she had last used it. He took her through the meals of each day, asking her which knives she had used in the preparation, and finally she became so confused he must have realized he was alienating the entire court-room by pressing her over something for which no one else could see a purpose.

O'Hare rose, smiling and smooth, to call the ladies' maid Mary to testify that the bloodstained peignoir was indeed Octavia's. She looked very pale, her usually rich olive complexion without a shred of its blushing cheeks, her voice uncharacteristically subdued. But she swore it was her mistress's. She had seen her wear it often enough, and ironed its satin and smoothed out its lace.

Rathbone did not bother her. There was nothing to contend.

Next O'Hare called the butler. Phillips looked positively cadaver-ous as he stepped into the witness box. His balding head shone in the light through his thin hair, his eyebrows appeared more ferocious than ever, but his expression was one of dignified wretchedness, a soldier on parade before an unruly mob and robbed of the weapons to defend himself.

O'Hare was far too practiced to insult him by discourtesy or con-descension. After establishing Phillips' position and his considerable credentials, he asked him about his seniority over the other servants in the house. This also established, for the jury and the crowd, he proceeded to draw him a highly unfavorable picture of Percival as a man, without ever impugning his abilities as a servant. Never once did he force Phillips into appearing malicious or negligent in his own duty. It was a masterly performance. There was almost nothing Rath-bone could do except ask Phillips if he had had the slightest idea that this objectionable and arrogant young man had raised his eyes as far as his master's daughter. To which Phillips replied with a horrified denial. But then no one would have expected him to admit such a thought—not now.

The only other servant O'Hare called was Rose.

She was dressed most becomingly. Black suited her, with her fair complexion and almost luminous blue eyes. The situation impressed her, but she was not overwhelmed, and her voice was steady and strong, crowded with emotion. With very little prompting she told O'Hare, who was oozing solicitude, how Percival had at first been friendly towards her, openly admiring but perfectly proper in his manner. Then gradually he had given her to believe his affections were engaged, and finally had made it quite plain that he desired to marry her.

All this she recounted with a modest manner and gentle tone. Then her chin hardened and she stood very rigid in the box; her voice darkened, thickening with emotion, and she told O'Hare, never looking at the jury or the spectators, how Percival's attentions had ceased and he had more and more frequently mentioned Miss Octavia, and how she had complimented him, sent for him for the most trivial duties as if she desired his company, how she had dressed more alluringly recently, and often remarked on his own dignity and appearance.

"Was this perhaps to make you jealous, Miss Watkins?" O'Hare asked innocently.

She remembered her decorum, lowered her eyes and answered meekly, the venom disappearing from her and injury returning.

"Jealous, sir? How could I be jealous of a lady like Miss Octavia?" she said demurely. "She was beautiful. She had all the manner and the learning, all the lovely gowns. What was there I could do against that?"

She hesitated a moment, and then went on. "And she would never have married him, that would be stupid even to think of it. If I were going to be jealous it would be of another maid like myself, someone who could have given him real love, and a home, and maybe a family in time." She looked down at her small, strong hands, and then up again suddenly. "No sir, she flattered him, and his head was turned. I thought that sort of thing only happened to parlormaids and the like, who got used by masters with no morals. I never thought of a footman being so daft. Or a lady—well . . ." She lowered her eyes.

"Are you saying that that is what you believe happened, Miss Watkins?" O'Hare asked.

Her eyes flew wide open again. "Oh no sir. I don't suppose for a moment Miss Octavia ever did anything like that! I think Percival was a vain and silly man who imagined it might. And then when he realized what a fool he'd made of himself—well—his conceit couldn't take it and he lost his temper."

"Did he have a temper, Miss Watkins?"

"Oh yes sir—I'm afraid so."

The last witness to be called regarding Percival's character, and its flaws, was Fenella Sandeman. She swept into the courtroom in a glory of black taffeta and lace, a large bonnet set well back, framing her face with its unnatural pallor, jet-black hair and rosy lips. At the distance from which most of the public saw her she was a startling and most effective sight, exuding glamour and the drama of grief—and extreme femininity sore pressed by dire circumstances.

To Hester, when a man was being tried for his life, it was at once pathetic and grotesque.

O'Hare rose and was almost exaggeratedly polite to her, as though she had been fragile and in need of all his tenderness.

"Mrs. Sandeman, I believe you are a widow, living in the house of your brother, Sir Basil Moidore?"

"I am," she conceded, hovering for a moment on the edge of an air of suffering bravely, and opting instead for a gallant kind of gaiety, a dazzling smile and a lift of her pointed chin.

"You have been there for"—he hesitated as if recalling with difficulty what to ask—"something like twelve years?"

"I have," she agreed.

"Then you will doubtless know the members of the household fairly well, having seen them in all their moods, their happiness and their misfortune, for a considerable time," he concluded. "You must have formed many opinions, based upon your observations."

"Indeed—one cannot help it." She gazed at him and a wry, slight smile hovered about her lips. There was a huskiness in her voice. Hester wanted to slide down in her seat and become invisible, but she was beside Beatrice, who was not to be called to testify, so there was nothing she could do but endure it. She looked sideways at Beatrice's face, but her veil was so heavy Hester could see nothing of her expression.

"Women are very sensitive to people," Fenella went on. "We have to be; people are our lives—"

"Exactly so." O'Hare smiled back at her. "In your own establishment you employed servants, before your husband . . . passed on?"

"Of course."

"So you are quite accustomed to judging their character and their worth," O'Hare concluded with a sidelong glance at Rathbone. "What did you observe of Percival Garrod, Mrs. Sandeman? What is your estimate of him?" He held up his pale hand as if to forestall any objection Rathbone might have. "Based, of course, upon what you saw of him during your time in Queen Anne Street?"

She lowered her eyes and a greater hush settled over the room.

"He was very competent at his work, Mr. O'Hare, but he was an arrogant man, and greedy. He liked his fine things in dress and food," she said softly but very clearly. "He had ideas and aspirations far beyond his station, and there was something of an anger in him that he should be limited to that walk of life in which God had seen fit to place him. He played with the affections of the poor girl Rose Watkins, and then when he imagined he could—" She looked up at him with a devastating stare and her voice grew even huskier. "I really don't know how to phrase this delicately. I would be so much obliged if you would assist me."

Beside Hester, Beatrice drew in her breath sharply, and in her lap her hands clenched in their kid gloves.

O'Hare came to Fenella's defense. "Are you wishing to say, ma'am, that he entertained amorous ideas about a member of the family, perhaps?"

"Yes," she said with exaggerated demureness. "That is unfortunately exactly what I—I am obliged to say. More than once I caught him speaking boldly about my niece Octavia, and I saw an expression on his face which a woman cannot misunderstand."

"I see. How distressing for you."

"Indeed," she assented.

"What did you do about it, ma'am?"

"Do?" She stared at him, blinking. "Why my dear Mr. O'Hare, there was nothing I could do. If Octavia herself did not object, what was there I could say to her, or to anyone?"

"And she did not object?" O'Hare's voice rose in amazement, and for an instant he glared around the crowd, then swung back to her. "Are you quite sure, Mrs. Sandeman?"

"Oh quite, Mr. O'Hare. I regret very deeply having to say this, and in such a very public place." Her voice had a slight catch in it now, and Beatrice was so tense Hester was afraid she was going to cry out. "But poor Octavia appeared to be flattered by his attentions," Fenella went on relentlessly. "Of course she could have no idea that he meant more than words—and neither had I, or I should have taken the matter to her father, of course, regardless of what she thought of me for it!"

"Naturally," O'Hare conceded soothingly. "I am sure we all understand that had you foreseen the tragic outcome of the infatuation you would have done all you could to prevent it. However your testimony now of your observations is most helpful in seeing justice for Mrs. Haslett, and we all appreciate how distressing it must be for you to come here and tell us." Then he pressed her for individual instances of behavior from Percival which bore out her judgment, which she duly gave in some detail. He then asked for the same regarding Octavia's encouragement of him, and she recounted them as well.

"Oh—just before you leave, Mrs. Sandeman." O'Hare looked up as if he had almost forgotten. "You said Percival was greedy. In what way?"

"Money, of course," she replied softly, her eyes bright and spiteful. "He liked fine things he could not afford on a footman's wages."

"How do you know this, ma'am?"

"He was a braggart," she said clearly. "He told me once how he got—little—extras."

"Indeed? And how was that?" O'Hare asked as innocently as if the reply might have been honorable and worthy of anyone.

"He knew things about people," she replied with a small, vicious smile. "Small things, trivial to most of us, just little vanities, but ones people would rather their fellows did not know about."

She shrugged delicately. "The parlormaid Dinah boasts about her family—actually she is a foundling and has no one at all. Her airs annoyed Percival, and he let her know he knew. The senior laundrymaid, Lizzie, is a bossy creature, very superior, but she had an affair once. He knew about that too, maybe from Rose, I don't know. Small things like that. The cook's brother is a drunkard; the kitchen maid has a sister who is a cretin."

O'Hare hid his distaste only partially, but whether it was entirely for Percival or included Fenella for betraying such small domestic tragedies it was impossible to tell.

"A most unpleasant man," he said aloud. "And how did he know all these things, Mrs. Sandeman?"

Fenella seemed unaware of the chill in him.

"I imagine he steamed open letters," she said with a shrug. "It was one of his duties to bring in the post."

"I see."

He thanked her again, and Oliver Rathbone rose to his feet and walked forward with almost feline grace.

"Mrs. Sandeman, your memory is much to be commended, and we owe a great deal to your accuracy and sensitivity."

She gazed at him with sharpened interest. There was an element in him which was more elusive, more challenging and more powerful than O'Hare, and she responded immediately.

"You are most kind."

"Not at all, Mrs. Sandeman." He waved his hand. "I assure you I am not. Did this amorous, greedy and conceited footman ever admire other ladies in the house? Mrs. Cyprian Moidore, for instance? Or Mrs. Kellard?"

"I have no idea." She was surprised.

"Or yourself, perhaps?"

"Well—" She lowered her eyelashes modestly.

"Please, Mrs. Sandeman," he urged. "This is not a time for self-effacement."

"Yes, he did step beyond the bounds of what is—merely courteous."

Several members of the jury looked expectant. One middle-aged man with side whiskers was obviously embarrassed.

"He expressed an amorous regard for you?" Rathbone pressed.

"Yes."

"What did you do about it, ma'am?"

Her eyes flew open and she glared at him. "I put him in his place, Mr. Rathbone. I am perfectly competent to deal with a servant who has got above himself."

Beside Hester, Beatrice stiffened in her seat.

"I am sure you are." Rathbone's voice was laden with meaning. "And at no danger to yourself. You did not find it necessary to go to bed carrying a carving knife?"

She paled visibly, and her mittened hands tightened on the rail of the box in front of her.

"Don't be absurd. Of course I didn't!"

"And yet you never felt constrained to counsel your niece in this very necessary art?"

"I—er—" Now she was acutely uncomfortable.

"You were aware that Percival was entertaining amorous intentions towards her." Rathbone moved very slightly, a graceful stride as he might use in a withdrawing room. He spoke softly, the sting in his incredulous contempt. "And you allowed her to be so alone in her fear that she resorted to taking a knife from the kitchen and carrying it to bed to defend herself, in case Percival should enter her room at night."

The jury was patently disturbed, and their expressions betrayed it.

"I had no idea he would do such a thing," she protested. "You are trying to say I deliberately allowed it to happen. That is monstrous!" She looked at O'Hare for help.

"No, Mrs. Sandeman," Rathbone corrected. "I am questioning how it is that a lady of your experience and sensitive observation and judgment of character should see that a footman was amorously drawn towards your niece, and that she had behaved foolishly in not making her distaste quite plain to him, and yet you did not take matters into your own hands sufficiently at least to speak to some other member of the household."

She stared at him with horror.

"Her mother, for example," he continued. "Or her sister, or even to warn Percival yourself that his behavior was observed. Any of those actions would almost certainly have prevented this tragedy. Or you might simply have taken Mrs. Haslett to one side and counseled her, as an older and wiser woman who had had to rebuff many inappropriate advances yourself, and offered her your assistance."

Fenella was flustered now.

"Of course—if I had r-realized—" she stammered. "But I didn't. I had no idea it—it would—"

"Hadn't you?" Rathbone challenged.

"No." Her voice was becoming shrill. "Your suggestion is appalling. I had not the slightest notion!"

Beatrice let out a little groan of disgust.

"But surely, Mrs. Sandeman," Rathbone resumed, turning and walking back to his place, "if Percival had made amorous advances to you—and you had seen all his offensive behavior towards Mrs. Haslett, you must have realized how it would end? You are not without experience in the world."

"I did not, Mr. Rathbone," Fenella protested. "What you are saying is that I deliberately allowed Octavia to be raped and murdered. That is scandalous, and totally untrue."

"I believe you, Mrs. Sandeman." Rathbone smiled suddenly, without a vestige of humor.

"I should think so!" Her voice shook a little. "You owe me an apology, sir."

"It would make perfect sense that you should not have any idea," he went on. "If this observation of yours did not in fact cover any of these things you relate to us. Percival was extremely ambitious and of an arrogant nature, but he made no advances towards you, Mrs. Sandeman. You are—forgive me, ma'am—of an age to be his mother!"

Fenella blanched with fury, and the crowd drew in an audible gasp. Someone tittered. A juryman covered his face with his handkerchief and appeared to be blowing his nose.

Rathbone's face was almost expressionless.

"And you did not witness all these distasteful and impertinent scenes with Mrs. Haslett either, or you would have reported them to Sir Basil without hesitation, for the protection of his daughter, as any decent woman would."

"Well—I—I . . ." She stumbled into silence, white-faced, wretched, and Rathbone returned to his seat. There was no need to humiliate her further or add explanation for her vanity or her foolishness, or the unnecessarily vicious exposure of the small secrets of the servants' hall. It was an acutely embarrassing scene, but it was the first doubt cast on the evidence against Percival.

The next day the courtroom was even more tightly packed, and Araminta took the witness stand. She was no vain woman displaying herself, as Fenella had been. She was soberly dressed and her composure was perfect. She said that she had never cared for Percival, but it was her father's house, and therefore not hers to question his choice of servants. She had hitherto considered her judgments of Percival to be colored by her personal distaste. Now of course she knew differently, and deeply regretted her silence.

When pressed by O'Hare she disclosed, with what appeared to be great difficulty, that her sister had not shared her distaste for the footman, and had been unwise in her laxity towards servants in general. This, she found it painful to admit, was sometimes due to the fact that since the death of her husband, Captain Haslett, in the recent conflict in the Crimea, her sister had on a large number of occasions taken rather more wine than was wise, and her judgment had been correspondingly disturbed, her manners a good deal easier than was becoming, or as it now transpired, well advised.

Rathbone asked if her sister had confided in her a fear of Percival, or of anyone else. Araminta said she had not, or she would naturally have taken steps to protect her.

Rathbone asked her if, as sisters, they were close. Araminta regretted deeply that since the death of Captain Haslett, Octavia had changed, and they were no longer as affectionate as they had been. Rathbone could find no flaw in her account, no single word or attitude to attack. Prudently he left it alone.

Myles added little to what was already in evidence. He substantiated that indeed Octavia had changed since her widowhood. Her behavior was unfortunate; she had frequently, it pained him to admit, been emotional and lacking in judgment as a result of rather too much wine. No doubt it was on such occasions she had failed to deal adequately with Percival's advances, and then in a soberer moment realized what she had done, but had been too ashamed to seek help, instead resorted to taking a carving knife to bed with her. It was all very tragic and they were deeply grieved.

Rathbone could not shake him, and was too aware of public sympathy to attempt it.

Sir Basil himself was the last witness O'Hare called. He took the stand with immense gravity, and there was a rustle of sympathy and respect right around the room. Even the jury sat up a little straighter, and one pushed back as if to present himself more respectfully.

Basil spoke with candor of his dead daughter, her bereavement when her husband had been killed, how it had unbalanced her emotions and caused her to seek solace in wine. He found it deeply shaming to have to admit to it—there was a ripple of profound sympathy for him. Many had lost someone themselves in the carnage at Balaclava, Inkermann, the Alma, or from hunger and cold in the heights above Sebastopol, or dead of disease in the fearful hospital at Scutari. They understood grief in all its manifestations, and his frank admission of it formed a bond between them. They admired his dignity and his openness. The warmth of it could be felt even from where Hester was sitting. She was aware of Beatrice beside her, but through the veil her face was all but invisible, her emotions concealed.

O'Hare was brilliant. Hester's heart sank.

At last it was Rathbone's turn to begin what defense he could.

He started with the housekeeper, Mrs. Willis. He was courteous to her, drawing from her her credentials for her senior position, the fact that she not only ran the household upstairs but was responsible for the female staff, apart from those in the kitchen itself. Their moral welfare was her concern.

Were they permitted to have amorous dalliances?

She bristled at the very suggestion. They most certainly were not. Nor would she allow to be employed any girl who entertained such ideas. Any girl of loose behavior would be dismissed on the spot—and without a character. It was not necessary to remind anyone what would happen to such a person.

And if a girl were found to be with child?

Instant dismissal, of course. What else was there?

Of course. And Mrs. Willis took her duties in the regard most earnestly?

Naturally. She was a Christian woman.

Had any of the girls ever come to her to say, in however round-about a manner, that any of the male staff, Percival or anyone else, had made improper advances to them?

No they had not. Percival fancied himself, to be true, and he was as vain as a peacock; she had seen his clothes and boots, and wondered where he got the money.

Rathbone returned her to the subject: had anyone complained of Percival?

No, it was all a lot of lip, nothing more; and most maids were quite able to deal with that for what it was worth—which was nothing at all.

O'Hare did not try to shake her. He simply pointed out that since Octavia Haslett was not part of her charge, all this was of peripheral importance.

Rathbone rose again to say that much of the character evidence as to Percival's behavior rested on the assessment of his treatment of the maids.

The judge observed that the jury would make up their own minds.

Rathbone called Cyprian, not asking him anything about either his sister or Percival. Instead he established that his bedroom in the house was next door to Octavia's, then he asked him if he had heard any sound or disturbance on the night she was killed.

"No—none at all, or I should have gone to see if she were all right," Cyprian said with some surprise.

"Are you an extremely heavy sleeper?" Rathbone asked.

"No."

"Did you indulge in much wine that evening?"

"No—very little." Cyprian frowned. "I don't see the point in your question, sir. My sister was undoubtedly killed in the room next to me. That I did not hear the struggle seems to me to be irrelevant. Percival is much stronger than she . . ." He looked very pale and had some difficulty in keeping his voice under control. "I presume he overpowered her quickly—"

"And she did not cry out?" Rathbone looked surprised.

"Apparently not."

"But Mr. O'Hare would have us believe she took a carving knife to bed with her to ward off these unwelcome attentions of the footman," Rathbone said reasonably. "And yet when he came into her room she rose out of her bed. She was not found lying in it but on it, across from a normal position in which to sleep—we have Mr. Monk's evidence for that. She rose, put on her peignoir, pulled out the carving knife from wherever she had put it, then there was a struggle in which she attempted to defend herself—"

He shook his head and moved a little, shrugging his shoulders. "Surely she must have warned him first? She would not simply run at him with dagger drawn. He struggled and wrested the knife from her"—he held up his hands—"and in the battle that ensued, he stabbed her to death. And yet in all this neither of them uttered a cry of any sort! This whole tableau was conducted in total silence? Do you not find that hard to believe, Mr. Moidore?"

The jury fidgeted, and Beatrice drew in her breath sharply.

"Yes!" Cyprian admitted with dawning surprise. "Yes, I do. It does seem most unnatural. I cannot see why she did not simply scream."

"Nor I, Mr. Moidore," Rathbone agreed. "It would surely have been a far more effective defense; and less dangerous, and more natural to a woman than a carving knife."

O'Hare rose to his feet.

"Nevertheless, Mr. Moidore, gentlemen of the jury, the fact remains that she did have the carving knife—and she was stabbed to death with it. We may never know what bizarre, whispered conversation took place that night. But we do know beyond doubt that Octavia Haslett was stabbed to death—and the bloodstained knife, and her robe gashed and dark with her blood, were found in Percival's room. Do we need to know every word and gesture to come to a conclusion?"

There was a rustle in the crowd. The jury nodded. Beside Hester, Beatrice let out a low moan.

Septimus was called, and recounted to them how he had met Octavia returning home on the day of her death, and how she had told him that she had discovered something startling and dreadful, and that she lacked only one final proof of its truth. But under O'Hare's insistence he had to admit that no one else had overheard this conversation, nor had he repeated it to anyone. Therefore, O'Hare concluded triumphantly, there was no reason to suppose this discovery, whatever it was, had had anything to do with her death. Septimus was unhappy. He pointed out that simply because he had not told anyone did not mean that Octavia herself had not.

But it was too late. The jury had already made up its mind, and nothing Rathbone could do in his final summation could sway their conviction. They were gone only a short while, and returned white-faced, eyes set and looking anywhere but at Percival. They gave the verdict of guilty. There were no mitigating circumstances.

The judge put on his black cap and pronounced sentence. Percival would be taken to the place from whence he came, and in three weeks he would be led out to the execution yard and hanged by the neck until he was dead. May God have mercy upon his soul, there was none other to look for on earth.

CHAPTER
TEN

——

"I am sorry," Rathbone said very gently, looking at Hester with intense concern. "I did everything I could, but the passion was rising too high and there was no other person whom I could suggest with a motive powerful enough."

"Maybe Kellard?" she said without hope or conviction. "Even if she was defending herself, it doesn't have to have been from Percival. In fact it would make more sense if it was Myles, then screaming wouldn't do much good. He would only say she'd cried out and he'd heard her and come to see what was wrong. He would have a far better excuse than Percival for being there. And Percival she could have crushed with a threat of having him dismissed. She could hardly do that with Myles, and she may not have wanted Araminta ever to know about his behavior."

"I know that." He was standing by the mantel in his office and she was only a few feet away from him, the defeat crushing her and making her feel vulnerable and an appalling failure. Perhaps she had misjudged, and Percival was guilty after all? Everyone else, apart from Monk, seemed to believe it. And yet there were things that made so little sense.

"Hester?"

"I'm sorry," she apologized. "My attention was wandering."

"I could not raise Myles Kellard as a suspect."

"Why not?"

He smiled very slightly. "My dear, what evidence should I call that he had the least amorous interest in his sister-in-law? Which of his family do you imagine would testify to that? Araminta? She would become the laughingstock of London society, and she knows that. If it were rumored she might be pitied, but if she openly admits she knows of it, she will be despised. From what I have seen of her, she would find them equally intolerable."

"I doubt Beatrice would lie," Hester said, and then knew instantly it was foolish. "Well, he raped the maid Martha Rivett. Percival knew that."

"And what?" he finished for her. "The jury will believe Percival? Or I should call Martha herself? Or Sir Basil, who dismissed her?"

"No, of course not," she said miserably, turning away. "I don't know what else we can do. I'm sorry if I seem unreasonable. It is just so—" She stopped and looked across at him. "They'll hang him, won't they?"

"Yes." He was watching her, his face grave and sad. "There are no mitigating circumstances this time. What can you say in defense of a footman who lusts after his master's daughter, and when she refuses him, knifes her to death?"

"Nothing," she said very quietly. "Nothing at all, except that he is human, and by hanging him we diminish ourselves as well."

"My dear Hester." Slowly and quite deliberately, his lashes lowered but his eyes open, he leaned forward until his lips touched hers, not with passion but with utmost gentleness and long, delicate intimacy.

When he drew away she felt both more and less alone than she ever had before, and she knew at once from his face that it had caught him in some way by surprise also.

He drew breath as if to speak, then changed his mind and turned away, going over to the window and standing with his back half towards her.

"I am truly sorry I could not do better for Percival," he said again, his voice a little rough and charged with a sincerity she could not doubt. "For him, and because you trusted me."

"You have discharged that trust completely," she said quickly. "I expected you to do all you could—I did not expect a miracle. I can see how passion is rising among the public. Perhaps we never had a chance. It was simply necessary that we try everything within our power. I am sorry I spoke so foolishly. Of course you could not have suggested Myles—or Araminta. It would only have turned the jury even more against Percival; I can see that if I free my mind from frustration and apply a little intelligence."

He smiled at her, his eyes bright. "How very practical."

"You are laughing at me," she said without resentment. "I know it is considered unwomanly, but I see nothing attractive in behaving like a fool when you don't have to."

His smile broadened. "My dear Hester, neither do I. It is extremely tedious. It is more than enough to do so when we cannot help ourselves. What are you going to do now? How will you survive, once Lady Moidore no longer considers herself in need of a nurse?"

"I shall advertise for someone else who does—until I am able to search for a job in administration somewhere."

"I am delighted. From what you say you have not abandoned your hope of reforming English medicine."

"Certainly not—although I do not expect to do it in the lifetime your tone suggests. If I initiate anything at all I will be satisfied."

"I am sure you will." His laughter vanished. "A determination like yours will not be thwarted long, even by the Pomeroys of the world."

"And I shall find Mr. Monk and go over the whole case again," she added. "Just so I am sure there is nothing whatever we can still do."

"If you find anything, bring it to me." He was very grave indeed now. "Will you promise me that? We have three weeks in which it might still be possible to appeal."

"I will," she said with a return of the hard, gray misery inside her. The moment's ineffable warmth was gone, Percival remembered. "I will." And she bade him good-bye and took her leave to seek Monk.

Hester returned to Queen Anne Street light-footed, but the leaden feeling was at the edge of her mind waiting to return now that she was forced to think of reality again.

She was surprised to learn from Mary, as soon as she was in the house, that Beatrice was still confining herself to her room and would take her evening meal upstairs. She had gone into the ironing room for a clean apron, and found Mary there folding the last of her own linen.

"Is she ill?" Hester said with some concern—and a pang of guilt, not only for what might be dereliction of her duty but because she had not believed the malady was now anything but a desire to be a trifle spoilt, and to draw from her family the attention she did not otherwise. And that in itself was something of a mystery. Beatrice was not only a lovely woman but vivid and individual, not made in the placid mold of Romola. She was also intelligent, imaginative and at times capable of considerable humor. Why should such a woman not be the very heartbeat of her home?

"She looked pale," Mary replied, pulling a little face. "But then she always does. I think she's in a temper, myself—although I shouldn't say that."

Hester smiled. The fact that Mary should not say something never stopped her, in fact it never even made her hesitate.

"With whom?" Hester asked curiously.

"Everyone in general, but Sir Basil in particular."

"Do you know why?"

Mary shrugged; it was a graceful gesture. "I should think over what they said about Miss Octavia at the trial." She scowled furiously. "Wasn't that awful! They made out she was so tipsy she encouraged the footman to make advances—" She stopped and looked at Hester meaningfully. "Makes you wonder, doesn't it?"

"Was that not true?"

"Not that I ever saw." Mary was indignant. "She was tipsy, certainly, but Miss Octavia was a lady. She wouldn't have let Percival touch her if he'd been the last man alive on a desert island. Actually it's my belief she wouldn't have let any man touch her after Captain Haslett died. Which is what made Mr. Myles so furious. Now if she'd stabbed him, I'd have believed it!"

"Did he really lust after her?" Hester asked, for the first time using the right word openly.

Mary's dark eyes widened a fraction, but she did not equivocate.

"Oh yes. You should have seen it in his face. Mind, she was very pretty, you know, in a quite different way from Miss Araminta. You never saw her, but she was so alive—" Suddenly misery gripped hold of her again, and all the realization of loss flooded back, and the anger she had been trying to suppress. "That was wicked, what they said about her! Why do people say things like that?" Her chin came up and her eyes were blazing. "Fancy her saying all those wretched things about Dinah, and Mrs. Willis and all. They won't ever forgive her for that, you know. Why did she do it?"

"Spite?" Hester suggested. "Or maybe just exhibitionism. She loves to be the center of attention. If anyone is looking at her she feels alive—important."

Mary looked confused.

"There are some people like that." Hester tried to explain what she had never put into words before. "They're empty, insecure alone; they only feel real when other people listen to them and take notice."

"Admiration." Mary laughed bitterly. "It's contempt. What she did was vicious. I can tell you, no one 'round here'll forgive her for it."

"I don't suppose that'll bother her," Hester said dryly, thinking of Fenella's opinion of servants.

Mary smiled. "Oh yes it will!" she said fiercely. "She won't get a hot cup of tea in the morning anymore; it will be lukewarm. We will be ever so sorry, we won't know how it happened, but it will go on happening. Her best clothes will be mislaid in the laundry, some will get torn, and no one will know who did it. Everyone will have found it like that. Her letters will be delivered to someone else, caught between the pages, messages for her or from her will be slow in delivery. The rooms she's in will get cold because footmen will be too busy to stoke the fires, and her afternoon tea will be late. Believe me, Miss Latterly, it will bother her. And Mrs. Willis nor Cook won't put a stop to it. They'll all be just as innocent and smug as the rest of us, and not have an idea how it happens. And Mr. Phillips won't do nothing either. He may have airs like he was a duke, but he's loyal when it comes down to it. He's one of us."

Hester could not help smiling. It was all incredibly trivial, but there was a kind of justice in it.

Mary saw her expression, and her own eased into one of satisfaction and something like conspiracy. "You see?" she said.

"I see," Hester agreed. "Yes—very appropriate." And still with a smile she took her linen and left.

Upstairs Hester found Beatrice sitting alone in her room in one of the dressing chairs, staring out of the window at the rain beginning to fall steadily into the bare garden. It was January, bleak, colorless, and promising fog before dark.

"Good afternoon, Lady Moidore," Hester said gently. "I am sorry you are unwell. Can I do anything to help?"

Beatrice did not move her head.

"Can you turn the clock back?" she asked with a tiny self-mocking smile.

"If I could, I would have done it many times," Hester answered. "But do you suppose it would really make a difference?"

Beatrice did not reply for several moments, then she sighed and stood up. She was dressed in a peach-colored robe, and with her blazing hair she had all the warmth of dying summer in her.

"No—probably none at all," she said wearily. "We would still be the same people, and that is what is wrong. We would all still be pursuing comfort, looking to save our own reputations and just as willing to hurt others." She stood by the window watching the water running down the panes. "I never realized Fenella was so consumed with vanity, so ridiculously trying to hold on to the trappings of youth. If she were not so prepared to destroy other people simply to get attention, I should feel more pity for her. As it is I am embarrassed by her."

"Perhaps it is all she feels she has." Hester spoke equally softly. She too found Fenella repellent in her willingness to hurt, especially to expose the foibles of the servants—that was gratuitous. But she understood the fear behind the need for some quality that would earn her survival, some material possessions, however come by, that were independent of Basil and his conditional charity, if *charity* was the word.

Beatrice swung around to face her, her eyes level, very wide.

"You understand, don't you? You know why we do these grubby things—"

Hester did not know whether to equivocate; tact was not what Beatrice needed now.

"Yes, it isn't difficult."

Beatrice dropped her eyes. "I'd rather not have known. I guessed some of it, of course. I knew Septimus gambled, and I thought he took wine occasionally from the cellars." She smiled. "In fact it rather amused me. Basil is so pompous about his claret." Her face darkened again and the humor vanished. "I didn't know Septimus took it for Fenella, and even then I wouldn't have cared about it if it were sympathy for her—but it isn't. I think he hates her. She's everything in a woman that is different from Christabel—that is the woman he loved. That isn't a good reason for hating anyone, though, is it?"

She hesitated, but Hester did not interrupt.

"Strange how being dependent, and being reminded of it all the time, sours you," Beatrice went on. "Because you feel helpless and inferior, you try to get power again by doing just the same to someone else. God how I hate investigations! It will take us years to forget all we've learned about each other—maybe by then it will be too late."

"Maybe you can learn to forgive instead?" Hester knew she was being impertinent, but it was the only thing she could say with any truth, and Beatrice not only deserved truth, she needed it.

Beatrice turned away and traced her finger on the dry inside of the window, following the racing drops.

"How do you forgive someone for not being what you wanted them to be, or what you thought they were? Especially when they are not sorry—perhaps they don't even understand?"

"Or again, perhaps they do?" Hester suggested. "And how do they forgive us for having expected too much of them, instead of looking to see what they really were, and loving that?"

Beatrice's finger stopped.

"You are very frank, aren't you!" It was not a question. "But it isn't as easy as that, Hester. You see, I am not even sure that Percival is guilty. Am I wicked still to have doubts in my mind when the court says he is, and he's been sentenced, and the world says it is all over? I dream, and wake up with my mind torn with suspicions. I look at people and wonder, and I hear double and triple meanings behind what they say."

Again Hester was racked with indecision. It would seem so much kinder to suggest that no one else could be guilty, that it was only the aftermath of all the fear still lingering on, and in time it would melt away. Daily life would comfort, and this extraordinary tragedy would ease until it became only the grief one feels for any loss.

But then she thought of Percival in Newgate prison, counting the few days left to him until one morning there was no more time at all.

"Well if Percival is not guilty, who else could it have been?" She heard the words spoken aloud and instantly regretted her judgment. It was brutal. She never for an instant thought Beatrice would believe it was Rose, and none of the other servants had even entered the field of possibility. But it could not be taken back. All she could do was wait for Beatrice's answer.

"I don't know." Beatrice measured each word. "I have lain in the dark each night, thinking this is my own house, where I came when I was married. I have been happy here, and wretched. I have borne five children here, and lost two, and now Octavia. I've watched them grow up, and themselves marry. I've watched their happiness and their misery. It is all as familiar as bread and butter, or the sound of carriage wheels. And yet perhaps I know only the skin of it all, and the flesh beneath is as strange to me as Japan."

She moved to the dressing table and began to take the pins from her hair and let it down in a shining stream like bright copper.

"The police came here and were full of sympathy and respectfully polite. Then they proved that no one could have broken in from outside, so whoever killed Octavia was one of us. For weeks they asked questions and forced us to find the answers—ugly answers, most of them, things about ourselves that were shabby, or selfish, or cowardly." She put the pins in a neat little pile in one of the cut glass trays and picked up the silver-backed brush.

"I had forgotten about Myles and that poor maid. That may seem incredible, but I had. I suppose I never thought about it much at the time, because Araminta didn't know." She pulled at her hair with the brush in long, hard strokes. "I am a coward, aren't I," she said very quietly. It was a statement, not a question. "I saw what I wanted to, and hid from the rest. And Cyprian, my beloved Cyprian—doing the same: never standing up to his father, just living in a dream world, gambling and idling his time instead of doing what he really wanted." She tugged even harder with the brush. "He's bored with Romola, you know. It used not to matter, but now he's suddenly realized how interesting companionship can be, and conversation that's real, where people say what they think instead of playing polite games. And of course it's far too late."

Without any forewarning Hester realized fully what she had woken in indulging her own vanity and pleasure in Cyprian's attention. She was only partly guilty, because she had not intended hurt, but it was enough. Neither had she thought, or cared, and she had sufficient intelligence that she could have.

"And poor Romola," Beatrice went on, still brushing fiercely. "She has not the slightest idea what is wrong. She has done precisely what she was taught to do, and it has ceased to work."

"It may again," Hester said feebly, and did not believe it.

But Beatrice was not listening for inflections of a voice. Her own thoughts clamored too loudly.

"And the police have arrested Percival and gone away, leaving us to wonder what really happened." She began to brush with long, even strokes. "Why did they do that, Hester? Monk didn't believe it was Percival, I'm sure of that." She swiveled around on the dresser seat and looked at Hester, the brush still in her hand. "You spoke to him. Did you think he believed it was Percival?"

Hester let out her breath slowly. "No—no, I thought not."

Beatrice turned back to the mirror again and regarded her hair critically. "Then why did the police arrest him? It wasn't Monk, you know. Annie told me it was someone else, not even the young sergeant either. Was it simply expediency, do you suppose? The newspapers were making a terrible fuss about it and blaming the police for not solving it, so Cyprian told me. And Basil wrote to the Home Secretary, I know." Her voice sank lower. "I imagine their superiors demanded they produce some result very quickly, but I did not think Monk would give in. I thought he was such a strong man—" She did not add that Percival was expendable when a senior officer's career was threatened, but Hester knew she was thinking it; the anger in her mouth and the misery in her eyes were sufficient.

"And of course they would never accuse one of us, unless they had absolute proof. But I can't help wondering if Monk suspected one of us and simply could not find any mistake large enough, or tangible enough, to justify his action."

"Oh I don't think so," Hester said quickly, then wondered how on earth she would explain knowing such a thing. Beatrice was so very nearly right in her estimate of what had happened, Runcorn's expediency over Monk's judgment, the quarrels and the pressure.

"Don't you?" Beatrice said bleakly, putting down the brush at last. "I am afraid I do. Sometimes I think I would give anything at all to know which one of us, just so I could stop suspecting the others. Then I shrink back in horror from it, like a hideous sight—a severed head in a bucketful of maggots—only worse." She swiveled around on the seat again and looked at Hester. "Someone in my own family murdered my daughter. You see, they all lied. Octavia wasn't as they said, and the idea of Percival taking such a liberty, or even imagining he could, is ridiculous."

She shrugged, her slender shoulders pulling at the silk of her gown.

"I know she drank a trifle too much sometimes—but nothing like as much as Fenella does. Now if it were Fenella that would make sense. She would encourage any man." Her face darkened. "Except she picks out those who are rich because she used to accept presents from them and then pawn the gifts for money to buy clothes and perfumes and things. Then she stopped bothering with the pretenses and simply took the money outright. Basil doesn't know, of course. He'd be horrified. He'd probably throw her out."

"Was that what Octavia discovered and told to Septimus?" Hester said eagerly. "Perhaps that was what happened?" Then she realized how insensitive such enthusiasm was. After all, Fenella was still one of the family, even if she was shallow and vicious, and now, after the trial, a public embarrassment. She composed her face into gravity again.

"No," Beatrice said flatly. "Octavia knew about it ages ago. So did Minta. We didn't tell Basil because we despised it but understood. It is surprising what one will do when one has no money. We devise little ways, and usually they are not attractive, sometimes not even honorable." She started to fiddle with a perfume bottle, pulling the stopper out. "We are such cowards at times. I wish I couldn't see that, but I can. But Fenella would not encourage a footman beyond silly flattery. She's vain and cruel, and terrified of growing old, but she is not a whore. At least—I mean, she does not take men simply because she enjoys it—" She gave a convulsive little shudder and jammed the perfume stopper in so hard she could not remove it again. She swore under her breath and pushed the bottle to the back of the dressing table.

"I used to think Minta didn't know about Myles having forced himself on the maid, but perhaps she did? And perhaps she knew that Myles was more than properly attracted to Octavia. He is very vain too, you know? He imagines all women find him pleasing." She smiled with a downward curl of her mouth, a curiously expressive gesture. "Of course a great many do. He is handsome and charming. But Octavia didn't like him. He found that very hard to take. Perhaps he was determined to make her change her mind. Some men find force quite justifiable, you know?"

She looked at Hester, then shook her head. "No, of course you don't know—you are not married. Forgive me for being so coarse. I hope I have not offended you. I think it is all a matter of degree. And Myles and Tavie thought very differently about it."

She was silent for a moment, then pulled her gown closer around her and stood up.

"Hester—I am so afraid. One of my family may be guilty. And Monk has gone off and left us, and I shall probably never know. I don't know which is worse—not knowing, and imagining everything— or knowing, and never again being able to forget, but being helpless to do anything about it. And what if they know I know? Would they murder me? How can we live together day after day?"

Hester had no answer. There was no possible comfort to give, and she did not belittle the pain by trying to find something to say.

It was another three days before the servants' revenge really began to bite and Fenella was sufficiently aware of it to complain to Basil. Quite by chance Hester overheard much of the conversation. She had become as invisible as the rest of the servants, and neither Basil nor Fenella was aware of her through the arch of the conservatory from the withdrawing room. She had gone there because it was the nearest she could come to a walk alone outside. She was permitted to use the ladies' maids' sitting room, which she did to read, but there was always the chance of being joined by Mary or Gladys and having to make conversation, or explain her very intellectual choice of reading.

"Basil." Fenella swept in, bristling with anger. "I really must complain to you about the servants in this house. You seem to be quite unaware of it, but ever since the trial of that wretched footman, the standards have declined appallingly. This is three days in a row my morning tea has been almost cold. That fool of a maid has lost my best lace peignoir. My bedroom fire has been allowed to go out. And now the room is like a morgue. I don't know how I am supposed to dress in it. I should catch my death."

"Appropriate for a morgue," Basil said dryly.

"Don't be a fool," she snapped. "I do not find this an occasion for humor. I don't know why on earth you tolerate it. You never used to. You used to be the most exacting person I ever knew—worse even than Papa."

From where Hester was she could see only Fenella's back, but

Basil's face was clearly visible. Now his expression changed and became pinched.

"My standards are as high as his ever were," he said coldly. "I don't know what you mean, Fenella. My tea was piping hot, my fire is blazing, and I have never missed anything in the laundry all the years I have lived here."

"And my toast was stale on my breakfast tray," she went on. "My bed linen has not been changed, and when I spoke to Mrs. Willis about it, all I got was a lot of limp excuses, and she barely even listened to what I said. You have not the command of the house you should have, Basil. I wouldn't tolerate it a moment. I know you aren't the man Papa was, but I didn't imagine you would go to pieces like this and allow everything around you to fall apart as well."

"If you don't care for it here, my dear," he said with viciousness, "you may always find somewhere that suits you better, and run it according to your own standards."

"That's just the sort of thing I would expect you to say," she retorted. "But you can hardly throw me out in the street now—too many people are looking at you, and what would they say? The fine Sir Basil, the rich Sir Basil"—her face was twisted with contempt—"the noble Sir Basil whom everyone respects, has thrown his widowed sister out of his home. I doubt it, my dear, I doubt it. You always wanted to live up to Papa, and then you wanted to exceed him. What people think of you matters more than anything else. I imagine that's why you hated poor Harry Haslett's father so much, even at school—he did with ease what you had to work so hard for. Well you've got it now—money, reputation, honors—you won't jeopardize it by putting me out. What would it look like?" She laughed abrasively. "What would people say? Just get your servants to do their duty."

"Has it occurred to you, Fenella, that they are treating you like this because you betrayed their vulnerabilities in public from the witness stand—and brought it upon yourself?" His face was set in an expression of loathing and disgust, but there was also a touch of pleasure in it, a satisfaction that he could hurt. "You made an exhibition of yourself, and servants don't forgive that."

She stiffened, and Hester could imagine the color rising up her cheeks.

"Are you going to speak to them or not? Or do they just do as they please in this house?"

"They do as I please, Fenella," he said very quietly. "And so does everyone else. No, I am not going to speak to them. It amuses me that they should take their revenge on you. As far as I am concerned, they are free to continue. Your tea will be cold, your breakfast burnt, your fire out and your linen lost as long as they like."

She was too furious to speak. She let out a gasp of rage, swung on her heel and stormed out, head high, skirts rattling and swinging so wide they caught an ornament on the side table and sent it crashing.

Basil smiled with deep, hard, inward pleasure.

Monk had already found two small jobs since he advertised his services as a private inquiry agent prepared to undertake investigations outside police interest, or to continue with cases from which the police had withdrawn. One was a matter of property, and of very little reward other than that of a quickly satisfied customer and a few pounds to make sure of at least another week's lodging. The second, upon which he was currently engaged, was more involved and promised some variety and pursuit—and possibly the questioning of several people, the art for which his natural talents fitted him. It concerned a young woman who had married unfortunately and been cut off by her family, who now wished to find her again and heal the rift. He was prospering well, but after the outcome of the trial of Percival he was deeply depressed and angry. Not that he had for a moment expected anything different, but there was always a stubborn hope, even until the last, more particularly when he heard Oliver Rathbone was engaged. He had very mixed emotions about the man; there was a personal quality in him which Monk found intensely irritating, but he had no reservations in the admiration of his skill or the conviction of his dedication.

He had written to Hester Latterly again, to arrange a meeting in the same chocolate house in Regent Street, although he had very little idea what it might accomplish.

He was unreasonably cheered when he saw her coming in, even though her face was sober and when she saw him her smile was only momentary, a matter of recognition, no more.

He rose to pull out her chair, then sat opposite, ordering hot chocolate for her. They knew each other too honestly to need the niceties of greeting or the pretense at inquiry after health. They could approach what burdened them without prevarication.

He looked at her gravely, the question in his eyes.

"No," she answered. "I haven't learned anything that I can see is of use. But I am certain beyond doubt at all that Lady Moidore does not believe that Percival is guilty, but neither does she know who is. At moments she wants more than anything else to know, at other times she dreads it, because it would finally condemn someone and shatter all the beliefs and the love she has felt for that person until now. The uncertainty is poisoning everything for her, yet she is afraid that if one day she learns who it is, then that person may realize she knows and she herself will be in danger."

His face was tight with inner pain and the knowledge that for all the effort and the struggle he had put forth, and the price it had cost him, he had failed.

"She is right," he said quietly. "Whoever it is has no mercy. They are prepared to allow Percival to hang. It would be a flight of fancy to suppose they will spare her if she endangers them."

"And I think she would." Now Hester's expression was pinched with anxiety. "Underneath the fashionable woman who retreated to her bedroom with grief there is someone of more courage, and a deeper horror at the cruelty and the lies."

"Then we still have something to fight for," he said simply. "If she wants to know badly enough, and the suspicion and the fear become unbearable to her, then one day she will."

The waiter appeared and set their chocolate in front of them. Monk thanked him.

"Something will fall into place in her memory," he continued to Hester. "A word, a gesture; someone's guilt will draw them into an error, and suddenly she will realize—and they will see it, because she will not possibly be able to be the same towards them—how could she?"

"Then we must find out—before she does." Hester stirred her chocolate vigorously, risking slopping it over with every round of the spoon. "She knows that almost everyone lied, in one degree or another, because Octavia was not as they described her in the trial." And she told him of everything that Beatrice had said the last time they spoke.

"Maybe." Monk was dubious. "But Octavia was her daughter; it is possible she simply did not want to see her as clearly as they did. If Octavia were indiscreet in her cups, perhaps vain, and did not keep the usual curb on her sensuality—her mother may not be prepared to accept that as true."

"What are you saying?" Hester demanded. "That what they all testified was right, and she encouraged Percival, and then changed her mind when she thought he would take her at her word? And instead of asking anyone for help, she took a carving knife to her bedroom?"

She picked up her chocolate but was too eager to finish the thought to stop. "And when Percival did intrude in the night, even though her brother was next door, she fought to the death with Percival and never cried out? I'd have screamed my lungs raw!" She sipped her chocolate. "And don't say she was embarrassed he'd say she had invited him. No one in her family would believe Percival instead of her—and it would be a lot easier to explain than either his injured body or his corpse."

Monk smiled with a harsh humor. "Perhaps she hoped the mere sight of the knife would send him away—silently?"

She paused an instant. "Yes," she agreed reluctantly. "That does make some sense. It is not what I believe though."

"Nor I," he assented. "There is too much else that is out of character. What we need is to discover the lies from the truths, and perhaps the reasons for the lies—that might be the most revealing."

"In order of testimony," she agreed quickly. "I doubt Annie lied. For one thing she said nothing of significance, merely that she found Octavia, and we all know that is true. Similarly the doctor had no interest in anything but the best accuracy of which he was capable." She screwed up her face in intense concentration. "What reasons do people who are innocent of the crime have to lie? We must consider them. Then of course there is always the possibility of error that is not malicious, simply a matter of ignorance, incorrect assumption, and simple mistake."

He smiled in spite of himself. "The cook? Do you think Mrs. Boden could be in error about her knife?"

She caught his amusement, but responded with only a moment's softening of her eyes.

"No—I cannot think how. She identified it most precisely. And anyway, what sense would there be in it being a knife from anywhere else? There was no intruder. The knife does not help us towards the identity of who took it."

"Mary?"

Hester considered for a moment. "She is a person of most decided opinions—which is not a criticism. I cannot bear wishy-washy people who agree with whoever spoke to them last—but she might make an error out of a previously held conviction, without the slightest mal intent!"

"That it was Octavia's peignoir?"

"No of course not. Besides, she was not the only person to identify it. At the time you found it you asked Araminta as well, and she not only identified it but said that she remembered that Octavia had worn it the night of her death. And I think Lizzie the head laundrymaid identified it too. Besides, whether it was Octavia's or not, she obviously wore it when she was stabbed—poor woman."

"Rose?"

"Ah—there is someone much more likely. She had been wooed by Percival—after a manner of speaking—and then passed over when he grew bored with her. And rightly or not, she imagined he might marry her—and he obviously had no such intention at all. She had a very powerful motive to see him in trouble. I think she might even have the passion and the hatred to want him hanged."

"Enough to lie to bring about the end?" He found it hard to believe such a terrible malice, even from a sexual obsession rejected. Even the stabbing of Octavia had been done in hot blood, at the moment of refusal, not carried out deliberately step by step, over weeks, even months afterwards. It was chilling to think of such a mind in a laundrymaid, a trim, pretty creature one would scarcely look at except with an absentminded appreciation. And yet she could desire a man, and when rejected, torture him to a judicial death.

Hester saw his doubt.

"Perhaps not with such a terrible end in mind," she conceded. "One lie begets another. She may have intended only to frighten him—as Araminta did with Myles—and then events took over and she could not retreat without endangering herself." She took another sip of chocolate; it was delicious, although she was becoming used to the best of foods. "Or of course, she may have believed him guilty," she added. "Some people do not consider it as in the least to bend the truth a little in order to bring about what they see as justice."

"She lied about Octavia's character?" He took up the thread. "If Lady Moidore is right. But she may also have done that from jealousy. Very well—let us assume Rose lied. What about the butler, Phillips? He bore out what everyone else said about Percival."

"He was probably largely right," she conceded. "Percival was arrogant and ambitious. He clearly blackmailed the other servants over their little secrets—and perhaps the family as well; we shall probably never know that. He is not at all likable—but that is not the issue. If we were to hang everyone in London who is unlikable we could probably get rid of a quarter of the population."

"At least," he agreed. "But Phillips may have embroidered his opinion a trifle out of obligation to his employer. This was obviously the conclusion Sir Basil wished, and he wished it speedily. Phillips is not a foolish man, and he is intensely aware of duty. He wouldn't see it as any form of untruth, simply as loyalty to his superior, a military ideal he admires. And Mrs. Willis testified for us."

"The family?" she prompted.

"Cyprian also testified for us, and so did Septimus. Romola—what is your opinion of her?"

A brief feeling of irritation troubled Hester, and one of guilt. "She enjoys the status of being Sir Basil's daughter-in-law, and of living in Queen Anne Street, but she frequently tries to persuade Cyprian to ask for more money. She is adept at making him feel guilty if she is not happy. She is confused, because he is bored by her and she does not know why. And sometimes I have been so frustrated that he does not tell her to behave like an adult and take responsibility for her own feelings. But I suppose I do not know enough about them to judge."

"But you do," he said without condemnation. He loathed women who put such a burden of emotional blackmail upon their father or their husbands, but he had no idea why the thought touched such a raw nerve in him.

"I suppose so," she admitted. "But it hardly matters. I think Romola would testify according to whatever she thought Sir Basil wanted. Sir Basil is the power in that house; he has the purse strings, and they all know it. He does not need to make a demand, it is implicit; all he has to do is allow them to know his wishes."

Monk let out his breath in a sharp sigh. "And he wishes the murder of Octavia to be closed as rapidly and discreetly as possible—of course. Have you seen what the newspapers are saying?"

Her eyebrows shot up. "Don't be absurd. Where in heaven's name would I see a newspaper? I am a servant—and a woman. Lady Moidore doesn't see anything but the social pages, and she is not interested in them at the moment."

"Of course—I forgot." He pulled a wry face. He had only remembered that she was a friend of a war correspondent in the Crimea, and when he had died in the hospital in Scutari, she had sent his last dispatches home and then, born out of the intensity of her feelings and observations, herself written the succeeding dispatches and sent them under his name. Since the casualty lists were unreliable, his editor had not been aware of the change.

"What are they saying?" she asked. "Anything that affects us?"

"Generally? They are bemoaning the state of the nation that a footman can murder his mistress, that servants are so above themselves that they entertain ideas of lust and depravity involving the well-born; that the social order is crumbling; that we must hang Percival and make an example of him, so that no such thing will ever happen again." He pulled his face into an expression of disgust. "And of course they are full of sympathy for Sir Basil. All his past services to the Queen and the nation have been religiously rehearsed, all his virtues paraded, and positively fulsome condolences written."

She sighed and stared into the dregs of her cup.

"All the vested interests are ranged against us," he said grimly. "Everyone wants it over quickly, society's vengeance taken as thoroughly as possible, and then the whole matter forgotten so we can pick up our lives and try to continue them as much like before as we can."

"Is there anything at all we can do?" she asked.

"I can't think of anything." He stood up and held her chair. "I shall go and see him."

She met his eyes with a quick pain, and admiration. There was no need either for her to ask or for him to answer. It was a duty, a last rite which failure did not excuse.

As soon as Monk stepped inside Newgate Prison and the doors clanged shut behind him he felt a sickening familiarity. It was the smell, the mixture of damp, mold, rank sewage and an all-pervading misery that hung in the stillness of the air. Too many men who entered here left only to go to the executioner's rope, and the terror and despair of their last days had soaked into the walls till he could feel it skin-crawling like ice as he followed the warder along the stone corridors to the appointed place where he could see Percival for the last time.

He had misrepresented himself only slightly. Apparently he had been here before, and as soon as the warder saw his face he leaped to a false conclusion about his errand, and Monk did not explain.

Percival was standing in a small stone cell with one high window to an overcast sky. He turned as the door opened and Monk was let in, the gaoler with his keys looming huge behind.

For the first moment Percival looked surprised, then his face hardened into anger.

"Come to gloat?" he said bitterly.

"Nothing to gloat about," Monk replied almost casually. "I've lost my career, and you will lose your life. I just haven't worked out who's won."

"Lost your career?" For a moment doubt flickered across Percival's face, then suspicion. "Thought you'd have been made. Gone on to something better! You solved the case to everyone's satisfaction—except mine. No ugly skeletons dragged out, no mention of Myles Kellard raping Martha, poor little bitch, no saying Aunt Fenella is a whore—just a jumped-up footman filled with lust for a drunken widow. Hang him and let's get on with our lives. What more could they ask of a dutiful policeman?"

Monk did not blame him for his rage or his hate. They were justified—only, at least in part, misdirected. It would have been fairer to blame him for incompetence.

"I had the evidence," he said slowly. "But I didn't arrest you. I refused to do it, and they threw me out."

"What?" Percival was confused, disbelieving.

Monk repeated it.

"For God's sake why?" There was no softness in Percival, no

relenting. Again Monk did not blame him. He was beyond the last hope now, perhaps there was no room in him for gentleness of any sort. If he once let go of the rage he might crumble and terror would win; the darkness of the night would be unbearable without the burning of hate.

"Because I don't think you killed her," Monk replied.

Percival laughed harshly, his eyes black and accusing. But he said nothing, just stared in helpless and terrible knowledge.

"But even if I were still on the case," Monk went on very quietly, "I don't know what I should do, because I have no idea who did." It was an overwhelming admission of failure, and he was stunned as he heard himself make it to Percival of all people. But honesty was the very least of all he owed him.

"Very impressive," Percival said sarcastically, but there was a brief flicker of something in his face, rapid as the sunlight let through the trees by a turning leaf, then gone again. "But since you are not there, and everyone else is busy covering their own petty sins, serving their grievances, or else obliged to Sir Basil, we'll never know—will we?"

"Hester Latterly isn't." Instantly Monk regretted he had said it. Percival might take it for hope, which was an illusion and unspeakably cruel now.

"Hester Latterly?" For an instant Percival looked confused, then he remembered her. "Oh—the terribly efficient nurse. Daunting woman, but you're probably right. I expect she is so virtuous it is painful. I doubt she knows how to smile, let alone laugh, and I shouldn't think any man ever looked at her," he said viciously. "She's taken her vengeance on us by spending her time ministering to us when we are at our most vulnerable—and most ridiculous."

Monk felt a deep uprush of rage for the cruel and unthinking prejudice, then he looked at Percival's haggard face and remembered where he was, and why, and the rage vanished like a match flame in a sea of ice. What if Percival did need to hurt someone, however remotely? His was going to be the ultimate pain.

"She came to the house because I sent her," Monk explained. "She is a friend of mine. I hoped that someone inside the household in a position where no one would pay much regard to them might observe things I could not."

Percival's amazement was as profound as anything could be over the surface of the enormous center of him, which knew nothing but the slow, relentless clock ticking away his days to the last walk, the hood, the hangman's rope around his neck, and the sharp drop to tearing, breaking pain and oblivion.

"But she didn't learn anything, did she?" For the first time his voice cracked and he lost control of it.

Monk loathed himself for stupidly giving this knife thrust of hope, which was not hope at all.

"No," he said quickly. "Nothing that helps. All sorts of trivial and ugly little weaknesses and sins—and that Lady Moidore believes the murderer is still in the house, and almost certainly one of her family—but she has no idea who either."

Percival turned away, hiding his face.

"What did you come for?"

"I'm not sure. Perhaps simply not to leave you alone, or to think no one believes you. I don't know if it helps, but you have the right to know. I hope it does."

Percival let out an explosion of curses, and swore over and over again until he was exhausted with repeating himself and the sheer, ugly futility of it. When he finished Monk had gone and the cell door was locked again, but through the tears and the bloodless skin, there was a very small light of gratitude, ease from one of the clenched and terrible knots inside him.

On the morning Percival was hanged Monk was working on the case of a stolen picture, more probably removed and sold by a member of the family in gambling debt. But at eight o'clock he stopped on the pavement in Cheapside and stood still in the cold wind amid the crowd of costers, street peddlers of bootlaces and matches and other fripperies, clerks on errands, a sweep, black-faced and carrying a ladder, and two women arguing over a length of cloth. The babble and clatter rolled on around him, oblivious of what was happening in Newgate Yard, but he stood motionless with a sense of finality and a wounding loss—not for Percival individually, although he felt the man's terror and rage and the snuffing out of his life. He had not liked him, but he had been acutely aware of his vitality, his intensity of feeling and thought, his identity. But his greatest loss was for justice which had failed. At the moment when the trapdoor opened and the noose jerked tight, another crime was being committed. He had been powerless to prevent it, for all the labor and thought he had put into it, but his was not the only loss, or even necessarily the main one. All London was diminished, perhaps all England, because the law which should protect had instead injured.

Hester was standing in the dining room. She had deliberately come to collect an apricot conserve from the table for Beatrice's tray at precisely this time. If she jeopardized her position, even if she lost it and were dismissed, she wanted to see the faces of the Moidores at the moment of hanging, and to be sure each one of them knew precisely what moment this was.

She excused herself past Fenella, uncharacteristically up so early; apparently she intended to ride in the park. Hester spooned a little of the conserve into a small dish.

"Good morning, Mrs. Sandeman," she said levelly. "I hope you have a pleasant ride. It will be very cold in the park this early, even though the sun is up. The frost will not have melted at all. It is three minutes to eight."

"How very precise you are," Fenella said with a touch of sarcasm. "Is that because you are a nurse—everything must be done to the instant, in strict routine? Take your medicine as the clock chimes or it will not do you good. How excruciatingly tedious." She laughed very slightly, a mocking, tinkly sound.

"No, Mrs. Sandeman," Hester said very distinctly. "It is because in two minutes now they will hang Percival. I believe they are very precise—I have no idea why. It can hardly matter; it is just a ritual they keep."

Fenella choked on a mouthful of eggs and went into a spasm of coughing. No one assisted her.

"Oh God!" Septimus stared ahead of him, bleak and unblinking, his thoughts unreadable.

Cyprian shut his eyes as if he would block out the world, and all his powers were concentrated on his inner turmoil.

Araminta was sheet white, her curious face frozen.

Myles Kellard slopped his tea, which he had just raised to his lips, sending splashes all over the tablecloth, and the stain spread out in a brown, irregular pattern. He looked furious and confused.

"Oh really," Romola exploded, her face pink. "What a tasteless and insensitive thing to have said. What is the matter with you, Miss Latterly? No one wishes to know that. You had better leave the room, and for goodness' sake don't be so crass as to mention it to Mama-in-law. Really—you are too stupid."

Basil's face was very pale and there was a nervous twitch in the muscles at the side of his cheek.

"It could not be helped," he said very quietly. "Society must be preserved, and the means are sometimes very harsh. Now I think we may call the matter closed and proceed with our lives as normal. Miss Latterly, you will not speak of it again. Please take the conserve, or whatever it is you came for, and carry Lady Moidore's breakfast to her."

"Yes, Sir Basil," Hester said obediently, but their faces remained in the mirror of her mind, the misery and finality of it like a patina of darkness upon everything.

CHAPTER
ELEVEN

————

Two days after Percival was hanged, Septimus Thirsk developed a
slight fever, not enough to fear some serious disease, but sufficient to
make him feel unwell and confine him to his room. Beatrice, who had
kept Hester more for her company than any genuine need of her
professional skills, dispatched her immediately to care for him, obtain
any medication she considered advisable, and do anything she could
to ease his discomfort and aid his recovery.

Hester found Septimus lying in bed and in his large, airy room.
The curtains were drawn wide open onto a fierce February day, with
the sleet dashing against the windows like grapeshot and a sky so low
and leaden it seemed to rest close above the rooftops. The room was
cluttered with army memorabilia, engravings of soldiers in dress uniform, mounted cavalry officers, and all along the west wall in a place
of honor, unflanked by anything else, a superb painting of the charge
of the Royal Scots Greys at Waterloo, horses with nostrils flared, white
manes flying in the clouds of smoke, and the whole sweep of battle
behind them. She felt her heart lurch and her stomach knot at the
sight of it. It was so real she could smell the gunsmoke and hear
the thunder of hooves, the shouting and the clash of steel, and feel
the sun burning her skin, and knew the warm odor of blood would fill
her nose and throat afterwards.

And then there would be the silence on the grass, the dead lying
waiting for burial or the carrion birds, the endless work, the helplessness and the few sudden flashes of victory when someone lived through
appalling wounds or found some ease from pain. It was all so vivid in
the moment she saw the picture, her body ached with the memory of
exhaustion and the fear, the pity, the anger and the exhilaration.

She looked and saw Septimus's faded blue eyes on her, and knew in that instant they understood each other as no one else in that house ever could. He smiled very slowly, a sweet, almost radiant look.

She hesitated, not to break the moment, then as it passed naturally, she went over to him and began a simple nursing routine, questions, feeling his brow, then the pulse in his bony wrist, his abdomen to see if it were causing him pain, listened carefully to his rather shallow breathing and for telltale rattling in his chest.

His skin was flushed, dry and a little rough, his eyes overbright, but beyond a chill she could find nothing gravely wrong with him. However a few days of care might do far more for him than any medication, and she was happy to give it. She liked Septimus, and felt the neglect and slight condescension he received from the rest of the family.

He looked at her, a quizzical expression on his face. She thought quite suddenly that if she had pronounced pneumonia or consumption he would not have been afraid—or even grievously shaken. He had long ago accepted that death comes to everyone, and he had seen the reality of it many times, both by violence and by disease. And he had no deep purpose in extending his life anymore. He was a passenger, a guest in his brother-in-law's house, tolerated but not needed. And he was a man born and trained to fight and to protect, to serve as a way of life.

She touched him very gently.

"A nasty chill, but if you are cared for it should pass without any lasting effect. I shall stay with you for a while, just to make sure." She saw his face brighten and realized how used he was to loneliness. It had become like the ache in the joints one moves so as to accommodate, tries to forget, but never quite succeeds. She smiled with quick, bright conspiracy. "And we shall be able to talk."

He smiled back, his eyes bright for once with pleasure and not the fever in him.

"I think you had better remain," he agreed. "In case I should take a sudden turn for the worse." And he coughed dramatically, although she could also see the real pain of a congested chest.

"Now I will go down to the kitchen and get you some milk and onion soup," she said briskly.

He pulled a face.

"It is very good for you," she assured him. "And really quite palatable. And while you eat it, I shall tell you about my experiences—and then you may tell me about yours!"

"For that," he conceded, "I will even eat milk and onion soup!"

Hester spent all that day with Septimus, bringing her own meals up on a tray and remaining quietly in the chair in the corner of the room while he slept fitfully in the afternoon, and then fetching him more soup, this time leek and celery mixed with creamed potato into a thick blend. When he had eaten it they sat through the evening and talked of things that had changed since his day on the battlefield—she telling him of the great conflicts she had witnessed from the grassy sward above, and he recounting to her the desperate cavalry battles he had fought in the Afghan War of 1839 to 1842—then in the conquest of Sind the year after, and in the later Sikh wars in the middle of the decade. They found endless emotions, sights and fears the same, and the wild pride and horror of victory, the weeping and the wounds, the beauty of courage, and the fearful, elemental indignity of dismemberment and death. And he told her something of the magnificent continent of India and its peoples.

They also remembered the laughter and the comradeship, the absurdities and the fierce sentimental moments, and the regimental rituals with their splendor, farcical at a glance, silver candelabra and full dinner service with crystal and porcelain for officers the night before battle, scarlet uniforms, gold braid, brasses like mirrors.

"You would have liked Harry Haslett," Septimus said with a sweet, sharp sadness. "He was one of the nicest men. He had all the qualities of a friend: honor without pomposity, generosity without condescension, humor without malice and courage without cruelty. And Octavia adored him. She spoke of him so passionately the very day she died, as if his death were still fresh in her mind." He smiled and stared up at the ceiling, blinking a little to hide the tears in his eyes.

Hester reached for his hand and held it. It was a natural gesture, quite spontaneous, and he understood it without explanation. His bony fingers tightened on hers, and for several minutes they were silent.

"They were going to move away," he said at last, when his voice was under control. "Tavie wasn't much like Araminta. She wanted her own house; she didn't care about the social status of being Sir

Basil Moidore's daughter or living in Queen Anne Street with the carriages and the staff, the ambassadors to dine, the members of Parliament, the foreign princes. Of course you haven't seen any of that because the house is in mourning for Tavie now—but before that it was quite different. There was something special almost every week."

"Is that why Myles Kellard stays?" Hester asked, understanding easily now.

"Of course," he agreed with a thin smile. "How could he possibly live in this manner on his own? He is quite well off, but nothing like the wealth or the rank of Basil. And Araminta is very close to her father. Myles never stood a chance—not that I am sure he wants it. He has much here he would never have anywhere else."

"Except the dignity of being master in his own house," Hester said. "The freedom to have his own opinions, to come and go without deference to anyone else's plans, and to choose his friends according to his own likes and emotions."

"Oh, there is a price," Septimus agreed wryly. "Sometimes I think a very high one."

Hester frowned. "What about conscience?" She said it gently, aware of the difficult road along which it would lead and the traps for both of them. "If you live on someone else's bounty, do you not risk compromising yourself so deeply with obligation that you surrender your own agency?"

He looked at her, his pale eyes sad. She had shaved him, and become aware how thin his skin was. He looked older than his years.

"You are thinking about Percival and the trial, aren't you." It was barely a question.

"Yes—they lied, didn't they?"

"Of course," he agreed. "Although perhaps they hardly saw it that way. They said what was in their best interest, for one reason or another. One would have to be very brave intentionally to defy Basil." He moved his legs a fraction to be more comfortable. "I don't suppose he would throw us out, but it would make life most unpleasant from day to day—endless restrictions, humiliations, little scratches on the sensitive skin of the mind." He looked across at the great picture. "To be dependent is to be so damned vulnerable."

"And Octavia wanted to leave?" she prompted after a moment.

He returned to the present. "Oh yes, she was all ready to, but Harry had not enough money to provide for her as she was used, which Basil pointed out to him. He was a younger son, you see. No inheritance. His father was very well-to-do. At school with Basil. In fact, I believe Basil was his fag—a junior who is sort of an amiable slave to a senior boy—but perhaps you knew that?"

"Yes," she acknowledged, thinking of her own brothers.

"Remarkable man, James Haslett," Septimus said thoughtfully. "Gifted in so many ways, and charming. Good athlete, fine musician, sort of minor poet, and a good mind. Shock of fair hair and a beautiful smile. Harry was like him. But he left his estate to his eldest son, naturally. Everyone does."

His voice took on a bitter edge. "Octavia would have forfeited a lot if she left Queen Anne Street. And should there be children, which they both wanted very much, then the restrictions upon their finances would be even greater. Octavia would suffer. Of course Harry could not accept that."

He moved again to make himself more comfortable. "Basil suggested the army as a career, and offered to buy him a commission—which he did. Harry was a natural soldier; he had the gift of command, and the men loved him. It was not what he wanted, and inevitably it meant a long separation—which I suppose was what Basil intended. He was against the marriage in the first place, because of his dislike for James Haslett."

"So Harry took the commission to obtain the finance for himself and Tavie to have their own house?" Hester could see it vividly. She had known so many young officers that she could picture Harry Haslett as a composite of a hundred she had seen in every mood, victory and defeat, courage and despair, triumph and exhaustion. It was as if she had known him and understood his dreams. Now Octavia was more real to her than Araminta downstairs in the withdrawing room with her tea and conversation, or Beatrice in her bedroom thinking and fearing, and immeasurably more than Romola with her children supervising the new governess in the schoolroom.

"Poor devil," Septimus said half to himself. "He was a brilliant officer—he earned promotion very quickly. And then he was killed at Balaclava. Octavia was never the same again, poor girl. Her whole world collapsed when the news came; the light fled out of her. It was as if she had nothing left even to hope for." He fell silent, absorbed in his memory of the day, the numbing grief and the long gray stretch of time afterwards. He looked old and very vulnerable himself.

There was nothing Hester could say to help, and she was wise enough not to try. Words of ease would only belittle his pain. Instead she set about trying to make him more physically comfortable, and spent the next several hours doing so. She fetched clean linen and remade the bed while he sat wrapped up and huddled in the dressing chair. Then she brought up hot water in the great ewer and filled the basin and helped him wash so that he felt fresh. She also brought from the laundry a clean nightshirt, and when he was back in bed again she returned to the kitchen, prepared and brought him up a light meal. After which he was quite ready to sleep for over three. hours.

He woke considerably restored, and so obliged to her she was embarrassed. After all, Sir Basil was paying her for her skill, and this was the first time she had exercised the latter in the manner in which he intended.

The following day Septimus was so much better she was able to attend to him in the early morning, then seek Beatrice's permission to leave Queen Anne Street for the entire afternoon, as long as she returned in sufficient time to prepare Septimus for the night and give him some slight medication to see he rested.

In a gray wind laden with sleet, and with ice on the footpaths, she walked to Harley Street and took a cab, requesting the driver take her to the War Office. There she paid him and alighted with all the aplomb of one who knows precisely where she is going, and that she will be admitted with pleasure, which was not at all the case. She intended to learn all she could about Captain Harry Haslett, without any clear idea of where it might lead, but he was the only member of the family about whom she had known almost nothing until yesterday. Septimus's account had brought him so sharply to life, and made him so likable and of such deep and abiding importance to Octavia, that Hester understood why two years after his death she still grieved with the same sharp and unendurable loneliness. Hester wished to know of his career.

Suddenly Octavia had become more than just the victim of the crime, a face Hester had never seen and therefore for whom she felt no sense of personality. Since listening to Septimus, Octavia's emotions had become real, her feelings those Hester might so easily have had herself, had she loved and been loved by any of the young officers she had known.

She climbed the steps of the War Office and addressed the man at the door with all the courtesy and charm she could muster, plus, of course, the due deference from a woman to a man of the military, and just a touch of her own authority, which was the least difficult, since it came to her quite naturally.

"Good afternoon, sir," she began with an inclination of her head and a smile of friendly openness. "I wonder if I might be permitted to speak with Major Geoffrey Tallis? If you would give him my name I believe he will know it. I was one of Miss Nightingale's nurses"— she was not above using that magic name if it would help—"and I had occasion to tend Major Tallis in Scutari when he was injured. It concerns the death of a widow of a former officer of distinction, and there is a matter to which Major Tallis may be able to assist—with information that would considerably ease the family's distress. Would you be good enough to have that message conveyed to him?"

It was apparently the right mixture of supplication, good reasoning, feminine appeal, and the authority of a nurse which draws from most well-bred men an automatic obedience.

"I will certainly have that message delivered to him, ma'am," he agreed, standing a trifle straighter. "What name shall I give?"

"Hester Latterly," she answered. "I regret seeking him at such short notice, but I am still nursing a gentleman late of active service, and he is not well enough that I should leave him for above a few hours." That was a very elastic version of the truth, but not quite a downright lie.

"Of course." His respect increased. He wrote down the name "Hester Latterly" and added a note as to her occupation and the urgency of her call, summoned an orderly and dispatched him with the message to Major Tallis.

Hester was quite happy to wait in silence, but the doorman seemed disposed to converse, so she answered his questions on the battles she had witnessed and found they had both been present at the battle of Inkermann. They were deep in reminiscences when the orderly returned to say Major Tallis would receive Miss Latterly in ten minutes, if she would care to wait upon him in his office.

She accepted with a trifle more haste than she had meant to; it was a definite subtraction from the dignity she had tried to establish, but she thanked the doorman for his courtesy. Then she walked very uprightly behind the orderly inside the entrance hall, up the wide staircase and into the endless corridors until she was shown into a waiting room with several chairs, and left.

It was rather more than ten minutes before Major Tallis opened the inner door. A dapper lieutenant walked out past Hester, apparently without seeing her, and she was shown in.

Geoffrey Tallis was a handsome man in his late thirties, an ex-cavalry officer who had been given an administrative post after a serious injury, from which he still walked with a limp. But without Hester's care he might well have lost his leg altogether and been unable to continue a career of any sort. His face lit with pleasure when he saw her, and he held out his hand in welcome.

She gave him hers and he grasped it hard.

"My dear Miss Latterly, what a remarkable pleasure to see you again, and in so much more agreeable circumstances. I hope you are well, and that things prosper with you?"

She was quite honest, not for any purpose but because the words were spoken before she thought otherwise.

"I am very well, thank you, and things prosper only moderately. My parents died, and I am obliged to make my way, but I have the means, so I am fortunate. But I admit it is hard to adjust to England again, and to peace, where everyone's preoccupations are so different—" She left the wealth of implication unsaid: the withdrawing room manners, the stiff skirts, the emphasis on social position and manners. She could see that he read it all in her face, and his own experiences had been sufficiently alike for more explanation to be redundant.

"Oh indeed." He sighed, letting go of her hand. "Please be seated and tell me what I may do to be of help to you."

She knew enough not to waste his time. The preliminaries had already been dealt with.

"What can you tell me of Captain Harry Haslett, who was killed at Balaclava? I ask because his widow has recently met a most tragic death. I am acquainted with her mother; indeed I have been nursing her through her time of bereavement, and am presently nursing her uncle, a retired officer." If he asked her Septimus's name she would affect not to know the circumstances of his "retirement."

Major Tallis's face clouded over immediately.

"An excellent officer, and one of the nicest men I ever knew. He was a fine commander of men. It came to him naturally because he had courage and a sense of justice that men admired. There was humor in him, and some love of adventure, but not bravado. He never took unnecessary chances." He smiled with great sadness. "I think more than most men, he wanted to live. He had a great love for his wife—in fact the army was not the career he would have chosen; he entered it only to earn himself the means to support his wife in the manner he wished and to make some peace with his father-in-law, Sir Basil Moidore—who paid for his commission as a wedding gift, I believe, and watched over his career with keen interest. What an ironic tragedy."

"Ironic?" she said quickly.

His face creased with pain and his voice lowered instinctively, but his words were perfectly clear.

"It was Sir Basil who arranged his promotion, and thus his transfer from the regiment in which he was to Lord Cardigan's Light Brigade, and of course they led the charge at Balaclava. If he had remained a lieutenant as he was, he would very probably be alive today."

"What happened?" An awful possibility was opening up in front of her, so ugly she could not bear to look at it, nor yet could she look away. "Do you know of whom Sir Basil asked his favor? A great deal of honor depends upon it," she pressed with all the gravity she could. "And, I am beginning to think, the truth of Octavia Haslett's death. Please, Major Tallis, tell me about Captain Haslett's promotion?"

He hesitated only a moment longer. The debt he owed her, their common memories, and his admiration and grief over Haslett's death prevailed.

"Sir Basil is a man of great power and influence, perhaps you are not aware quite how much. He has far more wealth than he displays, although that is considerable, but he also had obligations owed him, debts both of assistance and of finance from the past, and I think a great deal of knowledge—" He left the uses of that unspoken. "He would not find it difficult to accomplish the transfer of an officer from one regiment to another in order to achieve his promotion, if he wished it. A letter—sufficient money to purchase the new commission—"

"But how would Sir Basil know whom to approach in the new regiment?" she pressed, the idea taking firmer shape in her mind all the time.

"Oh—because he is quite well acquainted with Lord Cardigan, who would naturally be aware of all the possible vacancies in command."

"And of the nature of the regiment," she added.

"Of course." He looked puzzled.

"And their likely dispositions?"

"Lord Cardigan would—naturally. But Sir Basil hardly—"

"You mean Sir Basil was unaware of the course of the campaign and the personalities of the commanders?" She allowed the heavy doubt through her expression for him to see.

"Well—" He frowned, beginning to glimpse what he also found too ugly to contemplate. "Of course I am not privy to his communication with Lord Cardigan. Letters to and from the Crimea take a considerable time; even on the fastest packet boats it would not be less than ten or fourteen days. Things can change greatly in that time. Battles can be won or lost and a great deal of ground altered between opposing forces."

"But regiments do not change their natures, Major." She forced him to realism. "A competent commander knows which regiments he would choose to lead a charge, the more desperate the charge the more certain would he be to pick exactly the right man—and the right captain, who had courage, flair, and the absolute loyalty of his men. He would also choose someone tried in the field, yet uninjured so far, and not weary from defeat, or failure, or so scarred in spirit as to be uncertain of his mettle."

He stared at her without speaking.

"In fact once raised to captain, Harry Haslett would be ideal, would he not?"

"He would," he said almost under his breath.

"And Sir Basil saw to his promotion and his change of posting to Lord Cardigan's Light Brigade. Do you suppose any of the correspondence on the subject is still extant?"

"Why, Miss Latterly? What is it you are seeking?"

To lie to him would be contemptible—and also alienate his sympathies.

"The truth about Octavia Haslett's death," she answered.

He sighed heavily. "Was she not murdered by some servant or other? I seem to recollect seeing it in the newspapers. The man was just hanged, was he not?"

"Yes," she agreed with a heavy weariness of failure inside her. "But the day she died she learned something which shook her so deeply she told her uncle it was the most dreadful truth, and she wanted only one more piece of evidence to prove it. I am beginning to believe that it may have concerned the death of her husband. She was thinking of it the day of her own death. We had previously assumed that what she discovered concerned her family still living, but perhaps it did not. Major Tallis, would it be possible to learn if she came here that day—if she saw someone?"

Now he looked very troubled.

"What day was it?"

She told him.

He pulled a bell rope and a young officer appeared and snapped to attention.

"Payton, will you convey my compliments to Colonel Sidgewick and ask him if at any time around the end of November last year the widow of Captain Harry Haslett called upon his office. It is a matter of considerable importance, concerning both honor and life, and I would be most obliged if he would give me an answer of exactness as soon as may be possible. This lady, who is one of Miss Nightingale's nurses, is waiting upon the answer."

"Sir!" The junior snapped to attention once again, turned on his heel and departed.

While he was gone Major Tallis apologized for requiring Hester to spend her time in the waiting room, but he had other business obligations which he must discharge. She understood and assured him it was precisely what she expected and was perfectly content. She would write letters and otherwise occupy herself.

It was not long, a matter of fifteen or twenty minutes, before the door opened and the lieutenant returned. As soon as he left, Major Tallis called Hester in. His face was white, his eyes full of anxiety and fearful pity.

"You were perfectly correct," he said very quietly. "Octavia Haslett was here on the afternoon of her death, and she spoke with Colonel Sidgewick. She learned from him exactly what you learned from me, and from her words and expression on hearing, it appears she drew the same conclusions. I am most profoundly grieved, and I feel guilty—I am not sure for what. Perhaps that the whole matter occurred, and no one did anything to prevent it. Truly, Miss Latterly, I am deeply sorry."

"Thank you—thank you, Major Tallis." She forced a sickly smile, her mind whirling. "I am most grateful to you."

"What are you going to do?" he said urgently.

"I don't know. I'm not sure what I can do. I shall consult with the police officer on the case; I think that would be wisest."

"Please do, Miss Latterly—please be most careful. I—"

"I know," she said quickly. "I have learned much in confidence. Your name will not be mentioned, I give you my word. Now I must go. Thank you again." And without waiting for him to add anything further, she turned and left, almost running down the long corridor and making three wrong turnings before she finally came to the exit.

She found Monk at some inconvenience, and was obliged to wait at his lodgings until after dark, when he returned home. He was startled to see her.

"Hester! What has happened? You look fearful."

"Thank you," she said acidly, but she was too full of her news to carry even an irritation for more than an instant. "I have just been to the War Office—at least I was this afternoon. I have been waiting here for you interminably—"

"The War Office." He took off his wet hat and overcoat, the rain falling from them in a little puddle on the floor. "From your expression I assume you learned something of interest?"

Only hesitating to draw breath when it was strictly necessary, she told him everything she had learned from Septimus, then all that had been said from the instant of entering Major Tallis's office.

"If that was where Octavia had been on the afternoon of her death," she said urgently, "if she learned what I did today, then she must have gone back to Queen Anne Street believing that her father had deliberately contrived her husband's promotion and transfer from what was a fine middle-order regiment to Lord Cardigan's Light Brigade, where he would be honor- and duty-bound to lead a charge in which casualties would be murderous." She refused to visualize it, but it crowded close at the back of her mind. "Cardigan's reputation is well known. Many would be bound to die in the first onslaught itself, but even of those who survived it, many would be so seriously wounded the field surgeons could do little to help them. They'd be transferred piled one upon another in open carts to the hospital in Scutari, and there they'd face a long convalescence where gangrene, typhus, cholera and other fevers killed even more than the sword or the cannon had."

He did not interrupt her.

"Once he was promoted," she went on, "his chances of glory, which he did not want, were very slight; his chances of death, quick or slow, were appallingly high.

"If Octavia did learn this, no wonder she went home ashen-faced and did not speak at dinner. Previously she thought it fate and the chances of war which bereaved her of the husband she loved so deeply and left her a dependent widow in her father's house, without escape." She shivered. "Trapped even more surely than before."

Monk agreed tacitly, allowing her to go on uninterrupted.

"Now she discovered it was not a blind misfortune which had taken everything from her." She leaned forward. "But a deliberate betrayal, and she was imprisoned with her betrayer, day after day, for as far as she could see into a gray future.

"Then what did she do? Perhaps when everyone else was asleep, she went to her father's study and searched his desk for letters, the communication which would prove beyond doubt the terrible truth." She stopped.

"Yes," he said very slowly. "Yes—then what? Basil purchased Harry's commission, and then when he proved a fine officer, prevailed upon his friends and purchased him a higher commission in a gallant and reckless regiment. In whose eyes would that be more than a very understandable piece of favor seeking?"

"No one's," she answered bitterly. "He would protest innocence. How could he know Harry Haslett would lead in the charge and fall?"

"Exactly," he said quickly. "These are the fortunes of war. If you marry a soldier, it is the chance you take—all women do. He would say he grieved for her, but she was wickedly ungrateful to charge him with culpability in it all. Perhaps she had taken a little too much wine with dinner—a fault which she was apt to indulge rather often lately. I can imagine Basil's face as he said it, and his expression of distaste."

She looked at Monk urgently. "That would be useless. Octavia knew her father and was the only one who had ever had the courage to defy him—and reap his revenge.

"But what defiance was left her? She had no allies. Cyprian was content to remain a prisoner in Queen Anne Street. To an extent he had a hostage to fortune in Romola, who obeyed her own instinct for survival, which would never include disobeying Basil. Fenella was uninterested in anyone but herself, Araminta seemed to be on her father's side in apparently everything. Myles Kellard was an additional problem, hardly a solution. And he too would never override Basil's wishes; certainly he would not do it for someone else!"

"Lady Moidore?" he prompted.

"She seemed driven, or else had retreated, to the periphery of things. She fought for Octavia's marriage in the first place, but after that it seems her resources were spent. Septimus might have fought for her, but he had no weapons."

"And Harry was dead." He took up the thread. "Leaving a void in her life nothing else could begin to heal. She must have felt an overwhelming despair, grief, betrayal and a sense of being trapped that were almost beyond endurance, and she was without a weapon to fight back."

"Almost?" she demanded. "Almost beyond endurance? Tired, stunned, confused and alone—what is 'almost' about it? And she did have a weapon, whether she intended it as such or not. Perhaps the thought had never entered her mind, but scandal would hurt Basil more than anything else—the fearful scandal of a suicide." Her voice became harsh with the tragedy and the irony of it. "His daughter, living in his home, under his care, so wretched, so comfortless, so un-Christian as to take her own life, not peacefully with laudanum, not even over the rejection of a lover, and it was too late to be the shock of Harry's death, but deliberately and bloodily in her own bedroom. Or perhaps even in his study with the betraying letter in her hand.

"She would be buried in unhallowed ground, with other sinners beyond forgiveness. Can you imagine what people would say? The shame of it, the looks, the whispers, the sudden silences. The invitations that would no longer come, the people one calls upon who would be unaccountably not at home, in spite of the fact that their carriages were in the mews and all the lights blazing. And where there had been admiration and envy, now there would be contempt—and worst of all, derision."

His face was very grave, the dark tragedy of it utterly apparent.

"If it had not been Annie who had found her, but someone else,"

ANNE PERRY

he said, "one of the family, it would have been an easy thing to remove the knife, put her on the bed, tear her nightgown to make it seem as if there had been some struggle, however brief, then break the creeper outside the window and take a few ornaments and jewels. Then it would seem murder, appalling, grieving, but not shameful. There would be acute sympathy, no ostracism, no blame. It could happen to anyone.

"Then I seemed about to ruin it all by proving that no one had broken into the house, so a murderer must be found among the residents."

"So that is the crime—not the stabbing of Octavia, but the slow, judicial murder of Percival. How hideous, how immeasurably worse," she said slowly. "But how can we possibly prove it? They will go undiscovered and unpunished. They will get away with it! Whoever it is—"

"What a nightmare. But who? I still don't know. The scandal would harm them all. It could have been Cyprian and Romola, or even Cyprian alone. He is a big man, quite strong enough to carry Octavia from the study, if that was where it happened, up to her room and lay her on the bed. He would not even run much risk of disturbing anyone, since his room was next to hers."

It was a startlingly distressing thought. Cyprian's face with its imagination and capacity for humor and pain came sharply to her mind. It would be like him to want to conceal his sister's act, to save her name and see that she might be grieved for, and buried in holy ground.

But Percival had been hanged for it.

"Was Cyprian so weak he would have permitted that, knowing Percival could not be guilty?" she said aloud. She wished profoundly she could dismiss that as impossible, but Cyprian yielding to Romola's emotional pressure was too clear in her mind, as was the momentary desperation she had seen in his face when she had watched him unobserved. And he of all of them seemed to grieve most deeply for Octavia, with the most wounding pity.

"Septimus?" Monk asked.

It was the kind of reckless, compassionate act Septimus might perform.

"No," she denied vehemently. "No—he would never permit Percival to hang."

309

"Myles would." Monk was looking at her with intense emotion now, his face bleak and strained. "He would have done it to save the family name. His own status is tied inextricably with the Moidores'—in fact it is totally dependent on it. Araminta might have helped him—and might not."

A sharp memory returned to Hester of Araminta in the library, and of the charged emotion between her and Myles. Surely she knew he had not killed Octavia—and yet she was prepared to let Monk think he had, and watch Myles sweat with fear. That was a very peculiar kind of hatred—and power. Was it fueled by the horror of her own wedding night and its violence, or by his rape of the maid Martha—or by the fact that they were conspirators in concealing the manner of Octavia's death, and then of allowing Percival to hang for it?

"Or Basil himself?" she suggested.

"Or even Basil for reputation—and Lady Moidore for love?" he said. "In fact Fenella is the only one for whom I can find no reason and no means." His face was white, and there was a look of such grief and guilt in his eyes she felt the most intense admiration for his inner honesty, and a warmth towards the pity he was capable of but so rarely showed.

"Of course it is all only speculation," she said much more gently. "I know of no proof for any of it. Even if we had learned this before Percival was ever charged, I cannot even imagine how we might prove it. That is why I have come to you—and of course I wished to share the knowledge with you."

There was a look of profound concentration on his face. She waited, hearing the sounds of Mrs. Worley working in the kitchen and the rattle of hansoms and a dray cart passing in the street outside.

"If she killed herself," he said at last, "then someone removed the knife at the time they discovered her body, and presumably replaced it in the kitchen—or possibly kept it, but that seems unlikely. It does not seem, so far as we can see, the act of someone in panic. If they put the knife back . . . no." His face screwed up in impatience. "They certainly did not put the peignoir back. They must have hidden them both in some place we did not search. And yet we found no trace of anyone having left the house between the time of her death and the time the police constable and the doctor were called."

310

He stared at her, as if seeking her thoughts, and yet he continued to speak. "In a house with as many staff as that, and maids up at five, it would be difficult to leave unseen—and to be sure of being unseen."

"But surely there were places in the family's rooms you did not search?" she said.

"I imagine so." His face was dark with the ugliness of it. "God! How brutal! They must have kept the knife and the peignoir, stained with her blood, just in case they were needed—to incriminate some poor devil." He shuddered involuntarily, and she felt a sudden coldness in the room that had nothing to do with the meager fire or the steady sleet outside, now turning to snow.

"Perhaps if we could find the hiding place," she said tentatively, "we might know who it was who used it?"

He laughed, a jerky, painful sound.

"The person who put it in Percival's room behind the drawers in his dresser? I don't think we can assume that the hiding place incriminates them."

She felt foolish.

"Of course not," she admitted quietly. "Then what can we look for?"

He sank into silence again for a long time, and she waited, racking her brains.

"I don't know," he said at last, with obvious difficulty. "Blood in the study might be indicative—Percival would not have killed her there. The whole premise is that he forced his way into her bedroom and she fought him off and was killed in the process—"

She stood up, suddenly full of energy now that there was something to do.

"I will look for it. It won't be difficult—"

"Be careful," he said so sharply that it was almost a bark. "Hester!"

She opened her mouth to be dismissive, full of the excitement of at last having some idea to pursue.

"Hester!" He caught her by the shoulder, his hands hard.

She winced and would have pulled away had she the strength.

"Hester—listen to me!" he said urgently. "This man—or woman—has done far more than conceal a suicide. They have committed a slow and very deliberate murder." His face was tight with distress.

311

"Have you ever seen a man hanged? I have. And I watched Percival struggle as the net tightened around him for the weeks before—and then I visited him in Newgate. It is a terrible way to die."

She felt a little sick, but she did not retreat.

"They will have no pity for you," he went on relentlessly, "if you threaten them in even the slightest way. In fact I think now that you know this, it would be better if you were to send in your notice. Tell them by letter that you have had an accident and cannot return. No one is needing a nurse; a ladies' maid could perfectly well perform all that Lady Moidore wants."

"I will not." She stood almost chest to chest with him and glared. "I am going back to Queen Anne Street to see if I can discover what really happened to Octavia—and possibly who did it and caused Percival to be hanged." She realized the enormity of what she was saying, but she had left herself no retreat.

"Hester."

"What?"

He took a deep breath and let her go. "Then I will remain in the street nearby, and shall look to see you at least every hour at a window that gives to the street. If I don't, I shall call Evan at the police station and have him enter the place—"

"You can't!" she protested.

"I can!"

"On what pretext, for heaven's sake?"

He smiled with bitter humor. "That you are wanted in connection with a domestic theft. I can always release you afterwards—with unblemished character—a case of mistaken identity."

She was more relieved than she would show.

"I am obliged to you." She tried to say it stiffly, but her emotion showed through, and for a moment they stared at each other with that perfect understanding that occasionally flashed between them. Then she excused herself, picked up her coat again and allowed him to help her into it, and took her leave.

She entered the Queen Anne Street house discreetly and avoided all but the most essential conversation, going upstairs to check that Septimus was still recovering well. He was pleased to see her and greeted her with interest. She found it hard not to tell him anything of her discoveries or conclusions, and she made excuses to escape and go to Beatrice as soon as she could without hurting his feelings.

After she had brought up her dinner she asked permission to retire early, saying she had letters to write, and Beatrice was content to acquiesce.

She slept very restlessly, and it was no difficulty to rise at a little after two in the morning and creep downstairs with a candle. She dared not turn up the gas. It would glare like the sun and be too far away for her to reach to turn it down should she hear anyone else about. She slipped down the female servants' staircase to the landing, then down the main staircase to the hall and into Sir Basil's study. With an unsteady hand she knelt down, candle close to the floor, and searched the red-and-blue Turkey carpet to find an irregularity in the pattern that might mark a bloodstain.

It took her about ten minutes, and it seemed like half the night, before she heard the clock in the hall chime and it nearly startled her into dropping the candle. As it was she spilled hot wax and had to pick it off the wool with her fingernail.

It was then she realized the irregularity was not simply the nature of the carpet maker but an ugliness, an asymmetry nowhere else balanced, and on bending closer she saw how large it was, now nearly washed out, but still quite discernible. It was behind the large oak desk, where one might naturally stand to open any of the small side drawers, only three of which had locks.

She rose slowly to her feet. Her eye went straight to the second drawer, where she could see faint scoring marks around the keyhole, as if someone had forced it open with a crude tool and a replacement lock and repolishing of the bruised wood could not completely hide it.

There was no way in which she could open it; she had neither skill nor instrument—and more than that, she did not wish to alarm the one person who would most notice a further damage to the desk. But she could easily guess what Octavia had found—a letter, or more than one, from Lord Cardigan, and perhaps even the colonel of the regiment, which had confirmed beyond doubt what she already had learned from the War Office.

Hester stood motionless, staring at the desk with its neatly laid-out dish of sand for blotting ink on a letter, sticks of scarlet wax and tapers for seals, stand of carved sardonyx and red jasper for ink and quills, and long, exquisite paper knife in imitation of the legendary sword of King Arthur, embedded in its magical stone. It was a beautiful thing, at least ten inches long and with an engraved hilt. The stone itself which formed its stand was a single piece of yellow agate, the largest she had ever seen.

She stood, imagining Octavia in exactly the same spot, her mind whirling with misery, loneliness and the ultimate defeat. She must have stared at that beautiful thing as well.

Slowly Hester reached out her hand and took it. If she had been Octavia she would not have gone to the kitchen for Mrs. Boden's carving knife; she would have used this lovely thing. She took it out slowly, feeling its balance and the sharpness of its tip. It was many seconds in the silent house, the snow falling past the uncurtained window, before she noticed the faint dark line around the joint between the blade and the hilt. She moved it to within a few inches of the candle's flame. It was brown, not the gray darkness of tarnish or inlaid dirt, but the rich, reddish brown of dried blood.

No wonder Mrs. Boden had not missed her knife until just before she told Monk of it. It had probably been there in its rack all the time; she simply confused herself with what she assumed to be the facts.

But there had been blood on the knife they found. Whose blood, if this slender paper knife was what had killed Octavia?

Not whose. It was a kitchen knife—a good cook's kitchen would have plenty of blood available from time to time. One roast, one fish to be gutted, or a chicken. Who could tell the difference between one sort of blood and another?

And if it was not Octavia's blood on the knife, was it hers on the peignoir?

Then a sudden shaft of memory caught her with a shock like cold water. Had not Beatrice said something about Octavia having torn her peignoir, the lace, and not being skilled at such fine needlework, she had accepted Beatrice's offer to mend it for her? Which would mean she had not even been wearing it when she died. But no one knew that except Beatrice—and out of sensitivity to her grief, no one had shown her the blood-soaked garment. Araminta had identified it as being the one Octavia had worn to her room that night—and so it was—at least as far as the upstairs landing. Then she had gone to say good-night to her mother and left the garment there.

Rose too could be mistaken, for the same reason. She would only know it was Octavia's, not when she had worn it.

Or would she? She would at least know when it was last laundered. It was her duty to wash and iron such things—and to mend them should it be necessary. How had she overlooked mending the lace? A laundrymaid should do better.

She would have to ask her about it in the morning.

Suddenly she was returned to the present—and the realization that she was standing in her nightgown in Sir Basil's study, in exactly the same spot where Octavia in her despair must have killed herself— holding the same blade in her hand. If anyone found her here she would have not a shred of an excuse—and if it was whoever found Octavia, they would see immediately that she also knew.

The candle was low and the bowl filling with melted wax. She replaced the knife, setting it exactly as it had been, then picked up the candle and went as quickly as she could to the door and opened it almost soundlessly. The hallway was in darkness; she could make out only the dimmest luminescence from the window that faced onto the front of the house, and the falling snow.

Silently she tiptoed across the hall, the tiles cold on her bare feet, and up the stairs, seeing only a tiny pool of light around herself, barely enough to place her feet without tripping. At the top she crossed the landing and with difficulty found the bottom of the female servants' stairway.

At last in her own room she snuffed out the candle and climbed into her cold bed. She was chilled and shaking, the perspiration wet on her body and her stomach sick.

In the morning it took all the self-control she possessed to see first to Beatrice's comfort, and her breakfast, and then to Septimus, and to leave him without seeming hasty or neglectful in her duty. It was nearly ten o'clock before she was able to make her way to the laundry and find Rose.

"Rose," she began quietly, not to catch Lizzie's attention. She would certainly want to know what was going on, to supervise if it was any kind of work, and to prevent it until a more suitable time if it was not.

"What do you want?" Rose looked pale; her skin had lost its

porcelain clarity and bloom and her eyes were very dark, almost hollow. She had taken Percival's death hard. There was some part of her still intrigued by him, and perhaps she was haunted by her own evidence and the part she had played before the arrest, the petty malice and small straw of direction that might have led Monk to him.

"Rose," Hester spoke again, urgently, to draw Rose's attention away from the apron of Dinah's she was smoothing with the flatiron. "It is about Miss Octavia—"

"What about her?" Rose was uninterested, and her hand moved back and forth with the iron, her eyes bent on her work.

"You cared for her clothes, didn't you? Or was it Lizzie?"

"No." Still Rose did not look at her. "Lizzie usually cared for Lady Moidore's and Miss Araminta's, and sometimes Mrs. Cyprian's. I did Miss Octavia's, and the gentlemen's linens, and we split the maids' aprons and caps as the need came. Why? What does it matter now?"

"When was the last time you laundered Miss Octavia's peignoir with the lace lilies on it—before she was killed?"

Rose put down the iron at last and turned to Hester with a frown. She considered for several minutes before she answered.

"I ironed it the morning before, and took it up about noon. She wore it that night, I expect—" She took a deep breath. "And I heard she did the night after, and was killed in it."

"Was it torn?"

Rose's face tightened. "Of course not. Do you think I don't know my job?"

"If she had torn it the first night, would she have given it to you to mend?"

"More probably Mary, but then Mary might have brought it to me—she's competent, and pretty good at altering tailored things and dinner gowns, but those lilies are very fine work. Why? What does it matter now?" Her face screwed up. "Anyway, Mary must have mended it, because I didn't—and it wasn't torn when the police gave it to me to identify; the lilies and all the lace were perfect."

Hester felt a sick excitement.

"Are you sure? Are you absolutely sure—to swear someone's life on?"

Rose looked as if she had been struck; the last vestige of blood left her face.

"Who is there to swear for? Percival's already dead! You know that! What's wrong with you? Why do you care now about a piece of lace?"

"Are you?" Hester insisted. "Are you absolutely sure?"

"Yes I am." Rose was angry because she did not understand Hester's insistence and it frightened her. "It wasn't torn when the police showed it to me with the blood on it. That part of it wasn't stained, and it was perfectly all right."

"You couldn't be mistaken? Is there more than one piece of lace on it?"

"Not like that." She shook her head. "Look, Miss Latterly, whatever you may think of me, and it shows in your hoity-toity manners—I know my job and I know a shoulder from a hem of a peignoir. The lace was not torn when I sent it up from the laundry, and it was not torn when I identified it for the police—for any good that does anyone."

"It does a lot," Hester said quietly. "Now would you swear to it?"

"Why?"

"Would you?" Hester could have shaken her in sheer frustration.

"Swear to who?" Rose persisted. "What does it matter now?" Her face worked as if some tremendous emotion shook her. "You mean—" She could hardly find the words. "You mean—it wasn't Percival who killed her?"

"No—I don't think so."

Rose was very white, her skin pinched. "God! Then who?"

"I don't know—and if you've any sense at all, and any desire to keep your life, let alone your job, you'll say nothing to anyone."

"But how do you know?" Rose persisted.

"You are better not understanding—believe me!"

"What are you going to do?" Her voice was very quiet, but there was anxiety in it, and fear.

"Prove it—if I can."

At that moment Lizzie came over, her lips tight with irritation.

"If you need something laundered, Miss Latterly, please ask me and I will see it is done, but don't stand here gossiping with Rose—she has work to do."

"I'm sorry," Hester apologized, forcing a sweet smile, and fled.

She was back in the main house and halfway up the stairs to Beatrice's room before her thoughts cleared. If the peignoir was whole when Rose sent it up, and whole when it was found in Percival's room, but torn when Octavia went to say good-night to her mother, then she must have torn it some time during that day, and no one but Beatrice had noticed. She had not been wearing it when she died; it had been in Beatrice's room. Some time between Octavia leaving it there and its being discovered, someone had taken it, and a knife from the kitchen, covered the knife in blood and wrapped the peignoir around it, then hidden them in Percival's room.

But who?

When had Beatrice mended it? Surely that night? Why would she bother after she knew Octavia was dead?

Then where had it been? Presumably lying in the workbasket in Beatrice's room. No one would care about it greatly after that. Or was it returned to Octavia's room? Yes, surely returned, since otherwise whoever had taken it would realize their mistake and know Octavia had not been wearing it when she went to bed.

She was on the top stair on the landing now. It had stopped raining and the sharp, pale winter sun shone in through the windows, making patterns on the carpet. She had passed no one else. The maids were all busy about their duties, the ladies' maids attending to wardrobe, the housekeeper in her linen room, the upstairs maids making beds, turning mattresses and dusting everything, the tweeny somewhere in the passageway. Dinah and the footmen were somewhere in the front of the house, the family about their morning pleasures, Romola in the schoolroom with the children, Araminta writing letters in the boudoir, the men out, Beatrice still in her bedroom.

Beatrice was the only one who knew about the torn lily, so she would not make the mistake of staining that peignoir—not that Hester had ever suspected her in the first place, or certainly not alone. She might have done it with Sir Basil, but then she was also frightened that someone had murdered Octavia, and she did not know who. Indeed she feared it might have been Myles. Hester considered for only an instant that Beatrice might have been a superb actress, then she abandoned it. To begin with, why should she? She had no idea Hester would repeat anything she said, let alone everything.

Who knew which peignoir Octavia wore that evening? She had left the withdrawing room fully dressed in a dinner gown, as did all the women. Whom had she seen after changing for the night but before retiring?

Only Araminta—and her mother.

Proud, difficult, cold Araminta. It was she who had hidden her sister's suicide, and when it was inevitable that someone should be blamed for murder, contrived that it should be Percival.

But she could not have done it alone. She was thin, almost gaunt. She could never have carried Octavia's body upstairs. Who had helped her? Myles? Cyprian? Or Basil?

And how to prove it?

The only proof was Beatrice's word about the torn lace lilies. But would she swear to that when she knew what it meant?

Hester needed an ally in the house. She knew Monk was outside; she had seen his dark figure every time she had passed the window, but he could not help in this.

Septimus. He was the one person she was sure was not involved, and who might have the courage to fight. And it would take courage. Percival was dead and to everyone else the matter was closed. It would be so much easier to let it all lie.

She changed her direction and instead of going to Beatrice's room went on along the passage to Septimus's.

He was propped up on the bed reading with the book held far in front of him for his longsighted eyes. He looked up with surprise when she came in. He was so much better her attentions were more in the nature of friendship than any medical need. He saw instantly that there was something gravely concerning her.

"What has happened?" he asked anxiously. He set the book down without marking the page.

There was nothing to be served by prevarication. She closed the door and came over and sat on the bed.

"I have made a discovery about Octavia's death—in fact two."

"And they are very grave," he said earnestly. "I see that they trouble you. What are they?"

She took a deep breath. If she was mistaken, and he was implicated, or more loyal to the family, less brave than she believed, then she might be endangering herself more than she could cope with. But she would not retreat now.

"She did not die in her bedroom. I have found where she died." She watched his face. There was nothing but interest. No start of guilt. "In Sir Basil's study," she finished.

He was confused. "In Basil's study? But, my dear, that doesn't make any sense! Why would Percival have gone to her there? And what was she doing there in the middle of the night anyway?" Then slowly the light faded from his face. "Oh—you mean that she did learn something that day, and you know what it was? Something to do with Basil?"

She told him what she had learned at the War Office, and that Octavia had been there the day of her death and learned the same.

"Oh dear God!" he said quietly. "The poor child—poor, poor child." For several seconds he stared at the coverlet, then at last he looked up at her, his face pinched, his eyes grim and frightened. "Are you saying that Basil killed her?"

"No. I believe she killed herself—with the paper knife there in the study."

"Then how did she get up to the bedroom?"

"Someone found her, cleaned the knife and returned it to its stand, then carried her upstairs and broke the creeper outside the window, took a few items of jewelry and a silver vase, and left her there for Annie to discover in the morning."

"So that it should not be seen as suicide, with all the shame and scandal—" He drew a deep breath and his eyes widened in appalled horror. "But dear God! They let Percival hang for it!"

"I know."

"But that's monstrous. It's murder."

"I know that."

"Oh—dear heaven," he said very quietly. "What have we sunk to? Do you know who it was?"

She told him about the peignoir.

"Araminta," he said very quietly. "But not alone. Who helped her? Who carried poor Octavia up the stairs?"

"I don't know. It must have been a man—but I don't know who."

"And what are you going to do about this?"

"The only person who can prove any of it is Lady Moidore. I think she would want to. She knows it was not Percival, and I believe she might find any alternative better than the uncertainty and the fear eating away at all her relationships forever."

"Do you?" He thought about it for some time, his hand curling and uncurling on the bedspread. "Perhaps you are right. But whether you are or not, we cannot let it pass like this—whatever its cost."

"Then will you come with me to Lady Moidore and see if she will swear to the peignoir's being torn the night of Octavia's death and in her room all night, and then returned some time later?"

"Yes." He moved to climb to his feet, and she put out both her hands to help him. "Yes," he agreed again. "The least I can do is be there—poor Beatrice."

He had not yet fully understood.

"But will you swear to her answer, if need be before a judge? Will you strengthen her when she realizes what it means?"

He straightened up until he stood very erect, shoulders back, chest out.

"Yes, yes I will."

Beatrice was startled to see Septimus behind Hester when they entered her room. She was sitting at the dressing table brushing her hair. This was something which would ordinarily have been done by her maid, but since it was not necessary to dress it, she was going nowhere, she had chosen to do it herself.

"What is it?" she said quietly. "What has happened? Septimus, are you worse?"

"No, my dear." He moved closer to her. "I am perfectly well. But something has happened about which it is necessary that you make a decision, and I am here to lend you my support."

"A decision? What do you mean?" Already she was frightened. She looked from him to Hester. "Hester? What is it? You know something, don't you?" She drew in her breath and made as if to ask, then her voice died and no sound came. Slowly she put the hairbrush down.

"Lady Moidore," Hester began gently. It was cruel to spin it out. "On the night she died, you said Octavia came to your room to wish you good-night."

"Yes—" It was barely even a whisper.

"And that her peignoir was torn across the lace lilies on the shoulder?"

"Yes—"

"Are you absolutely sure?"

Beatrice was puzzled, some small fraction of her fear abating.

"Yes, of course I am. I offered to mend it for her." The tears welled up in her eyes, beyond her control. "I did—" She gulped and fought to master her emotion. "I did—that night, before I went to sleep. I mended them perfectly."

Hester wanted to touch her, to take her hands and hold them, but she was about to deal another terrible blow, and it seemed such hypocrisy, a Judas kiss.

"Would you swear to that, on your honor?"

"Of course—but who can care—now?"

"You are quite sure, Beatrice?" Septimus knelt down awkwardly in front of her, touching her with clumsy, tender hands. "You will not take that back, should it become painful in its meanings?"

She stared at him. "It is the truth—why? What are its meanings, Septimus?"

"That Octavia killed herself, my dear, and that Araminta and someone else conspired to conceal it, to protect the honor of the family." It was so easily encapsulated, all in one sentence.

"Killed herself? But why? Harry has been dead for—for two years."

"Because she learned that day how and why he died." He spared her the last, ugly details, at least for now. "It was more than she could bear."

"But Septimus." Now her mouth and throat were so dry she could scarcely force the words. "They hanged Percival for killing her!"

"I know that, my dear. That is why we must speak."

"Someone in my house—in my family—murdered Percival!"

"Yes."

"Septimus, I don't know how I can bear it!"

"There is nothing to do but bear it, Beatrice." His voice was very gentle, but there was no wavering in it. "We cannot run away. There is no way of denying it without making it immeasurably worse."

She clutched his hand and looked at Hester.

"Who was it?" she said, her voice barely trembling now, her eyes direct.

"Araminta," Hester replied.

"Not alone."

"No. I don't know who helped her."

Beatrice put her hands very slowly over her face. She knew—and Hester realized it when she saw her clenched knuckles and heard her gasp. But she did not ask. Instead she looked for a moment at Septimus, then turned and walked very slowly out of the room, down the main stairs, and out of the front door into the street to where Monk was standing in the rain.

Gravely, with the rain soaking her hair and her dress, oblivious of it, she told him.

Monk went straight to Evan, and Evan took it to Runcorn.

"Balderdash!" Runcorn said furiously. "Absolute balderdash! Whatever put such a farrago of total nonsense in your head? The Queen Anne Street case is closed. Now get on with your present case, and if I hear any more about this you will be in serious trouble. Do I make myself clear, Sergeant?" His long face was suffused with color. "You are a great deal too like Monk for your own good. The sooner you forget him and all his arrogance, the better chance you will have of making yourself a career in the police force."

"You won't question Lady Moidore again?" Evan persisted.

"Great guns, Evan. What is wrong with you? No I won't. Now get out of here and go and do your job."

Evan stood to attention for a moment, the words of disgust boiling up inside him, then turned on his heel and went out. But instead of returning to his new inspector, or to any part of his present case, he found a hansom cab and directed it to take him to the offices of Oliver Rathbone.

Rathbone received him as soon as he could decently dismiss his current, rather garrulous client.

"Yes?" he said with great curiosity. "What is it?"

Clearly and concisely Evan told him what Hester had done, and saw with a mixture of emotions the acute interest with which Rathbone listened, and the alternating fear and amusement in his face, the anger and the sudden gentleness. Young as Evan was, he recognized it as an involvement of more than intellectual or moral concern.

Then he recounted what Monk had added, and his own still smoldering experience with Runcorn.

"Indeed," Rathbone said slowly and with deep thought. "Indeed. Very slender, but it does not take a thick rope to hang a man, only a strong one—and I think this may indeed be strong enough."

"What will you do?" Evan asked. "Runcorn won't look at it."

Rathbone smiled, a neat, beautiful gesture. "Did you imagine he might?"

"No—but—" Evan shrugged.

"I shall take it to the Home Office." Rathbone crossed his legs and placed his fingers tip to tip. "Now tell me again, every detail, and let me be sure."

Obediently Evan repeated every word.

"Thank you." Rathbone rose to his feet. "Now if you will accompany me I shall do what I can—and if we are successful, you may choose yourself a constable and we shall make an arrest. I think perhaps we had better be quick." His face darkened. "From what you say, Lady Moidore at least is already aware of the tragedy to shatter her house."

Hester had told Monk all she knew. Against his wishes she had returned to the house, soaked and bedraggled and without an excuse. She met Araminta on the stairs.

"Good heavens," Araminta said with incredulity and amusement. "You look as if you have taken a bath with all your clothes on. Whatever possessed you to go out in this without your coat and bonnet?"

Hester scrambled for an excuse and found none at all.

"It was quite stupid of me," she said as if it were an apology for half-wittedness.

"Indeed it was idiotic!" Araminta agreed. "What were you thinking of?"

"I—er—"

Araminta's eyes narrowed. "Have you a follower, Miss Latterly?"

An excuse. A perfectly believable excuse. Hester breathed a prayer of gratitude and hung her head, blushing for her carelessness, not for being caught in forbidden behavior.

"Yes ma'am."

"Then you are very lucky," Araminta said tartly. "You are plain enough, and won't see twenty-five again. I should take whatever he offers you." And with that she swept past Hester and went on down the hall.

Hester swore under her breath and raced up the stairs, brushing past an astonished Cyprian without a word, and then up the next flight to her own room, where she changed every item of clothing from the skin out, and spread her wet things the best she could to dry.

Her mind raced. What would Monk do? Take it all to Evan, and thus to Runcorn. She could imagine Runcorn's fury from what Monk had told her of him. But surely now he would have no choice but to reopen the case?

She fiddled on with small duties. She dreaded returning to Beatrice after what she had done, but she had little else justification to be here, and now least of all could she afford to arouse suspicion. And she owed Beatrice something, for all the pain she was awakening, the destruction which could not now be avoided.

Heart lurching and clammy-handed, she went and knocked on Beatrice's door.

They both pretended the morning's conversation had not happened. Beatrice talked lightly of all sorts of things in the past, of her first meeting with Basil and how charmed she had been with him, and a little in awe. She spoke of her girlhood growing up in Buckinghamshire with her sisters, of her uncle's tales of Waterloo and the great eve of battle ball in Brussels, and the victory afterwards, the defeat of the emperor Napoleon and all Europe free again, the dancing, the fireworks, the laughter, the great gowns and the music and fine horses. Once as a child she had been presented to the Iron Duke himself. She recalled it with a smile and a faraway look of almost forgotten pleasure.

Then she spoke of the death of the old king, William IV, and the accession of the young Victoria. The coronation had been splendid beyond imagination. Beatrice had been in the prime of her beauty then, and without conceit she told of the celebrations she and Basil had attended, and how she had been admired.

Luncheon came and went, and tea also, and still she fought off reality with increasing fierceness, the color heightening in her cheeks, her eyes more feverish.

If anyone missed them, they made no sign of it, nor came to seek them.

It was half past four, and already dark, when there was a knock on the door.

Beatrice was ashen white. She looked at Hester once, then with a massive effort said quite levelly, "Come in."

Cyprian came in, his face furrowed with anxiety and puzzlement, not yet fear.

"Mama, the police are here again, not that fellow Monk, but Sergeant Evan and a constable—and that wretched lawyer who defended Percival."

Beatrice rose to her feet; only for a moment did she sway.

"I will come down."

"I am afraid they do wish to speak to all of us, and they refuse to say why. I suppose we had better oblige them, although I cannot think what it can be about now."

"I am afraid, my dear, that it is going to be extremely unpleasant."

"Why? What can there be left to say?"

"A great deal," she replied, and took his arm so that he might support her along the corridor and down the stairs to the withdrawing room, where everyone else was assembled, including Septimus and Fenella. Standing in the doorway were Evan and a uniformed constable. In the middle of the floor was Oliver Rathbone.

"Good afternoon, Lady Moidore," he said gravely. In the circumstances it was a ridiculous form of greeting.

"Good afternoon, Mr. Rathbone," she answered with a slight quiver in her voice. "I imagine you have come to ask me about the peignoir?"

"I have," he said quietly. "I regret that I must do this, but there is no alternative. The footman Harold has permitted me to examine the carpet in the study—" He stopped, and his eyes wandered around the assembled faces. No one moved or spoke.

"I have discovered the bloodstains on the carpet and on the handle of the paper knife." Elegantly he slid the knife out of his pocket and held it, turning it very slowly so its blade caught the light.

Myles Kellard stood motionless, his brows drawn down in disbelief.

Cyprian looked profoundly unhappy.

Basil stared without blinking.

Araminta clenched her hands so hard the knuckles showed, and her skin was as white as paper.

"I suppose there is some purpose to this?" Romola said irritably. "I hate melodrama. Please explain yourself and stop play-acting."

"Oh be quiet!" Fenella snapped. "You hate anything that isn't comfortable and decently domestic. If you can't say something useful, hold your tongue."

"Octavia Haslett died in the study," Rathbone said with a level, careful voice that carried above every other rustle or murmur in the room.

"Good God!" Fenella was incredulous and almost amused. "You don't mean Octavia had an assignation with the footman on the study

326

carpet. How totally absurd—and uncomfortable, when she has a perfectly good bed."

Beatrice swung around and slapped her so hard Fenella fell over sideways and collapsed into one of the armchairs.

"I've wanted to do that for years," Beatrice said with intense satisfaction. "That is probably the only thing that will give me any pleasure at all today. No—you fool. There was no assignation. Octavia discovered how Basil had Harry set at the head of the charge of Balaclava, where so many died, and she felt as trapped and defeated as we all do. She took her own life."

There was an appalled silence until Basil stepped forward, his face gray, his hand shaking. He made a supreme effort.

"That is quite untrue. You are unhinged with grief. Please go to your room, and I shall send for the doctor. For heaven's sake, Miss Latterly, don't stand there, do something!"

"It is true, Sir Basil." She stared at him levelly, for the first time not as a nurse to her employer but as an equal. "I went to the War Office myself, and learned what happened to Harry Haslett, and how you brought it about, and that Octavia had been there the afternoon of her death and heard the same."

Cyprian looked at his father, then at Evan, then at Rathbone.

"But then what was the knife and the peignoir in Percival's room?" he asked. "Papa is right. Whatever Octavia learned about Harry, it doesn't make any sense. The evidence was still there. That was Octavia's peignoir, with her blood on it, wrapped around the knife."

"It was Octavia's peignoir with blood on it," Rathbone agreed. "Wrapped around a knife from the kitchen—but it was not Octavia's blood. She was killed with the paper knife in the study, and when someone found her, they carried her upstairs and put her in her own room to make it seem as if she had been murdered." His fastidious face showed distress and contempt. "No doubt to save the shame of a suicide and the disgrace to the family and all it would cost socially and politically. Then they cleaned the knife and returned it to its place."

"But the kitchen knife," Cyprian repeated. "And the peignoir. It was hers. Rose identified it, and so did Mary, and more important, Minta saw her in it on the landing that night. And there is blood on it."

"The kitchen knife could have been taken any time," Rathbone said patiently. "The blood could have come from any piece of meat purchased in the course of ordering supplies for the table—a hare, a goose, a side of beef or mutton—"

"But the peignoir."

"That is the crux of the whole matter. You see, it was sent up from the laundry the day before, in perfect order, clean and without mark or tear—"

"Of course," Cyprian agreed angrily. "They wouldn't send it up in any other way. What are you talking about, man?"

"On the evening of her death"—Rathbone ignored the interruption, if anything he was even more polite—"Mrs. Haslett retired to her room and changed for the night. Unfortunately the peignoir was torn, we shall probably never know how. She met her sister, Mrs. Kellard, on the landing, and said good-night to her, as you pointed out, and as we know from Mrs. Kellard herself—" He glanced at Araminta and saw her nod so slightly only the play of light on her glorious hair showed the movement at all. "And then she went to say good-night to her mother. But Lady Moidore noticed the tear and offered to mend it for her—is that not so, ma'am?"

"Yes—yes it is." Beatrice's voice was intended to be low, but it was a hoarse whisper, painful in its grief.

"Octavia took it off and gave it to her mother to mend," Rathbone said softly, but every word was as distinct as a separate pebble falling into iced water. "She went to bed without it—and she was without it when she went to her father's study in the middle of the night. Lady Moidore mended it, and it was returned to Octavia's room. It was from there that someone took it, knowing Octavia had worn it to bid them good-night but not that she had left it in her mother's room—"

One by one, first Beatrice, then Cyprian, then the others, they turned to Araminta.

Araminta seemed frozen, her face haggard.

"Dear God in heaven. You let Percival hang for it," Cyprian said at last, his lips stiff, his body hunched as if he had been beaten.

Araminta said nothing; she was as pale as if she herself were dead.

"How did you get her upstairs?" Cyprian asked, his voice rising now as if anger could somehow release a fraction of the pain.

Araminta smiled a slow, ugly smile, a gesture of hate as well as hard, bitter hurt.

"I didn't—Papa did that. Sometimes I thought if it were discovered, I should say it was Myles, for what he did to me, and has done all the years we've been married. But no one would believe it." Her voice was laden with years of impotent contempt. "He hasn't the courage. And he wouldn't lie to protect the Moidores. Papa and I would do that—and Myles wouldn't protect us when it came to the end." She rose to her feet and turned to face Sir Basil. There was a thin trickle of blood running down her fingers from where her nails had gouged the skin of her palms.

"I've loved you all my life, Papa—and you married me to a man who took me by force and used me like a whore." Her bitterness and pain were overwhelming. "You wouldn't let me leave him, because Moidores don't do things like that. It would tarnish the family name, and that's all you care about—power. The power of money—the power of reputation—the power of rank."

Sir Basil stood motionless and appalled, as if he had been struck physically.

"Well, I hid Octavia's suicide to protect the Moidores," Araminta went on, staring at him as if he were the only one who could hear her. "And I helped you hang Percival for it. Well now that we're finished—a scandal—a mockery"—her voice shook on the edge of dreadful laughter—"a byword for murder and corruption—you'll come with me to the gallows for Percival. You're a Moidore, and you'll hang like one—with me!"

"I doubt it will come to that, Mrs. Kellard," Rathbone said, his voice wrung out with pity and disgust. "With a good lawyer you will probably spend the rest of your life in prison—for manslaughter, while distracted with grief—"

"I'd rather hang!" she spat out at him.

"I daresay," he agreed. "But the choice will not be yours." He swung around. "Nor yours, Sir Basil. Sergeant Evan, please do your duty."

Obediently Evan stepped forward and placed the iron manacles on Araminta's thin white wrists. The constable from the doorway did the same to Basil.

Romola began to cry, deep sobs of self-pity and utter confusion.

Cyprian ignored her and went to his mother, quietly putting his arms around her and holding her as if he had been the parent and she the child.

"Don't worry, my dear; we shall take care of you," Septimus said clearly. "I think perhaps we shall eat here tonight and make do with a little hot soup. We may wish to retire early, but I think it will be better if we spend the evening together by the fire. We need each other's company. It is not a time to be alone."

Hester smiled at him and walked over to the window and drew the curtain sufficiently to allow her to stand in the lighted alcove. She saw Monk outside in the snow, waiting, and raised her hand to him in a slight salute so that he would understand.

The front door opened and Evan and the constable led out Basil Moidore and his daughter for the last time.